Naked Fury

Naked Fury

◆

Jason Fury

Writers Club Press
San Jose New York Lincoln Shanghai

Naked Fury

Writers Club Press
an imprint of iUniverse.com, Inc.

For information address:
iUniverse.com, Inc.
5220 S 16th, Ste. 200
Lincoln, NE 68512
www.iuniverse.com

ISBN: 0-595-18593-2

Printed in the United States of America

Contents

◆

For Victor S…the most gorgeous man in the world—and the only one who got away…

Once more, I want to thank that valiant group of magazine editors who first brought out many of these tales in different forms during the late seventies and early eighties, and made it possible for me to reach audiences that appear to grow each year. Some of my mail today is from younger readers who received *Eric's Body* and my other books from older brothers, friends and uncles. Yes, even a few fathers. To *FirstHand, Manscape, InTouch, Advocate Men, Friction, Numbers, Blueboy, Mandate, Mach* and *Torso* magazines, I once again salute you.

Jery Tillotson
Autumn, 2001
Manhattan

WILD BOY

Nobody in town wanted anything to do with Larry, the "Wild Boy"...Larry, "that crazy kid!"..."that hoodlum who oughta be locked up."

People in my Bible-belt hometown of Carson City thought it a disgrace he roamed around like a stray dog, doing everything he wasn't supposed to. He should have been going to school everyday and to church every Sunday, like respectable people do.

I didn't blame him a bit for ignoring these institutions. Teachers and students treated him terrible. They laughed and jeered at his baggy, frayed clothes he received from charity groups.

His shoes were always too big and his hair uncombed and his body was dirty. Kids would whoop and hold their noses when they saw him coming. And since he bore the grand name of Lawrence St. Germain, the idiots had a field day with that, too:

"Hey, here comes the old St. Bernard, all covered with shit...here, boy here! Wanna bone? Was your Mama a bitch? Must have been to have a fuckin' polecat like you. Ha, ha, ha!"

And if he didn't respond to those taunts, the bigots would try even harder with such tender greetings as: "Been to the circus in those clown shoes? Huh, boy? Better answer when somebody talks to you, you fucking ass-hole!"

Then they ganged up on him and he tried to fight back and lost or he'd try desperately to escape but cowards derive their strengths in crowds, and they jumped on him with the joy, which comes to the weak who do everything in mobs.

I thought he was the most fascinating person in Carson City. Our whistle stop of a town was dead, with only 300 people, one stoplight and a church on every corner. During the 50s, just as it is today, the kids all wanted to dress and act alike, with the boys in jeans and tennis shoes and James Dean windbreakers and the girls in skirts, sweaters and frizzy permed hair.

Larry made me think of a scrungy looking Elvis Presley and I over-heard even some of the girls admitting this, although they were laughed at for even suggesting such a thing. Elvis was sleek and sexy and clean. Larry was a dirty bum who lived in a broken down trailer with his father, the town drunk.

In fact, one of the worst things they whispered about Larry was that since he had dark features and olive skin, he was probably a foreigner, or, even worse, there was "niggah" blood coursing through his veins. In my hometown, if you didn't have lilly white skin, you were an outcast.

He and his father had moved to our town the year before after being run out of High Point, North Carolina, about 15 miles away. They now lived in a rusting old trailer among some woods and weeds.

The sheriff's department was out there regularly because old Mr. St. Germain was real white trash. No store in town would allow him to enter since he was notorious for shoplifting.

With the food stamp money and welfare checks he got, he sold the first for booze and blew the rest of it on drugs and whores in neighboring towns. His son had to fend for himself.

He walked with his head down and had a way of jerking his face up and then glancing down fearfully when someone called out his name. Daddy said it was because his father beat him so badly that Larry had become conditioned to being frightened of being slapped and punched around.

He was in most of my classes where he always tried to disappear at the back of the room. Teachers ignored him but not Mrs. Evans, who taught English. She was an arrogant woman whose husband ran a used car lot, they lived in a nice house and she was known to enjoy insulting the poor farm kids who couldn't dress or act like their town cohorts.

My father and I despised her, considering her a disgrace to the school system and she and I had enjoyed numerous confrontations. I was the only one with enough guts to stand up to her. I had caught her several times doing imitations of me. You probably know the one rednecks use: flipping the wrist, patting the hair, twisting the hips, rolling the eyes and always getting laughs.

I made a point of shaking my ass, batting my eyes and flipping my wrists even more every time I passed her in the hallway. I died laughing watching her face turn red in anger. She also had a habit of chomping gum through every class period. I always made sure I had a mouth of gum and I chomped it like a maniac, making it snap and pop. Again, she flushed with rage.

In an ironic way, it was she who brought Larry and I together.

Although Larry was already 18, he was forced to attend his senior year in the town's one school. I had developed a fascination with him when one day, only a week after his enrollment, Mrs. Evans called out his name in class.

Someone had stolen $5 from her desk during the lunch period, she declared. She had gone home to eat and since it was a rainy day, the hallways were packed with kids and students had been going in and out of the room all during that time and so it could have been anybody. But she singled out the new boy.

"Mr. St. Germain—Lord, that's a mouthful to say, isn't it—Mr. St. Germain, would you know of anything about the $5 that was stolen from my desk? Did you hear me, young man? Stand up when I talk to you!"

I hated the way the kids were snickering and rolling their eyes and the tight sneer on the teacher's face. I also knew Larry could have had had nothing to do with the theft. I had tried talking to him during the break and found him miserable and scared and he had not gone near the room.

All eyes were now focused on our plump, short teacher and the tall, dark youth.

"Did you take the money from my desk, Mr. St. Germain? Someone said they saw you around my desk during lunch break."

Larry dropped his head even further against his chest and stared at the floor. He shook his head, muttering his denial.

I stood up. "Mrs. Evans, Larry was with me the whole time. We talked and he wasn't near the classroom."

She whirled on me, her fat face splotched with anger. "I didn't ask for any comments from you, Miss Know-it-all!" she snapped, glaring at me and her fat face grew purple. She batted her eyes and patted her hair and this, of course, had the classroom in stitches.

This teacher had a way of pooching out her lips when she was angry and now I imitated her.

"You're getting my comments, *Mister* Evans!" I retorted. "Larry was with me. I can promise you he was nowhere near your desk."

"Oh, you shut up!" she snarled and her face grew even pinker. "I'll deal with you later. Right now, I want to know who stole my money? I think we all know who did it, don't we, students?"

Everyone nodded and grinned and some of the girls giggled.

"Who did it, Mrs. Evans?" I asked again. "I don't know who stole your money. Why don't you tell us? Do you have any proof who took your $5?"

She whirled around and stared daggers at me. "One more crack out of you and we're going to the principal's office. I know who stole my money! It was this greasy, filthy bum!"

She waddled up to him, drew her hand back and slapped him so hard across the face it made us all wince. What startled me was that Larry hardly flinched. He was probably used to it, I thought, remembering what my father had told me of Larry's abuse.

Then she slapped him again and again and this time I jumped from my desk and went up to her.

"Let's go the principal's office, Mrs. Evans," I spat. "You just slapped a student with no good cause and that's a no-no according to the school's policy. Yes, I know them well, thanks to my father."

"Why, you damned little—"

She raised her hand and I patted my cheek. "Just put it right there, bitch, and I'll file a complaint with the board of education so fast you won't know who hit you. Let's see, how many complaints do they have on you now, Mrs. Evans?"

I took Larry's arm and started to lead him out of the room, with all the students staring at us with amazement. Nobody ever talked back to Bitch Evans.

She ran up to me and slammed her ruler across my shoulders so hard it broke but I whirled around and punched her in the stomach. I made a fist and smashed it against that fat, little face. Everyone screamed and shouted and by the time I got Larry to my father's office, our one-room school was in an uproar.

Nothing was done to me because the $5 Mrs. Evans thought was stolen was found in her pocket where she had forgotten she had put it. And Daddy saw to it that this louse was put on probation. She was assigned to work in the office, a real come down for this gum-chewing cow. Some of the faculty secretly praised me for both standing up to her, and looking out for Larry.

Thanks to my father, who was the high school coach, Larry began making money by doing odd jobs around our house on Main Street. He quickly brought a pair of new jeans and I thought he looked terrific. And he was so proud of them because they actually fitted him.

From my window, I'd watch him—a green strip of cloth tied around his black hair to keep it from his face…dark eyes almost hidden by thick lashes…and a scar on his cheek, which made him look tough and macho.

He and I had something in common. I was different, too. My father being a coach set me apart right there. I wasn't a big, macho stud, either, being of average height, with blonde hair and a definite swish.

Yes, I swished, which meant I was a natural born "sissy" but my father never criticized me for it. He seemed to accept the fact that I was happier staying in doors, not getting roughed up in sports, reading, drawing, cooking, making my own clothes.

I knew the slobs in town loved imitating me and gossiping like crazy but they never did it in front of me and God knows they knew better than to do in front of my big, handsome father. He'd tear their asses up.

My parent had taught me early on to be independent, to ignore peer and public opinion, to be my own self and stand up for what I believed was right.

When I suggested to him to let the "wild boy" stay for supper one afternoon after he had worked on the yard, he was happy to do so. I was always fixing Larry refreshments like iced tea and sandwiches when he was there during the day.

And he would flash me a gorgeous grin and a wink. At that first meal, he was terribly nervous, his hands trembled and he wouldn't look up at us.

But when he realized just how much my father and I liked him, he began to relax and open up. We were startled to say the least when he told us about his favorite writers. Not too many people in town had ever heard of Edith Wharton or Jack Kerouac.

Two days after this, I was coming home from school when I saw a circle of boys on the playground. They were howling and laughing and I saw them taking turns to dash into the middle and kick something.

I sensed someone was getting beaten up and when I hurried up to see who it was, I went crazy. Three boys were holding Larry down and others were trying to take off his new jeans.

Slapping and kicking him, someone hooted, "Looka the wild boy's new britches! Ain't they purty? Probably stole 'em, the fuckin', filthy sonofabtich! Let's see if he's got any underwear or if he's washed his ass today! Better hold your noses, buddies, 'cause he ain't washed in a year!"

I'd found a big tree branch nearby. And then I jumped in and slammed heads and bodies and everything else in my path.

Standing over Larry, I helped him stand up, with blood trickling from his nose and mouth and looked around at the wide-eyed hoodlums.

"You goddamned assholes!" I screamed. "Always so fucking brave when you're in a crowd, aren't you? You stupid pricks! You make me sick! You go to church every Sunday and give yourselves airs and you're nothing but white trash!"

Those goons rarely heard such language around school but my father had taught me quite a few colorful words when he and I discussed the hypocritical posturings of Carson City's deadbeats.

Now, he came running over to see what the hell I had gotten myself into. A big crowd had now gathered around us for the bullies were the school's most "popular" boys. Which meant no one ever fucked with them, but now my father joined me in giving these budding bigots an earful.

We saw that Larry got home safely to his dump of a trailer where his father sat in front of the black and white TV, drunk on his ass, watching the soaps.

At home, Daddy shook my hand and hugged me.

"You showed guts, son," he said proudly. "You made the Fury name proud."

And I wondered that night where I'd suddenly gotten the courage to stand up to the school's brawniest and most brainless meatheads. But then I had loved Larry St. Germain from the first day I set eyes on him so I vowed then that there had to be a way of us getting together on a more permanent basis.

I was ignored the next day at school, with everyone, including the "in crowd" giving me an icy shoulder but I nearly burst out laughing. What else was new? They would have nothing to do with me in the first place, even if my father was the school coach. They were furious because they couldn't dare gang up on me.

If they did, they had to face my father's wrath and nobody in their right mind wanted that to happen.

As I walked home that afternoon, someone stepped out from some bushes and faced me.

At first, I thought, uh oh, here we go again and prepared myself to do battle with some high school jerk. But it was Larry and solemn faced, beautiful and silent, he handed me a Snickers candy bar.

He had seen my father teasing me about this sacred delight since I was forbidden to eat them except on weekends. My face always broke out if I had more than a dozen.

Our eyes met—and something flashed between us and then he was gone. I told Daddy about the gift and we vowed to help him out. Between the beatings he got at school and the ones he received nightly at home, he wouldn't last long.

For the next week, I didn't see him at school. Gossip had it that his drunken down parent had beaten him so bad that he couldn't leave the trailer and when I went there, no one answered.

A month later, Larry's father died. He'd gone out on one binge too many and they found him lying beside the railroad tracks where a train had cut off his legs.

No one missed this sorry excuse for a man but now everyone wondered what would happen to Larry. Although 18, he was still considered a minor and there was talk of him being sent to the foster home in Thomasville. The Methodist Church had built a new one there.

But then my father shocked the hell out of everyone when he announced that he was adopting Larry as his own son.

So literally overnight, I had a brand new and very sexy new brother.

#

I remember that first day when Larry came to live with us.

For his first supper, I worked like a devil to make sure we had everything he would like: fried chicken, mashed potatoes, macaroni and cheese, all kinds of vegetables from our garden and gallons of iced tea. Of course, we had strawberry shortcake and peach cobbler. Real man food. And sissies like me enjoyed it, too.

Larry was thrilled to live with us and laughed and smiled at everything. When we finished eating, Daddy asked our newest family member: "When's the last time you took a bath, son?"

"I guess about two weeks ago."

"Well," my father drawled with a sparkle in his blue eyes, "I'm personally going to scrub you down and from now on, you're washing up once a day."

Larry just laughed. "Okay, Daddy-O! You're the boss!"

I trailed behind them as they went into the bathroom that Larry would share with me, along with my bedroom.

I watched him now strip. He was completely unabashed by his nudity or the fact that somebody was now scrubbing his ass and crotch. Slender and sensuous, he giggled as my father's hands rolled down his foreskin and ran the washcloth over his dick tip.

Larry was impressively endowed, with a thick, glossy length and a cock head that gleamed pink and glossy, like a mushroom. I was fascinated with how his egg-shaped balls danced around in their loose sac and every time Daddy ran the soap over them, they moved even more.

By this time, Larry had developed a growing erection, which caused us all to laugh. When he finally stepped from the tub, it looked like he had strapped a length of rubber hose around his hips. It flopped heavily as he walked over to the bed.

Daddy had laid out a new pair of pajamas and a blue robe for him.

"You two get some sleep now," Daddy said with a wink as he closed the door behind us. I had told him how much I loved Larry and he hugged me and said: "I'm very happy to hear that, son, because I think he's one of the finest guys I've ever met"

Now we were alone and the first thing Larry did was to strip down to his skin. I was delighted to see him slip in between the sheets, next to me, completely nude.

"I never wear anything when I sleep," he smiled and lit up a cigarette. His dark hair gleamed around his face and he looked down at me, as if seeing me for the first time. I wore a new pair of yellow pajamas that I thought would bring out the golden hue of my curls.

"Does it bother you if I'm naked and you aren't?" he asked. His young body gleamed and I saw drops of bathwater glisten on his chest and shoulders. I reached up and touched them.

"Not at all," I smiled. "It's not everyday I suddenly get a new brother. I—I really like you a lot, Larry."

He startled me by putting out his cigarette and suddenly pulling me close against him. Kissing me lightly, he stared down into my eyes; "We're brothers now. I'll always stand by you just like you've done for me."

I was even more surprised when he took my hand and guided it down to his privates. His dick felt even more thick and warm between his legs.

"You wanna play with my cock, Blondie? I want you to, anytime you want to. You can jerk it, suck it, stick it up your butt. Wanna play with my ass? It's all there, little brother."

I was trembling now for I'd never been in bed with another man before, except for my father. And now my new brother was saying things to me that a sane person never said in Carson City. You could get killed for just joking about such matters.

For all of us remembered the disappearance of little Gregory Jordan five years before. He lived alone with his mother but was so effeminate that each day of his life was made a hell at school.

And then one day he suddenly vanished. His mother never knew his fate but rumors were strong that a group of the town's most popular boys and fathers had tricked little Gregory into a car. He was taken out into the woods somewhere, raped, castrated and then thrown into the river.

Or so the rumors went for Gregory was never seen again. The sheriff's department never even looked for him. For the sheriff and his deputies were supposedly the ringleaders of the murder.

"Give me a little time, Larry," I managed to say. "But I want you to know something, brother. I love you a hell of a lot."

He kissed me on my cheek again and pulled me close to him. "I know, baby. Ever since that day on the playground—I knew then. Now, let's get some sleep. Remember, though. Whenever you want me, all you gotta do is tell me and I'm all yours."

Later, I watched his cigarette glow in the dark. Then I heard the steady creaking of the bedsprings and then a gasp from my brother—then silence.

#

My father had to attend a coaching seminar for the weekend in nearby Raleigh. He was hesitant about leaving us alone but Larry assured him that we'd be completely safe.

"I'll look after Jason," he promised.

"I'm hardly a weakling," I complained to Daddy. "Good God, I'll be going to college in five months."

"Okay, okay," Daddy laughed. "I'll buy you enough groceries for the next two days to feed an Army."

A thunderstorm blew up that afternoon and knocked the power out all over my neighborhood. But it was fun because Larry and I ate supper by candle light and then we played hide and seek in the dark and my new brother howled each time I screamed when he'd jump out and grab me.

"Come on," he said in a husky voice. "Let's get ready for bed."

My bedroom was charged with erotic tension for I had forgotten nothing of our first night together and the wonderful feel of his warm body—his young torso which I had felt and which he was eager to let me enjoy. How wonderful it was to awaken during the night and feel him right next to me, his warm breath kissing my neck and cheek.

He lit a candle and put it on our nightstand.

"Anything you want before we go to sleep?" he asked and stared at me, waiting for me to give the word.

I wanted like hell to shout, "Yes, Yes, it's you I want."

But I was so terribly shy back then and couldn't bring myself to put into words what I wanted. "Give me a little while, Larry, and then I'll tell you."

He said nothing, looking at me and then he winked and blew out the candle. Outside, the storm had grown worse. Winds groaned and knocked the branches against the house. Storms had always scared the hell out of me and I'd leave a light on. I sat up and whispered:

"Larry! Are you awake?"

"It's okay," he whispered. "You don't like the storm, do you? Well, I'm here now. Don't worry."

When I lay back down, he pulled me tight against him and this time I said nothing as he touched his mouth to mine.

Neither of us had been around and our lovemaking was awkward and simple but it was an important first step for us both. We writhed on the bed and then he guided me down to what I most wanted.

His foreskin was already sliding away from the tip of his hardness but I pushed it completely free and covered it with my mouth. He raised his hips slowly and inched more into me as my hands slid up and down his torso. I'd never realized a person could get so physically hot. Sweat gleamed on his skin and when I glanced up, his eyes were closed shut and his mouth opened.

"Play with my foreskin!" he whispered. "Stretch it out, honey and pretend its just rubber. It don't hurt none."

I obeyed with little prompting and was startled to see how far his rubbery overhang could go and I wrapped it halfway around my fist. Then he showed me how to tighten his sac by twisting it, until the two large testicles bulged out like twin apples, encased in pink rubber.

I sucked on him now and I loved it when he just lay there quietly, patiently, letting me slake my lust on him, and his fingers played with my curls.

"My dick's like rubber, too," he winked and I winced as he bent his organ in two, stretched it and even banged it hard several times on the wooden edge of the bed.

"When my Daddy was drunk, he used to like to see which of us had the toughest cock and we'd slap something hard until we were almost bleeding but man, mine got tough like that."

But after playing with his sexual wonders, it was time for get relief and I went down on Larry in earnest. His body trembled from the energy I put into it and he whistled silently, gasped and then I heard him mutter something and nod his head.

A sudden streak of whiteness into the air made me pause and this was followed by more. His flat stomach became a table for the glistening gobbets of semen.

Then he surprised me by laying me on my back and getting over me. He began talking in such a rapid, low monotone I couldn't quite make out all he was saying but it sounded like he'd only fucked a few girls, some whores in nearby towns with his father, so he wasn't all that experienced.

I grunted in pain when I felt him entering me and he paused for a minute until I could get used to him. After that, it went faster and smoother and he pulled me close as his hips lunged in and out in deep thrusts that had me gasping.

"Let me see you cum again, Larry!" I managed to say as he humped me and when he was ready, he pulled out and flapped his gleaming erection on my stomach.

Both of us watched as more whiteness spewed out in abundance. He looked from this sight to me, smiled and pulled me tight against him again.

So that was how my stepbrother and I spent that memorable night until it was nearly light outside.

He told me things in the dark, when we broke for cigarettes and Nehi Grape drinks, that no one had ever heard about: how his father had beat him so bad at times that Larry couldn't go to school and when he did, he felt like a total alien.

He would look around and see everyone all neat and clean and laughing and he knew that he had to go home each day to this raging, psycho who would bring his buddies by to suck and get fucked by Larry.

"I'd wake up and find a stranger sucking me and two more waiting," Larry remembered, "and there'd be my drunken old goat of a father standing there, taking their money so he could go out and guzzle booze."

After that night, it was like a veil had been pulled from my eyes. Everything appeared bright, beautiful and every time I looked at Larry and he'd look at me, we would both grin and laugh and hug each other.

In some mystical way, we believed that we really were brothers and may have lived like siblings in a former life period.

#

My father sensed something profound had happened between my new brother and me because after his return home that weekend, I'd catch him studying us, smiling and laughing with us.

He seemed pleased and one night, while I stood over the stove and Larry mowed the lawn, my father came up behind me and hugged me.

"Something tells me that you and Larry love each other," he whispered. "I mean, in more ways than just brothers."

I looked up at my father. "Daddy, he's the most wonderful thing to ever happen to me. Besides having you for a father, of course."

He pulled me close and kissed me just as Larry came in. "Hey, what do we have here?" he joked. "I didn't know you two were perverts."

"Come on over, son" laughed my father and embraced him, pulling him close so that all three of us stood there for a moment, hugging each other tight. "God, I'm proud to have such two fine sons!"

No one will ever persuade me differently but I know that during those special moments, something profound flowed between us all.

We were united forever in being a family and it was like Larry had always been there for both father and I.

#

In such a loving, positive home, Larry blossomed and became the person I thought he was always destined to be: an extraordinary individual.

Even the two-faced neighbors and the high school louts and bitches expressed amazement at how much he changed in just those few months.

Under Daddy's guidance, Larry began working out with weights, running, playing ball until his already tall, slender body filled out with rippling muscles.

In no time, he even became the school's star wrestler and boxer. He wore sharp, neat clothes that he brought with the money he earned painting houses on the weekends or mowing lawns. Daddy also gave him a generous allowance, just as I received.

His black, flowing hair now hung around his broad shoulders like jet silk.

His dark eyes seemed even more deeply set so that from a distance, it was like he had two slits for eyes. The new jeans he wore now fit him so snugly that his well-shaped rump and nicely packed box drew many admiring glances from the girls and guys.

Now, the very people who had tormented and beat him, who had shunned and ridiculed him wanted to be his friends. He was polite but distant to them.

"Why should I start kissing their asses now?" he said bitterly. "Just six months ago, I was the wild boy, the trailer trash bastard to them. Fuck them all."

On the night of the all-important junior-senior prom, one of the biggest snobs in school, Connie, the daughter of a preacher, actually asked Larry to take her to the prom.

"Sorry," he said. "I've got other plans."

She was totally unprepared for being rejected and her real self came out. "Other plans?" she sneered. "What other plans? Spending some more time with that faggot-step brother of yours?"

He slapped her hard.

"Don't ever say something like that about my brother. You think you fool everybody with this sweet, virgin shit. We all know you give blowjobs to the jocks and they've all got a pair of your stinking panties. So don't talk mean to me."

This created a scandal and she tried to bring criminal charges against him.

But my father threatened to bring all the jocks up and describe how she serviced them on the weekends. So, the poor little hypocrite was talked out of it and she ended up going to the prom with the school's slob, Ronnie, who loved to brag about how many girls he had fucked. Connie became his newest one.

Larry spent the night of the prom home in bed with me. My face remained buried between the tawny pillows of his rump and when I'd finished there, he would turn over and let me dine on his very experienced pecker. His cock didn't resemble that of a high school boy.

It was more like a grown man who had been around a few times and he once estimated that his father's buddies had probably blown him more than 1,000 times in a three year period, sometimes five to six times a night.

His drunken old Pappy would pick up $5 a shot. It was $10 if Larry fucked the human roaches.

"There was one weekend when my father wanted to go on a real toot over in Salisbury and he needed a lot of money for it," Larry told me. "He had me stay in bed from Friday until Sunday morning, letting every old scumbag he could find to come by and blow me."

"I'll bet you loved every minute of it," I teased him.

"Frankly, some of the guys were really good. They knew how to get me hard and keep it hard. I liked fucking a few of them, too. But most were so scrungy and drunk, I had to hold my breath so I wouldn't puke all over them."

#

I knew my father badly wanted to sleep with Larry but he told me he would never do it—unless Larry asked him.

"I don't want anyone to ever accuse me of seducing a kid like Larry, especially my own stepson," he would tell me.

But one night, as we lay in bed after a strenuous session of lust, Larry confessed to me that although he naturally loved me, my father had him climbing the walls because he was so damned handsome.

"When I see our Dad in those swimming trunks washing the car, I get a hard-on," he told me. "I mean, his muscles are so natural and big, I know he'd probably die if he ever knew how I felt."

I burst out laughing and told him of what my father had said about him.

"What?" Larry gasped. "You mean he really wants to do it with me, too?"

"Come on!" I snickered. "No, don't put a stitch on. No, not that towel, either. I want you to visit my father just as you look right now."

It was a little past nine o'clock at night but my father always read in bed until nearly midnight. I saw the light on under his door and tapped on it.

"Come in," he called out.

My father looked scrumptious, laying on his yellow sheets in just a pair of white jockey briefs. His chest was dusted with dark hair, his muscles gleamed impressively and the glasses he wore gave him a bookish air. I told Larry to wait outside the door.

"Daddy, I want to deliver to you a present," I said with a straight face.

He put his book down and squinted. "A present? What are you talking about? My birthday's not until August."

"But this present is for just being such a great father. Now close your eyes and hold out your hand."

"Now Jason, I'm trying to finish this book and—oh, all right," he grumped, good-naturedly. He put his book down and held out his right hand. I led Larry and guided him up to my father. Then I took my brother's relaxed length of manhood and placed it into my father's hand. Daddy opened his eyes.

He looked up at us, startled and dropped Larry's penis.

"What's going on?" he said lightly.

"Daddy," I hurried on, "Larry wants you as bad as you want him, so here you are and don't make any excuses."

Larry stood there, silently, staring at Daddy.

"Larry," my father began quietly, "do you really want this, too? You aren't being forced to do this."

"Yes, yes, I've wanted it from the first time I saw you in shorts and tee shirt on the ball court." I was moving back towards the door. Daddy pulled aside his sheet and beckoned to Larry. "Okay, son, why don't you just join me right now?"

Before I closed the door, I watched Larry peeling off my father's briefs, feeling of his privates and then burying his face in his lap.

That night began a feverish time for all three of us. Not a night passed that we didn't all get into bed with Daddy taking turns loving his two sexually charged sons—and then Larry and me taking turns giving him a great time.

Larry delighted in becoming master of our gatherings: he'd plow first me, then Daddy and then my parent and I would take turns paying oral homage to this new addition to our family.

#

Only a month before both of us graduated from high school.

I would be entering Columbia University in New York on a scholarship. Larry would enter the Marines Corps. College didn't interest him and the thoughts of spending four years in deep study and books were the last thing he wanted.

A week before he left for Camp Lejeune Marine Base, he and I walked along High Rock Dam and I snapped several Polaroid shots of my handsome, adorable step-brother.

In one particular picture, I caught Larry leaning against a tree, with the brown water of the river flowing in the background. Sun has painted his black hair with spatters of gold. His strong young physique is clearly outlined in the white shorts and red jersey he wore that afternoon.

His smile, though, was still that sad, lost expression that nothing my father or I could wholly eradicate. For the rest of his life, he'd be scarred by those nightmarish years with his monster of a father. And the taunts and beatings he'd received at school.

As the departure day grew nearer, he gave me and Daddy gifts that he had made with his own hands. Daddy received the striking leather wallet with genuine delight for it was obvious Larry had spent hours working in the exquisite detail of an Indian astride his horse.

For me, a ring carved out of wood, with a beautiful rock of pink, gold and aqua set in the center.

He waited until we were alone in our room for the last time before giving it to me.

I remember him coming out of the shower, the water still gleaming on his bronze hued skin, his eyes expectant as he handed me the small box of gold design that he had also created.

"Larry!" I murmured, looking at it. "It's–it's just incredibly beautiful. Will you put it on me?"

He obeyed and kissed me on the mouth.

"Thank you—Lawrence St. Germain. That's a beautiful name."

"When you say it," he answered, "It's even more beautiful."

Oh, that May night, with a chill in the air, with rain falling against the window, a soft lamp glowing in the corner, next to someone you love!

Larry literally throbbed with sexual energy for the next few hours. I began kissing him on his lips and face, then I moved downward, my favorite journey, passing over unique treasures which I would never encounter again: his boyish nipples, now erect, the long line of his stomach which was enfolded on either side by rows of chiseled muscles; his spread thighs, powerful and enticing, then to the muscle which had kept him alive when with his real father and which now brought us both such happiness.

"Love it up, baby," he moaned. "It'll have to last us for a long time."

And by saying that, he imbued the darkness of that room, the scene taking place on my bed, with a mystical energy. And although I was awake every second, I could see myself from up above, looking down at us on the white sheets, lost in time.

His hardness began to slip into my mouth and I cupped his testicles and brought them up hard, like a pulley to bring more of him into me. He lifted his hips slightly, too, and eventually my mouth pressed against his pubic hair.

I could feel him pulsing quickly, followed by a spatter of thick wetness and when I glanced up at Larry, his mouth hung open, his eyes closed and his arms laying out on either side of him.

But through a strange cast of light, he began to look old and gray, with deep pockets under his eyes and his teeth gone. But this illusion quickly left when he raised his head and grinned.

"First one of the night. Wanna take a trip on my back porch?"

We had begun to use all types of moronic sayings about our sexual desires like: "You got any cherries on your cherry tree that need picking…You got a flagpole that needs greased up?"

He turned over and for the last time in a long while I buried my face in delight in "his back porch." He had a wonderful, earthy scent and taste and I always enjoyed feeling his privates swelling up beneath my chin.

I pulled his pecker up from between his thighs and sucked on him like that. When he tensed up his dimples, I knew he was preparing to deliver me more of his "cream from the root of Lawrence St. Germain."

I watched him sleep that night and thought: remember this, because it'll be your only picture of him for months, maybe even a year or more.

He looked like a little boy as he slumbered, a kid who was scared but determined to show only a brave front.

Morning came too early. None of us felt like eating breakfast but I went through the motions of making coffee while Daddy put the hot oatmeal on. Our talk was strained; all three of us were sad and lost and didn't want to show it.

At the terminal, Daddy and I waited with Larry for his bus and when it came, he joined several other young men who were heading for Camp Lejeune.

I watched my father and his new son embrace, pat each other's backs and when they parted, both kissed each other passionately on the mouth. Their eyes were wet and when Larry took me into his arms, I couldn't control myself and broke down.

"Stop it, little brother!" he whispered, trying to joke. "You promised me."

Daddy came over and put his arm around me and we both looked at Larry.

"So long, son!" Daddy said softly. "We'll miss you. You'd better write."

"So long, Lawrence St. Germain," I managed to say. "What a beautiful name!"

He ducked his head and we heard him whisper: "When you say it, it sounds even more beautiful."

#

Neither Daddy nor I ever got over Larry's death in the Vietnam War.

When we visited the War Memorial in Washington a few months ago, his name was buried among the thousands chiseled upon the stone—of young men who left behind lovers and family to mourn them.

Daddy and I wept for a long time after that telegram came. Even when I left home that fall for college, all I had to do was to look at that picture I had taken of him that April day and break down.

I wear the ring he gave me everyday and will until I die. When I visit home, my father and I go to the small memorial grave we made for him behind our house.

It's only a tombstone that bears his name and Daddy makes sure the flowers are changed each week. Covered in waterproofed plastic on the stone is a picture of my brother.

Wearing a smart looking Marine uniform, he smiles out at us, his face that of a young man who is only starting out on his voyage of life. Yet, those dark eyes still glimmer with sadness as they stare out at us, as if asking in death: why me?

We think of the good times that are gone. We hope that everyone can be as lucky as we were for having known a man like Lawrence St. Germain .I whisper it now, even as I write this.

Lawrence St. Germain. What a beautiful name!

He is not forgotten.

THE POSTMAN ALWAYS COMES TWICE

◆

A thunderstorm is brewing and I've always had my best luck with men during bad weather.

Don't ask why. In this sizzling little spot on the Alabama map, everybody expects August to bring its worst microwaveable weather which means stormy weather can't be that far off.

So, perhaps I'll have better luck here with my choice of men than the animals who inhabit the concrete canyons of Manhattan.

But for some strange reason, known only to deep South farmers, I've noticed that the men I find here keep their shirts, jeans and workboots on, no matter if it's ll0 in the shade. And when they take them off, they look weird and grotesque: men with sun baked necks and faces and arms but bodies so white they look like they've been drained by a vampire.

My thoughts are straying, though, away from the mysterious creature that has tormented me: my hunky, brooding, and gorgeous postal carrier. He knows what I want but enjoys playing Mr. Innocent.

I can utter the most outlandishly sensual suggestions that reek of hot sex but he just blinks those strange eyes behind the Hollywood shades and goes into his Forrest Gump mode.

"No, suh," he drawls, chewing his gum. Or: "Sorry, but I ain't got time to have any iced tea or eh, fix your pipes, suh!"

Snapping his Juicy-Fruit, that idiotic smile on his rugged face, he knows I want to slap it off and scream: Get Real! Let's ball! Get out of those sweaty clothes and fuck the hell out of me.

Well, it's changing this afternoon when he brings me my mail. If he doesn't respond this time, then I'm slamming my door in his face and he can take that cute, postal uniformed ass elsewhere. I will just take my mail and that male can go straight to hell.

I moved into this small, wooden cottage outside of Hurtsboro, Alabama in early August. My New York shrink ordered me to leave the Big Apple for an extended period, as long as my finances held out.

"Go!" he thundered in his adorable Russian accent, while patting my head that rested on his broad chest. "You're burned out! You've been too long here in Manhattan."

I remember fondling the wonderful hardness pressed against his left thigh in those tight slacks. "Can't I have some more fun with you before I leave, Andrei?"

"No," he boomed again, pushing me away. "Find some Southern stud down there and settle down. You make me want to act in an unprofessional manner and I am a married man with four children."

Where upon, he kissed me passionately and we ended up as we always did on his couch, with Andrei giving me lavishly some of his Slavic energy to see me through my Dixie idyll.

And so through the grapevine, I heard about this area, where several other artists and writers have visited and for some bizarre reason enjoyed. The rent is dirt cheap, as is every other amenity of life. Two TV dinners for a dollar at the Piggly-Wiggly Supermarket, $2.00 for a gallon of wine—yes, the amenities of life which don't cost a fortune.

My cozy little abode is at the end of my mailman's route. There is no one else in this section once you turn the bend of the road there. Instead of concrete walls of condos stretching upwards in Manhattan, there is a vast field of corn stretching out before me, on the other side of the two-laned hard topped road where rarely a vehicle passes.

The nearest farmhouse is a mile down the road and beyond that a section of rusting trailers and decrepit shacks where black welfare mothers and their brood of kids sit on the front porch and stare at me when I take my walk each day at dusk.

In their front yards grow watermelons, tomatoes, and onions but most just lie there and rot. You get lonely living alone like this, with no one to talk to and any telephone or TV or radio. I can have no distractions since I am writing hard on a new book. It's about an eccentric Southern transsexual, who has become steadily reclusive over the years, who has four different personas, all of whom he uses in his writing. And he has this gift for attracting brooding, hunky males, all of them straight, who can bring him either heaven or hell.

So this is why I've taken such a hot interest in my daily visitor, guaranteed by Uncle Sam to make at least one visit, five days a week.

The first delivery he made came two days after I moved here. I was opening a can of Diet Pepsi when someone knocked on my door—two raps.

Curious and startled, I opened my door with some apprehension. I had met no one here except my landlady, an old Southern belle who was on her way to Miami. The locals gave me a wide berth at the supermarket, somewhat leery of my blonde hair and swish ways and eyes dramatic with a touch of lavender mascara.

The man stood there, silently, his face blank. We stared at one another for a moment with me having to look up at him. I came to his chest that was half-exposed by his unbuttoned shirt. Dark hair glistened with sweat on that broad expanse. Pools of wetness formed rings under his arms.

Beneath his postal cap, black curls gleamed with moisture. A diamond stud caught the glitter of the sun half-hidden by the thick layer of rain clouds. The short sleeves of his shirt bulged from powerful biceps. His shoulders were broad, swollen with virility.

He held several letters in his hand. Finally, he spoke in a soft Southern voice, almost a whisper.

"Are you Jason Fury?"

"That's me, just moved in three days ago."

"Well, I got some mail for you."

I opened the screen door and he gave me my mail, leaving damp fingerprints on the envelopes. He did not move but rested a hand on his black leather bag and tipped his cap back from his forehead. Big fingers smoothed the thick moustache.

I saw a particle of food in the corner of his full lips. What had he eaten just before he came here? Where did he eat? Maybe some woman along his route gave him something in return for a roll in the hay?

His voluptuous mouth quivered slightly—as if he were secretly amused at something.

"You must be burning up," I smiled. "Wouldn't you like a good cold beer? A Diet Pepsi? Some iced tea?"

"No thanks. What'd ya do? Just visiting? Gonna settle down?"

"I'm a writer," I drawled. "I write stories about gay men who get the hots for straight hunks."

His expression didn't change. "Where you get your ideas from?"

"I do my best research in bed."

This time the ghost of a grin poised at his mouth that he wiped with his hand. His hands looked so huge, like those of a machinist or farmer or boxer. What was he doing delivering mail?

"Gotta go. See ya."

I watched him swagger away hitching the strap of his bag over a broad, powerful shoulder. The pants weren't tight but the sweat had made the fabric sucked into the deep crack of his ass.

It was a firm, round pair of buns that undulated away from me. Very interesting, I thought. Unpredictable. Not one of the hayseeds I'd encountered at the small post office, with a wad of tobacco bulging from their cheek, or strains of brown snuff trickling down their chin.

His figure became smaller as it ambled down the road, but I forgot none of it. I imprinted it deeply into my memory: ham hock like hands, muscular thighs straining the material of his pants. Large nipples, stiff and thick, which pushed against the khaki shirt.

Other things…like the powerful odor of sweat and wet flesh and something else mixed in…a spermy bathroomish scent and tinged heavily with tobacco, stale beer, hamburger and onions, Lifebuoy soap…and sex…

I wanted to know this man, to see him naked and laying on my bed with his thighs spread wide, with his hands on the back of my head, mashing my mouth deeper, deeper onto his dark rod of virility which I sensed had guided his life, becoming the center of his universe…whatever that was…

On the weekends when he did not come, I became impatient and surly. I wondered how he spent his time and did he have a girl friend or was he…God Forbid!…married?

I fantasized about him fucking somebody and I could see clearly his gleaming, curvaceous butt pumping that dark thing into a hole. When he did make his brief, enigmatic visits daily—always knocking twice at my door, always holding my letters in his hand—he said little and I wondered if he were waiting for me to utter the magic words?

I never knew what he thought. I tried to find out one day.

"Am I the last person you see on this route?"

He nodded his head, half-smiling, as if amused at my clumsy attempts to draw him out.

"I'll bet you go straight home because your job is so exhausting."

He shrugged and scratched his butt. Then he startled me by drawling: "Usually have a few beers. Watch TV, ball games, wrestling, play pool, ride my motor-bike."

"Are you one of those wild bikers I read about? Do you dress in leather and have some hot Mama holding on to you?"

He shrugged, smiling strangely at some secret thoughts. What was he hiding?

"I would think your kids keep you busy?"

He laughed, a hot, deep-stomached laugh

"If you're asking if I'm married, the answer is no. Gotta go."

And off he went. But that afternoon, I discovered something startling about my Mr. Postman. My curiosity was at fever pitch and when he left me, I hurried to my bedroom and got out my binoculars. Yes, after you've lived in New York for awhile, you discover binoculars can often provide you with better entertainment than anything you could find at a bar, bath or movie house.

You've got all those windows of high rises around you to study, the men and boys passing below, hanging out on the sidewalks, and if they're Italian, then you've got a thrilling scene to watch.

Now, I saw him retrace his steps to the narrow two-laned black top. But instead of turning right, and heading toward town, he glanced briefly back at my place and then jumped over a narrow ditch and walked toward the wall of green cornstalks.

He dropped his mailbag to the red earth and moved slightly back until there were tall stalks of corn on either side of him.

I was thrilled to see him take off his cap, unbutton his shirt and strip it off. God, he was one muscular dude!

I squealed in delight when I beheld him unbuckling his belt and drop his pants and they settled around his string up boots. His manhood was dark and rough and very uncut, just like I had imagined it and then he delighted me by digging fingers deep into his foreskin and stretching it out, upwards towards his stomach.

Then, he began jerking off.

I was astonished at how brutal he was to his privates. He squeezed, scratched, twisted and pulled viciously at his pecker and groin between his fists until the tip bulged out like an over ripe plum—purple and sticky with strands of clear honey which dripped down over his fingers.

My breathing quickened as I watched this man close his eyes while cupping his balls in one hand, then twisting them around until they were like pink condoms swollen to the bursting point.

He looked so close to me I could imagine I heard him at that point groaning and gasping as a spurt of white wetness squirted out onto the bushes. More streams gushed forth and he watched it intently from behind his shades, smiling slightly, as if proud of his abundant outpourings.

Then, he stuffed this sticky mass of machismo back into his pants, buttoned up, pulled on his shirt and picked up his hat and bag and sauntered away. He ignored the moist splotches on the front of his slacks and the bits of earth and grass on the back.

I slumped to the floor, almost blacking out from the effect this secret ritual had on me. How many times had he done this and why did he do it? No wonder I detected the whiff of semen whenever he brought me my mail.

I hurried outside and soon approached the site where my dream lover had made love to himself, beneath the scalding sun, among the still trees and bushes and weeds.

Cum still glistened on the leaves, like vanilla pudding. I stooped down and licked it up, even the gobbets of whiteness that gleamed on the red earth.

It was good, thick and strong—like him.

But I had to do more than lick it up. I hurried back to my house and grabbed a bottle of cheap wine and stripped off my clothes. Then I returned to that silent place and lay down on the ground.

The sun was muted behind tan layers of clouds. It was so hot my head spun and as I guzzled the wine and lay upon the ground where my mysterious hunk dropped his seed, I had a strange fantasy: he was above me, naked and sweaty and still wearing his sunglasses. I reached up to grab him but he retreated slightly, smiling, as if taunting him.

I licked up more of his sex elixir and could feel it trickling down into me so that in some extraordinary way, he was now part of me.

I poured the cold wine over me and then tried to drink it before it sank into the earth where the semen had gone. Above me, the sky was turning ominous with huge banks of clouds the color of grapes.

As I lay there, I saw the weeds press down under the weight of some moving thing.

A snake, thick and the color of dirt and gravel, slithered along the red earth, just a few feet away from me. The eyes gazed at me for a moment and then the animal glided away.

It made me think of how close to nature one lives out here. At night, I can hear a wildcat wailing in the nearby woods, sounding like a baby. I can almost imagine dark figures of dead Indians moving around out there, too. Yes, it's very different out here from life in a metropolis.

I returned home, covered with red dust and wine and glimmers of another man's sperm: only minutes ago, his cream had simmered in those dark balls of his.

Now, it coated my stomach like balm. It meant that for better or for worse, we were somehow linked together and nothing would ever change that.

#

And for a week, we participated in this secret ritual, which he was unaware of. I would watch him go to that same spot and perform his unforgettable one-man routine and stroll away, his slacks soiled and moist.

And I would creep over there, with my bottle of wine and become slightly drunk as I licked up his offering and pretend he was there with me.

That is why I am sure something will happen this afternoon.

The sky here has loomed dark and dangerous each day but nothing happens. When I shopped at the Piggly-Wiggly this morning, I heard the cashiers agreeing that a storm was certain to break today.

"It shoah does look like it, don't it?" one of them nodded. "Gotta plant my squash and mater plants sometimes this week."

"I'm sewing me a dress pattern I got in that magazine. It's a purty dress I can wear to church or somethin' formal like. Donnie Lee Foy didn't like that last dress I made. It was red and he said it was—it was cheap looking."

The air was so hot and suffocating I thought I would faint before I reached home.

I've prepared myself for our first balling. The bed linen has been changed. Instead of regulation white, I've put on my swanky black silk sheets and comforter. A small lamp glows on the nightstand with copies of my books stacked casually. The big air-conditioner hums steadily so that it's cool and inviting in here.

I've put on a robe of gold lame that never fails to turn on my partner. It brings out the amber of my curls, the light blue of my eyes. There is wine and beer in the fridge.

He will step across my threshold today or I'm moving out tomorrow. I can no longer write because he has become an obsession.

The doorbell rings—twice.

#

He stands there as usual, quietly. A smile quivers on his lips. I want to kiss them real soon, like minutes away. How juicy they look! Through the glasses, his eyes study me intently.

"Hi!' I sing out. "What'cha got for me today?"

He hands me my letters and bills but he releases them slowly.

"What'cha want?" he asks softly. My heart quickens and I find it difficult to catch my breath. I pretend to study my mail. A bill from Bloomingdale's. A check from my publisher. Three other letters that look like love notes from some of my readers.

I glance up at him now. One hand rests on his mailbag. The other one is above, on the frame of the door.

He's so goddamned big!

"I want—a box," I murmur. "A big box."

"What you want in it?" he asks quietly. His fingers wipe sweat from his nose. A dab of catsup darkens the corner of his mouth.

"Something juicy and thick and dark. I want cream on it, too. Lots of cream. I want a surprise. It has to be unexpected."

It starts raining behind him. The air smells like wetness, soil and grass. I say nothing more. It is time for him to respond. It's part of the game he insists on playing.

He suddenly brushes past me into the living room. My hand feels moist where his body has touched it. He needs a bath. His body odor is powerful. But I like it like that.

"Where's your bathroom?"

"In there—in my bedroom."

I follow him and while he vanishes into the john, I sit on the edge of my bed, trembling.

At last, it's happening.

Next to my bed is a big window I closed because of the chance of rain. Now, I open it because I want to enjoy that cool, wet breeze sweep in. I turn off the air-conditioner. There is no screen on the window. I can lean out and pick honeysuckle that grows up the side of my cottage. I look down and see a huge Copperhead snake slithering off into the tall weeds.

It looks like the same one I saw in the cornfield. Why is it so close to where I live now? The Postman comes out of the toilet.

He has worn his dark glasses during all of his visits. Now, he removes them and puts them on my dresser.

His eyes are blue. And very cold. And suddenly I sense danger. I don't know this man at all. We're here completely alone, isolated from everything. No one knows I'm here—except my landlady, my publisher, my shrink, a friend or two—and this man whose name I don't even know.

He tears off his shirt and throws it into the corner of the room. His nipples are pink and thick. One has a metal ring gleaming from it. I didn't notice it before. Did he wear it just for me?

The biceps of his big arms swell impressively. On his shoulder is a blue tattoo that shows a heart and the words: *Born to Raise Hell.*

I start to get up, to put some space between us, for my unease grows. But he has moved closer, having kicked off his boots and stripped off his slacks and gray underwear. They're stained and dirty.

He mashes his privates against my face, grabbing the back of my head and grinding my nose and mouth against his warm tools. His hand, that huge hand, is squeezing and yanking brutally at his testicles.

Backing away slightly, he rips down his foreskin and crams the pink tip of his phallus into my mouth. I gag and try to push him away but he just grunts and slams me back against the mattress.

His big body now pins me against my bed, and his hips grind and push against my face, ramming his hardness past my tonsils. I feel like I'm going to suffocate but it doesn't bother him as I writhe and scratch to get away from him.

Suddenly, he rolls over on his back, pulling out of my mouth and yanking my face up to his. His mouth covers mine and now his tongue has replaced his erection as it shoots deep into my mouth, shutting off my air supply.

His spit tastes like tobacco, Juicy-Fruit gum, beer and hamburgers. He has a lot of spit and pushes wads of it into my mouth until it over-flows. It runs down my chin and onto my neck.

He spits onto my eyes and into my nostrils, and then lashes his tongue over all that wetness until all my features glisten with his saliva.

It is like he's found a big, rubber doll, the kind you find in the porno shops, where you inflate them up into life-size figures.

He says nothing and now rolls over on his back, pulling me on top of him and using his big hand, guides my face over and over his chest and then he guides my mouth over to his right tit.

It doesn't have a metal ring in it like the other one and he grinds it into my mouth. He mashes my head down so hard my teeth sink into his pectoral but it doesn't faze him.

"Bite it!" he suddenly growls. "Chew it off, buddy, just tear it off."

Repulsed, I try to escape but his hand tightens on the back of my neck until the pain is unbearable. So I chew and bite the nugget of flesh until I feel it free and rolling around my tongue.

"Swallow it!" he demands quietly. "Swallow that fucker!" Gagging, but prodded by his fingers biting viciously into my neck, I obey.

Now, he pushes my face on downwards, over his dirty, hard skin, into his lint-filled navel, on past the pubic hair and finally onto that sticky rod of power.

He holds it up and stuffs it into my mouth. He pushes his hips upward until I gag again. It doesn't bother him. His strange eyes roll backwards in joy as he unloads his sexual pressure into my mouth.

I want to get up and get him out of here but he has only started. He raises his hips and pushes his balls into my mouth. He fucks my mouth with them and it doesn't bother him when my teeth scrap them until blood seeps out.

This seems to excite him even more for he turns over, pulls me up towards the pillows and gets on top of me.

He pinions my hands down against the bed and raises his hips to position his hardness inside my cheeks.

"Don't!" I cry. "Use some lubricant, a condom! You'll rip me!"

`His response is to slap my face hard, then he pushes my legs up, holding them, and then he rams his tool up into me. I feel flesh tearing as he grunts and growls and crams it in deeper.

"Boo hoo!" he mimics me. "Little baby can't take no pain, can he, poah wittle babsy-wabsy!"

He throws himself so hard on me now that it knocks my breath out. His hips push and digs his dick in deeper. Between clenched teeth, I hear him gasping:

"Gotta get it twice, cocksucker. One time's not enough. Just won't do it. Gotta get it twice. Postman always comes twice."

I feel hot blood seeping out of me and into my black silk sheets. His cock is like an enemy's sword. For despite my pleas for him to stop, he slaps my ass, hard, violently, snickering and rips even deeper into me.

#

Finally, in my stupor, I hear those familiar gasps and moans coming from him. His face is close to mine. He bends down and bites my ear viciously. He whimpers in a high, keening sound and his frantic hip motions slow down.

The postman pulls himself out of me quickly.

Holding his instrument of torture, streaked with blood, just an inch from my face, he displays his second eruption. He rubs the white stickiness into my hair and into my nose with those swollen fingers of his. He coats my lips with it and inches his fingers into my mouth.

Suddenly, he shoots his hand hard into my mouth, so that bangs against the back of my throat. I gag and knock his hand away.

I lay there without moving, trying to catch my breath, knowing I should get up to stop my bleeding. My silk sheets are spattered with semen and spit and blood.

I feel dead.

He sits on the edge of the bed, staring at me, smiling and then to my horror, he reaches up to his left eye, gouges it out and holds it towards me.

"It's a glass eye. Put it in your mouth."

"No," I gasp. "Not that."

He grabs my head and pries open my mouth and crams the glass eye into it.

"Roll it around with your spit. Get it good and gooey with spit."

He looks like a demon with his one eye glittering, the other one black and vacant. He holds my chin still while he rams his fingers into my mouth to retrieve his eye.

Casually, he sticks it back in and stands up. He pulls on his clothes, his dark shades. Snorting snot onto his fingers, he wipes it against his pants.

"I'll be dropping by to see you tomorrow and everyday after that," he says quietly. "You ate my tittie and you put my eye in your mouth. That makes your ass mine. Understand?"

He cuts the air with his finger with each word. "Don't go fucking around with anybody else, know what I'm saying?? Don't even think of trying to leave here, you got that, good buddy? Know what I'm saying? I read your mail before you get it; I know what your plans are and where to find you. You better get your throat and ass greased up good because I always gotta cum twice. Always! And you'd better pray to God I do— or you won't have any ass left."

He walks over to me and jams a finger up into my anus. I cry out and recoil. Now he wiggles the finger in front of me. It is moist with blood. He puts it into his mouth and licks it clean.

"By the time I finish with you kid," he chuckles, "I'm gonna have that cunt of yours opened, wide, wide, wide. Even if I gotta use a knife."

He saunters out of my room and I watch him pick up his mailbag before closing my front door.

The storm is nearly over. I can smell the cornfield and the wet earth soaked with his seed and the old wine I spilt there. I still lay on the bed.

From the open window, the wind and rain blow over my face.

YOUNG SAVAGE

◆

When I was growing up down South, us kids were forever being warned to stay away from those swamp boys.

Oh, Lord! To hear the adults talk, those hulks that inhabited the Red Burr Swamp Community were scum, trash, worse than animals. They were so down in the dirt degenerate that good Christian folk—like my God-fearing parents—could be struck dead by lightning if they even whispered what all them sinners down yonder in the swamp did by night.

My feverish imagination rocketed into high gear at such gossip. What could those hot-blooded bucks do to make them candidates for hell fire?

Carson City, North Carolina, sat atop a small mountain. At its base surged the swampland. About 20 families lived down there, most of them so incestuous that no one could figure out their relationships. A few of the families, though, were rumored to be of gypsy blood—sharp and independent, owning prosperous farm spreads.

They traveled in big cars, lived in rambling old wood houses handed down through each generation from the Civil War. They stayed to themselves. They wanted nothing to do with us "townies," as anyone who lived in Carson City was called.

They lived by their own rules and saw life differently from the rest of us.

When I told my parents I thought the swamp studs were a heck lot more interesting than their white bread counterparts, my folks like to have died. Mama chased me out of the house with a broom.

Daddy got his leather strap ready. "Them Burr boys comes from a place the devil jus' loves!" screeched my Born Again Pappy. "Maybe you oughta join 'em."

"Whoopee!" I hooted. "Just tell me how, you damned ole ass-hole!"

And with that, he grabbed me, lowered my britches and before lashing them with his strap, took his damned good time rubbing my buns before drooling on them and watching them shiver beneath the lash of leather.

Those sultry outcasts and I shared the common bond of being different. Just as the snooty town kids hated them "swampers...Burr Boys...Jungle Coots," so was I loathed by the same bigots.

Why? Because I had zero desire in trying to be like them. Peer pressure meant nothing to one who was used to being called "queer...homo...cocksucker...she-boy...sissy."

Besides, I was proud of my gold curls, the way I could swish by the swamp boys and watch them wink and nod approvingly, while rubbing their crotches. Most were past 18 years old, actually young men, but those swamp parents really did believe in their kids getting an "edication", as they pronounced it.

What made them even more interested in me was that I didn't try to hide my fascination with their baskets. Those swamp studs wore the tightest jeans anywhere. I heard they helped each other squeeze into them, making sure their abundant male privates were outlined to a scandalous degree.

And some of them had butts so luscious I fantasized about perching a cup and saucer on those dimples.

Those swamp hunks always sprawled in their desks, their thighs spread wide and making a big pretext of not noticing how those big mounds in their britches made the girls and teachers blush, and their town enemies glower.

There were two swamp cuties in my senior class. And their undisputed leader was a stunning young animal by the name of Jimmy Jack Johnson. At six foot two, he evoked a vivid image of a dangerous but luscious panther, tamed just enough to wear painted on jeans that were molded lovingly around his shapely butt and heavy equipment. As if this wasn't enough, he offered even more goodies: a sleeveless tee shirt and an Elvis Presley pompadour slicked back into a gleaming helmet.

Jade eyes glowered out from beneath incredibly long lashes. His skin was tawny amber, giving credence to the legend that he came from real Indian ancestry. But even if a town girl drooled over this rippling collection of muscles, she wasted her time.

This young savage dated a 35-year-old divorcee in nearby Thomasville, while his fellow swamp "cooties" screwed the whores in High Point.

The very traits that repulsed the townies against me fascinated Jimmy Jack Johnson and company.

I'd pass him in the hallway where he'd be sipping his big Nehi Orange for breakfast. He'd throw me a wicked wink.

"So how's we doin' today, Goldilocks?" he'd drawl in that deep Southern groan, that sounded like it was coated with honey and bourbon. I'd give my ass a few extra wiggles and Jimmy Jack would rub himself in front of everybody and go: "Um. Um! UM!"

I loved watching him swing his beautiful rump around, drool over the huge swell of his arms and the bulge of his pectorals and nipples beneath his moist tee shirt.

His close buddy, Tater Head Johnson, was also in our senior class. People called him that because he had kinky red hair worn in a ponytail. Although shorter than Jimmy Jack, Tater Head was still trim and lean and something of a smart ass.

He was notorious for throwing fits. The girls shrieked when old Tater Head flopped around the floor like a Mexican Jumping bean. He'd jerk his head and roll his eyes and flip all over the place. I was sure he faked these convulsions just to get under the skin of his town enemies and to get attention from his swamp buddies.

One thing about the swamp boys, which embarrassed everyone except me was the animal sounds, they liked to make.

You'd hear them oinking like pigs, mooing like cows and bleating as if they were sheep. For some reason, when Jimmy Jack did his pig imitation, his buddies became hysterical.

They'd slide out of their desks, gasping for air and their faces all scrunched up into purple masks of hilarity. They'd stagger around, bounce off the walls and hold their stomachs, becoming helpless with hysteria as Jimmy Jack kept making his noises.

And people were shocked, *shocked* when Jimmy Jack's buddies felt him up in public.

I'd see them crowding around him in the hallways and as they talked, these studs would squeeze and caress his muscles, rub his stomach, his butt and then—and then his basket!

He never even blinked an eye. Sipping his Nehi Orange, he'd act like this was a natural way to act when you're the male knockout of the school—even if you are from the Red Burr Swamp.

And when you saw him standing there, brooding and gorgeous and dangerous looking, those jade eyes glinting, his pink lips all wet and full, it was easy to believe rumors that he was really in his twenties and his parents wouldn't let him get married unless he finished high school.

#

For a month, I noticed how the swamp boys vanished into a small wooded area next to the school during lunch breaks. What did they do there? Smoking? Drinking beer—the two biggest evils in Carson City? I finally went up to Jimmy.

It was our last day in school. Both of us had graduated the night before in a simple ceremony and I felt like I had nothing to lose.

He had just parked his Ford in the lot and was smoking a cigarette. Up close, his beauty was stunning. I watched his biceps swell as he lifted the cigarette up to his mouth.

With one foot beneath him, propped against the car, I saw a thick bulge in his pants. His strange, green eyes danced as I came closer and greeted him.

"Jimmy Jack, just what are you and your buddies doing in the woods everyday at lunch time?" I drawled. "Is it something nasty?"

His grin showed even white teeth. "Wanna come along today with me and find out? I don't know if you can handle it."

"Handle what, Jimmy Jack Johnson?"

His big hand with the red classroom ring on it brushed his crotch. My eyes followed this gesture. I blushed and he burst out laughing.

"I think you can handle it," he drawled and grinned, giving me a wink before he swung that gorgeous rump of his toward the classroom building.

And at noon that day, he escorted into the woods—and into a way of life I never knew existed.

#

His bosom buddy, Tater Head, and the other Swamp boys from our class were already there in a small clearing. Slurping their eternal Nehi Orange drinks, smoking cigarettes, they expressed delight at the sight of their sizzling leader—one who amazed me by quickly peeling off his tee shirt, his loafers and white socks, and then—his painted on jeans.

My eyes must have been big as saucers as the other boys saw my expression and laughed, but not in a mean way. Their eyes, too, gleamed with admiration when they beheld a completely bare assed Jimmy Jack Johnson.

He pulled at his very man-like privates, while one of the boys put a lit cigarette between the lips of the Adonis who smiled sweetly and gave me a wink that seemed to say: you ain't seen nothing yet.

"Whar's me a hole?" he barked.

"Rat cheer it is, good buddy!" grinned Tater Head, indicating an opening in the soft dirt. Jimmy strutted toward the hole and I saw what a fantastic rump. It jutted out dramatically from the base of his spine and I had no doubt that one could easily put a glass or cup on either cheek, and the contents of both wouldn't spill a drop.

We all gathered around as Jimmy Jack squatted above the hole. He grunted and strained and proceeded to relieve himself. All around me, his adoring worshippers were going crazy with excitement. Whooping and clapping their hands, they stooped down to watch Jimmy Jack fill up the cavity.

The boys ran their hands all over his muscles, through his hair, pulled at his genitals and covered his handsome face with kisses. One of them put a fresh cigarette between his lips and he seemed totally comfortable about the excitement he was causing.

A drowsy, thoughtful look was on his face as he stared off toward the school building. At that moment, I thought he looked like a king or a powerful warrior, squatting there in his entire stunning splendor.

And it was years later when I would read about ancient rituals, in which a king was worshipped for his abilities to procreate and dispense with body wastes in public. In fact, some American Indian tribes expected their leader to do everything before his people that most people would do in the privacy of their bathroom.

Jimmy turned his flushed face toward me and winked again. "You getting a good look at my butt, little Goldilocks? Get on down there and take a good look now. Don't be shy. Ohh, I got a big one coming out now and it's got your name all over it."

It was, indeed a big one, and while this was happening his buddies took turns wrapping their arms around his chest, nuzzling his face and kissing his body. When Jimmy Jack had finished, he sighed.

"Okay, somebody clean me up."

Tater Head pushed everyone else aside as he rushed forward with handful of dead leaves and tidied up his companion. But he didn't do so without a struggle. The other boys were all scuffling to bury their faces in Jimmy Jack's crack and he patiently let them take turns doing so.

He stood up, stretched and yawned and then went over to a big oak tree and leaned against it, smoking yet another fresh cigarette put between his lips. Another boy put a bottle of Nehi Orange drink in his hand. There was no doubt now that Jimmy Jack Johnson was their god, their leader, and their king.

Sweat dripped from his thick nipples, running down those powerful pecs, over the flatness of his stomach and then onto his privates. They looked swollen, almost grotesque in their darkness and thickness. It made me think of an over-ripe banana.

What made his beauty so unforgettable was that it was a natural look. There was nothing chiseled or artificial about his spectacular torso.

"Wanna play with my meat?" he asked shyly, with a sweet smile, like a rugged little boy offering you his favorite toy. "I got a grown man's dick," he added quietly. "Been using it like a man since I was seven. Just needs a few strong jerks, like you're milking a big cow teat, and you got me."

Before I could accept his extraordinary offer, furious voices rose up around me.

"You promised me I could pound your pud today, buddy!" squawked Tater Head. "You said all the cum in your balls was gonna be mine today!"

A scrawny swamp boy named Clem shook his fist at me. "You ain't getting that goober, Mr. Townie! I been waiting to gobble that goober all morning long! Ain't thought about nothing else but grabbing that big pickle of Jimmy Jack's and making it squirt out the good stuff! Jimmy Jack, I just gotta have it, old pal!"

"You all be quiet now!" growled our sweating Apollo. "Lil' Jason Fury here is our guest. You all know how's he wanted my dick. We done talked about how he just stares and stares at it like he's gonna die. And we all know his mouth hangs open when he sees my butt swing by in the hallway."

They grumbled and nodded their heads reluctantly. There was nothing sarcastic about the way Jimmy Jack noted these facts. It was as if it was to be expected and appreciated. I was shocked by the naturalness of his words. The townies would have crucified me and beat me to a pulp for even thinking something like that. With these boys, it was a natural part of life.

Now, he put his hand around his luscious manhood and held it up towards me. "Hep yo'self, lil' Jason boy. It's all yours, as much as you want. Now, boys, step back and give him some room to work on it."

"T'aint fair, t'aint fair, Mr. Jimmy Jack Johnson!" shrieked Tater Head. Angrily, he kicked dirt into the hole where his buddy had relieved himself. "How could you do this to me, buddy? I'm 'bout crazy for it. See how my hands are shaking and my head keeps bobbing around and my eyes are rolling and—I—I think I'm gonna have me a fit. A big fit!"

As he rolled his eyes and staggered around the clearing, the others muttered nervously. Tater Head Johnson was famous everywhere for his dramatic "fits" which could last for a few seconds to nearly an hour.

Someone said uneasily to Jimmy Jack: "Maybe you oughta let ole Tater Head have some of your dick for just a few seconds. We don't want him doing a flip-out on us out here."

But Tater Head had decided to have a full-fledged fit. He crumpled to the ground and flopped around, jerking his head and kicking and slapping the dirt.

That stupid little fake, I thought. I know what he's up to. Stepping over his convulsing body, I fell to my knees and startled Jimmy Jack by grabbing his warm, swollen meat and began jerking him so strenuously that the others ignored the writhing form of Tater Head.

"Pop him out a big one!" someone howled. "You can do it, Jimmy Jack! Show him how a swamp boy can do it!"

With his hands behind his head like a physique pin-up, Jimmy sucked in his breath and pursed his lips as I worked him up to a semi-hard. But suddenly Tater Head, aware that nobody was watching him, leaped to his feet, pushed me aside and used both his fists to build Jimmy Jack up to a purple, juicy stiff

Jimmy Jack gasped loudly, but he didn't resist the brutal mauling his manhood was receiving at the fists of his buddy. In fact, it looked like he thoroughly enjoyed this vicious workout.

Suddenly, our sweating stud muttered something unintelligible and Tater Head stopped his hand exercises and fell back.

We watched Jimmy Jack's puffed up beauty pulsate slightly against his rippling stomach. The erection was dark and dangerous; the bulbous tip a gleaming pink. It was an amazing sight. This enormous orgasm happening right there, in that small wooded area, just a hundred feet away from our school building.

When he finished, his eyes remained closed for several moments, while his stomach heaved in and out.

His comrades pushed up against him. Their hands slid over his butt and into his cleft, and even more grappled with his sticky erection.

Jimmy Jack cracked open his eyes, saw me and smiled. He held out his arms for me and I rushed up to them. Pulling me tight against him, he kissed me deep for a long time and thrust his phallus into my hands.

Without his arms around me, I would certainly have collapsed. For I had never seen anything like that before in my life, not even another naked man. And within an hour, I had witnessed my fantasies coming alive.

"You wanna go down on me, don't you, lil' Jason?" he whispered into my ear. "You want to suck old Jimmy Jack's big ole dick, don't you now? Everybody does. Men, women, children, animals. They all want it. You come home with me after school and you can do anything you want to with my body."

His father was planning a special celebration that evening because Jimmy Jack was the first Johnson boy to finish high school in 20 years. And for me, it was a perfect time for my parents were visiting friends in nearby Siler City until late that night.

And so two hours later, I was sitting between my gorgeous new lover and Tater Head, in the front seat of Jimmy Jack's green Ford, skimming away from Dullsville, USA, towards that sinful Red Burr Swamp Community.

#

A woman driving a red truck honked us to a stop.

We had turned off the main road into a narrow, dirt one which clearly led deeper into the swamp area. On either side of us were alligator infested bogs. A water moccasin fell from a tree onto the hood of our car. I snuggled up closer to Jimmy Jack who just snorted.

The woman had stuck her head out of the truck window.

"Whar you been, Mr. Jimmy Jack Johnson?" she called out angrily. "You ain't been by and I wanna know why?"

She was heavy but attractive with dark, frizzed hair, heavy make-up and a cigarette stuck between her lips. She was definitely no teenage girl. Bracelets clinked together on her wrist and on her ears were crimson earrings shaped like strawberries.

"Been busy, Ruby Mae," muttered my sullen Hercules.

Her tone changed to one of pleading. "Aw, come on over, honey. I'll have some Nehi Orange drinks, some tater chip sandwiches with lots of that mayonnaise you jus' love and lots of Spam. I even brought some

Baby Ruth candy bars for you. All the things you like, Jimmy Jack. How 'bout a deep fried peanut butter sandwich, dripping with butter and chocolate syrup?"

"Maybe," growled the young stud before pressing his foot down on the gas pedal. The car shot on down the road and Tater Head howled.

"All ole Ruby Mae wants is Jimmy Jack's big goober stuck up her cunt. I saw her one night trying to suck him off and she couldn't even get the tip inside her mouth. But when Jimmy Jack rammed that flagpole up her pussy, she squealed like a stuck pig."

Jimmy Jack smiled at the memory and I watched those startling eyes of lime flicker with a hot flame. Within a few minutes, we pulled up beside a big, rambling house.

It was unpainted but neat. All around the place were big trees with limbs dripping with curtains of Spanish moss. A half dozen dogs raced up to the car. They went crazy when Jimmy Jack made smacking sounds and clicked his fingers. I noticed how all of them licked his crotch and he just laughed.

"They know where to find a mouthful of juicy, dripping meat," cackled Tater Head. Later, I wondered about the meaning of his words. Jimmy's crotch was still stained with drying semen. That's what contributed to his intoxicating aroma. He wore no aftershave or deodorant. His skin gave off a scent that was musky, sweaty, woodsy, all male.

We entered a big kitchen. In the corner were a group of men, all sipping Nehi Orange drinks and watching Andy Griffin on the big TV in "Mayberry, RFD." They were husky, dark men in bib overalls with good-natured smiles on their faces as they greeted us.

Tater Head told me they were all neighbors who had come by for the special occasion. And standing at the stove was a tall, handsome man who was putting chicken into the oven to bake. His muscles were impressive and his chest broad. A pair of loose jeans hung low on his hips. On his bicep was an impressive tattoo of a valentine and in the middle were the words: *Mama's Boy*. His dark hair was pulled back into a ponytail.

With a dashing smile, he shook my hand and introduced himself as Sam Johnson, Jimmy Jack's father. With his moustache and dark, heavy eyes, he reminded me of a very sexy Clark Gable.

Then Jimmy Jack and Tater Head surprised me again by casually stripping off their clothes and folding them neatly, placing them on a table by the door.

"Daddy," drawled Jimmy Jack, "you know I've mentioned Jason quite a few times. He's the one whose been wanting to go down on me and have me fuck him. Now it's his first dick so could we do it rat cheer on the kitchen table where it's comfortable?"

Sam Johnson was putting sweet potatoes into the oven, too, and he just glanced up, smiling and nodded.

"You two boys go right ahead and do anything you want to. I won't be setting the table for a while. Just clean up your mess when you finish me, now, ya hear, Jimmy Jack? When you fucked Gurney this morning on the table I had to clean up after you. You shot cum all over the grits and gravy and I done told you I don't want any jism on my grits. That's about 5,000 calories more than I need."

"Yeah, Paw. I'll be careful."

Once more, I was dumbfounded by their casual attitude to something considered by Carson City as so evil and earth shaking. You were supposed to never even think about sex.

From the corner of my eye, I saw Tater Head going up to one of the swarthy men, unbuckled his bibb overalls, peeled them down and buried his face in the farmer's lap.

Before me, Jimmy Jack looked gorgeous as he sat down on the edge of the table, leaned back and held out his phallus to me. Knowing that nothing I could do could possibly shock these strange people, I got down on my knees and for the first time, put a man's goober into my mouth.

All the men had been watching me and Tater Head and now one of them came over to me and knelt down beside me. He pushed me gently aside.

"Ole buddy," he smiled, "I know this is your first dick and all but you got a stud here whose been used to somebody deep throating him since he was just a little boy. Here, let me show you. I'm his godfather, Gurney Bryce."

Jimmy Jack had laid back on the table with his mouth pursed and his face scrunched up in sexual joy. Another of the men had come over and sucked on Jimmy Jack's nipples and licked that chiseled stomach.

Sam, the father, paused for a moment as he stirred a pot of stew, to glance at the warm welcome his son was receiving.

"Gurney can deep throat my boy like nobody in the swamp community and they've all tried," he smiled. "When you can't find either Jimmy Jack or Gurney anywhere, all you gotta do and go outside near the outhouse. You'll find my son there with his legs wrapped around Gurney's neck and Gurney just sucking like a crazy pole cat on that man's dick."

Jimmy Jack was sweating profusely now as he continued to quiver and gasp at the attention being paid to his sex organ. Then, he began to tremble, a soft cry came up from his lips and Gurney gagged slightly.

Even the father paused in his cooking to watch his boy getting relief. The others had gathered around, including Tater Head, and Jimmy Jack didn't disappoint them. Gurney fell back, gasping, his mouth wet and a drop of white cream on his chin. His face was flushed as he stared with longing at the swollen wonder he had just worked on.

Jimmy Jack grinned and sat up, rubbing his tender privates. His balls were so big they made me thing of apples encased in silk.

"Nobody does it like, ole man Gurney here," he said fondly. "Say, I'm hungry as a pig. When we gonna eat, Paw?"

"Just as soon as Mr. Tater Head back there finishes gobbling up Luke. Tater Head, you hurry up now. Supper's about ready. Jimmy Jack, you left a big gobbet of stuff right there near that cup. Didn't I tell you to not leave a mess behind you?"

#

Nobody seemed to think it at all odd that Jimmy Jack and Tater Head sat at the long table bare butt while we dug into a feast. As Sam Johnson boasted, it was a special occasion for his son had finally gotten his high school diploma.

We gorged on baked chicken, platters of sliced tomatoes, cucumbers, creamed potatoes, homemade cottage cheese and butter and pitchers of fresh milk.

"Everything you're eating," smiled Sam Johnson, "comes from our farm. Including Jimmy Jack sitting there all big and sexed up."

Everyone chuckled and Jimmy Jack smiled, as if used to being commented on. After our dessert of watermelon, the men began cleaning off the table and putting things into the sink.

But every time they walked passed Jimmy Jack, they bent down to kiss his cheek, caress his nipples or reach down and fondle his impressive genitalia.

Jimmy Jack leaned back with a cigarette and a bottle of beer, a sensual half-smile on his lips, and his father joined us.

"This boy here," he began, "he reads the good book, the Bible, everyday of his life and if he doesn't, I'll wear that butt of his off. He found Jesus and he loves the Lard. The Lard, he done been good to me. Jimmy Jack, now you stand up and bend over this here table. I want to show lil' Jason something the good Lard done give to us all to enjoy."

The muscular buck obeyed and bent his rippling body over the edge of the table so that his stunning backside faced us. Mr. Johnson got up and ran his hands over the tawny dimples and deep into the crack.

"You see this boy's butt? Only God his self could have made an ass like this one 'cause I ain't never seen one as beautiful and I've seen hundreds of them, in the Navy, down here in the swamp."

The other men had gathered around us now and they all nodded solemnly in agreement. One of them murmured: "Amen, brother!"

"Sometimes I just can't think of nothing all day but young Jimmy Jack's backside," sighed Mr. Johnson. "I want to find him, pull his britches down and bury my face inside his crack."

The father suddenly fell to his knees and we lost sight of his face as he pressed it tight inside the cleft. He slobbered and groaned and Jimmy rested his face on his arms, his eyes closed and an angelic smile on his face.

Sam Johnson stood up, kicked off his loose jeans and showed to us his sturdy erection, one that stuck straight out in all its tanned glory. He stood behind his son and casually entered him from the rear. Jimmy gasped slightly and closed his eyes, a warm smile playing on his full lips. His father grunted and trembled as we all watched him penetrate deeper with each thrust.

Like his boy, Sam Johnson had a beautiful rear end, one lightly dusted with hair. While this was going on, Tater Head was sitting in a chair with his thighs parted and the reliable Gurney was giving him passionate head.

Two cars pulled up in front of the house. Through the window, I saw nearly a dozen rugged looking men of all sizes and ages amble up to the porch and into the kitchen.

All of them wore cowboy hats and boots and jeans but no shirts. Several had big tattoos on their shoulders, arms and chest and some could have won trophies in body building competitions.

When they saw Sam Johnson still loving Jimmy Jack, they all whooped and laughed. Jimmy Jack grinned and greeted them while his father was too busy screwing to look around.

When the father finished, he pulled out to show everyone his orgasm and it spattered onto the floor. His son turned over so that he lay on his back, showing no hurry to go anywhere.

"Sam, I just mopped the floor this afternoon," one of the men groused good-naturedly. Jimmy Jack remained laying there with his legs pulled back, smiling and smoking a cigarette and sipping from a new bottle of beer. His groin was so swollen and loose, it touched the table-top.

While I studied this scene, I was struck by how timeless it seemed: for at that moment, beneath the gold light of the overhead lamp, Jimmy Jack did resemble a type of swamp god—young, beautiful, big, his muscles swelled up and wet with sweat, his long hair now in tousled disarray, his face flushed with sexual heat.

"Your Daddy's gonna wear out your ass-hole," one of the swarthy newcomers cackled. "Every time I come here, he's got you on the table, just fucking you like he had a big, wet cunt."

"Yeah," grinned the sizzling beauty, "he does seem to get pleasure grinding it in every chance he's got."

All of the men were neighbors or relatives of the Johnsons. I couldn't tell who was who but there was something wild and dangerous and exciting about them.

All of them had dark eyes, an intense sensual aura around them with sturdy, rugged bodies. One of the younger men, Billy Joe, went up to Jimmy Jack who still lay naked on the table.

"You're giving me some of that ass tonight, Mr. Jimmy Jack," snarled Billy Joe. "Just because you got your diploma today don't make you any better than me. You let your Daddy fuck you anytime he wants to. But with me? Hell, no! Tonight, I'm getting some of it."

Jimmy mashed out his cigarette on top of a beer can and swung his feet to the floor. He stretched his body, an electrifying sight with his big hands reaching upwards, an act that sent all of his muscles into a dazzling dance. Sweat gleamed on his smooth skin and his privates swung heavy and swollen between his thighs.

"If you get my ass tonight," he drawled to Bill Joe, "you gotta go for it like all the others. I can't play favorites, you know that. Too many guys want me. I gotta give it to whoever gets me first."

From the moment they entered, the men had all been stripping off their clothes. Now, all were naked, including the rugged, dark-eyed Billy Joe who kept slapping his phallus across the palm of his hand like a rubber mallet.

His eyes never left Jimmy Jack who was now the center of attraction. But several had gathered around Tater Head who was on his back in a corner of the kitchen, getting screwed by a big, beefy man who resembled a wrestler.

"You ready to play the game?" Jimmy Jack asked softly and his words were like a bolt of lightning: all the men nodded eagerly, shifting their feet and pulling at themselves.

"Tater Head, get on over here now," called out Sam Johnson. "Mitch, you take your cock out of him for right now so's we can start playing the game."

Game? What type of weird game were the guys planning now? It had grown silent, everyone stared at Jimmy Jack who ran a hand over his gleaming body and with a smile he nodded.

"Alright men, the game has now begun."

With wild whoops and whistles, several of the guests picked Jimmy Jack up on their shoulders and carried him outside into the scalding darkness.

#

Although night, it was so light from the big full moon it was like twilight.

I followed the crowd and the men put Jimmy Jack down in the middle of a clearing. His father held up his hand for quiet.

"Now, we're gonna play a game of Squealing Pigs. I know you men want to have some fun with my boy and I know he wants to have some fun with you. But first, you gotta catch him and lil' ole Tater Head. If you catch either one, you make them squeal like a pig, then you get a gallon of my famous, home made Johnson Moonshine, I made it right out there behind the backhouse."

Tater Head joined Jimmy in the center of the clearing and the two young bucks taunted their admirers by flapping their cocks at them, slapping their butts and dancing around.

Their admirers, though, were dead serious. None of them smiled. All were breathing heavily, their eyes glittering and I saw one or two actually run a tongue over their lips, in anticipation of sexual fulfillment. The luscious objects of all these fantasies were aware of their attention and redoubled their mugging and dancing around.

Sam Johnson counted slowly to three and then as Jimmy Jack ran towards the water, his buddy, Tater Head, took off towards the barn. Both were pursued by a mob of men.

Surprisingly, Jimmy Jack was the first to be captured. I watched the men tackle him and cover him with their bodies. There was a lot of laughter, snorting and grumbling as he kicked and punched but they got his legs pulled back to his shoulder.

And the first to mount him was none other than the very determined Billy Joe.

"I told you I was getting some of your ass tonight," panted Billy Joe.

"You gotta make me squeal like a pig," gasped Jimmy Jack.

In the meantime, Tater Head was also captured. Instead of fighting, though, he was delighted to be caught and the first one to plug him up was none other than Sam Johnson, the host of the evening's revelry.

"Stick it in, Sammy!" hooted Tater Head. "Screw me 'til you drop!"

Furiously, the men drilled steadily, causing their partners to squirm around in the dirt. An hour passed, the screwing hadn't let up for a moment as one man pushed in, got relief and was replaced by another.

I think Jimmy Jack was acting when he suddenly let out a big squeal. The men around him cheered and the man who caused him to squeal was none other than Billy Joe, who had come around for seconds. And a few minutes later, Tater Head began to make pig noises.

Another car full of men had driven up and yet more handsome swamp men spilled out, stripped off their clothes and began swigging on moonshine they'd brought along in Mason jars.But they had a different idea of fun.

They found the strapping Sam Johnson, naked and feeling no pain and after wrestling around with him, they threw him to the ground and began gangbanging him. One after the other. And only after he made sounds like a porker did they give him a break, a very short one, for five minutes later, Sam was on his back again.

The men had crowded around him once more to get a chance to poke their erections up into his butt.

Covered with dirt and grass and sweat, Jimmy Jack had crawled over to an apple tree and eagerly took the beer I gave him. Someone else lit a cigarette and put it between his lips.

I got down on my stomach between his thighs and grabbed his hardness and tried to stuffing it into my mouth. But it had become much too large and my companion's admirer, Gurney, shoved me aside and once more took over.

A crowd had gathered around to watch this act and when Jimmy Jack was ready to blow, he aimed it for the stars and startled us all with the abundance and duration of his orgasm.

As soon as he finished spurting, though, the men forced his legs back and began another gang-bang. Jimmy Jack just smiled and winced with pleasure as his wet body trembled from the assault.

"Do it deeper, Elmer Lee!" he gasped as one hefty swamp boy took over. "You know how to do it now. Uh, you're getting there, good buddy."

Somebody had dragged out a mattress and Sam Johnson was carried over to it and plopped down. Nearly a dozen men were now waiting to mount him and then someone had the idea of carrying Jimmy Jack over there, too.

The ground was wet and rough, so my buddy was held high in the air as they carried him over to join his father.

Jars of white lightning were pressed against their lips, cigarettes were lit and other men were going off to different parts of the yard to have their own fun.

Tater Head was feeling so good he ran and jumped into the water but then he quickly leaped out of it. A big crocodile was out there, just waiting for a lean, young boy and Tater Head just barely missed being a meal for a rough skinned monster.

A strong arm wrapped around my waist and I looked up to see those dark, flashing eyes of Billy Joe looking down at me. He hugged me tight, kissed me and pulled me down to the ground.

"Aren't you afraid Jimmy Jack is going to miss you?" I joked.

"I've already done him three times tonight," grinned the handsome Billy Joe, whose teeth gleamed white beneath his moustache. "He won't mind if I give some of my love to his buddy."

And for an hour or more, I enjoyed this complete stranger, who was nearly as hot-blooded and dangerous and gorgeous as Jimmy Jack Johnson. And although that happened many years ago, all I can say is that a man from the Burr Swamp community makes love a hell of a lot different than normal people.

After one roll in the hay with them, you simply have to have more, more, more!

`Oh, what a night that was.

Yet, I was to visit the Johnson men only one time after that. On the second visit, they were doing something so outrageous they shocked even me. Even tonight, I have to laugh at how outrageous those swamp bucks were. I wish I had them all here with me right now.

Jimmy Jack got married, moved to Mobile, got divorced and returned to the Johnson homestead in the swamp. He eventually had four sons.

Crazy little Tater Head found the Lord, preached for awhile at the Mt. Zion Church in Carson City and then vanished with the church's building fund.

Not even his relatives know where that hunky little varmint is today.

Through the years, the Johnson clan has grown steadily. I've heard that Jimmy Jack's farmhouse is a favorite hangout for some of the most gorgeous swamp studs around, along with countless good-looking nephews and cousins.

They say, too, that on certain nights, when you're driving along the road that wounds close to the Red Swamp Community, you can hear the sounds of pig squeals—coming from the throats of men.

THE MEN WHO LIVE ON JUPITER HILL

◆

I always hated that one long block that stretched from my mother's house on Main Street to the Post Office.

When you strolled along that neat pavement, shadowed by ancient maple trees, you were on parade for everyone in Carson City—population 372—to see. On this particular freezing morning, last January, I walked it for the first time in 20 years.

Judy Mae's House of Fashion was still there, as was Old Clem's Esso Station and A Little Luck Poolroom. All of them lined the street, along with Ruby's Restaurant. "Genuine Home Cooked Meals!…Shrimp Platter Special!…Two Hot Dogs, $2.00!"

And like two decades before, I glimpsed curtains parting as dozens of eyes studied me with undisguised fascination.

Before, they liked watching "Miz Fury's" sissy boy with his swish walk and wild hair-do's and whisper about the latest rumors regarding the county's Number One Character.

Did he really give blowjobs in the church basement, was he really caught writing messages on the boy's bathroom stalls, advertising his skills for sucking cocks? Did he really dress up in his Mama's clothes when she was gone and wear her makeup?

Now, they wanted to glimpse the return of the prodigal son who had left town in a scandal no one would ever forget...one embellished a thousand times around fire places on cold nights, at supper tables before everyone grouped before the TV for the night.

#

As usual, Mama caused the trouble to happen. She was an expert at this.

Horrified that I was maturing into anything but an all-American boy, the one she had hoped would be the Jock King and the Popular Stud of dear ole Carson High, she had become a master at spotting my weaknesses that could bring disgrace upon her white head.

After all, she was "Ole Miz Fury," former principal of Carson City High. She had a reputation to keep up although why she cared what 372 rednecks thought of her was always a mystery to me.

She correctly perceived that the most gorgeous hunk in town, Harold Lee, and I were more than classmates. Why? Because back then, I was considered the town "freak...sissy...homo...cocksucker...girl-boy..." You name it and I was called it.

So, no boy in his right mind would be seen with me—unless he was a rebel and had so much money he could tell Carson City to go fuck itself.

Harold Lee was such a guy.

The girls were wild about him. He really did resemble in 1959 this stunning young buck who could have been a cross between Rock Hudson and Montgomery Clift.

I never forgot that black hair slicked back into a glossy ducktail, the blue eyes staring at me from between those jet lashes. That pouty, luscious mouth, moist and full, just made for passionate kisses.

And a torso that would have gotten an old maid in heat.

He was also heir to the huge Jupiter Hill Farms, the largest wheat, cattle and dairy spread in six counties. From the ninth grade on, he had flirted with me.

While my other classmates were transforming into either frogs or beauties or plain Janes or simple Simons, both Harold Lee and I had become like butterflies that had shed their cocoons.

He had been skinny and lanky up until that time before he blossomed into Sizzling Hunk. I had been pale and shy and short and had a face that looked like a pizza. But then, I, too, became blessed by nature. My skin had cleared up so much it was white and glowing.

My pudgy physique had become trim and girlish and when I walked, even my enemies studied my rump while rubbing themselves. I fashioned my hair into gold curls until I could have passed for Marilyn Monroe's brother.

Mama was horrified. She swore I used make-up because my lips were deliciously pink and my cheeks were touched with a glow. At that time, I used only a little mascara, some powder, but if I'd worn anything more, Mama would have jumped on me like a hound dog on a June bug. My "glow" resulted from having an intense crush on Harold Lee.

It was raining that afternoon in April of 1959 as I hurried home from school. I was startled when a familiar black Ford, complete with baby shoes dangling from the rear-view mirror, stopped and a familiar voice ordered me to get in.

Until then, we had communicated mostly by long stares, mysterious smiles, the silent method that we thought dramatic in that ancient era. Now, here he was, just inches away, wearing his James Dean red windbreaker, loose jeans and loafers and his hair all shiny and dark.

A cigarette dangled from his full lips and he gave me a wink that said more than a kiss. Instead of delivering me home to my watchful mother, though, Harold Lee took me to a log cabin that his family owned near their big farm.

It was cozy and very quiet and he turned on a gold lamp in the corner then put on a stack of 45 records on the turntable and asked if I could teach him how to do the "shag"—a popular 50's dance which I had learned by watching American Bandstand on TV and performing it at some of our sock hops.

With his arms around me, we quickly forgot about "shagging" and got down to basics. Rumors were confirmed that afternoon that Harold Lee was indeed an over-sexed Southern buck. In me, he found the perfect slut for I had done nothing with anyone until then.

He had never been "done" before. I had never "done" it. You could be castrated or killed in Carson City if people even suspected you did such ungodly things. I remember even now how casual he was about stripping off his clothes, showing me that Rock Hudson had nothing on him. Harold was stunning. Heavy, rugged, with powerful arms, chest and legs.

He laughed when I asked him if I could play with his wee wee.

"Play with it, squeeze it, kiss it, gobble it, I don't give a shit. I want you to, honey. Damn, but you give me a hard-on."

There was nothing childish about the way he held me close, kissing me passionately, getting over me and thrusting himself up into me. I held onto him tight and kept thinking: I've got Harold Lee—right inside me!

I spent hours worshipping his impressive endowment, twisting it, gobbling it, and watching it finally erupt. Each time was like a miracle. Harold loved watching my expression when he orgasmed. I've seen many since those days, but even now, his still remains burned into my memory. He was thrilled the way I grooved over his incredibly macho physique. The way he could barely move his arm and his big bicep bulged. The way he could relax and recline naked against the red and blue cushions, his sensuous pecs shimmering, his stomach rising and falling and his favorite play toy, drooping thick and heavy between his thighs—only to rise to its impressive hardness due to my handling and kissing and sucking.

Every time he came, I noticed how his nipples grew erect. Thick, pale and so suckable. Like having a miniature version of his phallus in my mouth again.

To keep people from talking, Harold Lee continued dating the girls, especially the preacher's daughter. I didn't care. None of them were doing with him the things I was doing. We became more than just sex buddies.

We had the same interests, we laughed at the same things, and we could be natural around each other. Mama was frantic to know where I was going each night and with whom.

As she enjoyed pointing out, I had to be up to no good since no respectable person in town would have anything to do with me. Graduation night loomed close. Harold Lee and I vowed that this ceremony should mark our escape from Carson City.

Both of us were 18, young adults, and I'd saved some money up from babysitting jobs and Harold Lee had a big trust fund we could dip into when he reached 21.

We agreed that right after the ceremony in the school auditorium, I would wait for him in my bedroom. He would do the age-old romantic thing of throwing a pebble or two against my window at midnight sharp and I would climb down a tree where he would swoop me up in his arms and we'd dash to his car.

We would then go to New York City or California where we could live the way we wanted to. We had no doubts he could be a movie star like Paul Newman or Tab Hunter. I would easily become a famous writer like Truman Capote or Tennessee Williams. I had a scrapbook of columns I'd written for our weekly newspaper, the The Carson City Courier.

He never came.

I watched my clock hands pass midnight and inch toward one then two and three and…

At dawn, I went downstairs for coffee only to find my mother already there, smirking, and watching with me with barely concealed delight.

"I seen that friend of yours, Mr. Harold Lee, driving off with Betty Mae after graduation last night."

I stared at my mother's sneering grin. What did she know about this? Betty Mae was the preacher's daughter. He had told me he would be telling her goodbye because she was so crazy about him.

"Okay, bitch face!" I snapped back. "What did you do? Don't tell me you don't know what I'm taking about. What did you say and what did you do? Let's have it out right now because I'm going to let you have it, too."

For long minutes, she spat out all the repulsion she had for me, how she and the parents of Harold Lee had gotten together and figured out what we were going to do. The old bitch gloated, cackling that they all laughed at me.

She pretended to wipe away fake tears and that was when I doubled up my fist and smashed it into her bony old face. I grabbed her hair and slammed it against the floor. She grabbed a butcher knife and tried to stab me but I knocked it out of her hand. For good measure, I punched her hard in the stomach and she went screaming out onto Main Street.

Before taking the bottle of sleeping pills, I called up the volunteer rescue squad. And when they found me, I managed to croak: "Harold Lee made me do it…I didn't want to do it…he stood me up for a girl…I've killed myself for Harold Lee…"

The town was rocked by this scandal. Not only had Ole Miz Fury's sissy boy tried killing both her and himself!

He did it over a boy! And the stud was none other than Harold Lee, heir to a dairy empire!

After I left the clinic, Mama refused to allow me back in the house. She destroyed all my personal property—from clothes, to records to my pictures of Harold Lee. If I ever tried setting foot in her house, she warned me, she'd have me arrested.

For I had brought disgrace to her and after she had worked so hard over the years to be considered "respectable!"

I beat her up again and warned her to never try to reach me. If she did, I'd come back and send her straight into the hospital again. I laughed at that shocked look on her bitter old puss. At last, someone had actually struck back at her.

I was 18 but managed to work my way through college and never saw her again until that January day a year ago when I stared down at her white, hard face in the coffin. She had died without making out a will and since I was her only kin, I inherited everything.

I wanted none of it. Not a stick of furniture or spoon from that house of misery. I was going to sell the house to the first bidder.

Good riddance, you old bitch!

For through the years, I discovered the role she had played on that tragic night when I had nearly killed myself. Somehow, she discovered my runaway plans, had gotten together with Harold Lee's mother.

So right after graduation that night, Harold's male relatives had locked him up his room. Worse, the preacher's daughter declared she was pregnant and so her father demanded Harold marry her right then and there.

Harold Lee, then, had been as much a victim as I had. I never saw him again. I heard that he and his wife had moved to Oregon, there had been a son born to them…

But the town never forgot any of this scandal.

Let them stare, I thought that cold, rainy morning and see how I've survived. If anything, my notoriety had grown with the years for it was well known that I had become an author of gay fiction.

Carson City had always boasted that it had never had either a "nigger" among its residents or a "fag." My existence proved they were all fools on at least one point.

So, giving my hips and my arms an extra swish, I swung into the corner Post Office.

#

Behind the counter was Postmaster Darrel Grubb who had been there as long as I could remember. A big grin broke over his face when he saw me.

"Well, I'll be darned! Jason Fury! And so when did you get in? Still living in North Dakota? Sorry about your Mom. Spry as a horse. Then bingo, that stroke got'er. Gonna be here long? I hear it snows in North Dakota."

I wanted to get the hell out of there and avoid the yokels who gathered there each morning for their hen party. And Darrel didn't miss a trick.

"I haven't lived in North Dakota for years, Darrel. I'm in New York now. I'm selling the house and then it's back to Manhattan. You got Mama's mail?"

As he handed me a big box of mail that had accumulated over the weeks, the door behind me opened and closed. Before I could turn around, the postmaster's words made me freeze.

"Mornin' Harold Lee! What can I do for you?"

"Nothing right now, Darrel."

That same voice—lower, deeper, a man's voice now. Trying to compose myself, I turned around.

In cowboy boots, a wide-brimmed hat, along with denim jeans and jacket, he leaned back against the wall, staring at me. A cigarette dangled from his lips like the Marlboro Man.

His Paul Newman eyes squinted as he smiled—a gesture that still had the power, two decades later, to dazzle and make me want to rape him. His dark moustache showed signs of silver, as did his thick hair.

His eyes were moist when he said softly: "So, you decided to finally come back, eh? You look wonderful. Welcome home."

I wanted to weep, to throw my arms around him right there but I managed to murmur: "Time's been good to you, too, Harold Lee. I didn't know you were living here now?"

"Moved back a few years ago after my wife died. Daddy kept wanting me here to help him run the old homestead so now it's just me, Daddy, my boy, Bruce, living at Jupiter Hill. Eh, got time for a little ride?"

The postmaster was thrilled at this encounter and leaned forward so he wouldn't miss a word. Oh, God, would he have some juicy gossip today for his cronies!

I wanted him to let everyone know that I had nothing to hide—or to be ashamed of. "I've got all the time in the world!"

And in his Ford pick-up, we were alone, together again, laughing, as if it was 20 years ago and neither of us had grown old.

#

Out in the countryside, he turned off into a dirt road and we bumped through the heavily wooded terrain. "Guess where's we a-going?" he grinned.

"Harold Lee! Don't tell me? The cabin's still there?"

"You bet your cute little ass, it's still there!"

And when we entered it, it was like visiting a time warp for nothing within had changed.

There were the same movie posters we'd swiped of *Jailhouse Rock* starring Elvis Presley and *Rebel Without a Cause*, with our god, James Dean.

There was our wall of beer cans we'd flattened and nailed onto one side of the cabin. And in the corner was our bed with the same patchwork quilt.

While I moved around, too moved to say anything, Harold had lit a fire in the big hearth and soon the cabin smelt of burning pine. Then he went to the old record player and put on a stack of 45s. I closed my eyes as the scratching, hissing sound of the Platters singing, "Winner Take All," purred forth, taking me back to all those nights we'd dance and have hot sex in that very bed by the window.

Harold came up to me and put his arms around me.

When I looked up, his cheeks, too, were wet. Like me, he whispered, he had wanted to kill himself that night of our graduation.

But his mother and three of her big brothers made sure he didn't. He'd been forced to marry Betty Mae and actually she wasn't that bad. But he knew how much I must've hated him and he had had never tried to reach me.

"I've thought about you everyday," he said. "And no one's been allowed inside this cabin. It's my shrine"

Our clothes fell to the floor. Time had made my old heart throb bigger and huskier—but his body was more powerful with big shoulders and arms. He picked me up easily and carried me to bed.

Time had not dimmed his ardor either, for as he kissed me, he groaned and writhed as if he were in a fever. When I made that unforgettable passage down his body with my tongue, he whistled silently, panting.

He was in superb condition. His skin, as of old, was still lustrous and hairless except for a light scattering around his big pectorals.

My hands wrapped around his manhood, my mouth followed. He had become a man during the passage of time. Bigger, huskier, ravishing. He grunted, grabbed the sides of the bed and his body began to tremble as my tongue tasted his hidden treasures.

That first orgasm would be the first of several that I knew Harold Lee to be capable of producing. And I was right. He sighed in contentment after his ejaculation faded but then he murmured his delight when I began sucking him again.

I had him to turn over and he presented me with the rump of a young man—smooth, white, rounded. When I complimented him on this achievement, he explained it away with both hard work on the farm and regular visits to a health spa in Asheboro.

I began licking his buttocks, then spread them and sank my face deep into the crevice. When my tongue found his opening, it bore deep until Harold Lee was once more squirming.

He suddenly rolled over on top of me and pulled my legs around his waist and pushed himself up into me. I'd forgotten how he felt but it was clear he had improved his technique over the years. Kissing me and nibbling my ears, he grunted and pulled out so I could see him unload again.

I lay in his arms as he kissed me for a long time, holding me tight, fearful I would vanish from him again.

"After all the guys you've known since me," he asked shyly, "am I still—okay?"

"You'll always be the king of the studs," I laughed, using my favorite nickname for him from the past.

He told me I would have to meet his son, Bruce, who was 21, and his father, Gerald, a still handsome 61. Harold Lee used to kid me about my crush on his handsome pappy.

He screwed me again and then another before we finally got up from the bed for it was growing late.

We agreed to meet for supper that night at seven. He'd pick me up and we'd go to one of the numerous little eating-places around Carson City.

As he told me this, a grin tugged at his mouth and his eyes danced impishly.

"Harold Lee, you're up to something! What are you planning?"

He burst out laughing. "Hey, give me a break! I've grown up some in 20 years."

"Ha, you've not changed that much. Something tells me you've got a surprise up your sleeve—or up your pants leg."

And he did.

#

I dressed carefully that night. In the mirror, I could have passed for someone in their early twenties. In the soft illumination, my hair glowed gold, my blue eyes sparkled. Because of my boyish height, I was often mistaken for a high school kid and had to show my I.D.

When the doorbell rang, I threw open the door. But instead of Harold Lee, someone much younger stood there. As he stepped forward, I could only stare in amazement. It might have been Harold Lee 20 years before.

"Hi," the stranger smiled sweetly, "I'm Bruce. My Daddy's Harold lee. He couldn't make it tonight. Had a last minute emergency at the dairy. He asked me to take his place. If—if that's okay with you?"

"Well, eh, Bruce, of course! I'm—I'm delighted to meet you."

Neither of us moved immediately, since we were both staring intently at each other.

It was like seeing Harold Lee again, the way he was two decades before. A black leather jacket and chino slacks hinted at the powerful young torso beneath. Jet hair and moustache made the light blue eyes and the white teeth gleam. He was young—but his expression and his aura was that of a charming rogue who had been around the block a few times.

He nodded his head, as if agreeing on something and then laughed: "Daddy was right. I just can't believe you're 20 years older than me. You look like somebody who just finished high school."

I took his hand and squeezed it. "Bruce, tonight, just pretend I'm a high school dropout so let's kick up our heels and do anything you wanna do. I'm in your hands."

He snapped his fingers and clapped his hands. "Ooo-weeeee! Let's get this show on the road then!"

#

As befitted a man who lived on Jupiter Hill, my "date," the scion of all those Lee millions, drove a sleek, black Continental. His easygoing charm and intense machismo relaxed me. I like a man who takes charge of the situation.

While the winter's wind whistled around the car, we were snug inside, especially when he withdrew a silver flask from the glove compartment and took several sips."Ah, good ole brandy!" he smiled. "Just what you need on a cold night. It's our house brand, Jupiter Dreams. " He handed it to me and I took a sip or two and gasped at its potency. I also felt dizzy from putting my lips on the same wet opening as he had.

"My Daddy talks about you all the time, Jason," he said quietly. "He always said you were the most original and fascinating guy he ever met."

With Bruce, I sensed I could say anything and not embarrass him. "Eh, did your father tell you about our graduation night, 20 years ago, when I tried to kill myself and he—"

I was relieved at his reaction. "Oh, ho, ho, the big scandal!" he hooted. "Everybody's heard about that."

Then he became serious, glancing over at me as he talked. "Sometimes Daddy told me he wished you and him had run off together—so he wouldn't have had to marry Mama. They never did get along too well. Mama was a religious fanatic and real jealous of Dad, because all the girls were always after him. He's so good-looking, as you well know."

"And you're certainly carrying on the Lee tradition with your good looks, Bruce."

"You really think so?" he drawled and when I nodded my head emphatically, we both burst out laughing.

Bruce took me to a chic little steakhouse in Salisbury and he proved a delightful date.

He had served in the Marines, had traveled the world so he wasn't a provincial small town boy whose only knowledge of life is from watching Oprah and MTV.

I had him laughing nonstop at some of the things his father and I had done in high school, especially the time he had sneaked me into his bedroom, thinking his parents were away.

To get me out of the house undetected, he had tied a rope around me and was lowering me from his second floor window when the rope snapped and I landed right in the arms of his father who was checking for burglars.

The senior Mr. Lee had merely laughed, holding me longer than necessary and promised to never say a thing to his wife.

"Yeah, grandpa is some guy," grinned Bruce. "Still looks like a movie star. Big shoulders, thick, white hair, good build. Like that guy on the TV show, Bonanza. Women do the damndest things to get noticed by him. But he's not interested. Likes being a bachelor again."

On the way home, Bruce asked if I'd mind stopping by the log cabin. Harold Lee had suggested it since he knew how much it meant to me.

"I'd love it," I murmured and felt a rush of excitement. Could be Bruce be thinking of the same thing I was?

He helped me over the tree stumps and rocks in the dark. Taking out a key, he carefully unlocked the door and stood for a moment on the threshold.

"Daddy's never let anybody in here," he said quietly. "He only let me look through the window. He said it was a special place. He'd never say why but this afternoon, he did."

He lit a fire in the hearth while I put on some of the old 45s. Bruce began swaying to strains of "Earth Angel" and "Over the Mountain." My companion came over and pulled me to him.

"Let's dance," he said softly. He had taken off his leather jacket. Beneath the gold crewneck sweater, I felt his solid warmth, mixed with the hardness of his muscles, smelt the ghost of a scent of musk, mixed with his own masculine aroma.

The record player kept repeating one of my favorites, the old golden oldie, "P.S. I Love You" by The Hilltoppers. It was like a shimmering dream, dancing in the shadowy light, the fire crackling in the hearth, this gorgeous hunk holding me close, in the very same place where I'd first become seriously in love with his father.

Outside, the wind blew harder and rain froze on the windowpanes.

Bruce pulled away slowly, smiling and still dancing sensuously. He stripped off his sweater, tee shirt, showing me a strong chest that was made even more macho by a light scattering of hair.

Still watching me, his eyes hot and impish, he kicked off his boots, unbuckled his slacks, pushed them down and kicked them into a corner.

Clad now only in his white BVD's and socks, he wriggled toward me. "If I'm with a special date, I let them take off my shorts. Go ahead." Putting his arms around me, he nodded his head in encouragement as my fingers slipped beneath the waistband and peeled the soft garment down his hips, past his ankles and he kicked them into the corner.

His hands were skilled as they quickly stripped me of my clothes and I could tell he was as thrilled with me as I was with him. I could easily see him as the rugged Marine he had been.

Laying me gently back on the bed, he quickly pulled me against him and began kissing me, gasping as my hands slid up and down his solid torso.

"You're my first guy," he whispered. "But you've gotta be special for Daddy to have loved you like he did."

His flesh was unusually warm, tasting faintly salty, as I licked his nipples and then down over his flat stomach that sank in deeply at the touch of my mouth.

Like his father, he was uncut and he sucked in his breath when I pulled down his fleshy sock and began loving his incredible phallus. It was uncanny how similar he was to Harold Lee, both in their torsos and their privates.

I had only sucked on him for a few minutes before he ejaculated. I didn't stop fellating him, though, and although he writhed and whimpered, I soon felt him growing hard once more. Sweat popped out on his beautiful physique and his mouth hung open as he came again.

A straight man is in heaven when someone rims him and Bruce turned over to offer me his dazzling posterior. When I began loving up his valley, he cried out and gripped the sheets.

Like his father, he liked reclining sexily and naked against the cushions, smoking a cigarette, sipping bourbon and watching me use my mouth to love him up. From his prominent nipples, down his flat stomach to his aroused package, I tasted and he closed his eyes, whimpering and gasping in joy.

"Jesus H. Christ!" he gasped. "No wonder my old man was crazy about you!"

On his back again, he wrapped his fists around mine as we masturbated him relentlessly, roughly, until he came again.

In his car, he pulled me close and kissed me for a long time, savoring this unique experience of "doing it" with another man. On the way home, he looked over at me and smiled. "You probably know how our family's a little bit different than most. Our philosophy is: a hard dick ain't got no conscience. Jason, don't leave town. I want us to get together every night and I want you to love my dick and my body until we're both old and gray."

"That sounds like a lot of fun—between you and your father, it shouldn't get boring."

He laughed and then said he wanted to drop by the farm to see how his Daddy was doing.

#

As we pulled up to the front entrance of the huge plantation house, which looked exactly like Tara in *Gone With the Wind*, the porch lights came on and Harold Lee strolled over to us. He was grinning from ear to ear as he stuck his head in the window.

"I trust my boy kept you entertained," he said dryly. Even in the shadows, I saw how his eyes danced.

"We had a wonderful time, Harold Lee," I drawled innocently. "He proved he's a chip off the old block."

Both men laughed and at that moment, we were joined by another man—a stunning looking older male with a shock of beautiful silver hair, broad shoulders and the same blue eyes of Harold and Bruce Lee. He reminded me of the legendary bodybuilder, Charles Atlas. Years in the made him look like he'd been dipped in bronze.

"Jason, you remember my Pappy, don't you?"

"Wow, of course I do! How could I forget?" I had long lusted for this older "Daddy" type who still looked glorious—tall, strong and warm.

Now, he pushed his face into the car window.

"My boy told me you were in town, Jason," he smiled. "I'd be flattered if I could take such a famous writer out to dinner tomorrow night. Are you free?"

"I'm free and I'd be delighted."

Harold Lee got in beside me as Bruce prepared to drive me home. As we headed toward town, I glanced from one to the other and could tell each was ready to explode with merriment.

"Somebody had better get more wood for the fireplace in that cabin," I said casually. "Because something tell's me I'm heading back there tomorrow night."

Both men burst into laughter. Then they began playfully fighting over whose arms would go around my shoulders and in whose lap my hand would rest.

I put my left hand in Bruce's lap, my right in Harold's and by the time we got to my house, I had their hardness firmly in my grasp.

Harold came first, followed only a minute or two later by his son. No wonder the son kept such a big roll of Bounty paper towels in his dashboard.

When they asked me to tell them who shot the most, I refused to say. I told them I didn't want to start a family feud.

And the following night, just when I had gotten into bed in the cabin with the sizzling patriarch of Jupiter Hill, the door suddenly flew open and who should come flying in?

Bruce and his father began stripping and grinning. My bed partner feigned outrage: "Why can't you two studs let me have some fun? Jason, I had no idea you were so popular?"

As Bruce got in beside me on my left, Harold Lee laid across all of us and made comical faces at our protests.

"Now I was here first," said the senior Mr. Lee, trying to keep from laughing.

"I was here last night," piped up Bruce, while pumping up his phallus into an impressive sight.

"But I was here 20 years ago," barked Harold Lee and to prove his point, he pulled me close and drove himself firmly up into me.

WARRIORS OF
THE SIDEWALK

◆

I knew nothing about Nightmare Alley until that freezing day when I first came to New York, was robbed and met Mickey.

It was he who led me into that sleazy darkness and started my year of living dangerously.

For it was in that notorious stretch of territory which runs behind a barricade of monolithic buildings near Times Square and 42nd Street that I was forced to work the streets as its star slut.

All for a man who became my pimp, my lover and my monster:

I remember:

Hurrying along the unlit alleys…past figures slumped against dirty brick walls, surrounded by used condoms and rusting syringes…past male and female hookers, turning tricks against the always clammy walls…of pausing beneath the all-night porno marquees, studying the Times Square regulars and wondering who of them would survive, and who would perish as they hustled their exhausted bodies for drugs and sex.

Only the rare fell into that first category of surviving. Most of them were trapped into the second where they vanished as if they had never existed.

This was a part of the life that haunted me. For a while, I saw certain characters all over that area. For days, you'd see them in the pizza parlors, coming out of the dirty movies, "hanging" out with their punks. Lost faced girls and boys, their eyes glazed, their hair frizzed and dyed in the latest punk style, their flashy mini-skirts and tight pants soiled and grungy. Everyone too skinny, hyper and frazzled.

And suddenly they vanished, leaving no trace that they were ever there. No one ever asked questions of where they might have gone to. Other lives meant little to the regulars. They were too busy trying to find the next sucker who would provide them money.

Carson City had hardly prepared me, a newly graduated high school senior, for the vastness of Manhattan. I discovered that it was only a small island, a few miles across and a few miles long. But it also contained 9 million people who lived on top of each other in the skyscrapers and high-rise apartment buildings.

The worst place of all, literally in the bowels of this vast metropolis, is life on the streets. And that was where I was convinced I would live until sudden death would put an end to it.

It was snowing the day I arrived at the Port Authority Bus Terminal.

In the main building, I remember going up to the big plate windows in the lobby and staring out. People and traffic hurtled both ways like living bullets through the whiteness. This was where I had always dreamed of coming.

Countless movies and TV shows had assured me of that. This would be my city where I'd become famous doing something. I just knew it deep inside me. Through some quirk of fate, I would soon be known around the world as a movie star, a legendary costume designer, a mythical kept boy, oh….you know how we dream when we're young and green and heading head first into hell.

As I looked out on 42nd Street, the sleaziest place in America—I admitted to myself that maybe this wasn't my city at all. I hadn't expected it to be—so big, so fast, so loud.

I patted my back pocket. There was $200 there, a fortune to me, enough to help me get started.

I was going to the 34th Street YMCA where I heard there were plenty of easy men and drugs. For the past year, those two magic items had controlled my life.

I would hitchhike to Greensboro or Charlotte, North Carolina, and there I would spend wild, dangerous days in bed with men who paid me so I could keep myself high.

My bachelor father had tried to beat my wild ways out of me but it was useless. Drugs were my best friends. Sex made me feel great. Of boyish height, with my blonde hair and big blue eyes, I was always popular with men.

They could fantasize that I was their naughty son.

Besides that, cock and coke made me forget my father's brutal beatings. I was in and out of the hospital because of his ferocious methods of discipline.

But even during these brutal rituals, I wanted like hell to suck him off. Swarthy, big, muscular, I was spellbound by his swollen balls which seemed to have a life of their own when I'd watch him in the shower and he'd squeeze and dry them off—always making sure I was around when he did this. If I could just knead those untouchable gems, I'd have him squirming for more. Oh, Daddy, just give me a chance!

So, I went in search of my Daddy surrogate, especially rough looking men who looked like him. With their hardness in my mouth, I would think: this is my Daddy, I'm blowing him. And when they'd fuck me, I'd nearly swoon in delight, thinking: this is my Daddy screwing the hell out of me.

But my Daddy was on the warpath now to find me.

He had taken all of the money I had earned after school working at McDonalds, which was to pay for my first year in college, and brought himself new clothes and a new whore.

I found Polaroid shots of her wearing the new dresses he'd brought her—with my money. When we fought about this, he beat me up and said if I ever went to the police, he'd have me locked up for doing drugs and sleeping with men.

Worse, he'd have the sheriff deputies find me and lock me away in a mental hospital.

The night before I caught my bus, I had crept into his bedroom and withdrew $200 from his wallet since he was paid that day. This was just a small pittance of what I had earned and he had stolen from me. I had no doubt that he now had the police looking for me and would have me locked up.

As I started to leave the bus terminal that wintry day, a small woman darted in front of me. She seemed to have trouble pushing the revolving door. As I leaned forward to assist her, a man behind me did the same. He pressed against my back and I thought: uh oh, he wants to have some fun and I've only been in New York for 10 minutes.

But as I headed for the line of yellow cabs, I felt of my back pocket.

It was empty. Whirling around, I thought I might have dropped it. I ran back into the terminal and tried to retrace my steps.

Only later did I learn that this was an old scam: a helpless woman tries to open a door, the sucker helps her while the woman's accomplice also pushes against the door, while dipping his hand into your pockets and robbing you.

In a daze, I leaned against the wall near the big windows, staring out at that miserable scene.

"Something wrong, kid?"

The man's face was swarthy, slightly pitted with acne scars. He was tall, slender, with broad shoulders, dressed in an expensive leather jacket and matching pants. He looked like my father in the way I had to look up at him. And those eyes. They were black, hot and very interested.

From my mouth to my eyes and hair his gaze traveled. He liked what he saw for I saw that telltale ghost of a smile touch his dark lips.

Smoking a cigarette, he listened to my plight and shook his head in sympathy. Pick pockets were all over the place. He was an undercover cop. He should know.

"You're really an undercover cop?" I gasped, relieved to have found someone who could help me. "What can I do, sir? I'm completely broke now. All I have are my clothes and duffel bag."

"Tell you what. I live nearby. Few blocks away. If you want a bite to eat, get cleaned up, I'll take you there and then you can go to headquarters and we'll file a report. Okay?"

"Wow, that would be really nice of you!"

I had been trying to keep tears from oozing up in my eyes. He smiled and gently wiped the moisture away with his finger. His name was Mickey and at that moment, he looked so strong and caring that I threw my arms around him.

"Don't mention it," he smiled and pulled me against him. "New York's not all that bad of a place."

His hand guided mine down to his crotch. He smiled knowingly as I squeezed it.

I felt safe with him as he guided me into the freezing snow and ice and across the street into Nightmare Alley.

#

I wondered why an undercover cop lived in a small room in a dingy hotel above Eighth Avenue, off 42nd Street.

It looked like wino and whore heaven. In the Hotel Rose, we had passed through a lobby filled with Puerto Rican and black women with screaming babies. Punks hung around in groups besides old rubber plants, smoking grass and sipping cans of beer.

Even though it was night, they stared at me through dark shades, making kissing noises and grabbing their tools. They resembled cockroaches: dressed in black, their sunglasses gleaming like huge, cold eyes.

My unease grew when we entered his room and two young girls—one white with bleached hair and the other black with braids—were sitting on the bed.

They looked terrified to see him and jumped up and he shoved them roughly out into the hallway. I heard his furious whispering to them and when he returned, he apologized.

"Just some deadbeat friends. Here, I'll bet you could use this."

He lit a joint, took a drag and handed it to me. It was what I needed and while gratefully drawing on it, he gave me a beer from his mini-fridge and then placed a McDonald's Hamburger into the microwave.

I was already feeling better and when he brought out a glass bowl and pipe, I was delighted for here was one of my favorite ways of getting high: smoking crack.

As had happened hundreds of times before, I saw myself stripping off my clothes and Mickey removed his.

"I'll bet I've got something else that'll make you feel good, too," he grinned. Mickey made me think of a juicy hot dog, especially after peeling off his blue bikinis, and holding out his privates to me—dark, strong and untrimmed—like a welcoming gift.

"You need this to make you feel fucking good," he stated.

"Mickey, you're some kind of wizard, you know? You give me everything I want before I even ask for it."

And somehow I was in bed, floating, smiling, as his full lips kissed me all over. I remember repeating the process on him, tasting his skin that had a sheen of coconut oil on it. His nipples were thick and his stomach rippled when I licked it.

He rammed his hips against my mouth, forcing his way into my throat.

I gasped for air and watched as he stroked his organ for a while and then casually came on my chest. It was only a modest orgasm—just a few drops of whiteness—but then I was startled when he suddenly got on top of me and began sliding his sticky phallus up into my anus.

He teased me at first, jabbing just the tip in, back and forth, and when I pleaded for him to push the whole thing in, he kept asking me: "You really want it all? My big thing up your little white butt? What'll you do for it, baby? Huh? You gonna be nice to Mickey?"

I nearly screamed when I said: "Yes, Mickey, yes, now fuck me!"

And when I felt it moving slowly up into me, I did cry out. No one had ever aroused me to the point of exploding like Mickey was doing.

It may have been hours—may have been one hour—that Mickey moved his well-exercised organ around within me. With his wet, warm lips constantly on mine, his hips moving relentlessly to satisfy me, he became within that time to be my god. I never wanted the sex to ever end.

The drugs made me lose all sense of time but when I did open my eyes, fully awake, a wintry light came through the window. I was laying in Mickey's arms and he looked down at me. How long had I been there? What had happened all during this time?

He needed money, he said. I could help him out and we'd be happy again if I would just do what he told me to. He wanted to make some of his male buddies happy. They would pay me and I could give him the money he needed and everything would be wonderful.

I had told him about my father and the cops looking for me. Well, he would make sure they never found me. He had powerful buddies in the NYPD.

Just an hour or two on my back or between a man's legs and that could bring us $50, $100 or more.

Although I had fallen under the spell of this swarthy seducer, and although my head still floated around, something warned me to get the hell out of there fast.

Hustling for a few bucks in Greensboro or Charlotte was fun. Ten or $15 wasn't that much. Men usually gladly gave it to me for bus fare or for cigarettes, beer after I had given them a great time in bed.

But $50 to $100 or more? This wasn't just having fun anymore. Sitting on the edge of the bed with the cheap red spread of rayon, I couldn't look at him when I shook my head.

"Mickey—don't ask me to do that! Please don't! I can't do it. I'll get a real job or something. I'll help you out. But no! Not that!"

There was a moment of complete silence—then a powerful slap knocked me to the floor.

My "god" suddenly turned into a hollering, shrieking monster. Kicking me, he grabbed my hair, yanked me up and made me get into my clothes. And then, he dragged me down the backstairs and out of the rear entrance into Nightmare Alley. There, he kicked me down the steps."If you come back here," he screamed, with the cords of his neck bulging out, "you fucking cocksucker, you'd better be ready to help me out!"

#

Sleet coated the sidewalks with a sheen of silver and in other circumstances I would have loved this sight, staring out of the window of a warm house, with something cooking on the stove, a soft bed waiting for me.

But now, I shivered beneath a movie marquee showing, *Inside Big Bill Jackson*, Triple XXX. My light jacket did nothing to protect me from the freezing winds. Mickey had kept my large duffel bag containing warm clothes.

Throughout that miserable afternoon, I cruised around the Port Authority Terminal and it became a game of staying out of sight from the policemen there. I watched them rounding up several young boys like me and taking them to the paddy wagon.

They could well be looking for me. My father would not think twice of having me arrested for getting my own money back. Although I hated Mickey for doing this to me, I couldn't keep out those vivid memories of him naked and rampant, kissing me and urging me to enjoy his body, to do anything I wanted to with his cock.

I thought of how warm and wonderful his torso would feel right now and how fantastic it would be to have some drugs and booze to help mute reality. His room and bed were snug and warm, he had powerful cop buddies and they would protect me.

The dark day had barely ended as I huddled against the bitter winds and made my way again into Nightmare Alley—and toward that room on the 15th floor of the Hotel Rose where Mickey awaited my return.

#

I stood in the shade of the billboard, out of the blazing sun.

For an hour I had watched the construction workers walk nimbly on the steel girders above me on 43rd Street.

Shirtless, many of them in cut-off jeans and work boots, they were providing the many gay men and women below with the best free show in town. These hunks knew it, too, and preened and posed outrageously.

And at lunchtime, it was even better. Sitting sprawled on the sidewalks with their broad backs propped against a building, they chewed their sandwiches and pizza and guzzled down cold bottles of beer while watching keenly everyone who passed by them.

Some of the younger ones were always eager to show off their bodies to the pretty girls. With their thighs wide apart, they rubbed their crotches and called out things like: "Say, how's about a date tonight?…Wanna have some fun? I'm hot and ready to trot…"

Although I was supposed to be out tricking for Mickey, I spent an hour or two each day checking out the various hard hats. And this particular site had the most handsome of any around.

Many of them sported tattoos of eagles or flags on their shoulders. When they stooped down to pick up something, their shorts slid halfway down their butts.

I'd watch them kid around, grab at each other and sometimes above me, one would take a piss, right there before dozens of lusty eyes.

The most gorgeous of these workers by far was a young Italian I saw each day. With black curly hair, a dazzling grin and light green eyes, his torso was stunning, like he had walked off the cover of Male Physique magazine.

I'd hear some of his buddies call him "Mr. Adonis," or "Pretty Boy" or "Mr. Beautiful." What made this so much fun to watch was to see him blush and grin. They obviously liked him a lot.

Even some of the haughty Manhattan babes would do a double take when they saw him in his skimpy chopped jeans. Sitting on the sidewalk eating his lunch, this hunk would spread his thighs while seemingly unaware of the sensation his muscles caused. What made him so electrifying was his quiet, sweet shyness. There was nothing crude, rough or redneck about him.

I was determined to get this luscious stud because by now, after four months in Manhattan as a sidewalk prostitute, I was convinced any male could be had—if you got him at the right time and in the right mood.

So far, I had experienced no rejections.

Mickey reinforced my appeal. We'd stand together on the sidewalks and he would ask me to choose any man I saw. And in amazement, I'd watch my pimp go up to the man—whether he was a young college stud or dapper businessman or handsome grandfatherly type—and bring his quarry back to me.

When I asked him what he told them, he said he told them to just look at me. That was all they needed. To have my "beauty" pointed out. For by this time, Mickey had helped enhance my natural good looks. He saw to it that my curls were lightened to a platinum blonde. A dash of mascara did wonders for my eyes. And since I was trying to fight my drug habit, my skin had become once again lustrous and smooth.

Anyone seeing me would have thought I was just an unusually cute boy from junior high in my shorts, Mickey Mouse wristwatch, sandals and solid color tee shirts.

Everything I made went to Mickey. He had an uncanny gift of knowing when I held back some money. When I did this, he beat me terribly but always careful not to damage my face. This was what attracted the johns—my innocent looking expression of innocence.

None of my tricks would have imagined I sometimes balled with as many as 20 men a day. I made sure our sex was safe. Condoms were mandatory and even then, I wouldn't let them enter me deeply on either end. Even when it was only kissing, I'd gargle like crazy with Listerine.

If I couldn't find the guys, Mickey would. One thing I did manage to keep private from him: my inner struggle to get off crack, cocaine and grass.

My decision came like this. During the first two months I worked for Mickey, my body was taking in nothing but junk food, soda pop, drugs and booze. I slowly realized my face looked like that of a corpse. All my natural sparkle had vanished.

Mickey kicked me out of the hotel again, warning me that the cops were looking for me. My father was determined to find me and he had somehow discovered I was hustling in New York.

So Mickey didn't want to see me until I had gotten myself "together." For weeks I lived in the parks, panhandled at Grand Central and the Port Authority and finally a kind man in his fifties took me home with him.

He was a surgeon and soon he had me looking healthy and fresh again. Nutrition was his specialty and he demanded I take mega-doses of vitamins and stay on a diet abundant with fruits and vegetables.

"I don't know what your story is and I don't want to know," he told me bluntly. "But if you go back to the streets and live again on dope and booze, you'll be dead within a year."

His words terrified me—but I returned to Mickey.

Even I couldn't give a rational explanation for his hold on me except that he had gotten my father's telephone number and threatened to call him and tell him where I was.

Few men could match Mickey in bed. He didn't fake his passion. He trembled and groaned when aroused and it took little to excite him. He never looked soft. You could see it bulging against his pants.

And when some of the men became serious about me, they were repelled by my addiction to sex and to drugs. Even when they offered me help, I rejected them. I had no desire to be sent to a rehab center.

I just knew I could do it on my own—when the right moment came. And when it did, I would leave Mickey and my life on the streets. But I had to do it on my own terms.

I knew now that I was only one of several members of his "stable" of whores. The two girls I saw that first day were part of his six female family. I think I was his only male slut. He kept us all separate. I had my own little room at the Hotel Rose.

On the streets, they called Mickey the Barracuda for the way he acquired his young whores. When they were exhausted or sick, he kicked them out or worse. They had this habit of dropping out of sight for good.

I wanted out of that lifestyle. And I finally figured out a way of saving money. In a plastic sandwich bag, I stuffed my money and put it into the hollowed out end of a tube of toothpaste. Each week I added to my kitty until I had acquired the grand sum of $1,000.

But each time I planned to escape, Mickey somehow sensed it and drew me back.

"You belong to me," he would tell me. "You'll never belong to anybody else—but me! I'll kill you if you ever try leaving me! I mean it. Ask anybody out there on the streets and they'll tell you I mean business. I've got friends on the police department. They'd love to pick you up and gang bang you before throwing you into the pen with those big dicked hogs."

And Mickey did have spies on the streets that told him everything I did. There was Carlos, a hulky, greasy slob with a frizzy beard, who was a pimp for seven young girls.

You always saw Carlos with a bunch of punks. Whenever they spotted me they'd call out: "Hey, Goldilocks…hey Blondie!" They'd smirk, make kissing sounds and all of them wanted me.Mickey knew my repulsion for them and he threatened me by promising a terminal gang bang by those creeps if I ever tried to get away.

Even worse than Carlos was "Copper Bob," a heavy, brutal faced policeman who sold drugs and got free use of Mickey's girls for free—in return for protection.

Copper Bob was fascinated with me. Mickey would force me to spend hours with the vicious, greasy cop and he told him everything about my past. So I had three devils watching me and always threatening me: Mickey, Carlos and Copper Bob.

It was lunchtime now and I saw Mr. Adonis sitting on the sidewalk eating his lunch. He wore no shirt and looked like Captain Marvel without the cape.

I walked toward him, deliberately swinging my hips more than usual, passing by a dozen or more half-naked workers. I saw them nudging each other from the corner of my eye. "Ooo-weee!" one of them snickered. "I think I know what he wants."

Nearer I got to the stunning young man who sat apart from the others. He looked up then, I smiled and said "Hi!" He looked surprised and then winked.

Since he sat near the curb, I pretended to wait for the light to change. "Wow! It's hot!" I said to him, fanning myself with my hand. "Don't you guys burn up working like this?"

"Naw!" he smiled. "We're used to it. You live around here?"

"Sure!" I laughed and let my hands skim over my hips. "Why don't you come up and see me sometimes? You won't be bored!"

He stared at me for a moment and then realized what I was suggesting. Shaking his head, he frowned. "Shi-yut. You oughta be in school, not hanging around here. It's rough and dangerous."

"I'm free, white and 18," I drawled. "And I support myself."

He snorted, amused but bothered by my personae. "How do you support yourself?" he then asked quietly.

"By having some fun. Come on up to my place and I'll show you."

He rolled beautiful green eyes and tried to look disgusted—but I sensed he was more than interested in me by this time. "Get off that!" he said. "You ain't no more than 13, 14 years. What's your name?"

"Jason Fury. What's yours?" He told me he was Victor from North Carolina. He and his buddies were all "good ole Southern rednecks," he joked and I noticed his buddies, who had all been listening to our conversation very intently, nodded their heads and whooped.

"I gotta go," he said and stood up, dusting the dirt from his jeans and rolling up his lunch bag and tossing it into a tin drum. The way his muscles rippled beneath the golden tan was a beautiful sight.

"Can I talk to you again, Victor? You seem real nice."

"Sure," he nodded. He held out his hand and I shook it. It was so warm, strong and rough. I felt better already.

"I'm out here everyday. Be careful, Jason. Stay out of trouble, ya hear?"

He sounded like an older brother and somehow I knew that Victor wouldn't forget me.

And he didn't. When I saw him again the next day, he raised a hand and smiled. He was sitting further away from the others this time and he looked even more gorgeous.

He seemed unaware of the lusty glances being thrown his way by both women and men. That day he wore just khaki shorts, work boots and a green sweatband around his black curls.

I wore pink shorts and a vivid red jersey. Yellow-framed sunglasses covered my eyes.

Snapping my gum, I was your typical cool Broadway cat.

"Sit down here, Jason," he said and patted the area next to him. "It's in the shade and cooler."

He offered me part of his ham and cheese sandwich but I thanked him and told him no because I always carried with me an apple or orange for lunch.

"I want to stay healthy and trim," I explained. When he handed me a bottle of orange juice, I accepted. "I don't want to get sick. I can't afford to. I don't want to ever get sick again. Not ever."

He glanced at me, his look full of questions and I sensed that I could confide in him for he was like both a big brother and a terrific candidate to add to my long list of bed partners.

Together, we must have made a very striking couple, indeed, for there were even more stares from pedestrians and in Manhattan, it takes something extraordinary to attract attention from those world-weary residents.

"Were, eh, you serious about having some fun?" he asked suddenly. "Are you really 18 or is that bullshit?"

So that was what was bothering him! My age. And even in Baghdad-on-the-Hudson, police didn't think much of older men having fun with underage minors.

I showed him my driver's license that carried my photo. That seemed to put him at ease because he leaned closer and said in a low voice: "Okay, then. You meet me right here at 5 p.m. sharp. Us guys have rooms at the Hotel Roosevelt around the corner. Know where it is?"

"I've been there many times, Victor," I joked.

He gave me another comical look of disapproval and left me with another of his cute winks. I watched his butt swing from left to right and a rare thrill made me smile: within a few hours, I would be seeing that ass—minus the jeans.

When he came off the worksite at 5 p.m., he wore a skimpy jersey over his brown shoulders. His yellow hardhat and lunch pail held against his side reminded me for some reason of a Roman warrior.

There was something so powerful and comforting in his very walk with his big shoulders thrown back, the wind blowing his jet curls. And when he saw me, he smiled in a way I had never seen a typical john smile.

To them, getting with me was something furtive and dirty. But with Victor, it was like he saw someone he liked. His hotel room was neat and cozy with underwear hanging on the closet door to dry.

After giving me a beer from his mini-fridge, he went into the bathroom to shower.

Quickly, I flew around the room to prepare it for love-making: I turned off the overhead light and clicked on the small lamp by the bed; I grabbed my make-up kit from my duffel and spritzed myself with *Eric's Body*, fluffed up my curls and dabbed on some pink lipstick and blue mascara so that by the time he emerged, I knew I looked my best.

And when Victor did appear dripping from the shower, I knew I had never seen a more beautiful male. Wearing only a brief white towel, his skin glowed like silk, water sparkled on his nipples and chest and as he came nearer, I could smell a whiff of Havana Weed Oil.

"Gee," he murmured, "you look real nice."

"And you look like Superman," I smiled. "You've probably got the girls beating down the door.

"Naw," he said. "I don't like these New York women. Too loud and aggressive. They sleep around too much. I don't want any of these diseases going around."

"You've got the right attitude," I agreed. "Don't waste it on these bitches. Save it for young sluts like me—because I'm free, white—and safe."

"Are you Jason? I hope so, because if you aren't—"

I whipped my HIV test card out of my duffel. "See? That's only a week old. I'm tested all the time because I don't want to die, either."

I pulled out a big bottle of Listerine from my bag. "I use about a quart of this a day so I won't have any germs anywhere."

And it was true. No matter how much Mickey beat me, I would perform no high-risk sex with anyone, unless they used condoms and even after the act, I showered and gargled and rubbed my private areas with Listerine.

He lay back on his bed and beckoned me to come to him. I sat on the edge and he took my hand and placed it on his right pec. While my fingers played with his thick nipples, he began to talk. His easy, Southern drawl sounded like music to my ears.

"Listen, honey, I ain't done it with a guy before. Yeah, I've been sucked off a few times while I was in the Marines at bus stations but that wasn't nothing. I didn't even see who they were. Just some nice, hot mouths. You're different, though. Cute, even pretty. You got me hard out there and—if you're really clean, like you said, maybe we can have some fun. Let's give it a try for a few minutes, and if things click, then maybe you can stick around awhile."

"May I take off your towel, Victor?"

"Yeah," he drawled, "I guess I'll let you do that."

When I did, I saw that his genitals were just as impressive as the rest of his body. The uncut organ was filling up, growing thicker and rising.

I bent down and took it in my mouth. Victor grunted and when I glanced up at him, his eyes were closed and his mouth pursed in a silent whistle.

My tongue pushed down the thick foreskin. Victor raised his hips slightly to push more of himself into my mouth and my lips eventually touched his pubic hair. My tonsils had pressed around the head and Victor made a sound of approval.

For several minutes more, I sucked hungrily for except with the exception of Mickey, I'd met no man who really turned me on. Victor was proving to be the man of my life. I loved everything about him—his attitude towards me, his quiet power, and a knockout torso.

"Get out of them clothes," he whispered. "I'd like you to stick around for awhile."

Hours passed as he kissed me and got over me and began to work his way up into me and when he finished fucking me, I went down on him again. And after he ejaculated, I had him to turn over.

His glorious white rump was as scintillating a treasure as his frontal jewels. Soon, I had him squirming and moaning and when he turned over, he was once more erect. I was startled by his intense machismo, the way he really adored getting done and then screwing me and then loving me up with his full, pink lips.

By midnight, I had to leave. Mickey would be on the warpath because I hadn't even called him like I was supposed to.

In Victor's arms, I explained my plight, how Mickey kept me a captive through his body and his threat of exposing me to my father. My new lover was outraged and threatened to find Mickey and break his neck.

"Don't!" I cried in alarm. "He'd kill you, Victor, and think nothing of it. He's got underground bozo's who love to murder."

"I'm giving you some money so he won't hurt you, then. If anybody lays a finger on you—"

"No money, Victor. You're special."

We promised to meet against the next night and we did all that week. Mickey said nothing. I gave him the money I made in the morning from my tricks, charging them extra, and that seemed to satisfy my pimp.

But I thought of nothing but Victor and when I was with one of my anonymous johns, having trouble feigning passion, I would only have to conjure up images of my construction doll to become aroused.

And the more he encouraged me to finally make a clean break with my life on the streets; I began to see a light at the end of my nightmare. I was almost completely clean of drugs. Now, a joint or two a day would suffice and the stuff Mickey and my partners gave me, I threw into the toilet.

On the fourth night with Victor, I lay in his arms, his mouth next to my ear and he said he and his other buddies from North Carolina would be finishing up their work in just a few days.

"You mean you're leaving?"

"We're leaving and so are you. I want you to come with me."

"Victor, I'd give anything to. But Mickey would kill me. You can't imagine the gang of hoodlums he hires for backup."

My boyfriend got up and put on a robe. "Just lay there a minute, honey. Let me show you my backup."

He was gone only for a few minutes and I was beginning to worry that maybe he worked for the vice squad, which was notorious for enjoying sexual favors free of charge, and then arresting the poor sluts—like me.

"Here's my backup team," Victor said from the doorway. In crowded six of his big, brawny construction buddies. I recognized them from the work site and Victor had often invited some of them to join us in his room for a beer.

They were sweet, rugged types who clearly adored Victor. And when he talked, they listened. As I lay in bed beneath the covers, Victor joined me without a stitch on, a fact that didn't seem to faze his friends at all.

Briefly, he told them of my situation, about the daily nightmare of facing possible death from Mickey or from members of his mob. Victor pulled me close to him and announced to the others:

"We're gonna help Jason escape—tonight. He's going back to North Carolina with us."

The men whooped and whistled and each one shook my hand and patted Victor on the back.

"We'll take care of him, Vic, good buddy!" they said. "Trust us."

"Listen, you guys," I cut in. "You'd better understand what you're going up against. Mickey ain't gonna let his best meal-ticket just leave. He'll put up a battle."

"Let'em!" my new buddies bragged. "We know how to take care of shit like that."

I had to return to my room, I told them to get my $1,000 cache. Victor and the others agreed to wait outside the building, so they wouldn't cause suspicion.

"We'll give you 10 minutes exactly," warned Victor. "If you aren't back by then, we're coming up for you. Here."

He slipped me a steel bar I could hide up my jacket sleeve. At least I'd have some kind of protection. Another buddy, Alfonso, a cute Latino type, handed me a whistle.

"You hide this inside your shirt. If anybody tries to stop you, just blow on this whistle and we'll come running."

"I've blown a lot of things lately, but a whistle?" I joked. The others laughed but it was laughter tinged with excitement. These men were looking forward to a good rumble and the fact that they could be instrumental in helping me out of my nightmare.

The lobby of the Hotel Rose, even at 10 p.m., was crammed with the lowest dregs of humanity. Since my mind was clear and I was in love and on my out, I suddenly saw it all in a new light.

I had long lost any pity to spare on the drug addicted women who produced babies like roaches for the city to keep up and slept around with more men than I did; their cretin descendants, the gaggle of black punks who all wore the latest fashions but turned up their noses at honest work, since selling drugs was so much more profitable—and then they'd bitch about being "victims of whitey."

How had I ever managed to exist here for four months? But I could answer that easily enough: drugs and sex and fear.

In just minutes, I would leave this world forever.

Were they looking at me with unusual scrutiny, I wondered as I took the elevator up to my floor? I attracted a lot of attention, anyway, because of my looks and by virtue of being white, blonde and looking like a high school kid. But I wasn't imagining the way everyone was staring, smirking and whispering about me.

I started to turn back and join my buddies who I could see across the street, pretending to be studying the front windows of a porno shop. It would only take two minutes and I would be out of here forever.

The hallway was empty when I slipped into my room. I hurried into the bathroom and grabbed my fake toothpaste tube with the money. But when I whirled around, I froze.

Mickey, and his towering bozo, Carlos, stood there, grinning at me. Behind them smirked Copper Bob, smacking his billy club across his palm. I watched Carlos pull a box cutter from his jacket pocket. He enjoyed slicing up the faces of his young whores when they displeased him.

My pimp grabbed my throat and threw me against the wall. "You've been having a lot of fun with your construction stud, haven't you, cocksucker?"

He whipped out a long, old-fashioned razor and held it before me. "When I finish making your face look like a map, you ain't ever gonna get any more tricks."

"You should know, you piece of shit!" I spat and rammed my knee up into his groin and shoved him aside. Carlos and Copper Bob were startled by my move, for both were bigger than me. I walloped his head with my steel pipe, whacked the faces of the other two, and lunged past them, racing out into the hallway.

Using my bar, I smashed the pane of glass of a window overlooking Eighth Avenue and blew my whistle. Tenants were opening doors, sticking their heads out but my three enemies had caught up with me and threw me toward the stairwell.

I smashed Carlos in the face again and then struck Mickey. This time, though, Copper Bob punched his fist into my stomach and I blacked out.

But not for long. When I came to, the trio had dragged me out into Nightmare Alley where a van waited for us. Four other hard-faced, rough looking animals, which I recognized from the lobby, were waiting there, smoking grass and grinning when they saw me.

I knew that if I were ever put into that van, I'd never get out alive.

Again, I grabbed my whistle and blew it before Mickey ripped it out of my hand. I kicked and scratched and when they knocked me to the ground, I found a broken beer bottle and slashed Mickey's hand when he tried to catch me.

"Help me!" I screamed over and over. "Somebody help me!"

Groups of black punks and welfare mothers had come out of the rear entrance of the hotel to watch the entertainment. For them, this was all in a typical night's fun at the Hotel Rose.

Some of the youths were laughing and imitating me and some were even dancing to rap music from a boom box radio. The women cackled and lit up cigarettes and guzzled beer. Life meant nothing to them. I was their live entertainment for tonight. It meant nothing to them if I was murdered right there before them.

By now, my captors had grabbed me and were loading me into the van when we all saw a large figure suddenly step out from behind a corner. He tapped a deadly looking crowbar cross his palm.

"You all planning on taking a trip with my buddy there?" drawled Victor.

"You fuckin' redneck yahoo!" shouted Mickey. "Go get'em, Carlos!"

That oversized goon rushed toward Victor but at that moment, a gang of a dozen of my lover's buddies rushed out around him. They were armed with metal bars, baseball bats and beer bottles.

I jumped on Mickey and managed to bang his head hard against the van. His feet slipped on the pavement and he fell down and I was on top of him, hammering him with my hands and feet, unloading four months of grief and frustration out on his miserable carcass.

Around me, there was a tremendous battle as bodies lunged, guns fired, men yelled. One of the weapons from the goons had fallen to the ground. I grabbed it and fired it toward the punks and welfare mothers who had been cheering my enemies on.

Like most cowards and street trash, they scattered fast. My boyfriend and his pals easily conquered the gangsters who were all out of shape. They had always depended on knives and guns to protect themselves. Victor and company had always depended on their bodies to carry them through the troubles of life.

Police cars were rushing down the hellish alleyway towards us. Behind them were TV vans carrying the media. Somehow, they had been tipped off that this 42nd Street rumble wasn't your ordinary gang battle.

Victor picked me up from the ground, brushed me off and hugged me close as his buddies whooped and cheered in triumph over their victory. And by the next morning, New Yorkers turned on their TVs and picked up their newspapers to read front-page stories about "The Warriors of the Sidewalks" who had helped capture a notorious pimp and his crew of criminals. And these "warriors" had done it without using any deadly weapons.

#

I returned to North Carolina with my buddies for a while, writing features for a Raleigh, North Carolina, newspaper. I also volunteered many hours of my spare time with young gay people who had problems with their sexual orientation and abusive parents. Even today here in Manhattan, I still spend every spare moment counseling these misfits. I've been through every trauma they describe.

Their confessions never shock me. No, not after my months on 42nd Street and not after my miserable home life.

I also enjoyed taking care of a big house on Chamberlain Avenue. I lived there with Victor and 12 of his construction buddies.

While I shared my bed with this adorable hunk, his buddies slept upstairs and so I never worried for my safety. I knew then I could take care of myself in most situations—but it did give me a good feeling to know I had more than a dozen big men who'll look after you.

I loved cooking up feasts for them and listening to their problems and taking care of them. They brought out the maternal instinct in me.

New York City was just a place on the map—an interesting place to see in movies and on TV. But as I told Victor: "It's a great place to visit— but I wouldn't want to live there."

Victor pulled me close and kissed me and guided my hands over his body and whispered: "You ain't never going back there—because you're always gonna be here with me."

In his powerful arms, against that magnificent body, I felt happy at last because it's not every lover whose been nicknamed by the New York media as a heroic "warrior of the sidewalks!"

The Monster

◆

I looked around me carefully before entering my apartment building that wintry day in December of 1955. Maybe I really was safe. No one moved on the snow-covered sidewalks of Fargo, North Dakota.

Even the old-timers who had lived here all their lives were holed up against the razor-sharp gales of wind, the thick blankets of sleet that pelted you like somebody shooting buckshot. Hills of snow covered everything. My car was buried somewhere out there. I needed to keep it clear of snow, and ready to race away fast—for a desperate escape.

I'd gotten my groceries for the week so now there was nothing else for me to do except get halfway drunk, smoke three packs-a-day of Chesterfields, whip me up stacks of cheese and boloney sandwiches and watch the soaps. There wasn't anything else on my small black and white TV, except for The Pewters—a mother and father and their three fat little kids who lectured you on finding God.

I couldn't hide out forever. This was supposed to be temporary. But until the heat cooled off and my name wasn't on the front pages of the Idaho newspapers, then I had no other recourse. Even now, the law was swarming into Minneapolis and the Dakotas in search of me—"the monster", as one politician labeled me.

According to him, I was supposed to be the ringleader of a gang of perverts in Boise who had seduced and destroyed the lives of thousands of young lads. Already, hundreds of my buddies had been arrested, tried in kangaroo courts and shipped off to prison to serve 25 years to life imprisonment—for being homosexual.

As I quickly slipped into my building, my heart beat so fast I could hardly breathe. I looked through the window to see if anyone had suddenly popped up. There was a bounty on my head of $25,000. The last call from my aunt a week ago disclosed that I had become the most wanted suspect in Idaho's history.

They demanded I return and "really blow the lid off the scandal" of that nightmarish secret world of pederasts that lived underground in that fine, all-American city of Boise. A world that needed to be wiped out and destroyed, its inhabitants locked up forever, said the witch-hunters.

Of all the places I had fantasized about living in, Fargo was not one of them. Yet, at that moment, it was the safest for a fugitive like myself. I was being looked for in surrounding towns. My face appeared everyday in the newspapers and on TV down there. It was like I was a million times worse than any killer, rapist, child abuser, bank robber or—worst of all—a communist. Because at that time, Senator Eugene McCarthy had created hysteria all across America that communists had infiltrated every aspect of life, from the church to work, and their number was in the millions.

Incredible as it sounds, people like me—male perverts—were referred to as something even lower than the communists.

In my building, I began to breathe normally. My money was dissolving at an alarming rate. But I'd had no time to sell my house or withdraw my savings. My aunt told me in that last furtive call that inspectors were watching anything she sent out in the mail. They correctly believed that she was in contact with me. They had questioned her for hours as to my whereabouts.

I had to remind myself. This is America, not Soviet Russia. Yet, here I was, running for my life. I had committed the unforgivable sin of putting my private parts into the wrong gender. Real, All-American men didn't do this. Only somebody insane, an abomination, a monster would sleep with his own sex. Women could do this without a blink of an eye. Holding hands, crying on one another's shoulder. Embracing each other. Only a perverted monster like me would do these unspeakable acts.

A frantic call at dawn from my aunt a month earlier warned me to run fast.

She worked as a clerk in the police department and a group of the city's finest was headed to my place to arrest me. Although my name was mentioned now and then, one hustler finally gave the inquisitors what they wanted. A trumped up seduction of the poor, innocent little eighteen-year-old when I'd never even laid eyes on him.

The politicians who were screaming the loudest about the "perverts" were also the biggest hypocrites you'd find anywhere. More than a few were known to enjoy kicking up their heels at all-male gatherings.

"Jeffrey Sahl is a monster!" shrieked Reverend Harriman from the pulpit of his Baptist Church, giving the face of this monster my name. "The number of innocent young men that he's ruined runs into the thousands!"

The local media picked up his sermon. In all the headlines, I was called 'The Monster' because the good reverend actually swore that I held underground classes for male perverts in how to seduce male children.

Reverend Harriman forgot to tell his congregation that he was a regular participant at the gay orgies—and that no young boys were present. And when our impeccable preacher had a few drinks under his belt, he stripped naked and adored having sex with an audience watching.

Yet, he and the treacherous hustlers were being believed. One of the most notorious of the male prostitutes, Luke, was dropping names all over the place. All the identities were of men he had never even met, had only heard about but it didn't bother him and his new cronies.

He was wined and dined by lunatic politicians and preachers and law enforcement officers. Ironically, I knew that the majority of these fanatics had very definitely enjoyed the gifts of the male tramps. But in true psychopathic fashion, they saw nothing wrong in what they were doing.

The Fargo building I lived in then was a typically solid, concrete/plaster structure. I didn't know who all resided there. Mostly retired people who rarely left their apartments. For the month of my stay, I kept mostly to myself, going out only when necessary. It drove me crazy for I was used to being a party boy to end all party boys, but at that moment I had no desire to trip up and do something stupid and be caught.

Although I had dyed my blonde hair brown, wore glasses over my blue eyes, and dressed in drab, conservative attire, some sharp-eyed crime stopper might recognize me and that'd be it. I now called myself Timmy. It was a name I had always wanted to be called. I was forced to leave my beloved convertible back home. My aunt gave me one of her three cars, an old Chevrolet that had brought me here.

In the lobby, one of the apartment doors opened and a handsome, half-naked giant came out with a bag of trash.

"Hey, Timmy!" he called out. "Better get plenty of vittles. Another blizzard's coming this way in a coupla hours." He deposited the trash bag in one of the metal cans and came toward me.

"My, my, Scott, that's really unusual," I joked. "That's all I've seen here for a month. Blizzards, blizzards."

Scott came up to me, smiling warmly, and I couldn't resist scanning his stunning physique.

I had met him a week before and was thrilled to have such a great looking hunk as a neighbor. My fear of being caught could hardly dampen my basic instincts. I had left a place where I had my pick of good-looking men and had come to this frozen city where the sun never shone, where it snowed every day, and your life was controlled by the wintry weather.

"Scott how do you look so damn good all the time? You remind me of a Viking! That red hair, beard, fair skin."

He grinned in pleasure. He wore just a pair of brief trunks. The frigid gust of air made his thick nipples harden. A light shadow of hair on his chest enhanced his intense virility. His beard and moustache were neatly trimmed.

He wasn't one of those bodybuilding freaks, with popping veins and sharply cut muscles. His impressive pecs hung naturally, his stomach was flat but not rippled, his arms and shoulders swollen with power.

"Lemme help you with those bags," he said and easily picked up my four parcels of groceries and I unlocked my door and let him in.

I had a simple studio apartment but it was warm and cozy and was easy to keep clean. I'd thrown up some big movie posters from *Gone With the Wind*, *Tarzan and the Leopard Woman* and *Bomba the Jungle Boy*.

While I stripped off my coat, heavy boots and gloves, he glanced at my poster of Bomba, showing that nearly naked Adonis with the blonde curls in all his glory.

"You like Bomba, eh?"

"He's the ultimate. I love the way his body's proportioned. It's not fakey or unreal like some of those bodybuilders are. You look like Bomba, Scott."

"You really think so?"

"All you need is a little loin cloth, a spear and you'd be a dead ringer. I wish I had loin cloth right now and I'd ask you to put it on now."

His eyes danced. A grin struggled on his mouth.

"Why don't I just fix me up with a loin cloth right here?"

"You wouldn't dare?"

Intrigued, I watched his push his shorts off so that he stood there completely bare-assed. His nudity was gorgeous. Hanging heavily between his thighs was his toolbox. A thick, slender phallus and plump balls.

He had grabbed a brief hand towel from over the sink and draped it around his narrow hips.

"What'd ya think, huh?"

The towel barely covered his privates. I knew like hell I should have resisted him but I was young and handsome and lonesome—and I wasn't used to going to bed alone at night. For although Boise might be a slow, folksy town, there were many luscious men more than ready to rock and roll in bed.

"Let me try to fix you a better loin cloth, my Viking Bomba."

I moved closer until I was just inches away from his clean, fair skin. His breathing had quickened. I became even more aware of his extraordinary torso, the way his waist tapered to his hips, and the way his glorious back porch reared up and away from his spine.

He had leaned against the counter, watching me with dancing eyes. As I draped the cloth across his genitalia, his big hand grasped my arm. "Would Bomba do this, do you think?"

He pulled me close against him as the towel dropped to the floor. My hands grasped his arms for support. His mouth covered mine hungrily. His right hand expertly guided my fingers over his tits, his stomach and then down to his manhood that had risen steadily.

"Scott, you're so big!" I gasped.

"You ain't seen nothing yet," he smiled. I grasped his sturdy endowment and led him over to my studio couch. My hand was warm from my Viking's sex muscle. It was all happening so fast. I was dizzy. I had never thought I'd find a hunk as luscious and hungry as Bauer, my boyfriend back in Boise, but Scott was proving himself to be the most attractive men I'd ever balled with.

For an hour or more, I sucked him, he sucked me, and he pushed himself up into me and stirred it around. I liked the soft whimpers he made when I mouthed his equipment, licking him and savoring his virility. It was fascinating to watch his stomach rise and fall rapidly before he spurted his passion out abundantly.

We lay there in each other's arms, me devouring his tits and playing with them, he stroking my curls.

"Are you really a writer?" he asked suddenly. "It's a weird place to come to and write."

My defenses went on alert. A gay lawyer had told me to never confide, never divulge if I ever had to go on the run. Fugitives were always caught when they opened up their mouths and yapped.

"But why not Fargo?" I said quickly. This was the alibi I was using—that I was a writer and needed complete privacy to create. "Nobody bothers you here."

"Timmy, listen," he broke in quietly. "You can trust me. Tell me the truth if you want to. If you don't want to, I'll understand."

I studied the cobalt blue of those eyes and sighed. "Scott, I wish I could. Maybe I will. Right now, I'm afraid to trust anybody."

"It's that bad, eh? Whatever happened?"

"I can't talk about it."

"I'll leave it alone, then."

He pulled me closer and I became lost once more in this macho surprise.

He left me an hour later, after loving me up again, promising to come back that night.

I took a long shower, tingling from our session, and went to my desk where I kept my daily journal. Although I might be a fugitive, I was certain that here, I had little to fear. I was still careful as hell, but the men I kept meeting were such simple, ordinary guys who wanted nothing more than bedroom gymnastics and company.

The Dakota male was proving to be a very pleasant surprise. I saw them on the sidewalks, in the Five Corners Bar I visited once a week. Rugged, wearing their wide-brimmed Stetson hats, jackets, a friendly, open expression on their weathered faces.

Even the young farm boys looked like mature men. I'd noticed quickly they didn't play games here. If you went into a bar, and a man sat beside you, he was usually straight. But friendly. And lonely. Within minutes, you had him in bed and having the time of your life. To them, there was nothing evil or sneaky associated with doing the deed that could have you locked behind prison bars for life.

They had fun, you did, and that was all they wanted. Several had returned and we'd grown closer but I had to be evasive without being hostile. How I wanted to be more open and loving with them. But I had to remind myself that I was a criminal fugitive. Hundreds of law enforcement men were eagerly seeking me. It'd be a feather in the cap of anyone who found me and dragged me back to Boise to stand trial.

I was the Monster who ran an underground school for other creatures to learn how to seduce children and innocent lads and turn them into fellow abominations.

I began to write in my journal. Even then, I planned to turn my experiences into a novel although I couldn't imagine any publisher wanting it. There just wasn't a big demand for books about homo's—unless they were portrayed as the devil's spawn.

Or some terrible creature on the verge of suicide from his demonic thoughts—and then he might be saved at the end by a good woman— or discovering the Lord. That was about the only kind of book you could find those days that dealt with monsters like me.

For in Boise, I had enjoyed a good life. An English teacher, I was highly respected. My students and I got along great. My dead parents had left me a beautiful mansion. I had a new Cadillac convertible, a huge wardrobe. I traveled and had an impressive network of friends— both male and female. But especially male.

Each party I threw, I met even more hunky looking guys. Like me, they were professional or in the arts. In private, we never thought for a second about being perverts or monsters. We joked about it. We laughed about having to put on our ordinary disguises by day, and becoming "fairies" by night.

But at my place, men were encouraged to dress up flamboyantly, wear cologne, some make-up if they wanted to. A few even brought suitcases where they changed into their female finery. My home soon became known as the place to go to if you wanted to make contact and meet some of the most handsome guys in Idaho.

That was why the tough hustlers hated me. I had nothing to do with them. Granted, they had a certain rough, macho sexuality but they were notorious for blackmailing their partners, draining them dry, and laughing about it.

Sometimes a few of them, especially the handsome devil, Luke, tried to crash my parties but I turned them away at the door.

Now, they had their revenge. They were squawking to the prosecutors about my orgies, how I lured underage juveniles there and seduced them, took pictures and home movies of them in all types of sexual acts. It was all a lie. Refusing to have underage youths at my parties was a rule stringently enforced. I liked a good time, but I wasn't crazy.

We all realized it was a game we had to play. We could have hot fun, but only behind locked doors, in certain places where the blinds were pulled shut. Then, the purge began in mid-1955. The local paper ran screaming headlines about "12 Perverts Arrested".

Their crime? They had confessed to having had sex with some of the tough hustlers who hung around the city park.

The next day, more "Perverts" were arrested. Among them: the handsome banker I had balled with, a used car salesman. Within a month, more than 100 "perverts" had been rounded up, tried in kangaroo courts and sentenced to 10 to 25 years in prison. The judges and jurors didn't care if the damning testimony came from tough male prostitutes who all had prison records.

I was teaching high school at the time. Naturally, I had become frightened at the virulence of the purge, where anyone could call up the newspaper or police station, drop a man's name and see him arrested within the hour. He could have done nothing at all. That wasn't the purpose, though. He just might have thought "perverted" thoughts. That's all they needed. My friends and I had discussed places to hide out in until things cooled down. Someone mentioned Fargo, North Dakota. Who in the world would head there? It was at the end of the world. Either there or a big city like Chicago. You could easily become lost there, impossible to single out. I'd heard there was a strong subculture of homosexuals there. There were bars, cafes, coffee shops, and movie theaters.

Men paid guys like me for a good time. I'd had buddies who moved there and were gifted with beautiful apartments, a lavish weekly allowance, a glittering wardrobe—from older gentlemen whose passion was buying the most beautiful of anything.

But that would be the first place for the law to look. So I chose Fargo.

I was already planning on leaving for Bois when I received a phone call from my favorite aunt who lived across town.

I had just put my breakfast on the table. Scrambled eggs, toast, coffee. I had already packed my bag for such an emergency. I was out of the house and on the main highway within fifteen minutes. I'd never even unplugged my coffee pot or shaved or showered.

It was incredibly easy to find a place to live here. There weren't that many moving into this ice-bound city.

At the library the next day, I was distressed to see the Minneapolis newspaper and its front-page article:

Hunt Continues for Fleeing Homos

I wasn't the only one the Idaho law was searching for. A dozen other men had also fled the city. I knew them well. Decent, hard-working guys who had often come to my parties. Where had they gone? Were they like me, living in disguise, worried about money and terrified of a knocking on the door and finding themselves hauled off in manacles to stand trial?

We'd all been shocked at how one of our friends had fled to Florida. A deputy from Boise found him there and promised him that all the law wanted to do was to question him. When he returned, he was promptly jailed, tried and sent to prison.

And the judge who sentenced him was one of the most notorious "perverts" in Boise!

My picture stared out again from page one, a photo from the school yearbook. I looked respectable, confident, and happy. But beneath my mug was again that incredible warning: that a $25,000 reward had gone out for my capture and arrest. Lawmen had gone through all my private documents and discovered photos of "orgies, men in female clothing, other signs of perversion."

My aunt had not had time to remove everything. The pictures were of innocent: men laughing, dancing, mugging for the cameras. Just like straight people did.

I glanced up suddenly. A man sat at the next table, facing me, and I saw that he was pretending to read a magazine. His right hand shaded his eyes but they had been studying me. My skin prickled. He didn't look like a Fargo man. He was too lightly dressed. A plain windbreaker, a flannel shirt, jeans, boots. His hair was dark and curly.

He was also handsome in a dark, intense way. I watched him get up to take the magazine back to the racks and he selected another one. The stranger looked rugged, broad shouldered, a man I would certainly like to get in bed.

But my guard was up. Am I getting paranoid? I glimpsed him flipping through the Time magazine before taking it back to the racks and leaving. He had pulled on a knit cap and gloves.

The next day, I was leaving the liquor store with my bottles of joy when I caught my breath. There he was again, standing across the street, waiting for the light to change. Fargo wasn't all that big but still it was strange to me that I'd see this man again. He must be following me.

Quickly, I slipped into the lobby of my building. The warmth, the stolid walls and gleaming floors reassured me. If there was a blizzard of any kind, I'd never have to worry as long as I stayed in my little apartment.

I was unlocking the door when suddenly, the stranger appeared.

"Are—are you Jeffrey?" he asked.

"No! My name is Timmy! Who are you?"

He came closer. In a whisper, he said: "Jeffrey! I didn't recognize you at first. Don't panic. I'm a friend from Boise. Some of your friends wanted me to find you. To see if you're okay or need anything. Your aunt says hello."

I was startled. I'd never seen this guy before. Only my close friends knew I was close to my Aunt Millie.

"Who—who're you?"

He did look vaguely familiar. But I couldn't place him.

"I'm Kim. Kim Robards. I was at one of your parties. But I also go to your aunt's church. We're friends. She knows about me, too. She hired me to try and find you here. I've got things she sent that she thought you might need."

"I'm sorry," I whispered, "I don't know what you're talking about, sir."

He sighed. "Your aunt's name is Millie. You live at 405 Evans Street. You have a two-story house there. You've got a real close buddy, Bauer. He sends you his love. He's worried to death about you."

Before I could catch myself, I blurted: "Why didn't Bauer come?"

"He's a teacher. It'd look suspicious. He's waiting to get out of Boise, too. He'll be running, too, if they drop his name."

My guard was dissolving. I'd been so lonely—and fearful.

"Okay, Kim. I guess I can trust you. Come on in."

I opened up cans of beer for us. After he took off his jacket and hat, he looked even handsome.

"I nearly didn't recognize you," he said. "Your hair's darker, you're wearing glasses."

I began to pour out all my bitterness and fears. When he put an arm around my shoulder, it felt so good. Then he pulled me closer against him and quickly we began to kiss, and his torso felt wonderful: firm and warm and comforting.

In bed, it was even better than when I'd been with Scott. Kim was much more intense, passionate and he proved to be an expert headman, bringing me to climax twice. He moaned for me to enter him and I did which surprised me. He sure didn't look like a bottom man to me. But his groans and whimpering told me everything about how much he thrilled to my prowess.

"You trust me now?" he smiled. We lay there, quietly, watching the pale light filter through the low windows of my basement home. Candlelight flickered and on the record-player turned my favorite album from the Hilltoppers. The beautiful voice of Johnny Sacca wailed, *"I'd rather die young, than grow old without you…"*

He got up to dress. "I'm staying at the Donaldson Hotel. I'll get some things your aunt wanted you to have. I'll let her know I made contact with you."

"Maybe I could call her—"

"And have them trace the call? You don't understand how bad they want you, Jeff! They're trying to find anyway they can of getting you back there. That means tapping phones, intercepting any mail you send. You'd better not think of trying to teach anywhere. They're alerting all the schools all over America to look out for you."

So they were strangling my means of making a living. I couldn't even try to teach—well, there was another way of making a living…one where fugitives like me could exist. If you were handsome, highly sexed and shrewd, your body could be your fortune.

#

Only a few minutes passed before someone knocked at my door.

"Who is it?"

"Scott!"

I was pleasantly surprised to find him there, only this time he was dressed in snug jeans, leather jacket and boots.

"I've missed you," he smiled simply and pulled me against him. "I came by several times. Man, I've been climbing the walls just thinking about our little get together."

While talking, he had quickly pulled off his jacket, his boots, his pants and briefs so that he was naked, a gesture that thrilled me. I have this thing about exhibitionists and I could see him easily at one of my parties, casually removing all of his clothes to strut around naked.

I was thrilled with my great luck. Still tingling from my encounter with Kim, I responded passionately to Scott's uninhibited lovemaking. He was the type who groaned when he was really aroused and gasped intensely when he found relief.

He pulled me close to him as he entered me roughly and lunged for a long time before he did it again.

"Whew!" he whispered. Laying in his arms, I ran my hand over his sweaty flesh, the heavy equipment and licked his hard nipples. "You are a real little sex machine, Jeffrey."

Jeffrey! I froze. He had called me by my real name.

I was pulling at his phallus again, studying the way it thickened and grew bigger. I raised my face to look at him:

"You called me Jeffrey? Why?"

He was smoking a cigarette. Now, he turned to glance at me. "You can trust me. That's your real name, ain't it?"

"My name's Timmy. Why did you call me Jeffrey?"

I watched him go over to his clothes. He felt for something in his jacket and pulled out an object that he kept hidden in his hand. His expression changed from warmth, desire—to a hard smirk.

"Hey, get up! I thought we'd go someplace."

"Where?"

"I thought we'd drive to Boise today"

"Boise? What—what are you talking about?"

He dangled a pair of metal manacles in front of me.

"I'm Bobby Armstrong with the Boise Police Department. I'm taking you in—for fleeing the scene of a crime?"

"What are you talking about? I'm Tim—"

"Oh, fuck that shit! I wasn't real sure at first it was but you'd disguised yourself. We got snitches in Boise, too. I just quietly moved into this building about a day after you did. You thought I'd lived here a long time, didn't you?"

"Why do you want me for? I've not done anything wrong? I didn't hurt anybody! All those parties I gave were for grown adults! Nobody was forced to do anything!"

His eyes that I had thought so striking were now completely iced over.

"I saw who visited you an hour or two ago. That was Vernon. He's from the Idaho state troopers. We all got kind of a contest to see who'd get the bounty money. Twenty-five thousand grand. Whoopee! Once I get you in my car, I'll have won it. I've already called headquarters. A planeload of my buddies is flying in tonight. Vernon is going to pure shit three ways when he finds out I've beat him."

"You forgot one thing!" I spat. "You fucked me all over the place, too. What're they going to do when they hear that?"

He snorted. "They'll say: 'Whatever it takes to bring him in.'"

"But you've been doing with me exactly what you're accusing those other guys of and railroading them into prison!"

He merely rolled his eyes and snickered.

"What fucking hypocrites you are!" I laughed. "I'll bet you're the type who can look at yourself in the mirror each morning and love what you see?"

"Hell, why shouldn't I? I caught you. All you wanted from me was a hot dick and a body and somebody to ball with. And look at where it landed you?"

I studied him and saw nothing human or warm about him. He was like a slug, with white skin, ice cubes for eyes, a vicious grin on his face. Suddenly, he looked ugly. What could I have ever seen him about him? It was like a screen were lifted and here was the real monster of Boise. All the men like him and Vernon. Monsters.

"You like sucking dick don't you, you fucker," I snorted. "And fucking another guy. What a jerk-off you've proved to be."

"I threw up every time I went back to my room!" he sniffed. "It was something I knew I had to do to handcuff you."

Outside, the wind had picked up and snow began hitting my windows. A new storm was on its way.

Still naked, he kept using one hand to play with himself. He studied me like I was something too repulsive to even get near. I was worse than a rat, a snake—a monster. Yet, there was the unmistakable glitter of lust that lit up his cold eyes.

He'd made himself hard again. He shook his stiff at me, grinning and giggling.

"Man, this is like bait to a pervert like you, ain't it? That's why they sent me. You homos always go after my meat bait. I shake it at a urinal or out in a park, and bingo, I've caught you!"

I wanted to murder him. But this was a matter of literal life or death. He was going to take me back to be tried and locked up in prison for life. For having done nothing but have a normal life among other males.

"I know it sounds crazy, Scott—I mean Bobby. But—could I have it just one last time? Nobody will know!"

It was such a lunatic suggestion, I expected him to laugh. But it was exactly the right thing to say for he cackled.

"Can't get enough of it, can you? You fucking, diseased pervert. But, hell, why not? Just don't you try anything, Miss Homo, is that clear? I could break your neck so easy and just tell the others that you tried to get away."

"Don't worry, Bobby. I wouldn't try that. You're a hell of a lot bigger than me, anyway! I just want to suck on it—"

"And if you try biting me—I'll dig my fingers in your eyes and pull'em out."

"Will you stop it? I won't try anything. I don't have anything to lose now. You might be the last guy I'll ever suck in the free world."

"Ha! You know something? You might just be right about that. So's let me give it to you one last time—before my buddies get here. Maybe ole Vernon will pop in. That'd really piss the hell out of him."

He lay down on the bed but for good measure, he'd rolled up one of his socks and stuck it between my teeth. "Just in case."

"I can't do anything with that damned sock in my mouth."

"Shut up and start sucking it."

He watched me carefully at first, but as my mouth worked on him, his face grew flushed and his eyes closed.

My hand slipped beneath the mattress where I kept my last weapon of defense.

I shot him twice with the small revolver I'd brought in St. Paul. I'll never forget that look in his eyes. Amazement, shock—sheer rage.

I pushed him onto the floor.

Groaning, he curled up and I thought how much he resembled a maggot. White, cold, writhing. Those eyes glazing over like cold jello. That mouth parting, closing, a fish gasping for air, no longer in his safe world. Piss formed a puddle around his hips.

"Why—why'd you do that?" he gasped. "Gimme help! I'm hurt bad!"

I put the gun beneath his chin and fired another bullet, so that his head with the red curly hair was destroyed. I felt nothing as I watched his handsome, virile body tremble. Then it stopped. So much blood flowed out from this lifeless piece of shit. His big fingers twitched, the same ones that had fondled himself just minutes before.

There was nothing good looking about him now.

Let that be waiting for my enemies when they came ready to manacle me and ship me off to prison for being who I was.

I threw my few things together and raced away, with the wind and snow howling around my old car, along that narrow two-lane highway that led to Chicago.

There, nobody would care who I was—nor what I became.

MY MAN

◆

His name was Emmanuel Harcourt Golinsky.

We all called him Man.

Not Mannie or Manuel—but Man. He demanded it. Failure to obey meant a flying bedpan that he could throw with startling accuracy. So I was therefore suspicious when Dr. Evers assigned me to do special duty with Emmanuel Golinsky. He had just been transferred to our VA Hospital in Wilmington, North Carolina, from a rehab center in New York.

We were famed for our successes in the rehabilitation of patients suffering from paralysis or loss of body parts.

My suspicions were aroused because whenever I was asked to do special duty—in other words, to look over only one patient and no others, to sit with them 8 to 12 hours a day—it meant no one else would.

From my experience as a student nurse, it meant the patient could often turn out to be a royal pain in the ass. This one turned out to be a lulu.

Before opening the door to his room on that hot, August day and waiting for Dr. Evers, I scanned my patient's chart once again. This guy had gone through a shattering experience. Just when he had gotten a big break in a TV series, *The Boys of Malibu,* a bad ski injury had left his legs paralyzed.

Before then, he had been a football star at Notre Dame, then an up and coming model, usually posed as the "rugged, older male", smoking a cigarette in the Marlboro ads or flexing his torso for body building commercials.

Then he had made a minor sensation as the nearly naked hunk that emerges from the water in a series of sensuous TV commercials for *Wow* perfume. These successes had given him a reputation for being arrogant and egotistical.

But while at Aspen, he had proved his arrogance by ignoring the warnings of his ski instructor and flew off into the air and smashed into a boulder. None of his beautiful torso had been injured: except his legs.

For six months, despite diligent work on the part of the hospital staff he still could not move a toe. Mostly it was because of his attitude. He had become so bitter and angry and full of self-pity that he had become a nightmare to the nurses.

All kinds of medication had been tried but instead of improving his mental condition, it had turned him into an insufferable wreck. He was now on Lithium, which had calmed him down some—but not much. Indeed, the report said it had made him even more irrational in some ways.

He had been transferred here because of our outstanding reputation—and because, the report said, the staff in New York had found him so obnoxious they couldn't find anyone to look after him.

I looked up from my chart when Dr. Evers hurried toward me. "Ready? Put on a smile now, Jason. And remember. He's going to test you and do anything he can to get under your skin. Ignore that. But he needs your help."

"Will you let me blow you as a reward?" I drawled.

He laughed. "There's a time and a place for everything."

Dr. Evers was a handsome man with silver hair but none of the male nurses had succeeded in bedding him down—yet.

When we opened the door and I first set my eyes on Emmanuel, I was completely stunned, not expecting to see this young, deeply bronzed giant. Most of my charges were white, weak, deteriorated, and sickly from medication and depression.

They looked like patients in desperate need of help.

But this hunk...he could easily have posed for a Chippendale Calendar and knocked all the other models out of the picture. At first, I thought he was naked but as I approached closer, I saw he wore a very brief bikini of flesh-tinted silk.

It bulged formidably at the crotch, outlining clearly the fact that he was not cut. He was heavily muscled, with tremendous pectorals, shoulders and arms. As part of his therapy, he was encouraged to work out with weights designed for the bedridden.

He also had the use of a sunlamp each day of the week, to keep his "Malibu" tan.

He kept the covers pulled up above his legs, though, and I dreaded to see what he was hiding. There were obvious physical signs that his mental state was in turmoil. Curls, unkept and dark, flared around a square, ugly-cute face, which reminded me of a bulldog.

It was half-hidden by a filthy beard. Even from where I stood, I could see it was matted with food. His eyes scowled ferociously at a paperback he was reading and I noticed the title, *Eighth Wonder,* by one of my favorite authors, "Big" Bill Jackson.

Dr. Evers went up to him. "Man, this is Jason Fury. You may remember I told you about him yesterday. He's interning here this summer. Both of you may have a lot in common. He wants to be a writer and you've been in the entertainment field—so you should have something to talk about."

"Hello, Man," I smiled and stuck out my hand. My patient's reply was to throw his book across the room and turn his big back to us. "I'm asleep!" he snorted. "Can't you fuck heads see I'm trying to sleep?"

He pretended to snore, waiting for us to leave. Dr. Evers put a finger to his mouth and motioned me to sit down. We nodded in understanding for both of us were experienced with the I'm-Asleep-So-Don't-Bother-Me routine. He opened the door and left me alone with this gorgeous Hercules.

Quickly, the "sleeping" patient turned over, sneering triumphantly—until he saw me. He smashed his big fists into the bedclothes and roared.

"So what's a shit head like you doing here, goddammit? You want me to get well, so I'll get well, but I won't do it with a muthafucker like you around me! You lazy, goddamned jerk! You look like a faggot with your blonde curls and those big blue eyes!"

He cleared his throat and spat, missing my foot by a fraction of an inch.

As I moved toward him, staring at him coolly while actually wanting to strangle him, he looked around wildly and tried to reach the water pitcher. I picked it up, and threw the water into his face.

He was shocked since everyone so far had treated him with kid gloves. But Dr. Evers had encouraged me to use my own techniques.

"If I could get on my feet," he screamed, "I'd break your fucking neck! I don't want you—"

"Shut up before I break *your* goddamn neck!" I snapped. "You arrogant, spoilt bastard! Why they're wasting a hospital bed for a prick like you is beyond me. Do you have any idea of the long, long line of male patients waiting to get in here? And these men really need it!"

My words startled him as I meant them to. I had learned that with some impossible patients, shoveling shit back on them is the only thing that works.

"How dare you curse at me?" he shouted. "Just wait until I get hold of the head nurse here. Where's my goddamned button?"

He looked around, trying to find the portable button panel he used to call the nurse station, but I held it before him and put it behind my back.

"Simmer down, Prince Charming, and let me describe what we hope to do with you here. You strike me as being more mature than you act. And the head nurse has got too many patients who really need her help. You're an egotistical asshole so admit it. You don't need her."

"I'm going to sue this hospital," he fumed, "and I'm gonna see that you're fired on your ass so fast—"

"Sure you will!" I taunted him. "You've got a great looking body, Man, but you ain't got the guts to learn how to use your legs. Now shut up or we'll have *you* shipped back to the New York hospital, okay? I understand you wore out your welcome up there."

He became suddenly silent, either from even more fury or fear. And when I saw the glint of anxiety in his tragic eyes, I became softer with him. My shock method seemed to have worked for he said nothing as I explained the routine we had planned for him.

"You've been in therapy and rehab for six months since your accident," I pointed out. "Yet, you've refused to cooperate with anyone. You're wasting everybody's time, Emmanuel—"

"Don't you call me that name," he hissed. "I won't answer to that name. You're supposed to call me Man. That's spelt—"

"I can spell, Emma—I mean Man. Why do you want us to call you that?"

"Because that's the name I was using when I was a model and about to become a TV star. Man O'Day. Get it? I was a man for day and now I'm just a vegetable. Mr. Part-Time Man. The Man Who Was."

"Oh, stop wallowing in your self-pity!" I exploded. "You've got your body at least, even though you can't use your legs. We've got men here who've lost half their torsos, their manhood. Get off your ass and try to help yourself, you overgrown crybaby."

He let out a scream and this time managed to lunge toward his nightstand where he picked up the telephone and threw it at me. "Get out of here, you fuckin' goody-two-shoes! Don't you show your ass around me again or I'll sue this place!"

In the doorway I paused and taunted him: "Sue all you want to, Mr. Man. But you're going to be seeing me for better or for worse. So get used to it. And you ain't suing nobody when you refuse to learn how to walk."

At the nurse's station, I was the center of attention. All the other interns and nurses gathered around me. You poor thing, they sighed. How horrible to have that egotistical monster for a patient all summer. They'd been terrified they would be the unlucky victim.

For Man had already acquired nicknames. The Bearded Terror. The Bawling Baby. Even more cruel: the Gimpy-Legged Monster. Yet, all of them, including the gay guys, admitted that if he were just a tiny bit less of an S.O.B., they wouldn't mind giving him a rubdown in the least.

But as the days passed, I came to look forward to my sessions with the Man. He had finally stopped screaming and cursing and trying to insult and hurt me.

He learned that I would just gaze upon him with repulsion while he ranted and raved or I could suddenly come back with an insult which floored even him. I had learned how to dish it out while in college that year. As the campus "freak and faggot", I had no intention of letting meat headed yahoos put me down when I knew I had more on the ball than a dozen of them rolled in together.

So after a week, he became almost human, someone who could be boyish and spoilt but also very, very attractive.

"Watch out!" warned Dr. Evers. "He's so filled with bitterness and hurt that he's become treacherous. He'll fool you and then suddenly pull the rug from out under you. I'm serious, Jason. Don't let his charm fool you. He's psychotic in many ways."

I discovered this the hard way that is often the best way when confronting truths about someone you're attracted to.

It was one week after our fiery first meeting. He was taking a stronger dose of medication now, which seemed to calm him down some. The afternoon was another scorcher and I was passing a wet sponge down over his broad back until my fingers reached his waistband.

He wore another very brief bikini that afternoon which exposed nearly all of his very curvaceous rump. As I passed the sponge along the waistband, he looked over his shoulder and whispered: "Take it off. I don't like wearing clothes anyway. As a model, I was used to being naked. So please take my bikini off."

I obeyed and seeing his ass completely revealed was a breathtaking sight. Somehow, he had kept his buttocks completely free of bedsores. They both gleamed in perfect symmetry and whiteness. Water trickled into the crevice of his cheeks.

Between his thighs bulged two pink balls, the size of large eggs, and his penis, with its dark, uncut sock of flesh, looked swollen and thick.

All of this beautiful flesh and muscle therefore made the spindly, thin legs below grotesque looking. How he could resemble a Hollywood hunk for most of his physique—and then have those two helpless match sticks which were useless?

"Help me turn over, Jason," he murmured.

I loved putting my hands around his waist and chest and rolling him over—but then I had to drag the lifeless legs, too. They felt like boneless rubber.

He put his arms behind his head and watched me, smiling strangely, as I continued sponging him off. His phallus had risen up now so that its moist tip brushed against my arm.

I looked down to see the head pushing out of its covering. It was pink, gleaming, like a light bulb and from its opening glistened a thick bubble of transparent sap.

From his over-sized pecs, my sponge moved down to the stomach, which rippled, from the faster breathing of my patient. Lower went my sponge, until I moved it around his steadily thickening organ and the two testicles which jumped now and then.

He smelt wonderful, like warm flesh and a citrus cologne he put on in the morning. Beneath his forearms, the skin was ivory and I could make out faint traces of blue veins.

"You've been really nice to me, Jason," he whispered in a hoarse voice, "and I've been a fuckin' asshole. I know I have. So I want to give you something. It ain't much. But it's all I got. Do you want it?"

I was supposed to be the cool professional, but in that hot, little room, with this gorgeous creature laying beneath my hands, completely nude and very erect, I nodded my head.

"Anything you want to give, Man," I said weakly, "I'd be happy to take."

He put a fist around his phallus and I was startled by how glossy and delectable it looked. "I want you to have—this!"

A stream of piss spattered my face, going into my mouth and nose. I betrayed no emotion as he tossed his head, laughing so hard he could barely breathe.

He did have trouble breathing when I dumped the pan of soapy water into his face. "I thought you might really want that, too, Emmanuel!"

He sat up, fuming and ranting and flinging the water from him and even more outraged because I had actually called him "Emmanuel."

I started to stalk out of the room but then I remembered something. I hadn't emptied Man's urinal and when he took a piss, it really filled up that metal container so much I often had to make two trips to dump the contents.

"You called me Emmanuel!" he was snarling, glaring at me. "You fucking two bit twerp! You're probably the dumbest student in college. You—"

"Oh, Emmanuel!" I cut in. "I'm so sorry. I forgot to empty your pissary. Well, I haven't got time to flush it down the toilet. Do you mind?"

I dashed the urine full in his face. This time he was so shocked he said nothing as I left. I was overjoyed to hear him gasping and muttering. The staff applauded me. Even Dr. Evers, although he didn't say whether or not he approved of my unorthodox method of discipline, just shook his head with an amused snort.

But after that incident, Man cooled down very quickly. No longer did he try and insult me. I could just make a gesture toward the urinal or the wash pan and he'd look nervous.

However, he did not loose his arrogance—or his outrageous charm. After all, he was Irish, as he confided one day, and like most of the Irish men I'd met in school, his machismo could be extraordinary. He liked to see how much he could get by with. For instance:

"What're you doing with those scissors?" he asked one morning.

"You're getting that bush of a beard and hair trimmed."

He covered his head with his hands. "Oh, no I'm not! You're not touching a hair on my body."

An hour later, though, he looked at the results in a mirror. He couldn't hide the gleam of satisfaction in his dark eyes.

"Shit. You'd make a lousy barber."

"Can it, Mr. Man. You like it and don't deny it. I've never met such a narcissistic bastard in my life. You love yourself so much!"

He snorted and when I caught him fondling his new beard and curls, he started to bitch but then sighed. "Well, it doesn't look that bad."

Without thinking, I reached over to caress his thick, pink nipples that were always erect.

"They're always stiff, Man. Like you might be thinking of something hot and sexy."

My fingers caressed his enormous pecs that hung heavy and voluptuous over his chest like twin balconies.

"I'm not dead all over, my friend," he teased and watched his hot, dark eyes dance impishly.

A day later, he had just used the bedpan and called out from behind the curtain. "Jason, come here and wipe me."

"Wipe your own ass, you lazy idiot."

"I'm just a poor cripple."

"You really want me to?"

"Yes, I do," he said with finality.

And as I performed the task, he raised his hips upwards towards me, putting his impressive genitalia only inches away from my nose. I smelt the intoxicating scent of him, which was tinged with freshly spilt semen.

"Something tells me you've been using your trusty right hand," I drawled and pulled his bikini briefs back up.

"I'm only normal," he said quietly. "Just laying here can make a guy real horny."

"But you're supposed to be a hopeless cripple," I mocked. "I didn't think you kind of guys did that stuff."

He snickered and slid a hand beneath the band of his bikinis and squeezed himself. "Everybody in the hospital wants my meat. I know they do. Especially those little student nurses who bring me my meals."

"And you aren't going to let anybody touch it?"

His eyes glinted with a hot expression. "Maybe I'm saving it for somebody special."

"Gee, now isn't that special?" I joked and even he laughed, a gesture which transferred his usually glowering looks into that of an impish little boy.

During the third week, I came in with a wheelchair and got out one of his robes.

"Let's get cleaned up, Mr. Man!" I sang out. "We're going visiting today."

"I'm not going anywhere," He grumped. "I don't want to see anybody."

"Out of those filthy bikini briefs and let's get spruced up, you stubborn cover boy."

But in less than an hour, with my constant prodding, the staff was amazed when a dapper looking Man O'Day could be seen in a wheelchair, wearing a navy blue robe, being pushed toward therapy.

His dark hair was swept dashingly away from his square face. His moustache and beard enhanced his aura of intense virility. Even the robe could hardly disguise the enormous shoulders, arms and chest of this particular patient.

Until then, he worked an hour or more each day in his bed with weights and barbells, refusing to have any interaction with other patients. But we visited the gym, saw men just like him working out, yelling good-natured barbs at each other, and behaving like normal people.

From there, I gave him a tour of the other wards. His unusual good looks drew much attention, for he did indeed look like a visiting movie star.

He enjoyed this tremendously, although he wouldn't admit it, but he became quiet when he met men who fought in the Vietnam and Persian Gulf wars. They had no legs, some had no arms, some had neither.

A few had their manhood destroyed in the fighting. Yet, they fought valiantly each day to try to live a full life as far as possible from their beds and wheelchairs.

My patient was unusually quiet after that experience. He didn't say much and I could see him staring thoughtfully into the distance. From his immature world of narcissism, he finally saw that although he might be handicapped for life, his existence was far from over.

By this time, the doctors had decided that the nerves to his legs were not entirely dead. If the operations were successful, and he applied himself, there was a strong chance of him walking again one day.

Instead of leaving his room at the end of a shift, feeling like I would explode with anger, I now found myself lingering even after quitting time. He was proving to be charming, boyish, witty and it was not difficult to understand how attractive he must have been during his brief heyday.

And of course, much of his attraction lay within his extraordinary body. I'd rarely seen skin as smooth as his, almost without blemish, and beneath its gold hue, it was even more seductive.

When I gave him a sponge bath, I loved to run the cloth over his over-sized nipples, watching them swell up and when I reached his hips, he quietly raised his hips while I peeled down his briefs.

He seemed to enjoy this ritual, too, saying very little as his breathing quickened. When I cleansed the area of his scrotum, Man would grasp his privates together with both fists to hold them taut while my cloth moved around.

And when I finished there, he would release his pride and joy, which was now in a more swollen state than before.

"Wanna see something?" he said one afternoon when I was drying off his groin. "Bet'cha never seen this with a man before?"

"Wanna bet? I've seen quite a few things, Man, so it takes a lot for me to be surprised."

"Shut up for a second and watch my cock."

With his hands behind his dark curls, he closed his eyes and strained. I saw his penis begin to stir, saw the balls dance in their loose sac, then beheld his organ swelling up and slowly rise up.

It became bigger as Man continued grunting and gasping, and then the pink head suddenly popped out of its foreskin.

"See?" he said. "I can get hard without touching it."

"And when it gets that hard, Man, do you have some fun with it?"

"Maybe," he smiled. "But—I won't say how."

He pulled up his briefs and turned his back to me. This meant he wanted to be alone. But it was hard to look away from that spectacular rump.

#

Dr. Evers and the other doctors would warn us interns to beware of becoming involved with patients.

"Do your work," we'd be instructed, "but leave your emotions out of it. They have to leave here someday. You can't."

But none of us believed this. All of us became more than just professionally involved with our patients. And I knew that Man was proving to be more than just a hopeless case. I thought about him all the time and a bond of some kind grew between us. When he told me he had actually gotten a degree in architecture from Notre Dame, I urged him to think of entering that profession. He had actually worked summers in a top architectural firm in Chicago and so he had experience.

"Nobody's gonna hire a cripple like me," he muttered.

"You're nuts, Man O'Day. Most businesses would love to have a handicapped person with real talent. It makes them look good."

"Oh, you mean I'd be their token wheelchair boy?"

"You're pitying yourself again, Man. Don't do it. Think reality. It's hard and grubby and not very sensitive but it's the way the world goes round these days. You'd get top consideration from any architectural firm. Besides that, you know you're gorgeous."

He chuckled softly and when I kissed his cheek, he blushed beautifully.

We had discussed many times his weak points and I always pointed out this tendency to feel pity for himself. It wasn't good for him and it made him look less of a person.

But we got together and studied the want ad sections of the paper each day, and I got him a list of area architectural firms. Since I was a good word processor, I offered to create him a resume and cover letter.

"You'd do that for me?" he asked. "What are you getting out of this, Jason? Is it just being a good intern or you want something more? Tell me?"

Something warned me about confessing how much I wanted him both physically and as a person. There were still dark areas about Man I couldn't figure out and as Dr. Evers warned me at least once a week: "Be careful with him, Jason. He's still psychotic in some ways. He might just be playing a game with all of us. Be on guard."

"Isn't it obvious?" I tried to joke. "I just want to get my hands and mouth on your great looking tits, your white ass and that big thing you got swinging between your thighs."

He didn't smile. He studied me with unnerving intensity. "Is that all?"

"Isn't that enough? Oh, let's cut it out, Man. I'll make you a great resume tonight."

Man was going to therapy now and actually began to play wheelchair basketball and other games with his cohorts. He became a popular figure with his mocking sense of humor and his outstanding physical strength.

And one afternoon when I was supposed to be off, I dropped by to see him. Dr. Evers met me in the corridor and asked me to come along with him.

He took me to a one-way window—where we could look through but no one could see us—and we stared down at the therapy room. A dozen or more men were there, receiving therapy from staffers.

"Look over there, in the corner, Jason," murmured Dr. Evers. "He doesn't want you to know he's here. It's a surprise he's planning but I thought you'd want to see it."

There was Man alone at a double bar: the type one walks between while holding on to keep one's balance. One of the staffers was at the other end.

"Come on, Man," he was saying. "It's going to hurt you some but just keep on moving. Yeah, that's it."

I had grabbed Dr. Ever's arm. "My God, he's really walking, doc!"

It was so painful watching him trying to drag his legs along that my eyes watered. And by the time he reached the end with his arm around the therapist, I felt wetness on my cheeks.

I looked at the doctor. He, too, was choked up.

"We're not supposed to get emotionally involved," he managed to say dryly and then we hugged each other.

Man was making his first steps towards success.

\#

Each week after that, my patient looked more splendid.

He worked out even more with weights since we went down to the gym several times a day. The other patients were calling him Conan the Barbarian, a nickname he accepted with amusement.

He also enjoyed showing me his "cock trick," the ability to make it erect with no manual massage. How I wanted to put my hands on it, if not my mouth, and what made it so frustrating was that I sensed he wanted it to. But I didn't dare.

For although he was physically improving, his mind was still unsettled. He could still throw screaming fits and sink into dark depressions and refuse to go anywhere or even brush his teeth. And then he'd snap out of it so completely you wondered if you had imagined the whole thing.

But it became common knowledge throughout the hospital that Man would let no one touch him but me. Man O'Day was Jason Fury's pet. When he went into one of his sulks, I was the only one who could coax him out of it.

He had also become incredibly jealous.

When he saw me talking to other male patients in the gym or in therapy, he pouted like a little boy. One day I had talked and laughed with one of the handsome young doctors while in the cafeteria.

Later, in his room, Man exploded. "You fuckin' cocksucker! All you wanna do here in the hospital is suck dick."

"Yeah, yeah," I mocked, "that's the only reason I spend hours being yelled at by an asshole like you so I can run around sucking all the men's cocks. Gee, I need one right now. Hey, there goes one now! That black orderly's supposed to have a bull dick!"

I pretended to dash for the door and heard Man laugh. When I looked around, he had pushed the sheets down and had taken out his own impressive equipment.

"You don't have to look far for a cock, Jason," he smiled. "I ain't had any complaints about mine. Look at it. Wouldn't you like to have some fun with this one?"

He was playing his cock game again and we watched it begin to swell up, then it rose thicker and bigger until it pulsed against his flat stomach.

"Mmm," he groaned, "it could use some relief. Why don't you just run your hand over it? Feel how hot it is. How hard! Umm, it's gonna explode!"

I had moved closer, unable to say anything for it had never looked more desirable. The tip gleamed like hard candy, the color of dark pink.

But I forced myself to sigh and quip: "Wow, Man, if I ate that monster, I'd put on 10 pounds and I'm trying to lose weight."

He snorted and pulled the sheets up over his hips. The chance was gone. All that night I cussed at myself: you lost it! Here you had Man literally giving it to you, and you turned it down.

Dr. Evers and his other doctors would have been proud of me.

I wanted to scream and vowed that if the chance came again, I would definitely go for it.

For physical beauty of that type comes along only a few times in a lifetime. I wanted to enjoy every morsel of it.

#

A month had passed since that incident and one morning I found him elated. He was getting positive response from the letters we sent out for employment with architectural firms. The three firms who answered said that they would definitely keep his resume at the top of their list. Things were slow now—but in spring…

And in the meantime, his legs were operated on. The doctors were hopeful they had cured him of at least some of his paralysis.

And as he worked steadily with his therapists, we could actually see his legs beginning to fill out some. He could even move his toes and feet.

Finally, one of his letters received a very positive response. The architectural firm of Lars and Brown, the biggest in Wilmington, wanted him to come for an interview the following morning.

I had never seen him so excited, sparkling with hope.

"Jason, listen, buddy, you've got to come by tonight and help me get ready for tomorrow. I need my beard and hair trimmed, my clothes laid out and—"

"I know, I know," I laughed, "I get the picture. You'd better believe I'll be here."

"And if you do," he grinned with a sparkle in his eyes," I'll do something nice for you."

He rubbed his crotch suggestively."

"Hmmm," I went, pretending to be puzzled. "I just can't imagine what you have in mind."

But I playfully ran my fingers over his bulge and he groaned and I nearly did him right there with the door open and the hallway bustling with staff.

As I was leaving his room, one of the younger specialists, Dr. Hamilton, who I had laughed with in the gym, bumped into me and he playfully grabbed me close.

"We've got to stop meeting like this," he joked.

I caressed his face and pretended to feel of his arms. "I know, Dr. Hamilton. Everyone's gossiping!"

I glanced back at Man and he was staring at us, unsmiling, and his dark eyes stormy.

Oh, God, I thought. He's so jealous!

#

I was two hours late that night.

My car had broken down on the outskirts of town, there was a terrible rainstorm and by the time I got to the hospital, it was nearly nine.

Man was furious.

"Man, I'm terribly sorry!" I began. "My car broke down and—"

He listened to my apologies, his face white with anger beneath the tan, and then he broke in: "You mind rubbing my legs, Jason. They feel strange. A little pain."

I pulled the covers down. He was naked. This wasn't unusual since he hated wearing anything. But I could sniff the *Havana Weed Oil* he liked to wear and I could tell he had rubbed coconut oil into his skin.

He had done all this for me.

But now I massaged his legs, beginning with his ankles and working my hands on up. He lay there relaxed, like a centerfold for a gay magazine, his black hair gleaming with mousse, his beard and moustache trimmed and his muscles looking even more impressive.

If possible, his daily workouts had swelled his chest and shoulders and arms to even bigger proportions.

His stomach was sinking in and out so that his phallus looked stunning. Man had begun shaving his pubic each day, thus making his manhood loom even bigger and darker.

When my hands reached his upper thighs, my fingers brushed against his sac where his testicles bulged out as if they were twin balloons, tucked within the pink groin.

His hand grasped his erection and pulled the foreskin down, so the tip slid out like a small apple.

"I've been a sonofabitch," he whispered. "Nobody would have taken the abuse I've given you and you've given so much in return. If you want this—it's yours. It's all I can give you—now."

I had closed and locked the door. It was late anyway and few people were around.

This time I had no pangs of hesitation. My fist replaced his and I began to use my mouth.

Rarely did I feel dizzy when having sex with a handsome man but I was now. I had fantasized so long about doing this—and it was proving to be even more wonderful than in my dreams. His phallus was so incredibly glossy and smooth—and warm. It fitted perfectly into my mouth and I was amazed at how much of it I could take. For long minutes, I slathered it with my tongue and my spit. His enormous testicles bulged—rising and falling with each movement of my mouth.

I felt his relief pulsing and I glanced up to see him watching me.

I put my arm on his stomach and looked up at him, thrilled that this had finally happened and now I could enjoy him whenever I wanted to. But his eyes were studying me intently.

"Did you and your doctor friend have a good time tonight?" he smiled bitterly.

"Doctor? What do you mean? There wasn't any doctor. My car—"

"Don't give me that shit!" he muttered, sitting up and pushing me violently to the floor. "I know you've been balling with that meathead of a doctor. And since you had a few extra minutes, you came in here to ball with a cripple."

I couldn't believe what I was hearing. Now, his face blazed with anger and bitterness as he pulled the sheets up to his neck.

"You're as nuts as Dr. Evers said you were," I shot back. "The only person I want to ball with is you, Man. You're not a cripple to me. You're a fantastic guy. I've been dreaming this would happen—"

He turned his back to me, a sure sign he had locked me out of his mind. "When you leave, faggot, put your $50 on the dresser."

It was worse than if he had slapped me. Only then did I realize how suddenly love can turn to hate. And what he said made me hate him so much I grabbed a handful of his carefully combed hair and yanked his face around.

"Fifty dollars? I thought surely a two-bit cripple like you would charge more? I mean what else do you have going for you besides that lousy cock of yours."

I gave him a slap across the face that made my hand burn but oh, did it feel good. Especially when I saw the expression on his face.

I walked to the door. "I'll make sure that blowjob you got will be put on your bill. Only I charge $100 per shot. You'd better let your insurance company know."

And on that dramatic note, I slammed the door behind me, just as he threw a bedpan at me that bounced off the wall.

#

Man was proving impossible, the staff told me on the phone.

He wouldn't let anybody near him. He refused to leave his room and it looked like he was retreating in his improvement instead of moving ahead.

Wouldn't I please come back?

I had the flu, I told them. As for Man, he was in the past. I wanted nothing more to do with him.

On the 4th day of my absence, Dr. Evers phoned me. Man had vanished. He had tipped one of the young volunteers to help him slip out of the hospital and all of his things were gone.

"Do you know where he could be, Jason?"

"Yes, I hope with all my heart he's frying somewhere in hell."

Dr. Evers laughed but caught himself. "Now is that anyway to talk about such a charming patient? Seriously, I think he's trying to find you."

"Oh, really? Great! When he gets up here in his wheelchair, I'll gladly kick it down the 4 flights of stairs with him in it!"

I knew I was hardly acting as a professional but what he had said and done to me had devastated me. If I drank, I was sure I'd be in bed that moment, drunk out of my skull.

The doorbell to my studio apartment rang. A short cab driver stood there. He had a crippled man in the car but he wouldn't get out. Would I persuade him to leave?

Of course I hurried out into the freezing cold and there sat Man, in the back of the cab, looking like some ruined Hercules. The driver and I got him into his wheelchair and into my elevator and pushed him into my room.

At last, we were alone away from the hospital setting.

He wore a yellow jacket, brown cords and looked fabulous with his tousled curls and haunted eyes and those great, big shoulders.

We said nothing. He wheeled his chair to the wall and turned it around. On the back of his chair was a pair of crutches. He reached back, got them out and I watched him strain as he struggled to get to his feet.

When he stood there, propped up on his crutches, he finally raised his face to look at me.

"I'm an asshole," he muttered nervously. "I'm trouble and a bastard. But—could you help me?"

I went up to him and threw my arms around him. "Yes, Mr. Asshole," I laughed. "I'll do more than help you. I want to love you."

"Me?" he asked, looking startled. "After all I said? I'm warning you now; I'm a fucking nightmare. You'd better think twice before you take me on."

"You're right, Man. Give me one second. Okay, I've thought about it and—I want to take you on."

#

The door to my bedroom bangs open.

Man, using only one crutch now, hobbles in. As usual, he's naked as a jaybird, a fact that bothers me not at all. I encourage him to never wear any clothes around me.

"You jerk!" I call out, pretending to be furious. "Can't you see I'm trying to sleep?"

It's seven in the morning. Man ignores me since he knows I'm joking and worriedly looks around.

"Where's my shirt?"

"It's hanging up on the closet door where I put it last night. You're wearing your gray one today along with your black slacks and silver tie."

"Where's the tie?"

"It's with your, oh, never mind, you little boy! You couldn't find anything unless it was hanging on your pecker."

I throw my arms around him but he's still looking around the room. "Where's my—?"

"Oh, shut up!" I laugh.

He stares down at me and his cute-ugly face breaks up into a grin. He sits on the edge of the bed and pulls me down into his lap. Then we kiss like two high school sluts.

He's calmed down a lot since moving in with me three months ago. Medication has something to do with this but my combination of "tough love" and genuine passion has also contributed profoundly to his new maturity.

We still holler and yell at each other a few times a week but there's nothing mean or negative behind it. You might even call it a love game. Because when I call him a "bastard," he knows I mean "beautiful."

When he calls me a "swish fag," he means "you adorable guy, you."

My hand slides down his stomach and into his lap. His always healthy privates are nice and swollen from his hot shower.

He guides me onto my back, lays on top of me and pushes himself in. He's learned to do this so smoothly I become dizzy with delight.

"More, more," I whisper. And finally he's in all the way.

"I've gotta be at work in an hour."

He's become an outstanding architect in one of the biggest offices in town. And now I grab his neck tighter and whisper: "You architects are all alike. Hurry, hurry, hurry. Which is more important? Them or me. Don't answer."

He smells like a healthy, young animal and that haunting oil he loves me to rub into his skin.

He's breathing heavier now and I know what that means.

"Oh, God!" I gasp. "Oh, Man!"

I GOT YOU, BABE

◆

I was alone.

While everyone else had long fled the campus that day for Christmas holidays, I had holed up in the faculty building, grading papers.

When I flew to London in January for a needed get-away I wanted nothing laying on my desk when I returned—except the framed photograph of my boyfriend/husband, "Big" Bill Jackson, staring back impishly at me.

His baby blue eyes seemed to dance as if he knew that he was the only man I should be thinking of—-but since he was intimate with every facet of my body, and my personality, he was aware that I could no more resist becoming involved with macho hunks with problems than Cleopatra could have helped being the most desirable woman in the world.

"They need my help and friendship," I would explain to him.

His reaction? An amused snort. "They also make great stories, too, lil' dahlin.'" He liked using all those old Southern nicknames of affection.

We were getting together in Manhattan at our place before traveling together to London. He was visiting relatives in Denton, North Carolina but both of us were looking forward to meeting some of our readers in England. In a curious way, the same readers who enjoyed my stories loved his, too.

But now, as I prepared to leave the warmth and security of the administration building at the University of North Carolina at Wilmington, I peered through the big glass windows of the lobby.

It was nearly nine o'clock, a freezing, wintry night, with frozen mounds of snow still glistening from our storm of two days before.

Was *he* out there waiting for me? My car was parked in that remote corner of the lot, on the side of the building. Two hours before, there had been other faculty members near me, trying to do the same thing I was doing before heading for the hills.

We'd even broken out some champagne, turned on a rock radio station, shown off some wild dance steps and I even went through "some" of my hottest routine I used at my occasional appearances at the Ritz Male Follies where I was a star stripper in New York City.

I use the word "some" because I only took off my boots and sweater. "The rest," I told several of the cute young Profs and their assistants, "I'll show you in private some night."

Their hot-eyed appreciation and wild whoops encouraged me to think they would all want to see more. But now it was like a mausoleum here. Andy could be out there at that moment, waiting to jump out and do anything. Where was the damned security guard?

I, more than most, thought of security since Andy Dexter had entered my life two months before, turning my world into a war zone of emotions. Why was he doing this to me? I had been warned, but like most of the characters in my stories, I was a sucker for these complex hunks.As "Big" Bill had said to me more than once: "Can't you ever get interested in some nice all-American boy whose not fucked up?"

"Well, of course!" I would answer. "I've got you, babe!"

When you come to a college, trailing behind you the reputation of being a "gay writer," you can expect problems. The day it was announced in the local newspaper that I would be Writer-in-Residence at the university, and then gave a rundown on the types of books I'd written, and that I appeared often as a stripper at the notorious Ritz Male Follies, rabid groups of fundamentalist zealots went into high gear.

They got up petitions to forbid my presence. They added the usual homophobic crap that at the top of my "agenda" (why are open gays always supposed to have an "agenda"?") was the "brain washing" of pure young boys into "perverts."

I had never known of any gay guy forcing a younger man to do anything, although I'm sure that happened, just as straight men seduce young girls with hardly any fanfare.

But my proponents outnumbered my enemies and so there was heated controversy when I made my appearance on campus.

I was interviewed by the campus and local press as the "first openly gay" instructor on campus—as if I were a trained seal or an African headhunter.

And it was during my first month at the university that I met the two men who would change my life around, for better or for worse.

Let's start with the good stuff first, in the six foot five form of one Butch Johnson—former Marine, golden gloves boxer, Mr. America runner-up who had somehow evolved into a brilliant geologist.

Greedily, I listened to the gossip about the faculty's 44-year-old hunk…how his wife threw him out of the house regularly for his inability to keep his pants on when around pretty coeds…how he liked to brag that he was "born with a hard-on"…how he was reputed to be hung like a bull.

Since people were telling him how much he resembled that movie super hero, Indiana Jones, as portrayed by hunky Harrison Ford, Butch adopted an identical guise of wide-rimmed Fedora Hat, leather jacket lined with fur, loose corduroy slacks and work boots. A dark stubble enhanced the square jaw and brought out the cobalt blue of his Paul Newman eyes. Framing these startling orbs were thick, dark lashes.

Against his golden tan, his white teeth blazed in lascivious grins. It was like he was telling the world: I'm the last of the red-hot lovers.

It was during the ritual of faculty reception—where the old profs met the young ones—that I finally set eyes on the luscious Dr. Butch Johnson.

Good God, I thought, he is one sexy stud. And big, too. While I was surrounded by the curious and by those who had actually read my fiction, Butch was lost in a harem of females with his wife glowering by the punch bowl. She was plain and plump, which seems to be the type ravishing dolls like Butch Johnson usually end up marrying.

His eyes met mine. He winked and when everyone galloped into the dining room for buffet, he sauntered over to me. Since I'm only five foot seven, I had to look up, up into the rugged face of this powerful bronzed bruiser.

A wicked smile played around his lips with a small scar on the upper one giving him a dashing edge. Brown hair was combed back into a ponytail. His white shirt was unbuttoned halfway down his chest to show the world that he had a chest to be proud of, along with just the right amount of hair to prove his virility, without looking like a gorilla.

A black cigarillo was clenched between that row of dazzling Chiclets like teeth and as he took my hand, his eyes danced impishly.

"My, my, my," he joked, "am I really meeting the notorious Jason Fury? Is the rumor true that you plan to deflower all the young male virgins on campus."

"Oh, I never bother with boy virgins anymore, Butchie-Woochie," I drawled. "I gave that up years ago. Too much trouble. No, I hope I can seduce a man who looks like The Terminator and is supposed to have a pecker as thick as a beer can and as long as a big banana. Any suggestions?"

His eyes widened in shock and amusement. "Good luck, Goldilocks," he cooed. "The Terminator look-a-like you're thinking of doesn't swing with the lads. Only the lassies."

"Famous last words," I smiled. "From what I hear, his cock has no morals at all when it's hard. Like this."

I reached down and grasped his crotch. He backed away, trying to keep from grimacing and rubbing himself. "Don't! I get hard so fucking quick—see what you made me do?"

We both stared down at an impressive swelling in his pants leg.

"My, my, I am so very sorry," I mocked. "That's something I would love to get down. Wouldn't you like to see how I research my stories?"

He laughed and shook his head in disbelief. Looking around and seeing we were alone, he jerked his head for me to come closer.

"Eh, why don't we go somewhere and talk-in private? My van's parked out back, behind the garage. It's red with blue curtains on the windows. I'll go first and you join me in 15 minutes."

I burst out laughing. He said this with such skill I knew this was a much tired-and-true proposition.

"Maybe I can fit you into my schedule, Butchie-Woochie."

As the minutes ticked away, my pulse raced faster. What was he planning? Surely I couldn't be this lucky within just minutes of meeting the faculty stud, whose groupies and affairs were already legendary?

As I stepped into the back of the van, 15 minutes later, I found out what Butch had been up to.

Like a stunning cover boy of a skin magazine he lay stark naked on a blanket of white fur. A small spotlight had been arranged above to bath his spectacular torso in gold hues, outlining his flat stomach, the impressive pecs and shoulders.

But it was his hips that hypnotized me. Butch had grasped the base of one of the biggest erections I had seen in some time. He shook his dark, veined organ at me like he was offering me a succulent sucker.

"Ever seen one this big, Blondie?" he whispered. "Christ, it's hurting me. You said you could take something like this down? Let's see what you can do."

So much for his credo of never "swinging with the boys." I had been stripping off my sweater, slacks and boots all this time until I was naked and he whistled when he saw what I had to offer, too: hours under the sunlamp had given me a golden glow, and my privates and rump nearly always pleased my partner. I turned around so he could see my butt and this caused Butch to whistle.

He grabbed my hand and pulled me down hard against him. Even as he proved a wild, uninhibited lover, I wondered: how many dozens of times has he done this with his bevy of groupies, with other professors? Will I be just another one nightstand?

Well, I was going to give him a workout where once would never be enough. If I used all my expertise, I would have him coming around every night and afternoon.

As he kissed me, his hardness rubbed against my stomach. I discovered that much of what I heard wasn't exaggeration. He really was a satyr, for as I sucked on his nipples, his stomach and finely shaven pubic area, he gasped and grunted in joy.

And when my hands grasped his erection, proving that he did, indeed, have two handfuls, he covered his eyes with his arm and spread his thighs.

"Oh, man, take it all, you're incredible, Jason, simply incredible."

He was thrilled by the way I nibbled and tickled his toy, while my hands moved up and down on his stalk.

"Don't get off," he pleaded. "That was just the first one. I've got backed up."

He came again a few minutes later but instead of exhausting him, Butch pulled me to him and rolled over on top of me. I felt him positioning the sticky organ up into me.

And with the skill born of long practice, he slid it up easily into me. I frankly never liked getting screwed since some huge football player in college had raped me one time and nearly killed me.

But Butch was so careful and enthusiastic, I forgot to resist and let him have his way and somehow, I began to love it, too. He moved and ground his hips until sweat dripped from his body onto me.His mouth tasted delicious—wet, warm, hungry and when he grunted: "Wanna see me cum?" I said yes.

He pulled out and slapped his wonder onto my stomach. A few strokes of the hand produced a sudden burst of semen onto my flesh and before it finished, it looked like he had spilled a half-cup of cream over me.

"There's something I want to do, Butch," I demanded. "Turn over on your stomach."

"Yes, sir," he grinned. "You know something, you're better than anything in your stories."

"Wait'll you try this, stud, and you'll go out of your skull."

His rump was a masterpiece of white smoothness, high, lustrous and when I buried my face deep inside until my tongue was tickling his opening.

Butch gasped and raised his head while I worked even harder to tongue him. Beneath my chin, I felt his privates begin to swell again and as my tongue went deeper, I suddenly felt a gush of warmth on my chin. Looking down, I saw where he had ejaculated again.

He bent down and gave me a quick peck on the cheek. "Okay, that's it. Sorry, but the old lady is gonna be looking for me."

"Butch, you were fantastic. You know where I live, don't you? It's—"

He held up his hand. "Sorry, honey. We can't do this again. I shouldn't have done that. You're my first man. Don't laugh now. I'm serious. Well, maybe a few times in the Marines. But my old lady keeps me on such a short lease—"

"Butch?" a voice called out in the darkness. "Are you out there, Butch?

"Oh, shit, it's the little woman," he gulped. "Gotta go, Goldilocks. Enjoyed it. Bye now."

Driving home, I had to laugh. Big macho Butch Johnson, dancing to the tune of his wife. What a riot! But God, he was a wonderful sex machine. And I'm sure other men before me had heard that one about, "I've never done it with a guy before."

This, I thought that night, will certainly be a fun place to teach. That is, until I met Andy Dexter.

I had heard rumors of this student before he signed up for my Creative Writing course.

Although his father was Dean of Student Affairs, his son ran around with a bunch of wild-eyed, pill-popping bikers. Spoilt rotten, he had a history of problems with dope and booze, had been in and out of rehab centers.

In other words, the other teachers told me, watch out! He's trouble with a capital T.

But he was so cute, I thought, when I saw him at the back of my classroom that first day.

As many of my stories proved, I'm a sucker for troubled men. I just know I can help them out and set them on the right path. Many times I had. A few times had been disasters. I didn't know then that Andy would fall into the latter group.

While I gave my budding writers tips on how to prepare their manuscripts for submission to publishers, I was entranced with the tall, slender boy with dark curls, dressed all in denim except for his black turtleneck.

His dark eyes were tormented, though, and a bad case of acne had given his face a permanent flush that I found very sensual. It was like he was in a perpetual state of heat.

In my classroom, his striking eyes followed me everywhere and when I saw him move down the hallway, that beautiful butt fascinated me. His jeans outlined his dimples with loving care.

During that first week, he turned in a number of poems and stories and all of them graphically described how he wanted to rape a certain blonde-haired instructor of Creative Writing.

"At night I stare at his picture," he panted in a story, "and my fists grasp myself so hard that I cover his features with my balm. But then, too, I imagine wrapping him up securely and then forcing my dick into his mouth and up into that ass which keeps all the boys hard because he swings it by us, as if saying to us: come on and feed me, fellows and plug me up."

Another poem that disturbed me was written without any skill but it was the meaning behind it, which chilled me:

I watch you every night when
You think you're alone but I have ways
of entering places which are locked up.
I watch you for hours, laying there, beneath
a gold comforter, with your TV and DVD remotes and I play with myself
And I've decided that you will have
No one but me. I'll make you my
Prisoner and perhaps in death,
You and I will always be together."

Chills ran over me. Big Bill had given me a fabulous gold comforter for my bed. He knew one of my rituals before sleep was to surround myself on my bed with favorite books, my remote for the VCR and DVD players.

This is one student, I thought, whom I had better not tease or I'll end up in a body bag.

#

He sauntered into my office on the first day after Halloween. It had turned brutally cold and I wore a heavy sweater of black cashmere, leather slacks, and a red muffler around my neck. My floor heater was on for it was still freezing.

Andy wore his usual uniform of denim and work boots and the way he sat down and smiled at me, I thought: this guy has got sex on his mind. His crotch looked so full, you would have thought he had stuffed a pair of socks there but the way his right hand brushed it, I knew it was the real thing.

"Hi, Andy," I smiled. "Wow, isn't it freezing? My office is like a fridge."

He slumped down further in his chair, directly across from me and spread his legs even wider. "Naw, I'm never cold. I'm always too steamed up, like I say in my writing."

He had slid a hand down beneath his waistband and I could see his fingers massaging himself. His smile had turned into a grin, his dark eyes glittered and it was at that moment I realized that this guy was indeed, trouble.

My enemies had made certain that my office would be under 24-hour surveillance by both student and faculty spies, determined to "crush the enemy!" This was how the religious bigots had described me and I was struck by how similar their threats were as one newspaper headline had phrased it during the notorious Boise, Idaho homosexual witch hunt of 1955. In 1995, we were still "the enemy" in the warped minds of homophobes, whose tribe is still legion.

I had already turned down more than six suspiciously timed overtures of an erotic nature from male students, whose true motives were so transparent I laughed in their faces.

"Andy, eh, would you not do that please? People are walking by and—just don't, okay?"

"Okay," he smiled, "but I do this all the time. I can't get enough of it. My shrinks call me a satyr. That means I'm horny every second, even when I'm asleep and—"

"Let's discuss your writing," I cut in quickly for it was becoming increasingly clear, this kid was fucked up in a bad way. His mouth and hands trembled, as if he were ready to explode, and now he sat on the edge of his chair, leaning forward, staring at me.

"I've read everything you've written," he interrupted. "You've known hundreds of men! *Hundreds* of them. Like that Vietnam vet in your story, 'Barbed Wire', that criminal in 'Kiss Me, Kill Me,' that cop in 'Miracle on 55th Street.' But you know? All of them were fantasy!"

He had leaped to his feet, shut my door and now slammed his fist down on my desk. "All fucking fantasy! We've got to really make these stories real! You tell us to write from experience. I want to experience it, goddammit! Are you ready to do it with me?"

A chill swept over me as I realized how naïve I had been in believing Andy was just an interesting hunk with a few frustrations. I got to my feet and moved around the desk towards the door. But he jumped up and stood against it.

"Andy, you don't have to experience everything to write," I smiled. "I mean, if you're writing about murder, you don't go out and kill somebody just to describe. Look now, I've got a meeting I have to go to. Maybe we can—"

I was startled by his swiftness. He threw himself against me, while pushing down his jeans.

"Feel how big I am," he panted. "You love it, you know you do. I see you looking down at my meat every time you walk by me. Christ, you're giving all us guys big hard-ons, the way you swish and the way your mouth moves, like you wanna suck us all off."

I shoved him away but he pushed against me harder and ordered me to look down at his hands.

"Shit, I'm cumming," he grinned. "See? Just being close to you makes me do this. I've got your pictures all over my room. I beat off every night staring at you. I know where you live and sometimes I sneak in and watch you sleep."

He seemed impervious to the gobs of semen spattering his jeans and hands. I shoved him aside and threw open the door. "Get out! Just get the fuck out before I call security."

At that moment, Butch Jenkins walked by and when he saw me, he came up. "What's going on?"

His physical presence alone made me want to hug him.

He easily towered over both me and my new stalker.

"I'm inviting this jerk to get out of my office."

"Andy?" Butch said, moving toward him. "You causing some more trouble?"

The young man snorted and walked past us, rubbing sperm into his hands and over his face, lolling his tongue at us.

"Why don't you complain to my old man?" he sneered. "He'd love to hear how you tried seducing me just then. We all got bets on who'll be the first guy you ball with here. And the minute you do, you're out. You know something else? I'm fucking that ass of yours, too, man. I'm fucking you so hard my cock and your butt will be bleeding by the time I finish."

"Go fuck yourself, sleazebag!" I spat. "You're the only one who wants your cock. When I want one, I'll get a man, not a fucked up jerk like you."

"Yeah, Andy," Butch added." Just get. And don't bother Jason here or you'll have me to tangle with, too."

"Oh," he mocked us, "you really got me scared, Mr. Big Dick Stud."

After he left, Butch came into my office and I showed him the congealing spots of semen on the floor.

"You mean he came that much?" whistled Butch. "I'll bet he's a tiger in bed."

"You mean a shark or a king cobra," I retorted. "Butch, he's not getting away with this. That kid's crazy. I'm filing a complaint with his father."

Butch's response was a cynical snort. "Ha! I can tell you what the outcome will be before you even do it. Zero. Nothing."

But Andy's parent, our Dean of Affairs, merely sat there and glared at me while I spoke. His expression of revulsion toward me was so exaggerated I would have laughed if I hadn't been so angry. Instead, I mimicked him, twisting my mouth down and narrowing my eyes.

Finally, he blew up.

"Well, what do you expect?" he snarled. "When all you do is write stories about perverts and AIDS-ridden degenerates?"

"You know you're right, Dean Dexter," I answered. "Now that I know your son's a pervert, I'll have to write a story about him. Have you had the moron tested for AIDS? Have you? I've heard your skirts aren't so clean. Don't you hang out at that gay rest area outside Wilmington? I hear you're the one who always wears pink bikinis!"

"Get out!" shouted the dean .

I had heard many rumors about the hypocritical dean—who foamed at the mouth about "fags and homo's" but who, typically, was wilder than the poor souls he put down.

Later, I discovered that this man had been one of my most virulent opponents in coming to teach there. And soon after that, Andy vanished from campus. No one knew where he was, but he certainly kept in contact with me."

Over the Internet, he sent me obscene drawings showing me being sexually attacked by a humungous monster. "Your day's coming," he warned, "when you'll get the fucking of your life."

And then he began to telephone me at both work and at home. But instead of saying anything, he played that old top 40 hit of years gone, the Sonny and Cher theme song, *I Got You, Babe*.

The campus police said they could do nothing until my psychopathic admirer actually threatened me physically. The telephone company gave me a private number but a day later, the calls resumed.

Somehow, he had found out what my number was. Butch was concerned but he couldn't pay me too much attention. His wife was giving him an unusually hard time. Some coeds had sent her Polaroid shots of them and Butch doing what comes naturally, in living color.

\#

I thought of all these things that night as I stepped out of the administration building and headed for the parking lot. My keys were gripped between my fingers like I had seen it done on TV where I could use them as a weapon if necessary.

Why hadn't I gone out earlier with the others and moved it near the entrance? Now, my Lexus was covered with snow and sat alone at the far end of the lot.

So far, so good, I thought and grasped my can of mace and steel hammer bar Butch had given me for protection. Just as I put my key into the door lock, it suddenly swung open.

Out stepped Andy Dexter.

"Howdy do, ma'm!" he sang out. "You sure took your time getting out here. Thought I'd freeze my ass off."

"How the hell did you get into my car?" I cried, moving backward and preparing for battle. "What are you doing here? I'm calling the cops."

He grabbed for me but I slashed his hand with the keys and he cried out, clutching his hands and glaring up at me. If I could just get off the frozen ice and onto the cleared path I could run for it. He moved toward me, grinning and stretching out his arms, like he were getting ready for some heavy exercise.

"Ah, why get mean and bitchy?" he cooed. "I wanted to offer myself as a Christmas present to you. You don't know what you're missing with a sex machine like me. You can gobble my cock, twist it, pull it, man, the rougher you get with it, the better I like it. I've got this cock machine that you pump and makes the dick bigger. You can make it as big as you want. Now, come on, and gimme some of your queer pussy!"

He lunged for me but I slammed my hammer against his shoulders and yanked out my mace can but Andy was incredibly swift.

Just as I swung my hammer again and shot mace at him, he leaped forward, throwing me hard to the ground. I smashed my fist into his face, then brought up my knee hard into his groin and he rolled off, whimpering in pain.

Half falling, I scrambled to my feet and raced to the administration building. Behind me, I heard Andy shrieking: "You fucking queer pussy! You want it rough, I'll give it to you, damn you! Don 't you know I love pain, man? Oh, now, I've really got to have you, babe!"

I ran around the corner of the building and straight into the big arms of Butch.

"Hey, where's the fire?" he joked.

"Butch, it's that basketcase, Andy Dexter! He's just tried attacking me out in the parking lot."

"Stay here," ordered Butch but I went with him. Of course, there was no sign of Andy but Butch got into my car with me and told me to drive straight to the campus police.

The two officers, used to nothing more dangerous than stopping snowball fights or taking drunken students back to their dorms, listened to my case.

They couldn't do anything, they said. Andy would have to really do me physical harm before they could move in. Also, the kid's father was a big shot on campus. They had to be very careful and...

"Good Almighty Damn!" roared Butch. "What's a guy got to do to get some protection around this shit-hole? Get killed?"

When I took Butch back to his van in front of the administration building, I noticed it was piled high with suitcases and boxes.

"You going away for the holidays, Butch?"

"Yep," he snorted, "around the corner to the Holiday Inn. The old lady kicked me out again tonight."

"Gee, what a bummer. The Holiday Inn for the holidays. Butch, I've got a great idea. I've got plenty of space at my house on the beach. Stay there until things cool down."

"Hmm," he muttered thoughtfully. "That is a possibility. Well, maybe for just a night or two. And, eh, I don't want to sound mean, but let's just be buddies and nothing more. I mean, I was drinking that night that we did something together. You understand. I don't swing that way."

"Of course, Butchie-Woochie," I laughed for I had often listened to these very same words coming from straight men I had bedded down. "Just having you there would make me feel better. I don't like being alone with Norman Bates' brother running around."

In truth, the house I was renting that winter did resemble the notorious homestead of Norman Bates and his weird old mother in the movie, *Psycho.*

Once a large building, the top floors were shut off from the first and second floors which were all mine. It would make a perfect hideaway for any nut or criminal for the constant wail of the wind made the house creak all the time.

What made it even spookier was that the house was the only one at the tip of the small island of Wrightsville Beach. There were other cottages nearby but they were boarded up through the winter months. I was completely alone out here.

Butch thought the same thing when I showed him around.

"Shit, man, if I were you, I wouldn't stay out here alone. Too easy for somebody to break into."

"I think Andy already has. He wrote me poetry about watching me sleep and coming through a window."

"You'd better keep your mace can and steel bar within easy grabbing distance," suggested Butch.

But just having him there, big, strong and confident, made me instantly at ease. An intruder would have a formidable enemy if Butch ever caught him.

I made us a big steak and hash browns feast, along with a pitcher of very potent Bloody Marys. He had chosen one of the four bedrooms for himself. It was right next door to mine.

He had stripped off his sweater and tee shirt and wore just slacks held up by bright red suspenders. In the candlelight, his resemblance to Indiana Jones was even more marked.

I loved watching the way his biceps bulged each time he moved his arm and he entertained me afterwards by displaying his ability to jiggle his pecs.

"You need to wear a bra," I teased.

"You know actually, sometimes my nipples get so raw brushing against my shirt because I guess they're so abnormally large."

They were unusually thick and long and stuck out as if he had pasted candy kisses on his chest.

When he showed me the room he had fixed up, I had to laugh. Instead of a bed, he had hung a hammock.

"I got to really like a hammock when I was living over in the Amazon and the ground was crawling with snakes and lizards and spiders."

"Butch, listen!"

I held up my hand and we heard the whistling of the wind, the boards creaking.

"What is it?" he whispered.

"I could have sworn I heard footsteps overhead."

"It's closed off, isn't it?"

"It's supposed to be but anyone could take down the boards."

He grabbed a baseball bat and I followed with my steel pipe and we tiptoed toward the stairs. They had been shut off with a wooden door so it was impossible to continue upwards.

My hand had gripped Butch's arm and now he looked down at me and winked. "Just the wind. Now I'm just next door. If you need anything, just holler."

I pretended to be in heat. "Oh, Butchie," I gasped, running my hands along his shoulders and chest. "You know exactly what I want and need."

I laughed as he blushed and rolled his eyes. "Now we promised to behave ourselves," he said nervously. "I don't swing that way. I was just drunk—"

"Oh, I know, I know," I laughed again. "Don't worry, handsome. I was just joking."

He pretended to glare but winked before closing his door. Many straight hunks I'd slept with in the past behaved in the identical manner of my Indiana Jones clone. But only Butch looked like a centerfold with those snug britches outlining his amazing tush, the bulge in the crotch, those glorious muscles—all bronzed and made even more luscious by those boyish red suspenders.

It was impossible for me to sleep.

I kept thinking of my brutal encounter with Andy and then especially of that bronzed Tarzan only a wall way from me.

A loud thump shook the floor, followed by a loud bellow. I leapt from my bed, threw on my black robe of cashmere, trimmed in gold, and hurried into Butch's room.

Stark naked, thank the Lord, he was sitting on the floor with the hammock collapsed around him. Rubbing his nose and cursing, he got to his feet and kicked the hammock.

"Christ Almighty Damn!" he roared. "My fucking bed's done broke and so is my nose!"

"Come on Butchie-Woochie!" I smiled, putting my arm around his waist and touching his nose. "Let's go into the bathroom and I'll fix it up."

As we walked, I saw how his thick penis flopped from his left thigh to his right, like he had a dildo strapped to his waist.

After getting out my iodine and band-aid, I sat down on the edge of the sink and had him come closer. He obeyed, bracing his big hands on either side of me on the wall, so that he was just an inch or two away.

His dong brushed against my knees as he bent his face down for me to examine. Behind him, his buttocks jutted out in all their ivory splendor. Oh, if only someone had a camera, the pictures would be snatched up by any of the skin magazines.

A sheen of sweat made his muscles gleam and I noticed how thick his nipples had become.

His nose was only scratched but I turned it into a major production. I loved feeling his warm breath on my face, the way he closed his eyes like a little boy, his mouth partly opened, wincing when the iodine touched the raw area.

I also loved watching his organ grow thicker. His breathing had quickened and I could even feel his body heat growing more intense, with even more sweat oozing out over his glowing skin.

As I dabbed his nose and tried on several band-aids, his organ had risen until it bulged against my knee. I glanced down. The tip had slid out of its sock and a bubble of wetness gleamed.

"Do you always get a hard-on, Butch whenever you bust your nose?" I drawled.

His answer was to suddenly pull my face against his and he kissed me. With a moan his arms went around me and he picked me up, carrying me to my bed.

"I just can't control my wee-wee," he joked as he lay on his back and I began licking his body. "When it gets hard, it don't care whose around although I try to tell it to just stick with women."

"You hypocrite," I teased. "If there were an elephant or a hole in a tree, you'd have your cock buried in each of them."

This time there was no hurry to enjoy ourselves and it was wonderful licking his armpits, his tits and stomach and watching it sink in to an incredible depth when my lips touched it.

By this time, his hardness was pulsing against his stomach with the head almost touching his navel.

I took it into my mouth, startled by how deep I could bury my tongue into it.

When I finally gulped it all down, yes, even to the smooth pubic area, Butch let out a whoop.

"Wow, I thought I'd died and gone to heaven!" he muttered.

He quickly filled my mouth to overflowing and then he flipped me over on my back and began kissing me wildly while preparing to enter me.

"I'm surprised you ain't screaming in pain," he panted. "Most girls, okay, a few guys, too, can't take it all. Too fucking big."

"But I'm the notorious Jason Fury whose been fucked by the biggest. Remember?"

"Is mine one of the bigger ones from your repertoire?"

"Yes, yes, how did you guess?" I laughed and he lunged in so deeply I cried out.

At breakfast the next morning, he was still in a highly charged state for when I danced over with a platter of cinnamon rolls to him at the breakfast table, both of us naked, he pulled me down into his lap, and onto his erection.

"Butch!" I gasped. " Wow! That was so sudden!"

He said nothing for he was too busy screwing. His lunges grew faster and I looked down to see his wetness dripping onto the floor.

"You must keep your wife happy?" I observed.

"Naw, that's just the problem. She wants it only about once a week, sometimes less."

"Ditch her, handsome, and find somebody, like me, who could really appreciate it."

"That's an idea. I—"

The phone rang and I jumped up to get it. As soon as I picked up the receiver, though, I heard that dreaded sound.

"*I got you, Babe!*"

And singing over the music was Andy. I held the receiver for Butch to listen to. He put his ear next to mine and then we heard Andy screaming: "Just a matter of time, Jason! Keep your ass wet an open for me, 'cause I'm gonna drive right on into it!"

The phone went dead.

"Isn't it great to have such an obsessed admirer?" I sighed.

Butch was rubbing his neck in agitation and pulled me to him. "It's time you and me whipped that boy's ass. You ready?"

That was easier said than done. When we called up the residence of Dean Dexter, a recording said they were down in Florida for the Christmas holidays.

Butch and I then visited the city police but they gave us the same spill as the campus police. They could do nothing unless Andy actually tried to harm me physically.

"But he did!" I protested. "In the parking lot, in my office. He used violent force."

"Did he injure you?" asked the bored looking officer. "Did you have to go to the hospital? If he tries anything again, hold on to him and call us."

Outside the station, Butch said: "You're moving out of the Bates Motel today. You're asking for trouble, living alone in that remote old house."

He knew of a cottage in town which one of the professors might rent out. After talking to him on the phone, Butch looked at me and smiled.

"There is a God. The professor said we can move in tomorrow morning. He'll air it out today and tonight because it hasn't been used for a while. You can live there through spring."

"Butch, that'd be perfect because that's when my time is up here."

"One more night in the Bates Motel," he said, "and then we're out."

I was putting groceries away when Butch stuck his head in the door and told me to come with him. He had something to show me.

"Seems like we've had a visitor while we were in town."

On the mirror of the bathroom, someone had scrawled a "happy face", in what looked like male semen. And on my pillow, more sperm was congealing.

Arming ourselves with bats and steel rods, we searched the house but found nothing. How could Andy have gotten in? We had fastened all the windows and doors before leaving.

And all through that the rest of that day, I had the strange sensation that someone watched me. Limbs of bushes scratched the windows and the wind snapped the screen door like someone was banging to get in.

Butch saw my nervousness and pulled me to him.

"Okay, baby, time for beddy by. Ole Butch has a sure fire way of making you forget all about this creep."

"Oh, really, Butch. And what is this sure fire way?"

"Let's get in bed and I'll demonstrate."

"Do you promise to quench my fire?"

"Oh, I'll quench you, alright. Better make that drench!"

And as hard as it sounds, he did make my mind move away from Andy and concentrate on what Butch was doing to me.

Years of experience, which he claimed started at the age of nine, had made him a master love maker. He knew how to kiss, how to lick my body and then suck me in a way that left me light headed.

With a wonderful sex machine like Butch, I forgot all about time and felt completely and secure with him pressed against me. When he pushed himself up into me, it was like we had become one person and I hated when he pulled out.

"Nature's calling," he whispered.

"Well, I'm calling, too. Butch, I want you!"

"You just keep your legs pulled back and your butt-hole nice and juicy and before you know it, I'll be plugging you back up."

He clicked out the lamp so the room was in total darkness. This was one of the games he liked to play. He'd leave me alone in the pitch dark, nervous, with my legs pulled back and then suddenly I would feel his organ sliding in so perfectly, it was like magic. How could he see that well to not even have to feel around?

I heard the toilet flush. In the dark, I could make out his figure tip-toeing up the bed.

And within just a few seconds, he was performing that extraordinary technique of quietly sliding up, up into me until I felt his balls hanging outside me.

I put my hands up to his face.

And I knew something was wrong. *Very* wrong.

"Butch?" I began as my fingers moved along his face, touched his hair. Sharp teeth suddenly bit into my hand.

"I've *finally* got you, Babe!"

Andy mashed his body down harder on me, pinioning my hands against the bed. But I brought my knees up hard into his groin.

He screeched and then I shoved him aside, leaping to the floor and running into the hallway.

I bumped into Butch who was rubbing his head where Andy had conked him.

"When I get my hands on that prick…?" he muttered.

He and I turned to see Andy trying to escape by leaping for the stairs but we caught him.

When the cops arrived, they laughed at the sight of our "guest" who by now had received a blackened eye, bloody lip and a few bruises on his body.

And then we all laughed really hard when he complained that he was filing charges of assault.

"Oh, please do, sir!" I mocked. "I'll be the first in court so I can file my charges against you."

Thanks to his father, Andy never spent a day in jail. He was shipped off to yet another mental hospital up north. From what I understand, his massive intake of drugs accounted for much of his bizarre behavior but that didn't help me out any.

If he wanted to take drugs, then great. But why make innocent people share the downside of them? I saw to it that the hypocritical dean was fired from his position. Numerous gay students, both male and female, testified during a hearing how he had tried every trick in the book to get them to leave the school.

He's now president of some hick Bible college in the Midwest and appears on TV every Sunday with a sermon that urges his members to punish gay people.

Butch never returned to his wife. I had finally persuaded him to stop being a hypocrite. He was the type who should never stay married and even after he and I began living together for the rest of my stay, I was hardly surprised to find other boys and girls undies in his pockets and handkerchiefs stiff from spunk.

"You were born with a hard-on, Butchie-Woochie," I would drawl as he tried to explain what had happened. "Your cock doesn't have a fucking conscience. You need to beat some sense into it."

"Yeah, you're right," he'd agree. "Before you start beating it, how about loving it some."

We see each other now and then these days because he hates New York City and felt nervous around my companion, "Big" Bill. They were so much alike that Butch felt threatened. Where he lived, everyone considered him the big, strapping stud.

In New York, home of thousands of big, strapping studs, "Big" Bill was considered the biggest, and the most desirable, but he only had eyes for me. And occasional dalliances with others. Although most people consider us married, we understand each other too well. Even when he does play around, he always comes back to me. And I always return to his massive arms and thighs.

When I saw Butch last Christmas, I brought him the DVD movie of Indiana Jones.

I had an artist friend to create me a special movie case and on the front, we put one of my pictures of a very naked, very aroused Butch and then superimposed a picture of a very naked and aroused me, holding on to him as he swings through trees.

I'm shown holding on to his hard-on and the video is entitled: *Indiana Butch and his Cock That Never Sleeps.*

SCARLETT, MACK AND ME

◆

From eight that morning until 10 that night in the year 1939, I had been among the heavily made-up dancers in MGM's exhausting, trouble-prone production of *Wizard of Oz*.

As one of the green-faced inhabitants of the Emerald City, I had sweltered along with nearly a hundred others beneath the hellish lights. Because this was being filmed in Technicolor, there were even more huge banks of scalding light than usual. Our make-up melted, cast members and dancers fainted through the days, the crew could only film for brief minutes and at each break, we all raced to the big tin tubs of ice water to drink.

The "stars" were treated to icy Cokes or could retreat to their trailers. Even child star Judy Garland was coddled like the Queen of England but us poor extras? Ha!

We had one hour to try and grab a bite in the packed commissary and by the time we got our food, it was time to race back to the sound stage. God help any of us who had to use the john. We weren't supposed to even think about such base needs.

And just when our sequence seemed to finally flow smoothly, one of the dancers would slip, a wig or hat would fall off, a microphone got in the picture, oh, God, anything that could go wrong, had gone wrong through the day.

And all during this time, all costumes were so soaked with sweat you could actually see the steam at times wafting upwards from our bodies. No fans were allowed during filming because the microphones would have picked it up. God knows there was no air-conditioning back then either. So you can imagine the rich odors all of us carried beneath those smoldering hot costumes and wigs and paint.

When I arrived in Hollywood in 1929, with a six-month movie contract with MGM as a musical "star," I knew my name would be up in lights all over the world after my first appearance in the studio's "All-Singing! All-Talking! All-Dancing!" extravaganza, Night of Stars.

With an black jazz band behind me, I sang and danced up a storm to some silly tune called "The Chincochita Stomp!" But when I caught myself for the first time in a preview showing of the film, I was laughed off the screen.

I looked like a beautiful little girl with blonde curls bouncing, wrists flapping and hips twisting.

The audience screamed with hilarity and that was the end of my star career. But I had stuck it out and become a popular dance extra, the kind you saw whirling a partner around behind Eleanor Powell or Fred Astaire and Ginger Rogers in all those classics like *Born to Dance, Top Hat, Swing Time.*

I also had one hell of a wardrobe so I was always on call to wear my own clothes as one of the guests seen in the lobby of 1932's *Grand Hotel* or as one of the unlucky subway riders hurled to their death by a giant ape named King Kong.

Is this how I want to spend the rest of my life, I asked myself again as I drove my snappy little Roadster along Sunset Boulevard that cold, rainy night in January?

I had stopped to buy some groceries and here it was, nearly midnight and my face felt like sandpaper after I had scrubbed for an hour to get all of that green make-up off.

A few blocks from my house, I saw the hustler leaning against the building—a favorite spot to make contact. On clear nights, sidewalk sluts could be spotted all along this area. The boys knew dozens of movie people would be leaving the studios after dark and that many of these film people were on the lookout for a quickie.

Although exhausted, I wasn't dead and this particular stud was enough to energize even a zombie-like dance extra.

Wearing a cowboy hat, he was a big guy, with his arms folded across his chest. What instantly aroused my interest was that he looked so much older—and certainly bigger—than the usual sidewalk hustlers of Hollywood.

As if sensing my interest, he shifted his stance and moved more into the light from the clothing store window. Dark hair peeped out from under his hat, a moustache made him look like Clark Gable and unless he had used padding—not unusual back then in 1939—he had one hell of a body.

I could easily see him naked, between sheets, holding me in those big arms and making me feel better with what I hoped swung between his thighs.

I stopped my car and rolled down the window. He came over to me and leaned forward.

"Hi!" he smiled shyly.

"Hi yourself! Aren't you afraid of getting a cold out here?"

"It sure ain't too warm," he said in a low, Southern voice. "I've been waiting for a buddy to pick me up but I guess he's forgotten about me."

"Well, until he comes, why don't you join me at my place around the corner for something hot to drink. Maybe some soup and sandwiches? You can keep a lookout from my house down the blocks. See, it's the white one with the little turrets."

The stranger made a pretext of looking around for his imaginary friend and then he opened the car door and hopped in.

God, he was big, like a young giant. If he proved to be trouble, I'd have one hell of a problem getting him out of my place but his smile was sweet and gentle when he held out his hand and said: "Hi, I'm Mack."

"And I'm Sunny St. James."

#

My place really was one of those gorgeous little dreams you see in magazines. It had once belonged to lesbian super star, Nazimova, she of the startling blue eyes, boy's figure, the creator of such classics as *Camille, Billions, War Brides* but who lost every penny in her wildly gay art film, the 1922 *Salome* which used only an all-homosexual cast and crew.

Hollywood still whispered about *Salome* and the orgies, which reportedly took place before and off the camera.

When I tried opening the door, it was stuck because of the dampness but Mack merely nudged it with his shoulder and it flew open.

While I went into the kitchen to whip us up a snack, Mack knelt before my hearth and soon had a cozy fire crackling in the hearth.

In my eating nook, I got a good look at him and was even more impressed. You're used to meeting "beautiful...gorgeous...fantastic..." looking would be stars in Hollywood but Mack was—breathtaking.

Having removed his thin jacket and hat, he looked even more like Clark Gable if he had stood at six feet five or six. Huge shoulders, arms and pectorals strained against his thin jersey.

This was striking because at that time, the physical style for men was slender, if not skinny types with hardly any musculature. Look at Tyrone Power, Gable, Bogart and Cagney in their movies and see what I mean. Only heroic personalities like Buster Crabbe or Johnny Weismuller could get away with looking like bigger-than-life men.

With his wide-opened eye look of innocence, Mack told me he couldn't find work, even as an extra, because of his physical size. All female stars back then were tiny and if he were in the same scene, his towering physique would overshadow everyone else.

I had seen first hand some of the film legends since coming to the film colony in 1929 and knew what he meant: Gloria Swanson, Kay Francis and Bette Davis were like little schoolgirls. Gloria and Mary Pick ford, in particular, were barely five feet tall.

Their male counterparts like George Brent, Charles Boyer and Paul Mona could have been mistaken for boys. So the only work Mack could find now was as a boxer, a truck driver, a bodyguard and bar room bouncer.

"I'm still waiting for that big break," he sighed, "maybe as Tarzan or Flash Gordon—one of those big movie heroes."

I told him about my nightmarish film debut in *Night of Stars*, and MGM had forced me to leave after putting me into horrible bit parts: as a butler, a messenger boy, a hair dresser, all of them walk-ons that went to the lowliest extra.

"Why?" Mack asked. "You look like Jean Harlow except, of course, you're a man."

"That's the problem," I said. "I've got a great voice, I'm a great dancer but when people saw me on the screen, they died laughing. I was too swish. A big joke. People thought I was the comedy relief."

I was so obviously a fruit, I joked, that my singing and dance routine with the adorable Anita Page, who had electrified the screen in *Broadway Melody*, had been cut after that horrendous preview.

For another hour we traded mutual tragedies of near chances that never worked and when there was a lull, Mack studied his fingers.

"You've been real nice to me, Sunny," he said shyly, "and since I don't have any money, maybe I could do something else for you."

It was hardly a subtle offer but what it promised was thrilling.

"Could I ask anything, Mack?"

He smiled sweetly and nodded his head. "Anything I can physically do."

"I want you to do a strip tease for me."

His blue eyes became even bigger. "You mean—take off my clothes? Sure, that ain't such a big deal."

"Not just take off your clothes. Sometimes when I've got some buddies over, we take turns stripping off our things to music. Come on into the den. I've got a Mae West record we always play for our strip shows."

I placed him before the burning fire and told him to turn his back to me and then "do what comes naturally. Just a second, Mack, while I put on the record. Are you ready?"

"Let the music play," he drawled. I settled down on some silk cushions and as Mae West began belting out her raucous theme song, "Sister Honkytonk", I watched one of the hottest strips in my life.

Like most natural athletes, Mack had great physical grace. To the music, he began to sway and clicked his fingers.

He turned around, not looking at me, but wearing a look of concentration on his little boy face. Off came his boots, his jacket and then he pulled out his belt.

He moved his hips sensuously and turned to wriggle his cute tush in my face. Still just inches away, he pushed down his light slacks so that he now wore only black socks and white boxer shorts.

"Wow!" I murmured for he made the famous muscleman, Sandow, who had been such a hit on Broadway back in the 1900s, look like a pigmy. Mack made his enormous pecs jiggle, caused his flat stomach sink in and then he peeled down his shorts and threw them into the corner.

He had turned his back to me again, twitching his ravishing, white behind, and now turned to face me. I whooped and clapped for he had grasped his organ with his fist and was whirling it around like a rubber hose.

"Is that real?" I gasped.

He grinned and took his hand away. His phallus swung thick and swollen between his thighs. Then he startled me by grabbing it again and then smashing it hard against the wooden arm of my chair.

Twice he did this, as if he had a hammer in his hands, and he struck it with such force, the tip of his erection bounced like a rubber ball. This unusual routine had also made his manhood puff up to a truly impressive size.

"Oh, God," I muttered, "if they could get this on film, you'd become king of the stag film studs."

He shuffled over to where I sat now, swiveling his hips and then he handed me his very virile treasure.

"See?" he whispered. "I've gotten it all nice and big for you."

He dragged the drooling tip back and forth across my cheeks and nose and I grabbed his hips and brought him hard against my face.

He grunted in pleasure and fell to his knees before leaning backwards, giving me maximum ease in sucking him.

My mouth ain't all that big and usually I can do little orally with a big weenie. But although in the "large" category, Mack's equipment was beautifully malleable and supple. You could cram and bend it until most of it was secure inside the mouth.

While I was doing this, my hands massaged his equally large testicles and with all this stimulation going on, I watched his chiseled stomach begin to move faster as his breathing quickened.

I took out his pride and glory in time to watch it fire off some very impressive streams of whiteness and the fact it ended up on my bear skin rug didn't bother me at all. Mack was proving to be someone I wanted around for more than a one-night stand.

He proved it when he turned over on his stomach and jutted his adorable rump up in the air. He looked over his shoulder and winked and then placed his hands back there to part his cheeks and show me his smoothly shaven cleft.

I got the message alright and ran to get my dildo box. I got out a really big one, licked it and began to work it deep into my muscle man.

In just a few minutes, he suddenly grabbed his shorts and thrust them beneath him, barely in time for once more, he began spurting.

"Whew, that was close!" he smiled. Getting to his feet, he stooped down and picked me easily up into those brawny arms.

"Hey, it's time to hit the sack," he murmured.

And in my big brass bed, with the feather mattress, with dozens of black and white glossies autographed by the stars I had worked with, we loved each other some more and then fell asleep.

And the next day, he moved in with me

#

For five years he had scrambled and schemed to stay alive in the film colony but he had no luck.

It was always his great physical size which held him back. Even Joan Crawford, Marion Davies and Norman Shearer had all agreed he was better looking than any of the movie idols, but they simply couldn't have him in their scenes when they saw his screen tests.

Even if they dug a trench or elevated the star several inches into the air, which wasn't unusual then, Mack would make them resemble ants.

He had been the leading contender for MGM's Tarzan, but Louis B. Mayer, chief honcho and rabidly conservative, deemed Mack a "freak" because of his tremendous pectorals.

"They're bigger than Mae West!" he screamed. "This guy needs a brassiere!"

He tried working as a stuntman in cheapjack westerns but quit after nearly breaking his neck and being on his back for nearly six months.

Since he could handle a horse, he had been one of the hundreds of riders in the Errol Flynn actioner, *Charge of the Light Brigade.* When Clark Gable rebelled against the brutal Charles Laughton in *Mutiny on the Bounty,* Mack was among the brawny rebels.

Booze was his enemy, though. An audition for an important role in the James Cagney gangster picture, 1931's *Public Enemy,* went down the drain because Mack got drunk before his test.

In desperation, he had even done a sexy "apache" dance routine with a female partner at one of the theaters between films but had to quit after police said it "was too dirty."

Lately, he had supported himself by starring as "Donkey Dan" in a series of stag films, using his talented equipment in such smut epics as Donkey Dan, the Handyman and Donkey Dan, the Plumber. His "tools" had helped unplug the pipes of everyone in these spectaculars from the wife, the daughter, even the father and son.

When I had asked Mack to perform his amateur strip tease that memorable night, it wasn't just from lusty motivations.

For besides being a popular song and dance extra before the cameras, I had also become over the years the queen of drag queens and I ruled every weekend over the notorious and legendary Club Purple, right next to MGM.

Some of the most famous male faces on film could be seen crowding into that ultra exclusive cabaret, including William "Billy" Haines, once the prince of the Jazz Age in MGM movies but who had been kicked off the lot after he was found in bed at the YMCA with a cute sailor.

Valentino had often come there during the 20s, with his bosom buddy, the sultry Latin lover, Ramon Navarro, and I understand that when they performed a sizzling tango together, the temperatures rose to the boiling point.

In my blonde wig, sequined gowns and silk stockings and heels, I brought down the house with my imitations of Mae West, Alice Faye, Jean Harlow and even Garbo. Other fantastic queens, supported me all in the movie business, and our audience was a heady combination of not only film performers but also hunky carpenters, stunt doubles, cowboys, photographers.

I had been looking for a big, muscle stud for a new routine I was cooking up—and Mack was an answer to my prayer.

A week after our first night together, and after rehearsing with him for hours, word spread through the studios from Warner Brothers to RKO to the small independents on Poverty Row that the Purple Club was going to showcase a spectacular surprise, featuring myself and a "handsome newcomer."

We were famous for mixing classy singing and dance routines with down and out sleaze, which made the Purple Club a legend around the world.

More than a thousand men, and gay women, clamored to be admitted that night. Hundreds were turned away. Looking through a hole in the curtain "Kitty," a cute guy from the story department of Paramount, and who specialized in "doing" Garbo, called me over.

"Honey, get a load of the big shots!" he whistled. "As I live and breathe, isn't that Ramon Navarro over there? Wow, looka the gorgeous thing against the wall in the beret and black sweater. That's Errol Flynn and he's stuck on a moustache to disguise himself."

I joined him at the hole and I giggled. "Tyrone Power just came in and look—he's heading straight for Errol!"

Our black Dixie Jazz band struck up the music and the entertainment began. "Kitty," who had borrowed an actual gown worn by Garbo in her classic, *Mata Hari*, had everyone howling with her very raunchy routine called "I Don't Vant To Evah Be Alone!"

Finally, it was my turn. I knew all the costume designers in Hollywood by this time, having worked for all the major studios since 1929, so I could borrow any gown I wanted.

That night, I wore a slinky number Joan Crawford had worn in *Dancing Ladies*, a creation coated with thousands of sequins. In my blonde wig, full make-pup, I swiveled out onto the stage and sang Mae West's old standard, "Some of These Days."

The large room was dark, except for a gold spotlight on me. Suddenly, a second light picked up another figure, standing with his back facing the crowd.

He was huge, powerful, and wearing pants and jersey so tight, you saw instantly that this was no ordinary dancer.

Mack wriggled up to me, smoking a cigarette, a beret pulled low over his brows. We moved sensuously together and he threw his hat out into the crowd.

There was a gasp of delight when I suddenly ripped off his thin jersey to reveal those phenomenal pecs and shoulders and arms.

The crowd screamed and cheered for he wore only suspenders and slacks now. But soon, I had pulled down the suspenders, unbuttoned him and before I peeled down his pants, Mack turned and bent forward, offering everyone drooling in the dark to feast their eyes on his stunning backside, which was quickly exposed after I ripped away the pants.

Completely naked now, he rubbed against me, put his arms around me as I kept crooning the words to Mae West's anthem.

You could hear the sudden intake of breath from everyone when I grabbed Mack's heroic organ and began massaging it. He leaned up against the wall, my hands ran all over him, especially his privates.

By the time I led him off the stage by pulling his cock, it had swollen up into an unforgettable erection. The audience, the other performers, went crazy.

They screamed and clapped and whistled until me and my new partner had to come out and do an encore. Only this time, we gave everyone what they wanted.

As the band played, Mack embraced me tight and parted the front of my gown and guided his phallus in there.

While I clung to him he entered me right there, before hundreds of eyes, and proved to everyone that he wasn't just a knockout performer. He left no doubt that he knew how to drill like a champion.

Live sex shows were hardly rare there at the Purple Club and we had some of the best performers in the world to come there and display their prowess. But in Mack, they found a wide-eyed young giant, who had the face of a little boy, and a body Charles Atlas would have killed for.

Starting with that night, a golden cycle began for Mack and I'll admit, I was a major factor in making it happen.

By 1939, all the studio casting directors recognized me as a real professional—always on time, always dressed perfectly for my bit part (dress extras had to provide their own attire for all those party and theater scenes), so I was instrumental in getting Mack extra work.

I had been cast as a party-gore in the Bette Davis tearjerker supreme, *Dark Victory*.

So I found a tuxedo big enough for Mack and he appeared with me in two of the sequences: at a bar with Ronald Reagan and others and at the welcoming party when Bette returns home from the hospital.

Some of the other gay extras and I agreed that "Little Ronnie Reagan" was a hunky dish but although he was pleasant to us, he made it clear that he was straight, although our director, the flaming Edmund Goulding, was anything but.

Mack and I were seen briefly as vacationers on the Riviera in the comedy, *Topper Takes a Trip*. A friend phoned me they were looking for a giant to play in a Little Rascal's comedy short at the Mack Sennett Studio. I sent Mack over and he got the part, although he was loaded with so much make-up, a huge wig and hair, none of my buddies recognized him.

But like everyone in Hollywood and America during that time, we were obsessed with the casting of David O.Selznick's ambitious production of the Civil War classic, *Gone With the Wind*, or called simply, Wind, for short.

All of us queen's fantasized about playing Scarlett O'Hara, the beautiful Southern vixen who snares the sexy Rhett Butler. A crowd of us had come back to my place one night right after Mack had made his sensational debut.

There were two costume designers in the crowd, a make-up genius from Universal, a few extras and a casting director. While I sat in Mack's naked lap, wearing a white silk robe, we began joking about what a scream it would be if I got dolled up as an actress and got a test for Scarlett.

And since Mack looked so uncannily like Clark Gable who everyone wanted for the role, why couldn't he test for the role of Rhett Butler? Gable had announced he would never play Rhett Butler and it was widely known Selznick was desperate. More importantly, he kept stressing that he would love to use complete unknowns in all the key roles.

"Well, why don't you two do it?" drawled Nelson Harriman, the brilliant costume designer for Tiffany Studio. "I could whip you two up fantastic outfits to wear."

"I know Selznick personally," cried Jonathan Sage, a handsome but ruthless casting director. "I could arrange the screen tests."

"I could create your make-up," declared Whitney Factor, a master at transforming the beautiful into the hideous at Universal or the ghastly into the ravishing.

By the next afternoon, it had been arranged with the brilliant and gay director George Cukor who was in on the secret and who was in charge of the screen tests for Wind.

I would be tested the following week as Angel Dawn, a young actress from Broadway. Mack wouldn't need a phony background. He had worked in westerns and horror films and had done stunt work. A big plus in his favor was his genuine Southern accent. It was deliciously slow and soft and oh, so very sexy.

When I appeared for my test I have to admit I really did look "ravishing," thanks to the work performed on me by my buddies. My gold curls were hidden beneath a dark wig, my make-up made me look more beautiful than Hedy Lamarr, who was considered the most beautiful gal in Hollywood at that time.

And I was attired in Scarlett O'Hara's favorite color: red. From my hat to my sheath dress to my slippers, I was completely scarlet.

So then the flamboyant director, George Cukor, directed me in the corset scene with Mammy and the scene with Ashley in the orchard, begging him to run away from his wife, Melanie.

I poured my heart into those scenes, which I played with actor Douglass Montgomery.

When I finished the last test, with my face still wet with tears, Cukor just stared at me. "Where in the world have you been, Miss Dawn?" he teased but with genuine shock in his eyes. "You were quite good."

Coming from him, that was quite a compliment. He was known for being notoriously sharp tongued, "bitchy" but also for getting superb performances from his performers.

My elation couldn't be contained and I raced home to wait for Mack's return. He had been outfitted in rugged, virile clothes for the part of Rhett and had even worn a wide-brimmed hat, which the dashing blockade-runner was never without in the book.

We knew his size alone was extraordinary but Selznick was a genius. Surely, if he liked him, he could find some way of fitting Mack brilliantly within the camera lens.

When Mack came home that night, he, too, was dazzled.

"They liked me," he said quietly. "Sunny, they told me I was great. They discussed my size, but they think they could work around that before the cameras."

Later, I heard from George Cukor that both my test and that of Sam's were "electrifying." Something about our personalities "flashed" out on film. We supposedly possessed that phenomena described as "flesh magic." No one could quite explain it, only that Garbo, Crawford and Davis had it. When we were on the screen, you saw nobody else.

Through the studio grapevine, to which I was directly plugged into because of my contacts, we became hysterical when we heard that Selznick was thrilled with both our screen tests. He played and replayed mine repeatedly, and did the same for Mack who had come across as a perfect Rhett.

Even Louella Parsons gasped in her movie column: "Do the names Angel Dawn and Mack Johnson ring a bell? They may become household words if David O. Selznick decides to star them in his gigantic spectacular. Their screen tests are the talk of the studio!"

I heard that all the women on the Selznick lot and within the studio had made excuses to come by when Mack was preparing for his test. His dynamic virility and looks had them all atwitter.

Of course, both of us were turned down since Selznick discovered that British vixen, Vivien Leigh, and MGM agreed to permit Gable to portray Rhett Butler.

It had been mostly a fun game for the dozen or more of us who were in on the escapade so Mack and I didn't exactly cut our throats.

But for just a few hours, we had both seen our dreams begin to actually form on the horizon. If Carole Lombard and Dorothy Lamour and Clark Gable all began as extras, look at them now? They were more famous than European royalty. School children in Japan and Russia knew their names but couldn't name the President of the United States.

While we didn't star in this epic, we were called out to Selznick Studios to play in a number of the big scenes for the spectacular: especially the one where Scarlett sees thousands of dying soldiers in the rail yard of Atlanta.

Mack and I laid there in the broiling sun for hours as soldiers while the terribly complicated scene was set up. We played cards with the other men and dished about the cast and other movies being made.

Was it true Gable had been a gay hustler when he first came to Hollywood during the late 20s? Was that why he had Cukor fired as director because the swish director knew only too well of Gable's brief fling with MGM's badboy, Billy Haines, who had also been fired because of his fling with a sailor in a YMCA?

And was it true members of the gay crew were blowing some of the strapping black extras while fitting them with costumes? Mack had certainly been groped and handled while trying on his soldier costumes.

When he stripped and showered after a day of work, he was the center of attention. One of the handsome black extras returned home with us one night and proved a delight when he got in bed with Mack and me.

We were also among the dancers in the waltz sequences, as well as among the visitors at the barbecue at Twelve Oaks, standing behind Vivien Leigh as she flirts with all her "beaus." And I was clearly visible in the birthday party for Ashley Wilkes as we stand around Leslie Howard singing "For He's A Jolly Good Fellow."

Although blue from losing the role of Scarlett (as were hundreds, if not thousands of other hopefuls), I just shrugged and kept working. This was the way of life in Hollywood. It happened to everybody. Mack, though, took his rejection very hard, indeed. He became quieter around me and he began drinking again.

I tried to give him more to do at the Purple Club where both he and I were definitely the major star attractions. We even had him stripping naked to a hot jazz number and then going out into the audience where the men went crazy.

He encouraged them to handle him, to do him right there and then he would bring some lucky customer to the stage and go at it right on a bed we had dragged in. That Christmas, some lucky patron got a lucky number at the door and had Mack as his holiday present that night.

I knew that he was getting done by everyone from the handsome bartenders to the movie gods he worshipped. But I also knew that I was the one he really loved.

And then I was called back to do more extra work on, believe it or not, *Wizard of Oz* which was still in production after nearly a year. I got Mack a juicy part, as one of the witch's guards who chase Dorothy and her friends through the castle and up to the turret and the witch dies a watery death.

And then his spirits really shot up the morning he got a call from the casting director at the tiny independent studio, Mascot. It was planning to do a serial called *Tonga, the Jungle King.*

Someone who had seen Mack in all his unclothed glory at the Purple Club had recommended him for the star role.

I helped him get ready, packing his duffel bag with a bathing suit and robe since they wanted to test his swimming and athletic ability, in addition to wearing regular street clothes.

That night, he bounded into my den and swung me around. He didn't know if he got the role but the director, Yakima Cannutt was very impressed.

"When I put on the G-string they had for me, you could have heard a pin drop," he laughed. "They were dumbfounded. Everybody joked about how if I got the role, they'd have to strap my privates down with tape because it did, eh, kind of bulge out."

Exactly four days later, I returned home from the *Wizard of Oz* set, completely exhausted and relieved that the movie had been wrapped that afternoon. It was finished. This was one movie set where you literally saw the floor glistening from human sweat.

I found Mack laying on our bed, completely drunk.

He had lost the role of Tonga. They wanted a bigger name and so Tom Tyler, the rugged stuntman and cowboy actor, would be playing Tonga. Also, one of the crew had told him bluntly that he looked just "too damned sexy. Your tits are huge. Your nipples always look hard. It looks like you're packing a bread loaf beneath that G-string. You'd have the censors screaming bloody murder."

I left him there for I sensed he wanted to be alone.

At breakfast the next day, he joined me and I looked up at him anxiously. He was sober and looked beautiful in a black jersey and white pants.

We talked about how horrible Hollywood could be to people like us but then we had done this many times. He seemed unusually quiet, though, and when he finished his coffee, he got to his feet and held out his hand.

"So long, honey. It's been nice. You've been wonderful. But I'm moving on. I've had it here. No one's ever going to put me into anything important because I'm just too goddamned big."

He didn't want to waste the rest of his best years by playing a man in a gorilla suit, as a bunch of "blurs" in the background where nobody would ever recognize him.

"I just know I've got special gifts that I can't waste anymore by being in the background."

He hugged me briefly. Then he picked up his paper bag, which held his possessions and left.

Mack didn't like emotional scenes.

But I remember it was a foggy morning when he left the house, just like the scene in *Wind*, where Scarlett realizes she loves Rhett Butler and runs out into the mist to find and tell him so. I watched him vanish into the mist and then collapsed in bed. True, I had had many men. But Mack was the only one who I really loved. It wasn't just his fantastic body and lovemaking.

I felt like we were part of each other. At night, when we were joined together, I felt like a wife with an incredible husband.

When *Gone With the Wind* opened for Christmas in 1939, I thrilled to it like everyone else did. Naturally, I looked for me and Mack and although we were seen and gone in seconds, we were still frozen permanently on celluloid.

By the early forties, just as World War II began, I, too, grew tired of being just another blur. For although I had become a featured dancer in Betty Grable movies, you barely saw me. Betty was the star and nobody else would be featured in her musical numbers.

I returned to Carson City where I opened my own dance studio, which proved a big success. I lived with my handsome father on our big plantation on the outskirts of town and knew that this was where I really wanted to be. Hollywood had been a fun part of my life. But it wasn't a place I wanted to retire in.

One Saturday afternoon in 1948, my father and I went to our town's only theater, the little Jewel, to see the usual double feature. The first one was *The Mummy's Bride* and the second one was *Smoking Guns* starring a new cowboy star, Buck Montana.

Looking powerful and handsome in tight black pants and shirt, he was introduced by firing his guns at the camera. And as it moved steadily up to his face, my hand stopped midway between my box of popcorn and my mouth.

"Daddy!" I gasped. "It's him! It's my Mack! He made it!"

Somehow he had returned to Hollywood after the war and it was the right time and the right place for big men like himself. In 1949, he was making personal appearances for his new movie, *The Indians Are Coming* and he delighted my father and I when he came to visit us for the weekend.

It was like old times again and my father enjoyed Mack's extraordinary bedroom prowess so much that we both begged the cowboy star to return and stay longer.

When Mack retired from movies in 1955, he did just that and he and my father and I became an intimate little family, living an opulent life on our plantation and his homes in Santa Monica and New York City.

We spent hours, until his death in 1978, watching dozens of old movie videos in which we had bit roles, freezing the scenes so we could briefly study ourselves in our golden days. Even more fun was viewing Mack's ancient, scratchy stag films he had unearthed in a storage building in San Francisco.

Daddy was spell bound by Mack's phenomenal beauty and prowess in those crude movies. He agreed that it was like watching a very well built, and extremely hung Clark Gable, performing with those long gone female and male co-stars.

We donated the collection of Mack's stag films to the Playboy Foundation, which has built up a treasure trove of adult movies from the past. For over the years, a myth had grown up about the notorious "Donkey Dan" movies, which were believed to have vanished forever.

Some archivists swore he never existed and only a figment of someone's imagination.

Now, modern day viewers can see with their own eyes that there was most definitely a stag film star named "Donkey Dan" and that he was blessed with spectacular gifts, which throws the late Johnny Holmes and Long Dong Silver into the shade.

My father died in 1974 and my wonderful Mack passed away in 1989. Even on his deathbed, he was a spectacular beauty: his black hair had turned silver and although his legendary muscles were not as powerful as before, he was a stunning figure as he lay in his coffin.

And when I watch *Gone With the Wind*, I naturally adore the performances of that magical cast, but I also think: if Mack and I had been cast, it would have been even more magical.

(**Author's Note:** This story first appeared in "InTouch" Magazine in 1979 and later served as the basis for my novel, *The Kiss of King Kong*.)

BURNT ORANGES

◆

The explosion between my father and myself that April morning in 1912 had been a long time coming.

And when it did it was ignited by such a trivial incident. He found me in bed with his best friend.

Now, why should that have bothered him, one of the most notorious cocksmen of America's robber barons? Twice I had caught him plunging our cook and once with my governess who was fondling him.

After all, he was the famous "Black Jack" Sarelle—the powerful, dashing self-made millionaire. Famed for his physical size as well as his extraordinary gift for making money, he was the Steve Reeves of his day, often painted by the masters and sketched in countless newspapers and magazines.

A black beard and moustache made him resemble a pirate, especially with those dark, wicked eyes and thick brows. A schoolboy fight had left a scar above his upper lip, which like his lower one was full and sensual.

He was also famed for being an outstanding athlete and often invited his fellow millionaires over to our mansion on Fifth Avenue to boxing matches held in his private gym.

There, he would hire the top pugilists in New York to come and fight him and he always won. These stag gatherings were considered scandalous because my father and his partner fought stark naked. The fact that he invited Broadway's prettiest, and most uninhibited chorines, to join in the festivities, didn't help his reputation.

But he didn't give a damn. He'd made his money on his own, he held nothing but contempt for New York's hypocritical social doings and this made him the darling of the press and the ordinary citizens.

"Black Jack" Sarelle was celebrated in ribald songs and poems for a time and there were even a stream of penny novels about a "dashing, handsome millionaire who resembled a pirate." These books never failed to give graphic details about why he was such a popular man with the women.

Whispers were rampant about my stepfather's extraordinary physique. He kept it in such rippling, muscular condition that he finally consented to pose for world famous sculptor, Rodin, who created his most famous work, Power, with my father the model.

When it was unveiled, though, in 1910, it created a tremendous scandal. There was my stepfather, immortalized forever in granite—completely naked and showing everyone the heroic endowment between his thighs.

Many male reporters accused the famous sculptor of exaggerating the "male organ." But Rodin declared that what you saw was reality. Black Jack Sarelle was a phenomenal male beauty. So why not show him as he really was?

The monument finally appeared before the public but with a very large fig leaf over my father's most proud possession. I had seen it many a time and thought: if they think what they see in his statue is shocking, what would they do if they saw him with a hard-on?

I had seen it many a time because Father hated to wear clothes. He was ahead of his time, a passionate nudist. Our female staff was under strict orders not to intrude into his private suite in our Fifth Avenue mansion. If they did, they would have seen one of the great male beauties of his time.

Yet, he treated me with intense contempt for my reputation as an equally notorious pervert. To be honest, it had gotten so bad that women who saw me on the streets invariably tightened the grasp on their husband's arm—especially if he were handsome and had a bold sparkle in his eyes.

No one could believe that I was Black Jack's only son. He was like an Indian, a pirate while I had gold curls and big blue eyes and a boyish figure, which featured an ass so curvaceous men would stop and watch me, pass by.

If they were street boys or rough trade, they would make whistling noises and bawdy comments, encouraged no doubt by my smiles and winks.

In winter of 1911, I left America to live in London as an artist. Since I had shown zero interest in becoming part of my father's vast Sarelle & Co., America's foremost producer of coffee pots and toilet seats, he agreed to support me for a year "until I came to my senses."

Instead of becoming an artist, however, I became London's most popular party boy and slut—until my father burst into my room one morning, kicked out the husky Royal guardsman from my bed and announced I would stay with him at the Ritz Hotel while he was in London.

Was it true, he snarled, that I had brought street urchins, chimney sweeps and criminal hoodlums up to my room? Yes, I drawled, in addition to two very handsome detectives from Scotland Yard, some lusty stable hands and even a member of the royal family.

"Behave yourself or you'll be cut off without a penny!" roared my father.

"Yes, Daddy, anything you say," Daddy, I wept.

But the minute he went out on business, I turned once more into London's most notorious male whore. There were such cute men in London during this time. The blanket of repression, which had hung over London since the Oscar Wilde scandal of 1895, was lifting with a vengeance.

If you had cigarettes and liquor to entice, you could have your pick of the farm boys and ex-cons or the hundreds of lonely men who hung out at Piccadilly Circus.

Secretly, I did have qualms for my treachery to my father. When he accused me of being completely unreliable, he was right. I was willful and perverse because I resented his coldness to me all of my life.

You couldn't imagine two people more different. As I've described him, he stood out in any crowd because of his powerful size. This was during an era when men rarely grew more than five feet five. Women were usually smaller.

I looked like a high school boy, one very well proportioned with a shapely rump, smokey blue eyes and curls the color of copper and sandalwood which I wore in ringlets. Since I was regarded as the most dandy of the dandies in London at that time, I also sported a moustache.

When I look at those faded photographs today, I could have passed for a mature looking lad of 13 or slightly older. My father stands behind me in that darkened photographer's studio of London in 1912. He could easily have been a movie star...the way his full lips are slightly parted, moist, the glitter of those black eyes, staring down at me, his thick brows, black curly hair, shoulders that belonged to a boxer or stevedore.

Countless days in the sun swimming and rowing had bronzed his body. This, and the thick moustache, made his white teeth dazzle. Deeply set eyes glinted dark and bold from between long lashes.

He was outrageously vain about his looks—and body.

In 1910, he caused a scandal at Newport, the favorite watering hole of New York's rich, where we had a mansion so big it was called "Black Jack's Castle."

He agreed to appear in a charity pageant as the ancient god Atlas—naked, except for a pair of paper-thin silk tights, which emphasized every swelling, and curve of his lower torso to an extraordinary degree.

I remember one of the servants giggling to the other that "you can tell that Master Sarelle was circumcised."

So, the day of our confrontation before the nightmare began started off quietly.

Daddy had gone to the Ascot races in London with some of the Astors and Vanderbilts—and while he was away, I enticed into my bed my father's best friend, the snooty but very oversexed aristocrat, Sir Edmund Orme.

To most people, he was your usual London snob, slender and heavy-lidded, but to me, he was a wonderful flirter with a hot glow in his gray eyes.

In bed that afternoon, he became a real sex tiger when he plunged his white, slender manhood up into me and moaned: "Oh, God, little Reggie! I've been wanting to fuck you since the day I saw your father giving you a bath as a baby!"

His skin felt soft, warm, smelling of a floral scent and when he kissed me, his mouth was moist and hot. I enjoyed the way he moved his hardness around, then pulled it almost out, teasing me, and then plunged it in with all his energy.

He did this for several minutes, causing me to cry out and hold tighter to him. I had sucked him off several times in the back of carriages and in hotel rooms he would rent for our encounters. Edmund became feverish with lust when I allowed him to shave my body so that it now looked like that of a teenage boy.

Behind his bobbing buns, I watched the door open silently.

My father said nothing as he casually approached the bed, in his black cape, smoking his long cigar, and coolly studying the area where his bosom buddy had plunged his erection.

"Eh, Edmund?" I whispered. "Me thinks we have company."

Let me say this for Edmund. He was one cool dude. Glancing over his naked butt, he gave a slight start when he saw my father.

"Why, Jack!" he sang out lightly. "How jolly nice to see you, old boy! I just dropped in to say hello to Reggie."

He lost some of his coolness when father threw him and his clothes out into the hallway where a startled group of maids had been listening.

I heard Edmund cry out: "Jack, don't be such a bloody beast about this! It's not what you think!"

Ripping away the silk sheets from around me, Father picked me up and shoved me to the closet.

"Start packing!" he roared. "I knew I couldn't trust you. So we leave for America tomorrow. And if I ever see you again in such a position—with a man's cock stuck up your ass, I'll—"

"You'll what?" I spat, whirling around and moving toward him. "I saw you in the same position last month when I caught you fucking your sweet little duchess out in the garden. And a week before that, you had her daughter playing with your cock in the library when you didn't think anybody was around, showing her that book of dirty pictures of you."

"That's different!" shouted Black Jack Sarelle. "They're women. They've got a hole between their legs to be fucked. It's natural!"

"God gave me a hole, too, and the most gorgeous studs in London can't get enough of it! I can take a shit with it, too! Can your cunts do that?"

I knew there were even more maids outside our door, listening to every word and probably having coronaries. For a moment, I thought my father was having one. His face had flushed a deep red, he began to tremble, his hands opening and closing and he slumped against the wall.

Then, I realized he was laughing hysterically. He half staggered across the room until he had collapsed on the edge of the bed.

"Yes, I can see why they'd find your bung-hole so very attractive," he gasped. Then his voice became more gentle: "Okay, now, let's get packed up. Our ship leaves tomorrow from Southampton."

"Which ship is it, Daddy?"

"The one everyone says is unsinkable. The Titanic."

#

All of us had read the torrent of articles about the Titanic–"the engineering marvel of the new century!"

With a flip of a switch, the captain could supposedly make the mammoth liner unsinkable by closing up all the lower compartments from water.

None of us, however, were prepared for what greeted us that brilliant morning in April, 1912, in Southampton. As tall as a four-story building, it gleamed white and silver against the cobalt blue of a spring sky.

A small band aboard played snappy dance tunes while a steward showed my father and I to our deluxe suite in the First Class section. On the way, we met so many friends from America that it was like a traveling party.

John Jacob Astor and his wife sang out a cheery "Hello!" as they walked their little Airedale, Kitty. I was thrilled to see one of my favorite movie serial queens, Dorothy Gibson, who was signing autographs for her younger fans.

A muscular young stevedore caught my eye as he helped bring luggage up to our deck and when I winked at him, he returned it with a knowing grin. Daddy gave my arm a painful twist.

"If you do that again, I'll shout at the top of my lungs!" I warned him, "and scream out that you're a dirty pervert and rapist."

"Can't you think of anything worse?" he drawled. "And stop staring at that boy like that! You're absolutely disgraceful."

"I was taught by a master," I snorted, giving him an accusing look. "Ha! Look at you, staring at those young women like you want to rip off their panties. Knowing you, you probably will before the trip is over."

"Shut up and get inside the suite," he said absently for our sparring was typical of our relationship. Frankly, I thought my dangerous, sensuous father the most ravishing man I had ever seen and when I was balling with other men, I always compared them physically with father.

I watched him now move into the suite and look around, like a little boy, spoilt outrageously who expected only the best. He seemed pleased with what we found. Dark walls of walnut gleamed from the glow of small French lamps, covered with shades of pink and gold crystal. A marble topped dresser, thick carpeting of rose and a big, square window, which opened upon the sea.

But there was only one big, brass bed.

"Daddy, where do I sleep?"

He was in a testy mood and had already stripped off all his clothes except his trousers and socks.

I had seen him naked countless times but each time was always a stunning shock. He seemed totally indifferent to his staggering physical beauty. As he paced around the room in his bare feet, putting his belongings away, he was as graceful as a savage Indian, a dark cigar stuck between his teeth, his stunning back dancing with muscles.

He turned to me, scratching his tits, which in turn made his pecs and biceps jiggle.

"You're sleeping with me on this trip," he muttered, looking me up and down, "because I'm going to make damned sure you don't go dragging half the men in here, turning it into a male whorehouse!"

"Oh, really?" I sniffed. "I'm having the carpenters make me a big sign to hang over our door here: Reggie Sarelle's Whorehouse! Specials Every Hour! Seafood Treats Galore! Sailors and Stevedores Special Rates!"

He listened to me, glowering and shaking his head while he peeled off his socks and slacks. Only the best silk boxer trunks ever touched the skin of Black Jack Sarelle.

"I saw that greasy seaman you flirted with. God knows what diseases he's got but you wouldn't care, would you? You'd fuck anything with a cock! Can't you control your disgusting appetites for once in your life? Especially aboard this ship?"

I forgot his heroic beauty as rage engulfed me. What a goddamned hypocrite my father could be! Him, calling me names?

"My appetites?" I screamed. "What about yours? You've made abortionists in London and New York rich! How many other bastards have you fathered? What about the number of maids we lose each year because they go off to have your bastards, you bastard?"

I tore out of the room, determined to return to London and find Sir Edmund Orme and live in the apartment he wanted to rent for me. Pushing my way through the hundreds of passengers and visitors, I was nearly at the ramp when a strong hand grabbed my shoulder, whirled me around and I found myself being thrown over the naked shoulder of my father, as if I were a bag of flour.

He had yanked on his trousers, which meant everyone on deck saw first hand his much talked about and discussed torso. This little melodrama electrified the crowd. Oh, wow, they thought. The ship hasn't even left yet and the colorful Sarelles are already feeding grist to the gossip mills.

In our suite, he threw me on the bed and watched me carefully, as he yanked off his slacks. Absently, as he lit up another black cigar, he pulled at his dark length of manhood and scratched his butt.

"What is wrong with you?" he asked in genuine alarm. "Please don't make any more scenes, son! You act like you're crazy."

"I'm sorry, Daddy," I lied. "I'll be a good little boy."

"I'm glad to hear that," he responded with obvious relief. As he shook his head at me, studying me with concern, he went to the sink and prepared to shave.

I lay there, watching this familiar ritual of my big, strong father, not wearing a stitch, humming to himself and covering his square jaw with foam.

He dropped his brush on the floor and as he bent down to retrieve it, I made another mad dash for the door. Again, his big hands grabbed me and whirled me around. Pinning my arms behind my back, his wet, hard body pressed against me.

"You're hurting me, Daddy!" I cried out.

"I want to hurt you, goddammit!" he muttered angrily. "I wanted this trip to bring us closer together because I know I've been a lousy parent to you. It's not too late, though, is it? I'm only 41. You're 18. Won't you meet me at least halfway?"

The sincere pleading in his eyes and voice was so unusual that I was shocked.

Black Jack Sarelle never pleaded or showed sensitivity. He always brutally took what he wanted and to hell with bruised feelings. How else had he become a multi-millionaire by the time he was 23?

At the same time, I became acutely aware of his body. A lock of black hair had fallen over his forehead, making him look like a young giant. His privates pressed against my stomach. They felt so firm, large and warm. From his big biceps, where I had gripped them, my hands slid up around his neck.

He bent his face down and began kissing me. His tongue went deep into my mouth, his lips were so warm, moist and soft and I threw my arms around him.

And from him emanated a wonderful aroma, which was more than just clean skin, breath and hair.

Two years before, a close friend of my father's, a French perfume maker, had concocted a cologne especially for my parent. No one else had it and Daddy called it *Burnt Oranges*.

A haunting mixture of citrus, musk and flowers, it meshed beautifully with my father's flesh and the exhilarating results always had people asking him the name of this rare elixir.

Where could they buy some like it? But this belonged only to my father. There was one bottle of jade crystal containing this precious substance. It was the one beautiful thing in his life. Even when I asked if could put a drop on, he refused.

It was his and to me, it captured his essence—splendid, dangerous and mysterious.

He seemed to remember himself and drew his face away but his breathing was rapid, he looked at my hands massaging his round pectorals and then I glanced down at his privates that swelled up suspiciously fast.

"Daddy, if you would only treat me like a son, and not as a spoilt brat," I pleaded, kissing his chin and then his chest. He pulled me against him again, as if suddenly discovering me.

"Maybe I always want you to remain a little boy," he smiled. As he nuzzled my face, giving my cheek several small kisses, my hands slid down his broad back, to his hips and then over that spectacular rump.

High, white and rounded, it was drooled over by not only women but by the homosexual men of our social set. As my fingers slid into his cleft, he tensed and his penis was definitely growing harder against me.

I moved back slightly and slid my hand along its swollen surface. "Hmm, I think you need some relief, Pappy."

He snorted and drew back, not trying to hide his state of arousal but suggesting he was proud for me to see how big he could get.

"Let's get dressed and see what kind of food they have on this cattle boat," he grinned.

I didn't move right away. I watched him saunter in that animal-like walk to his dresser. Artists and sculptors would give much to see him at that moment, his ass undulating lazily from left to right, his organ bobbing out like he had affixed a big roll of dark socks to his hips.

Then I saw him pick up his precious bottle of *Burnt Oranges* and dab a drop along his neck. Even where I stood, I could sniff that intoxicating aroma. That and my father were perfectly matched.

#

Two days passed and we discovered that the "in" place on the Titanic was the smart little Parisian Café. After drinks and gossip, we usually adjourned to the lounge where a marathon game of cards would begin.

Daddy was in heaven for he had won small fortunes at poker. I hated cards and all that smoke so would usually slip away to explore the fabulous liner.

It was on the second day when I broke my vow to my father to behave myself.

The main foyer featured a tremendous dome of glass overhead. I loved to sit there and watch the women in their latest fashions. Frankly, I thought the huge hats, the corseted figures and baggy coats hideous. But then the men didn't dress any more interesting. We all had to wear bob tailed slacks, ankle boots and high, round collars.

Even in that wretched attire, though, I attracted much attention because of my unusual coloring of silver, pink and gold.

Two young men came up to me, looking like your typical teenage millionaires. Alex and Boris were the heirs to a copper fortune and I had seen them at bars in London so we weren't really strangers.

They invited me for cocktails in their suite and as soon as we'd had a few, our clothes naturally dropped to the floor and they wanted me to demonstrate with them some of the techniques I was supposed to be so skilled at.

While I buried my face in the lap of Alex, his boyfriend, Boris, came up behind me and mounted me. He'd had only a little experience fucking a man so I had to direct him how to go about doing it.

Alex was a bore. Although I enjoyed his pecker, he only wanted to get his rocks off. "Hurry, Reggie, Hurry, don't take your mouth off! I've nearly got it."

Boris, too, only wanted to get his relief and he banged me hard and it was over in just minutes. These American youths simply didn't have the expertise of the older men I was used to in London and Paris. There, I found men who had spent a lifetime perfecting their love making techniques.

I quickly dressed and hurried to our suite. Thank God Daddy hadn't returned yet.

But barely had I washed up, put on a robe and gotten into bed than my dashing parent swept in.

He removed his cape and hat, and then stripped off the rest of his clothes as we small talked about the evening. He was completely naked now and slipped into bed next to me.

He never covered himself up and enjoyed laying there, nude and smoking a cigar, and sipping his customary brandy.

I couldn't keep my eyes from his thick penis, uncut and thick, draped over the side of his hip.

"Did you have fun tonight, son?"

"Oh, I did! I met a friend and—"

"You fucked and sucked each other!"

He had smashed out his cigar into a tray and suddenly rolled over on top of me, holding my hands down against the mattress.

"Get off me!" I cried out. "You're crushing me to death!"

"Why do you keep wanting to hurt me?" he hissed. "What do I have to do to keep you from fucking around with every man you meet? Tell me? We all heard about the orgy with the American boys!"

"Find me someone who'll kiss me and fuck me and let me suck the hell out of him whenever I want to! You wanted the truth, now you got it!"

His eyes flicked over my face, and moistening his lips he nodded.

"Okay, you found one."

His mouth touched mine and pressed against it, and I nearly fainted. It was finally happening. For hundreds of hours I had fantasized my gorgeous father doing exactly this and now it had transcended fantasy.

Soft, warm, moist, he moaned as his kiss became even more passionate and I threw my arms around his back and slid my hands down to his buttocks and into their warm, moist cleft.

He rolled over on his back and my mouth left his to travel down that magnificent terrain of Black Jack Sarelle. With both hands, he had grasped his manhood, holding it ready for me to savor and love.

I nearly blacked out from finally achieving my fantasy: of being loved and possessed by our extraordinary father. The next hour was one of feverish passion. Saying nothing, the only sounds in our suite was of his heavy panting, his groaning, whimpering which all joined with mine.

His flesh was warm, ravishing, and succulent and I devoured him from his nipples—thick, erect—down his rippling stomach, his deeply set navel, to his tools that had swollen to an incredible degree.

He encouraged me to be rough with him, to nibble and bite and stretch and pull. I gathered his groin up in my hands and we both studied it in wonder: his balls bulging like ripe tomatoes in a thin sac of pink silk.

His tool had to be grasped with both hands and it was like a work of art: gleaming, hard, hot and pulsing steadily as I made it swell up to the bursting point. When he did erupt, my fists, face and neck were spattered with his warm nectar.

On his stomach, he moaned even more as I buried my face in his deep cleft and became lost there in a world of dark sensuality, his hole throbbing as my tongue worked itself deeper into it. It was no wonder that I became drunk on this part of his body, one that the sculptor Rodin had pronounced, "The Eighth Wonder of the World."

His testicles swelled up again and suddenly, there was yet another release of his rare wetness that made it look as if he had spilt a cup of custard on our sheets.

By this time, we had become more relaxed with each other, for there were no more questions about what was really on our minds. With a black cigar in his mouth, a crystal tumbler of brandy in hand, he lay there quietly and smiling as I gulped and savored the core of his phenomenal virility.

And then I lay wrapped in his arms, as he kissed my face and then my mouth again and we talked in that whispering, low voices that very sensual men do with their new partners.

Many times he had dreamed of this happening but he was terrified of my possible rejection. After all, I had the cream of British and American aristocracy as my bedmates. He had seen the street urchins and rough trade on the streets go crazy when I walked by, flirting with them.

"And I was terrified that if you found out how I felt about you," I confessed, "that you would become a cold stranger and want nothing to do with me."

When I said that, he snickered like a sensual little boy who positioned himself between my buttocks.

"Hold to me tight now," he grunted as he slipped into me, "because a lot of people can't take what I've got."

When he discovered I could not only take it but I wanted it in even deeper, he murmured prayers to whatever power had finally thrown us into bed together.

"The Titanic did this," he laughed as we poured a toast of champagne. "May we never forget the Titanic!"

We were to discover the irony of his words in less than 24 hours.

#

Like a small family, the people in "our" set knew something had happened between Black Jack Sarelle and his beautiful but wild son.

We usually bickered and fought and glared at each other in public, displaying an icy politeness that was more deadly than a screaming match.

Now, we spent every moment together ignoring the pleas of others to join them for cocktails, cards or dinner. My father's female "groupies" back then, beautiful women who had heard of Black Jack's extraordinary bedroom talents, were sad and bitter at his indifference.

The good-looking male passengers and crewmembers that looked upon me as a fascinating and naughty bird of paradise, couldn't understand why I ignored them. I was supposed to be such a slut that I would do men in closets and in dark corners.

Now, both of us could only be gazed upon and drooled over. Which made us even more desirable. The more sophisticated guessed at the truth and gave us knowing smiles when we passed them by on the deck. My gorgeous father now always kept his big arm around my waist, my shoulders, and often nuzzled his face against mine.

Dressed in warm clothes and wool caps, my father and I would stand at the railings, looking out at the freezing ocean, and he would roar with laughter over my descriptions of the sex habits of some of the men we knew. Nothing shocked him, nor did he forbid me anything now.

He patiently let me have him for breakfast while he sat eating his and I was in heaven on my knees, my face buried between his thighs.

My favorite sight was for him to be bent over the sink, brushing his teeth or shaving, with that knockout set of buns thrust toward me. I would rush over and bury my face there, which would always produce an erection an then I scoot before him and take it down.

The ship's captain invited us to join him for supper.

As we dressed for this special occasion, I looked out the window where the water glistened darkly. A strange sensation came over me and I could suddenly see people in the folds of that dark green void, screaming for help. I could almost smell the ocean closing over my head. I hurried over to my father who stood there like a Russian prince: all dark and glistening and big and beautiful. He was trimming his moustache and even beneath the starched white of his shirt, his arms strained the fine linen.

"Daddy, I'm scared! Something is going to happen! I just know it."

He put his scissors down and held me close, kissing me.

"Whatever happens, you don't have to worry. I'll always be here to look after you."

Hoping to throw off my sense of approaching doom, I tried to lighten up the mood. "Oh, sure, Daddy dearest. I can see you swimming in the ocean with me held over your head."

He smiled as he put on his black dinner jacket. "You'd be surprised at what I can do. I'm the Strongest Man on Wall Street. That's what they said last years in the papers when I held up the front of that car."

I remembered the sensation he had caused when one of his friends was hit as they crossed the street by one of the new electric cars. My father had pulled up the front of the machine while others rolled his friend from out under it.

I checked my light make-up I liked wearing—some mascara, a touch of lip rouge, some powder—and now my father permitted me to make his brows even darker with my eyebrow pencil.

"Is there anything in the world you want right now that you don't have," he said softly, holding me and kissing me again.

"*Burnt Oranges*," I laughed, knowing he would never part with the most beautiful possession he owned.

"Ha, I'm sure you would," he smiled. I watched him take out his bottle of the perfume from its velvet pouch and he opened the vial to press a drop of the precious elixir against his neck.

Then he startled me by touching my throat with it so that now, for the first time, one other person shared this haunting fragrance.

"Happy now?" he asked. "That proves that you and I are now bound together forever."

And with the perfume creating an aura of shimmering beauty around us like an invisible rainbow, he took my hand and pressed it against his arm and we went to find the ship's captain.

Dinner proved to be a stilted affair and I waited impatiently the moment my father and I could hurry back to bed. Captain Smith was a haughty bore and to break the icy monotony, I asked him:

"Is this ship really unsinkable? It sounds too good to be true?"

Acting as if I had asked him if there was really a God, he gave me a look of disbelief: "Nothing can sink this ship. Technology has made sure of that. Why, even God couldn't sink this ship."

Once more, that terrible sense of icy foreboding passed over me. I saw huge waves and icy water flooding this vivid, glittering restaurant, the people in there scrambling desperately to escape, the women dragged down beneath by their heavy gowns and corsets and jewels…the men unable to swim fast enough because of their starched shirts and high collars and boots and heavy tuxedos.

My father saw my expression and murmured his apologies to everyone, telling them I was experiencing a case of seasickness. But I caught one of the Astor women winking impishly at me, along with her husband, who glanced from me to my father.

It was clear they knew why we were in such a hurry to return to our suite.

As soon as we stripped, and slid beneath the sheets, my father opened some champagne and we sipped it before we began our hours of strenuous lovemaking.

"Daddy, that same premonition came over me there at the dinner table," I whispered to him. "Something horrible is going to happen to us before we ever see land."

"Now, I told you not to worry," he chided me and held me closer so that my face was pressed against that magnificent hairy chest and I covered his right nipple with my mouth.

Against me, I felt his phallus begin to swell and I was ready for it, anything to get my mind off my imaginary terrors.

But then, we heard it.

A sound that made me think of a great bolt of cloth being ripped. Our room shuddered. At that moment, chunks of ice clattered through our half-opened window.

"What the hell is going on?" Daddy muttered and we both bounded out of bed and hurried to the window. A huge shape out there in the dark could be seen receding into the distance.

We heard signs of a commotion. People running outside on the deck, voices raised, and then something even more ominous occurred.

The ship had shuddered to a stop.

And in that moment, all my fears of the unknown flooded my mind.

"Daddy, Daddy, it's what I've been fearful of! The ship will go down!"

He looked at me with a face pale with concern but he didn't joke now. Both of us quickly pulled on our warmest clothes—tweed suits over thermal underwear, our long socks and boots, caps, scarves and dashed outside.

One of the Vanderbilt men was rushing past us. "The ship's struck an iceberg! Terrible damage. We're going down!"

Out on the deck, a few dozen passengers milled around but no one seemed upset. I grabbed the arm of our steward and asked him if the ship was going down.

He sniffed and declared: "Not even God could sink this ship."

Not even God.

I wasn't religious but when he used the very same words the captain had, my fear grew. And within an hour, the bantering, laughing passengers who had been throwing ice at each other were now silent and women were crying.

The deck was already tilting downward toward that freezing, black water. The din of noise was now deafening, the confusion massive. Sirens wailed, steam blasted from the pipes at ear-splitting levels.

Rescue rockets exploded against the black sky, spattered with thousands of brilliant stars. But even through the noise, we all heard the ship's band playing ragtime tunes.

On the boat deck, lifeboats were uncovered and prepared for loading. We knew for sure the ship would sink when the captain shouted through a megaphone: "Children and women first! Please, get in! There's not a second to lose! Only experienced boatmen will be allowed in with the others."

Daddy and I labored to help the frantic crewmen push the first of the craft into the davits and then out above the water. At first, no one would go near the flimsy looking boats. Why leave the warmth of the lounge and solid floor of the ship to risk falling three miles down to the ocean's floor?

Finally, the first boat splashed into the water, only half filled. A second one eventually hit the surface. This one contained only 12 passengers in a boat built for 40.

Suddenly, from the stairwell surged a swarm of hundreds of seamen, crewmen and third class passengers laden down with boxes and suitcases.

The chaos grew even worse and during this din, my father and I became separated. For frantic seconds I sought him and then hurried back to our suite. Perhaps he had returned to retrieve our valuables.

Seawater already lapped several feet deep in the corridor. That frightening water I had looked down on a hundred times, had wondered about, was now actually around my boots.

And below were miles more of the freezing water, filled with sharks, squids and other nightmare creatures of the deep.

Our suite was empty but here the sea, too, was nearly up to our bed, with water pouring through our window. No time to waste, I thought frantically. Get out, get out!

But something held me there for one long moment. I looked around, not wanting to forget anything about this place where my stepfather and I had discovered our love for each other.

Our bed was still mussed where our bodies had just lain...clothes still strewn around the floor...the night wind blowing the curtains...on the dresser gleamed his gold backed brushes and toilet kit, inset with jade...his gold cufflinks and ring with the small ruby...his small bottle of *Burnt Oranges.*

Water was up to my waist now and I thrust the bottle into my coat pocket and raced outside.

The ship had slanted so low that I couldn't stand straight and with the water surging around me, I struggled toward the deck. I bumped into my father who grabbed me and held me tight.

"Good God, I've been looking for your everywhere," he shouted above the din of screaming passengers, steam blasts and the explosion of overhead rockets. "There're only two boats left. You're leaving on one of them!"

"But what about you, Daddy?" I cried. "I'm not leaving this boat without you."

Staring down at me, he smiled and kissed me. "I'll get on the last one. Don't you worry now, son."

He pulled away and stared down at me. This time, his dark eyes were wet with emotion. "God, I'm glad we got to know each other. It'll get even better when we get back to New York together and I'll build us a big, rich new mansion on Fifth Avenue. Come on now, son!"

A huge crowd of men and women were fighting to get into the seats of the two small boats.There were nearly 2,000 people left aboard and we all knew that unless we could get into one of the craft, it would mean certain death once the sea overtook us.

A dozen men had formed a circle around the two boats and the atmosphere was explosive. An officer held a gun in the air and threatened to shoot anyone who tried to force their ways into the boats.

The law was still women and children and two seaworthy men to guide the boat.

This time there was no trouble getting passengers to enter. The deck now dipped into the water and waves were lapping on the very surface where my father and I had strolled just hours before.

He now thrust me forward and told everyone I was an expert oarsman and swimmer and they would need me to help them to safety. People were fighting to get past the human barrier but Daddy pushed me into the boat and immediately it swung out above the water. As we lowered, people lined the decks, shrieking: "Take me, take me, too! Please God, don't leave me here!"

Several men leaped from the deck into the wintry water and flailed desperately toward us. We managed to pick up two but the others went down instantly and one of those rescued had fainted from the cold.

As we rowed away, I saw my father standing there at the railing, watching me quietly, a handsome, glowering giant who I had just come to know.

Lighting up a cigar, he pulled the collar of his overcoat up to his chin, smiled and gave me a wave of his hand before turning and vanishing into the milling crowd of doomed souls.

#

A strange silence settled over this incredible scene. Sirens and rockets had stopped now. Through this eerie calm, the band could be heard clearing playing its dance tunes.

Then, we heard a pause and over the roiling water and chunks of ice, beneath a sky spattered with stars, the mournful strains of "Nearer My God to Thee" drifted out to us.

All of us had been too shocked and too busy handling the boats to stop and let emotion take over. Now, as we watched the people lining the rails of the sinking ship, staring at us, many of us joined them in the hymn.

"Nearer my God to thee,

"Nearer to thee…"

This couldn't be happening, I thought as I tried to mouth the words of the song. Two hours before, my father and I were preparing for bed, in the luxury of the great white ship.

Now, the water had inched steadily up the main deck. We jumped as an explosion from within the ship shook it. Even from where we bobbed in the darkness, we heard people screaming and shouting and watched them scramble for their lives on the deck, which was rising up into the air.

We watched the doomed as they fled the water which greedily devoured them.

"Daddy!" I screamed. "Daddy, jump, jump now, damn it! I'll save you!" The women in my boat covered their faces and wept as I continued shouting out my father's name, praying for some miracle to bring him to me.

But I knew there was no hope when the Titanic suddenly tilted straight up into the air, with people sliding down its decks into the freezing water and then it moved straight down to the ocean's bottom, more than three miles below.

#

In the winter of 2001, I forced myself to watch a two-hour special about the Titanic on television.

Unable to turn away, I viewed an expedition showing millions of us some of the relics recovered from the grave of that ship in which 1,503 women, children and men had perished.

Just two years after the disaster, I was dining in a restaurant in London with a friend when my skin prickled and I looked around fearfully, suddenly remembering that nightmarish night. And then I realized the orchestra was playing "The Tales of Hoffman". This was the very same music the doomed band aboard the Titanic had played that last night at supper.

Now, the horror returned as I watched on TV how the camera revealed a swaying chandelier, which I remembered, had hung in the restaurant. It was now coated with decades of algae and rust...a metal cooking bowl...some bottles of champagne...the actual deck where I had once trod with my father...

I had no interest in seeing the movie, *Titanic*, which took the world by storm in 1998.

Unlike some of the survivors, I never wanted to talk about my experiences aboard the jinxed vessel. The memories were too bitter. For close friends, though, and they're all nearly dead now, I will show them the actual tweed suit and coat I wore that last night and the life jacket I saved.

I visit the Metropolitan Museum of Art here in New York sometimes in winter and stand before the statue of my father as *Power*.

It still draws admiring crowds. Few would believe the statue is no exaggeration of the magnificent man who posed for it nearly a century ago. Through the magic of metal, he is frozen forever with his heroic figure thrusting forward, his muscled arms holding up a flag, whipped by a long ago wind.

And sometimes I take out the crystal vial from my leather bound case of valuables.

Its contents have long since evaporated. There is still enough ghostly whisper of scent left to conjure up *Burnt Oranges*, though, to evoke vividly the man who once wore it—as if it were the most beautiful thing in the world.

DEMON LOVER

◆

Every few years, usually on the most God-awful night in winter, some-body knocks at my door.

And no matter how many times I may have moved during that time, I find my demon lover standing there.

"Hey!" he says quietly. His square face is inscrutable, yet his strange brown eyes gleam with triumph. Against all odds, he's found me again. "So what's happening, Blondie?"

"Cochise!" I squeal and my emotions intertwine with both joy and fear. Throwing my arms around his strong neck, I give him a big kiss. "Where in hell have you been?"

"Looking for you," he always drawls lazily, as if he's just casually turned off the highway and cruised through town to find me in my usual remote abode. That's all he will say for a moment as he tears off his ice-covered cowboy hat, the denim jacket and red wool scarf. He puts his guitar case carefully against the wall.

This is his talisman for one day soon he's going to be on the Country Western Top 10…another Billy Ray Cyrus. And Garth Brooks? Watch out, Garth! A new kid's heading your way, even though he is getting up there in years.

And then he grabs me to him, wrapping those big arms around me like he is never letting me out of his sight again. He smells of cold highways and the wind, of bourbon and chocolate candy, of cigarettes and Old Spice aftershave. And that intoxicating aroma of himself.

Cochise…my dream lover and my tormentor, my earthly god and my demon, a man who would never fit in anywhere and who seems to roam the earth trying to find some elusive gift and failing to, always returns to me no matter where I've moved over the years.

While kissing me, he moans deep down like a male Dixie redneck that's finally returned to his roots after seeing what the outside world has to offer and wanting none of it.

"Ya miss me, huh? Huh? Ya miss me, huh? Huh?" he babbles.

Standing over six feet tall, he picks me up easily, seeming to know by magic where my bedroom is. Tearing off our clothes, we then proceed to the next stage of our ritual, one begun nearly 30 years before.

He rams his Georgia hammer of flesh up into me.

There, he's got me pinioned now so there can't be a chance in hell of my going anywhere for a while. Thus anchored, he drives it in deeper, making me cry out and hold on to him because he knows I've let few go where he's now traveling.

Because no one can do it like Cochise.

He cums quickly but enjoys letting all that good ole Southern stuff soak inside me. In the meantime, he takes my face between his hands and studies it like an explorer checking to see if any signposts have changed. Slowly, he pulls out, lies on his back and pushes my face down on top of his swollen wonder.

He likes to watch me use both hands to grasp this sticky, dark wand and cover it with my mouth. And one thing I find unique about him is that Cochise likes it rough.

You can pull it, stretch it, bite it and it tickles him. To him, this is proof that he is 100 percent man and he has used his fleshy staff to decide important turning points in his life.

Once, when we were driving across country in his van and became lost, he slapped his love muscle across the map and said: "My cock says we go that way!"

We did and got even more lost, which says something about the journey of his life.

And after several hours of grunting and mumbling and writhing on my usually neat bed, we talk quietly, my face resting on his right pectoral where I can suck on his nipple. The ashtrays fill up with cigarette butts, the bottles of liquor are emptied, and this is the pattern that takes hold over the next few days.

We rarely leave the bedroom except to eat and shower and use the bathroom and order in tons of groceries and even more junk food.

And with the curtains pulled tight, we've sealed off reality, creating a time warp where nothing has changed since the first time we met in 1962. Ribbons of smoke from my cherry incense rise up out of the mouth of a copper dragon on the bamboo nightstand, next to the Tiffany lamp with the gold light. Amber rays illuminate a few pictures of men I've loved...Eric of the stunning body...Carson, my adorable cock of the walk....Bobby Rob, that gorgeous bastard of the county...Jimmy Jack Johnson, leader of the pack of swamp cuties...with the one of Cochise standing out because of that irresistible grin of impish little boy planning more of his deviltry.

He stares from the frame with those brandy hued eyes seeming to watch every move I make. Cochise always turns the picture down so that his younger self won't be watching us. Why, I wonder? For he is now 42. I'm 38. Age seems to have ignored Cochise while punishing others.

In a bizarre way, it is like Cochise and I have been married for three decades and if it true, it is a pairing born in heaven and hell.

Whenever he arrives, he destroys the serenity of my reclusive life. He hates to see me "settled down." He begins to needle me, and then he grows more intense, meaner when I refuse to give up all I've got and join him on his wanderings on the highways of America.

And so he leaves me after a week, both of us shouting at each other. I'm the "fucked up fag...queer...sissy...no talent writer." He's the "fucked up basket cases...two-bit bum...parasite...moocher..." And then I fall onto my bed, relieved he has gone once again.

But when I smell his fragrance on the sheets, see the ash tray full of his smashed cigarettes, the liquor glass where his lips had touched, a cheap comb, with a strand of his black hair, then I....

#

Cochise is truly a devastating mixture of devil and angel—that extraordinary species of redneck stud and tender lover found nowhere on earth but in the South. And that's where he found me.

My life as a student at East Carolina University in Greenville, N.C., had become a nightmare.

This was during the early 60s when gay people were still locked up tightly away in their millions of closets.

But not me. I had this passion, even then, of being myself, come hell or high water, but so far it had brought me mostly hell. Just within a few months after arriving there in January, 1962, I realized it was a major mistake. The campus was a hotbed of homophobes in V-neck sweaters and polished loafers and short haircuts, parted neatly on the side.

Dear ole ECU, as it was called, was ruled by fraternity fuckups and sorority bitches. For them, to see a swish, very open homosexual was simply astounding. If they even suspected someone was a queer, then they made damned sure the offending creature stayed out of sight.

But when they realized that they had no chance of having my life dictated by them, they went out for blood. They taunted me, harassed me at every chance, to hasten my flight from campus. Many of my tormentors were closet queers. When I asked one why he was doing this, he shrugged and sniffed: "Because if I acted friendly to you, they'd think I was a fag, too. So if I give you hell, that protects my ass."

"You lousy two-bit cocksucker," I snarled. "I hope you end of frying in hell." And that's still my attitude toward the closet queers who beat up on other gays either verbally or by inference by day, but turn themselves into flaming sluts at night.

Yes, this type of logic enraged, even more than the more obvious brainless meatheads whose life would be empty unless they had someone to pick on. Since it was the height of the Civil Rights Movement, they couldn't very well pick on a black as their scapegoat or risk exposing to the world what scum they were.

But an out-and-out queer? In me, they found the perfect target.

The worst of the bashers was a pimply-faced pig named Gene Schmidt. He seemed to have changed his major from education to Let's Get The Queer. He would gather his fellow bigots together and plot ways to show their peers just how much they hated the freak.

On one scalding afternoon in 1962, I was walking by a construction site on my way to class. Several times before, I had noticed that these workers included a few very hunky looking studs. And when I swished by, they would pause in their work to stare at me.

Strangely, I sensed hostility from them. And they didn't scream out, "Looka the cocksucker!" or "Hey, ain't she pretty today?" as my other admirers did.

Suddenly, a group of my enemies stepped out from behind a large bush where they had been waiting. My main enemy, the pizza faced Gene, pranced around me, mincing his hair, batting his eyes, flipping his wrist.

"Oh, my boys, isn't she positively divine today? Say, cocksucker, we could all use a blowjob today. What'd ya say?"

They were all bigger than me but that hardly prevented my fury from boiling over. "You mean you've got a cock, Mr. Pizza Face? From what I hear, fatso, you've been giving the clap to all the campus whores."

"You fuckin' fag!" he screamed. This creep and the others had hidden their baseball bats behind them but now brought them out as Gene swung at me.

I dodged and rammed my shoulder into his jiggling stomach and with a cry, he stumbled back among his admirers.

None of them had expected the sissy to strike back and now they lunged for me with their weapons. I barely had time to throw dirt in their eyes before they surrounded me.Suddenly, I saw them all crying out and cursing as four, big figures waded in, punching them with their fists and using wooden boards as clubs. I watched the bashers run like the cowards they were, led by Gene, and then I looked up to see my heroes.

They were the construction workers I had seen several times before, led by the biggest of them who now helped me to my feet. The others brushed the dirt off me and gathered my books for me.

The big worker wore only a red sweatband around black hair, work boots and dirty jeans so wet form his sweat that they molded themselves to his muscular form like leotards.

From his heroic shoulders, chest and arms, sweat gleamed and his fists were still balled into fists.

"You okay, honey?" he asked with no hint of sarcasm. His dark eyes were large and child-like and he gave me a sweet smile. "My name's Cochise. If those shit-holes come bothering you again, you let me know and we'll take care of 'em."

"Yeah," the others muttered, staring at me, "you let Cochise or us know and we'll show them what a real fight's all about."

Their hands were big and rough as they shook mine but they felt wonderful. I thanked them again and hurried on toward campus but I glanced back once to give them a final wave. They still stood there, staring at me and they grinned and gave me a wave, too.

Through the day, I thought about Cochise. Why was he being so nice to me? I was to discover through the years, though, that manual workers and jocks were always friendly to me. Peer opinion meant little to them. This is more than I can say for the hypocritical Christians and Catholics I've had the misfortune of knowing.

I was walking along Main Street that afternoon when someone brushed up against my arm.Startled, I looked up into the beaming face of Cochise. With the bland looking shoppers and students passing by, he really did look like a comic book hero. He was still nearly nude except for his jeans and work boots. The red sunset gleamed off his sweating flesh and I watched a drop of perspiration roll off his right nipple, then dribble over the flat stomach and beneath the low-hung jeans.

Even more striking was how he had let his mane of dark hair flow down to his shoulders. Boys still sported short hair and crewcuts. Hippies had yet to become mainstream. Yet, he showed no nervousness at all in having lots of beautiful hair and showing it.

"Hi," he grinned. "I thought I recognized you from across the street. Me and the guys were having some beers. Come on. I'll drive you *home*."

He drove like a maniac. His van was a rat's nest, jammed with empty beer cans, potato chip bags and candy wrappers and the butts of hundreds of cigarettes.

He got us cans of cold beer form his cooler and lit up a Salem. On the radio, "Good Golly, Miss Molly!" blared out and Cochise screamed and howled along while banging the dashboard with his hand.

Then he swerved off the main road onto a crude trail that led out into a wooded area. A thunderstorm had come up and rain lashed the windows.

"Gotta take a piss," he explained. Out into the rain he jumped, shucking off his boots and jeans and tossing them into the back of the van.

Like someone totally out of the conventional populace I had been exposed to, he was alien. With his head thrown back and his mouth open to catch the rainwater, he held out an impressive length of muscle to relieve himself.

Then with a howl and a grin, he jumped into the back of the van and gestured me to join him. He had spread his wet clothes on top the dozens of cans and pulled me on top of him.

He talked softly, like a child, which proved an exhilarating contrast to that macho physique of his.

"Ever since I saw you walking by us out there on the site, you've been giving us all hadrons and we bet who'd fuck you first. Is your sister Marilyn Monroe? You sure to hell look like her."

He was a wild, bucking stud who guided my hands all over his muscles while kissing me so good I felt dizzy. His nipples tasted as luscious as they looked and flipping his hair away from his face, he took his hands to guide my lips on down his sensuous torso....past the stomach with the suggestion of a beer gut, to the white hips and then to the dark phallus which already pulsed against his abdomen.

It tasted like rain and sex and muscle and he smelt even better, like woods and musk and that intangible quality of pure male. Sitting up now, he stared with great interest as I covered the tip of his erection with my mouth.

There was still plenty of stalk for me to wrap my fists around, and they pressed against the groin, which outlined testicles so round they were shaped like big figs.

I heard him make short sighs of pleasure as I enjoyed him. My chin rested on his sac and on either side of my face was those masculine thighs. I'd never felt so secure as I had at that moment for I knew that my partner would kill anyone who dared interrupt our coupling.

Without any warning, I felt his organ begin to pulse and my mouth overflowed with an abundance of his elixir. When I glanced up, his head was thrust back as it had beneath the rain and his mouth was opened again.

He pushed me back suddenly and covered my body with his.

"You ain't lived until you've been fucked by Cochise," he panted and with no tenderness, pushed himself up so fast I was amazed. The boys I had balled with on campus were so virginal and innocent that I was their first partner. All they knew about sex was jerking off. The majority had never even got it on with a girl before.

And here was this master who acted like he had being going at it from child hood and I learned later, he had.

He covered my face with kisses, urging me to feel how tight his buns were, how long his shaft was and he pulled out slightly to let me feel of it.

With the rain and wind now battering the van, and with this ravishing savage above me, his dark hair flowing over his temples, I thought: remember this because there will be times in the future when you'll want like hell to have it again.

He pulled out to let me see him ejaculate and let me suck him off once more. Instead of being furtive or mean or repulsed by what he was doing, as my other partners had been, he treated sex so naturally and so much fun that I protested when he said it was time for us to go.

I had buried my face between the cheeks of his high, smooth butt and he smiled and murmured: "Okay, you lick my butt-hole and then blow me and then we get back to town."

His reddish, tawny skin looked even more succulent wet that drove me to new heights of rimming and sucking a man's dick. On the way back to town, he lit up a cigarette and glanced at me, laughing.

"Wow, you are one fucking little sex machine! You're my kind of slut."

I pretended to pant and drool. "And wow-wee, so are you, man! You've got a bod and a cock and an ass that I wouldn't enjoying a few dozen times a day."

He threw his head back and whooped like an Indian and then held out his big hand that I shook. It felt so warm and sexy it made me think of how I felt when I buried my face between his butt cheeks.

This set the tone for the future.

Twice each week, he'd pick me up in his van and we'd go out to our trysting place and go crazy. I did persuade him to at least find a mattress for us to lay on. Those empty beer cans were murder on the back.

Cochise seemed fascinated by what all his cock could do. He made me think of a little boy with a fascinating toy. He liked me stretching out his abnormally loose foreskin and forms it into a small bowl.

Then he would fill it full of baby oil and tie it up with a leather thong and fuck me like that.

We did more than become sex crazies. I loved it when he'd hold me in his arms, a cigarette dangling from his moth, and he'd tell me about his life.

As the son of a 100 percent Cherokee Indian, he was thrown into a foster home when he was small. By the age of nine, the staff was fighting over his sexual favors. He was already proving to be a hung little mule.

"I guess I knew even then I'd always be a big-dicked Indian stud!" he drawled and cackling crazily, he'd hug and kiss me.

He loved me. There could be no doubt. He told me this all the time now.

Yet, I wondered what he did in his time away from me. When I asked him, he shocked me by admitting with no qualms the fact that he had a wife and two kids living with him in a trailer. He laughed himself sick at my reaction and showed absolutely no shame at all.

One night he forced me to meet his brood. I found his wife, Mona, to be a beautiful Georgia girl who had been a schoolteacher before meeting the love of her life. She was beautiful and wise, with a striking mane of red hair and delicate skin.

The kids, Cochise, Jr., and Daisy, were adorable and bright.

While we watched the high-spirited father do tricks with his children in the backyard, I looked at Mona who was smoking and sipping a beer with a sad expression.

"You're so lucky to have a husband like Cochise."

She glanced at me and smiled. "Everybody who balls with him and comes with him to visit me tells me that."

Cochise insisted we attend a gay bar one night. He didn't hide his outrageous pride in his body and privates. He ran ads in gay and straight magazines and boasted that he had met hundreds of partners like that.

There was only one queer bar in Greenville at that time, which I thought was the pits because it was usually filled with arrogant frat types or snooty closet queens. None of them dared let on that they were there to find sex. The manager threw you out if you even suggested you were cruising. All your flirting had to be done by long, dramatic facial expressions…raising your brow…licking the opening of your beer bottle.

I went there once and was given the definite cold shoulder. I was simply too obvious for their tastes.

But the night Cochise and I entered the bar, no one there would ever forget it, even though it happened in 1962.

My wild savage wore a black headband, his hair newly washed and swinging around those big shoulders. Handmade sandals, painted on jeans with a hole in the rear to disclose he wore no underwear and a sleeveless white jersey comprised his rape outfit.

I wore light make-up with blue shorts and shirt to bring out the azure color of my eyes and the gleam of my curls. Everyone there craned their necks to watch us in amazement. It was that notorious campus fag but who was this magnificent Adonis?

The jukebox began screaming, "Good Golly, Miss Molly" and with an Indian war whoop that would have made Geronimo proud, Cochise threw me out on the small floor where no one had ever dared dance before.

Before the manager knew what was happening, my partner and I twisted our hips, squealed and rubbed up hard against each other. The bartender looked wide-eyed and aghast. The clientele there always acted like polite zombies.

And then Cochise proved that night that the future Chippendale's missed a super star on that little dance floor.

While I twisted and humped, Cochise stripped off his tee shirt, swung it around his head and then kicked off his sandals. Everyone had frozen on their stools as my lover-boy expertly peeled off his jeans, to show that he most definitely did not wear undies.

Whistling and growling, he grabbed his heroic organ and whirled it around like he had a rubber dildo. The bar manager staggered out to scream for us to leave. Cochise planted a big, wet kiss on that fat face and then we danced out into the night.

They still talk about that night.

A few weeks later, I felt like killing myself.

Cochise had stopped coming around and I was packing up my things to spend the summer with my bitch of a mother. There were no summer jobs available. I'd heard, though, that word had gotten around to anyone hiring summer help that I was completely unsuitable. Why, I'd give my employers a terrible reputation and hurt business. I was a flagrant queer who the cops watched because I went around campus soliciting tricks.

Cochise burst into my room without any explanation. He saw my packed suitcases and putting them beneath his arm, he used his other hand to drag me out to his van.

"Come on, honey. You're going with me."

He was leaving his wife and kids and was going to roar across America. He hated everything about marriage and wanted freedom. I was his mate now. He'd find us a good place to live and I'd stay home and take care of him while he worked.

But it was a disaster. Living out of a van, week after week, can be the pits. With our money gone, we lived on apples, peanut butter sandwiches, canned beans. But at first, it was pure joy.

Cochise sat behind the wheel of his even more grungy van, completely bare assed. Now and then, we'd pull over to the side of the road where I'd do him and bury my face in that moist, dark cleft.

He would take out his guitar and strum and sing old legends: "Copper Kettle," "Strange Young Man," and even a teary-eyed "Puff, the Magic Dragon."

Sometimes we'd pick up a hunky looking hitcher whose eyes would widen when they got a look at the naked stud behind the wheel. More than likely, all three of us would wind up in the back, with Cochise humping both of us and then each of us taking turns sucking out his always abundant supply of sex cream.

And then when he drove, I loved rubbing his hardness and balls over the bottom of the steering wheel, bearing down so hard that he'd finally ejaculate. The dashboard became incrusted with his outpourings.

Better still was getting down between his thighs while he was steering the wheel and eat him. Sweat trickled down onto my face from the thighs on either side of me. More than one passing truck driver would nearly go off the road when they glanced down to see this Indian warrior getting done.

Wearing his dark glasses, Cochise would glance up at them and just hoot and wave and swig from a never-ending supply of Black Label beer.

After a month though, we were down to our last dollar bills. He proved adept at draining gas from other parked cars into our van. Another skill he unveiled was swiping candy bars and cigarettes and baloney from high way stops. I discovered there were many things about my partner that I would never know and didn't want to.

He told me only what he thought I wanted to hear. Once he hinted that he may have well served some time in the pen. Naturally, I wanted to hear more and he joked that quite possibly he had murdered another man while serving in the military.

With Cochise, I could never tell when he joked or fantasized or spoke the truth.

We then began arguing—him calling me a lazy assed fag because I wouldn't hustle the truck drivers at the rest areas and earn us some needed money. Strangely, he would ball with countless guys, but he wouldn't charge them. "I'm not like that," he'd explain mysteriously.

It gave him a kick for me to watch him getting done. Instead of watching the head between his thighs, his eyes would be fixed on me, studying my reaction, an unpleasant smile on his sweaty face.

We'd stop and pick fruit in Alabama and then Cochise dropped all pretexts of using drugs. I'd suspected as much when he'd babble for hours, his eyes glazed and I'd drift asleep.

He was a speed freak.

Now, he blew in any money we had left on booze and drugs. More importantly, our personalities clashed. Cochise could live in a pigpen and be happy. All he worried about was his own body that he'd keep in top condition. I was neat and orderly and hated a mess. Our van was a moving trash dump.

It got to the point toward the end that one morning he announced I couldn't touch him unless I wrote my old bitch of a mother and asked for money. I told him that was one thing I wouldn't even do for Jesus H. Christ.

"No money," he sneered, "no cock."

"That's all you've got as your claim to fame, stud," I sneered for by now, I was sick of our whole "trip across America" jag and my illusions about Cochise had vanished when our last money had gone for his dosage of speed and beer.

"That'll cost you, Miss Fury," he sneered. He then reneged on his stance of not taking money from truckers who did him. He parked our van in a rest area and then using his blazing charm, rounded up a group of truckers who blew him at $5 a shot.

I fell asleep, only to be awakened by the squeals of a fat blob being screwed by Cochise. And after they finished and were drinking some beer, I heard the blob ask Cochise about me:

"Jason? Oh, he's just some Nellie little fag I brought along to give me blow jobs."

I jumped out of the van and hitched back home to my hated old bitch of a mother, with my ex-boyfriend's taunt ringing in my memory: "Ha! Well, there goes another one of my cocksuckers."

Still, like most Southern studs, Cochise had incredible charm and fascination. I hated him passionately for a long time but all I had to do to become aroused was to think of him. For he really was a demon lover, one who made every other man a wimp.

Three years later, I had just started my first newspaper job in Wilmington. For some reason, everyone liked me immediately and my flamboyant personality fit in well except for my city editor, who was a handsome but brutal bastard.

He tried every way he could imagine to make me quit and go elsewhere since he had a well-known repulsion for "queers." After one major skirmish with him, I had locked myself up at my beach apartment, trying to cool down.

I had almost no money saved, jobs for people like me were harder to find than the real Santa Claus. I had brought a bottle of champagne, one of my favorite cures for worry when I heard a knock on my door.

It was winter, I lived alone at my tip of the beach and was hoping it would be Eddie, the cute photographer who had been promising to come around one night "for a drink."

It was Cochise. His old van was parked behind him. He wore the same denim outfit I had seen on him three years before. All those brutal, slicing things I was going to say to him vanished.

He looked gorgeous but scruffy, his denim jacket and jeans frayed, a new lost expression of weariness, of disillusionment in his eyes that looked older. His guitar case hung over his shoulder.

I called in sick the rest of the week and my demon lover made me forget my troubles.

He told me of settling down briefly in Mississippi where he had married a girl called Pattie and they had had two kids. But marriage bored him and he didn't like being tied down and…

It was a week of fantastic love and he had even grown better in bed. On the sixth day, I knew trouble had entered our paradise because he was taking so much speed he hadn't slept a wink since first arriving. He also told me he was getting restless and he had to go and I was going with him.

I told him I loved him but I wasn't crazy. I couldn't just skip out of my first job. He was furious and tied me up with sheets and was carrying me out to his van when the beach's one police car cruised along just at that moment.

Cochise was jailed overnight and I was fired from my job since another paper had written a page one feature showing me trussed up like a turkey and my "male friend" who looked like a wild-eyed fugitive.

Cochise found me again, two years later. This time I lived in Fargo, North Dakota, for God's sake, and worked in a miserable job as a reporter for the Associated Press there.

When I opened my door, he stood there, trying not to grin while one the city's usual blizzards raged behind him. Snow coated his cowboy hat and denim jacket, but his eyes danced with glee and he tired not to burst out laughing.

"What's happening, Blondie?"

This time I was determined he wasn't going to get so easily and I made a few meows of protest but he just grinned, shrugged and gave me a kiss that made me nearly faint.

The few friends I had made among the young cowboy types were astonished to see this magnificent looking creature camped out in my tiny studio. He dwarfed everything around him.

But he charmed everyone and began bringing home men and women he met at some of the numerous bars around the city. He went back to doing speed, began pestering me for money and when I wouldn't give it to him, he turned tricks at the bus and train station, bringing them all back to my place.

I told him to get out and when he insisted I leave with him, I refused, he slapped me hard and stole my color TV.

The next time I saw Cochise three years, I worked in Montgomery, Alabama as a newspaper reporter. When I opened the door to my high-rise cocoon on 7 Clayton Street, he had his arms crossed, his cowboy hat tilted low over his brow and wore no shirt.

He was more bronzed than ever and his pecs billowed out like the dimples of his butt.

"Hey, what's happening , Blondie?" he grinned.

"Cochise, you damned—I can't believe—oh, Good God!"

He had since married a girl named June in Pensacola, Florida and they'd had two little kids. But he was bored with the marriage game and had become restless so…

It was wonderful. He found a job doing construction, had stopped taking speed and seemed to have become more serious. His body had slimmed down so that he was big, very well built but much more sensuous.

Naturally, he lived to ball and we began doing it so much I called in sick and was out for two weeks "with the flu…"

Our only argument this time was with the people he was bringing home. When I returned home from work, I found signs of his lust here and there…a lipstick stain on my towel, the smell of perfume…wads of toilet paper stiff with semen beside my bed.

A month later, he left a note on my kitchen table. His handwriting was like that of a child and I could picture him, sitting there, bare assed, his tongue stuck between his teeth as he concentrated on his words.

He had met a beautiful bar maid named Melanie and they were heading to California to "find themselves."

I have no doubt that at this very minute, there is a girl called Melanie with two children whose father has suddenly split again. And like the countless other women, male lovers, she finds it impossible to hate him.

#

It's been snowing here in the mountains of North Carolina for two days now. Asheville is a beautiful old city but a boring one. The mountain men are nice, though. A few remind me of Cochise.

I got a post card from him a year ago. He was working on a construction site in New Orleans. He loved me the best of any person he had ever known.

One day, real soon, we'll be together again. He just knew it. As an Indian, he saw it in the stars.

A car passes by slowly on the lonely road that runs below my remote cabin.

The vehicle vanishes around the bend. I know I'm crazy but a demon lover can do these things to you, yet, I keep hoping that one of these wintry nights, a van will stop, and a big figure in a cowboy hat will lope up to my door and knock.

And when I answer it, I'll hear the most beautiful four words, I've ever heard.

"Hey, what's happening, Blondie?"

THE MAN WHO WAS TOO HANDSOME

◆

My father was "too handsome."

Incredible as it sounds, this was the main reason my mother gave the court for wanting to divorce him after an 18-year marriage marked by continuous turbulence.

She told the judge she could no longer endure all those sex-starved coeds who left nude pictures and "filthy" propositions in his office at the University where he was a professor of philosophy. Some of his most rabid fans had created a website devoted to the phenomenal sensuality of the ravishing Dr. Edwin Fury.

Mother admitted, too, that it was not altogether his fault that he was "so attractive." God had been good to him so she couldn't place the blame entirely on her husband, Dr. Edwin Fury.

It was just that he had this phenomenal sex appeal that charged the atmosphere wherever he went and people responded to it. If she and "The Ivy League Hunk", as one newspaper called him, went out to enjoy a meal, the waitresses fawned all over him.

If they went shopping, the clerks nearly raped him. At parties, women practically forced him into a spare room to sexually attack him. Men, too, were hardly spared form his charisma.

She had no proof that he was a "bi" but she informed the judge that my father was the type who would turn no one down. It was just in his nature. He had something people wanted and he saw no reason why he should keep chaste and untouched except for one person—his wife.

"Does your husband encourage this attention?" the judge asked.

"Not exactly," my mother had stammered. "He just exists, he lets people do what they want to do to him and—I can't stand it anymore!"

What's worse, she added, was how he acted like an animal in the bedroom. No, he wasn't brutal or dirty. It was just that he was a satyr. He could never get enough sex. He wanted it two to three times every night!

The last straw, she concluded in her divorce papers, was when he had posed naked for a photographer in "very provocative poses" (translated: with one hell of a hard-on) and which he distributed to his groupies on campus.

He claimed he had the photographs made for "artistic purposes." But I understand they became the hottest item on the campus of North Carolina State University. They were drooled over and Xeroxed and enlarged until they were being sold underground.

And did this upset my father? He actually autographed the damned things!

I was 18 when all this was going on. I remember well how the local paper in Raleigh ran a witty feature on the professor who was divorced by his wife on the grounds he was "too handsome."

A picture ran alongside the article, showing the object of all this palpitations and turmoil but many wondered: is this the red-hot stud that likes to show off his hard-on in bare butt photos?

Never let a photograph form your opinions about the attractive or sexual quotient of the subject. In the newspaper picture, he was handsome but certainly no Tom Cruise or Jean Claude Van Damme.

Wearing just a pair of tennis shorts and shoes, he was slender but very well proportioned, with sharply defined pectorals and a flat tummy and strong looking thighs.

But it was his face, which gave some hint of his killer charm. A lock of dark hair fell over his brows and his smile was shy and sweet. His eyes, though, told much more about this satyr: behind tortoise glasses, his blue eyes danced with impish glee, as if saying: I may look like an innocent little tyke but just wait'll until we get in bed!

For weeks after that article, our phone rang with calls from women and men, all wanting to become my father's keeper. The postman staggered under mailbags with letters and Polaroid's from people of all sexes who graphically described how they could relieve Dr. Fury's problem of being relentlessly horny.

Nearly all of them said they would give up anything to live with a man "who was too handsome."

Daddy loved all this attention! Talk show hosts begged him to appear on their shows. The *National Enquirer* and every other tabloid tried to arrange interviews—and revealing photographs.

But the university made it clear that once he did any of that, his teaching days were over. And my father really did enjoy teaching—and all the chances of meeting an endless line of curvaceous cuties each semester.

Although mother had painted him as a raving sex maniac, he was actually very shy. I will admit, though, that he had scads of girlfriends just waiting to give him sexual relief.

And mother was right when she accused him of being oversexed to an alarming degree: he seems born with an erection.

In a crowd, he would be considered just another handsome man. But close-up was when one actually became acutely aware of his blazing charm, warmth and intense sexual heat.

A key factor in trying to understanding the image he presented was that helpless air of being vulnerable. Every woman who met him wanted to take care of my father. They wanted to press his wrinkled shirts, sew a button on his jacket, tie the lace of his untied shoes and unzip his pants. Although physically strong and macho, his pink lips were usually half open and the slightly puzzled expression in his eyes suggested someone who needed help. Added to that was his ability to blush. Oh, how beautiful he was when something would tickle or surprise him and his square, macho face became suffused with a glorious pink.

I was 18 when Mama left us. Naturally, I assumed care of my father. People had always done so, from his Southern mother and five sisters who spoiled him rotten to countless girlfriends. He was a wonderful protector and provider but when it came to realities, he was completely lost. Ask him to boil an egg and he would nearly set the kitchen on fire.

Seeing him bare-assed was no surprise to me but as I got older and realized I sexually desired men, I knew that he would forever be the only man in my life. Around the house, he lived in a skimpy little bikini. His bulge shook like a bowl of jello. When little, I liked climbing into his lap and he would read the cartoons to me.

He didn't object at all when I'd play with his nipples, trace the ridges in his stomach or rub the nice bulge in his briefs. I would wonder then why my rubbing that mound would cause it to grow bigger and harder. Or why he would place a hand over it when it began swelling up. Only later did I realize how easily he was aroused.

After taking his nightly shower, he liked to stretch out on his bed naked and lay on his stomach. He directed me on how to massage lotion into his skin—from his neck on down to his feet.

I was fascinated by how his "wee wee" would jut between his thighs and then it swelled up and become bigger. One night when he dozed, I began playing with it and it grew even larger.

Playfully, I rolled down the foreskin from the tip of his erection and out slid the head that was big and pink and glossy. The tip sparkled with thick moisture.

And then to my amazement, out spurted streams of thick whiteness. What had I done? The wetness had formed a puddle between his thighs and at that moment, he turned over and saw my fright.

"Daddy, I didn't mean to hurt you?" I wailed. He had been asleep and blinked his eyes in confusion. Then realizing what had caused my alarm, he took me into his arms and held me close while explaining the facts of life.

He seemed completely unfazed that his swollen organ protruded against me and the whiteness continued to ooze out.

But after that night, he always stuffed his privates up beneath his stomach so I wouldn't have anything to play with while he snoozed. He saw nothing wrong with my playing with that beautiful rump of his and so while he dozed, I played with his hole and squeezed his dimples to my heart's content.

And then one night, he and I attended an amateur physique competition at the school in which faculty and students competed. He didn't win but after we got home, he kept talking about how beautiful and smooth some of the bodies were with their clean-shaven sheen.

And so that night, I began shaving his body—trimming every hair on his body except for his chest. But I was more interested in making smooth his pubic area and the light dusting of hair in the cleft of his butt. He would reach back and spread his buttocks so I could really get down deep and make him all glossy and smooth.

And when I removed the hair around his genitals, he would hold the tip of his foreskin tight so the head would not be exposed. After shaving him, he loved for me to massage creams and oils into his skin, even his privates.

He was quirky about me seeing the cusp of his penis exposed. He mumbled something about how even the touch of air on his head could make him hard.

When it came to his testicles, Daddy squeezed the sac so tight that his balls bulged out like apples. I massaged oil into all these goodies and when I got to his ass-hole, he didn't object when I slid my fingers up there and in doing so, I would watch his manhood puff up to an alarming degree and then he would tell me "that's enough" because it was time we slept.

But I would wait outside his door and listen. Sure enough, I would hear the bedsprings creaking and the sounds of his panting and then a soft "Ohhhhh!"

The next morning when I emptied his trash can, I found wadded up balls of Kleenex, all stiff from his macho outpourings.

#

People in Raleigh always talked about us.

They gabbled even more the night Daddy and I attended a Halloween party given by some of the art professors. These affairs were always raunchy and wild with everyone drinking and doping too much.

But I can safely say that when Daddy and I walked into the large living room of the host, people whooped and whistled and surrounded us.

I had dressed up like Marilyn Monroe in the beaded flapper dress she wore in her film classic, Some Like it Hot. With my light blonde hair, trim, boyish figure and shapely butt, it wasn't hard for me to duplicate to an uncanny degree the very image of my screen goddess.

Mona, one of the art students and a groupie of my father, had fixed me up with the wig, dress and make-up, including a long cigarette holder.

If I was a sensation, Daddy made tongues hang out and the hands come out to fondle and caress him for he was a living invitation for rape.

I had sewn a narrow strip of green silk over the front and back of his jock strap. That was all he wore and the faintest breeze would lift both panels to disclose his luscious basket and his gorgeous bare butt. He and I entered the room arm-in-arm.

Instantly, all the guys knocked each other over to dance with me. His flock of male and female admirers surrounded daddy and so he went out in the middle of the floor to do a frenzied dance with one of the girls, the silk panels did nothing to protect his modesty.

Everyone saw his basket and his backside and soon afterwards, he vanished into one of the bedrooms, coming out for air now and then, as his groupies lined up for servicing. Even I had to laugh when someone pointed out lipstick smears on his butt and thighs and hickies all around his nipples.

When I saw him nude that night after his shower and he had stretched out for his massage, I teased him about the remnants of make-up on his balls and cocks.

Daddy just giggled impishly and winked at me, as if saying: "I had a hell of a good time tonight."

From that moment on, I was determined to have a good time with him, too. But I would have to let him know in the most graphic of terms. It was the only way to communicate with this lovable, dreamy eyed sex machine.

#

It was two weeks later that I took my stand with him to reveal what was going through my mind.

Although 18, I looked much younger and could have passed for either a beautiful young girl or a ravishing young man. I didn't 't wear make-up but some people thought I did because my eyes were so blue and the lashes so long.

My mouth was naturally pink and gleaming and even Daddy studied my lips when I talked and he would run a tongue over his own. He treated me exactly as if I were his daughter, instead of his son.

He was overly protective, kissed me many times a day on my cheek and held my hand when we walked out in our garden in the back.

So when he would sigh on occasions that he hoped I would marry a nice woman and raise a family so he could become a grandfather, I would die laughing and say: "No way."

It was a November morning when I unloaded what was on my mind.

As usual, Daddy sat at the table, nibbling breakfast while giggling over the comic strips.

He looked like a boy with his unpressed shirt, a button missing at the collar, his tie badly knotted and his hair mussed. I was on holiday break from the private school I attended and after refilling his cup with coffee, I went up to him and pushed his newspaper away and sat in his lap.

"Hey, I'm trying to read, honey," he groused. "Don't bother me."

He tried grabbing the comic section again but I had put my arms around his neck and made him look at me.

"Daddy, there's something I want to tell you."

The comics had fallen to the floor and he put on his glasses to read them from where he sat. He giggled.

"Daddy, are you listening to me?" His eyes were racing along the "Little Orphan Annie" panel now and he was lost to everything else. I grabbed his face and forced him to look at me.

He made comical faces and rolled his eyes before kissing me on the cheek.

"What's your problem, Marilyn?" Ever since our big splash at the party, he had called me Marilyn and I called him Tarzan. "It'd better be important or I'm whipping that little butt of yours."

"Daddy, I want you to know I—I'm attracted to men."

The smile froze on his face. "You're—what?"

"I want to have sex with men, Daddy. I like to dress up like a woman and have men flirt with me and I want to ball with them."

He rolled his eyes and leaned forward to bury his face on his arm. He began to slap the table and to shake his head.

"Ha, ha, my son is queer. Oh, God, that's all I need. I'm killing myself paying alimony to your Mom, Debbie Stockham is threatening to kill me if I don't marry her, five different girls have told me I'm the father of their babies. And now my son says he's into men."

I knew my father well. Whenever he was confronted by something big and unexpected, he liked to put on a big show. Like the time Mama found those nude pictures of him. Sure enough, he leaned back in his chair and took my hand and kissed it.

A sour grin played around those pink lips that had kissed countless women besides my mother. Soon, I vowed, they'll kiss me in a most unfatherly manner.

"Eh, well, have you been diddling with the boys?"

"No, I've been saving myself for just one man, Daddy."

"Oh," he asked sadly, "and who is this man?"

"It's you, Daddy. You and nobody else. I want an older man as my lover and you'd be perfect."

He jumped form the chair, nearly dumping me on the floor and began to pace back and forth. "I—I don't believe I'm hearing this!" he cried dramatically. "You have to be joking!"

"You always bragged how you fucked your first girl when you were 12 so what's the big difference? I'm still a virgin!"

"That's different! I was a red-hot stud and not a goddamned— deviant!"

I threw a box of Wheaties at him and he slung the morning papers at me and we hollered and yelled and then ended up laughing. Trying to look serious, he suddenly unzipped his pants and pulled out his stunning genitalia, shaking them.

"Look, son, I got this cock, you got yours, and they were made for women. Listen, I know this girl student, she'd be perfect for you to experiment with and—"

I threw my arms around his neck. "I don't want a female, you idiot! I want you and nobody else!"

"Stop it! Not one more word about this! Do you understand me? This is the darkest day of my life!"

He pushed me away and continued pacing, running his hand through his curls that made him look even cuter. He knew this, too, for he paused before a mirror to see how he looked.

The tangled "do" appealed to him for he smiled slightly to see how his teeth looked but then, remembering it was the darkest day of his life, he fell back into his chair and now attempted an air of some great tragedian.

But he wasn't very successful, and in fact a glimmer of interest sparkled in his wide opened, innocent eyes.

He announced he had a solution for my problem. He would line me up with one of his male grad students. I could get it out of my system because it was only a passing thing.

"Everybody goes through this phase," he lectured, 'when they think they want their own sex but you get over it. Yes, I think I've got just the boy for you."

I was thrilled. Of course, I wanted Daddy but if not him, then…

#

Mike arrived at the appointed time the following night.

Both Daddy and I agreed on Mike as the "stud" who would be my first and—Daddy hoped—last male lover.

You have to understand that my father was very conservative in some ways and although he hardly put down alternative lifestyles and knew a number of sexually adventuresome people, he still hoped I would do the "right thing" by eventually marrying and having some children.

In his eyes, he wouldn't be a successful "father" unless he had grandchildren he could look at and know his name would regenerate into the future.

Fortunately, I adored Mike. Husky, rugged and radiating the warmth of a big teddy bear, he was like an older brother and for the past four years had been called in by Daddy to pick me up from school, to take me shopping, to baby sit with me until my father got home.

He and Daddy double dated, too, and sometimes my parent would drawl to me "Mike is completely over-sexed. He'd fuck a rattlesnake if you held its mouth open."

With his dark eyes snapping, Mike looked from Daddy to me. "Well, baby brother, you ready for our hot date?"

I was amazed at his casual attitude because I was sick with nerves. And poor Daddy looked pale with anxiety. It was his son's first boy-boy date!

"Look Mike," Daddy pleaded again, "like I've discussed with you, this is Jason's first date. Be gentle with him. If he wants to suck, just let him suck. If he wants you to fuck him, don't get carried away and send him to the hospital. Use those Trojans I gave you—"

"You told me those were your last," teased Mike. "You'd better get another supply. Jesus, doc, you used a dozen last week."

"Mike, please shut up!" snapped my father. "Why don't you just let Jason hand jerk you to start off with? Don't try to rape him like you did—"

"Daddy!" I cried out. "Would you please shut the hell up?"

I was shocked by his candor but Mike just laughed.

"Don't worry," he grinned. "Whatever I've got, he can have."

"And you have him back here by 12 midnight sharp!" warned my parent, pushing his glasses back on his nose and checking his watch.

#

Mike proved the perfect stud to break in any willing virgin.

After he parked his car on a deserted road in the country, he stripped off his clothes with no trace of awkwardness and urged me out of mine.

"I'm basically straight, honey," he told me before pulling me against him and kissing me. "But I like your Dad a lot and I'm doing this as a favor to him."

First, he said it was always good for a couple to get "warmed up" and he meant lots of kissing and caressing. He urged me to sit in his lap and kissed up a storm.

I felt him growing erect beneath me and before I knew it, he had slipped the tip of his phallus up into me.

It made me gasp for I was still a virgin. I'd never even jerked off anyone before and here was Big Mike thrusting up into me as casually as if this was a normal part of his daily routine.

He laid me back on the seat and got over me and he lunged his hips up into me, making me cry out even louder. I threw my arms around his back and he buried his mouth on mine.

His kissing didn't electrify me for this wasn't his favorite thing. But Mike certainly knew how to screw. Just when I didn't think he could push in any deeper, he did so and I kept up a steady stream of cries and gasps.

My fingers slid down his broad back to his rump and he paused long enough for me to squeeze his balls and the base of his shaft. Wow, he was swollen.

He pulled out suddenly and plopped his organ onto my lap where it began to pulse and rise and then out spurted his semen. It was impressive and again, Mike merely grunted, like it wasn't a big deal, that this happened all the time, and then he laid back, with his thighs spread and encouraged me to "do" him.

It was exciting to lower my face between his thighs, to have that forbidden part of his body right in my hands and then in my mouth. He kept whispering me to do "rougher" and I kneaded his balls like they were made of rubber, and this seemed to help induce his next orgasm.

It spilled from my mouth onto his pubic hair and he sighed in contentment. He pulled me up again and kissed me and then held me against his chest while he lit up a cigarette.

"So how did you like your first man?" he asked pleasantly.

"I loved it, Mike—but Daddy's the one I really want to ball with"

"Yeah, he told me that," Mike said, "and so would about a hundred other gals and guys. When we double date, he doesn't waste much time in chitchat. He gets out of his clothes as soon as possible, and when I watch him fucking, it even gives me a hard-on. His cock gets so swollen and wet looking and that cute butt of his? Um uh!"

Just remembering my stepfather in action was making him stiff and I stroked it while licking the sticky slit: "Mike, what can I do? I've simply got to make my Daddy my lover!"

While I sucked Mike once more, he suddenly came up with an idea that he promised would work. And before he escorted me to the front door at 11:58 p.m., with my father standing there, waiting, we had devised a seduction plot that even Hollywood would have rejected as too bizarre to believe.

Believe me, this actually happened but nothing worked out like we thought it would.

#

The motel room was in almost total darkness.

Mike led me inside and guided me to the bed where a naked man lay.

"I'll now leave you two alone," whispered my escort and shut the door behind him.

I sat on the edge of the bed. A warm, strong hand pulled mine onto a stiff erection. I squeezed it and without a word, I bent down and worked it into my mouth.

"Oh, Judy! Judy! That feels fantastic!" gasped my father.

Yes, my father!

I was trembling so hard I'm sure he felt it, fearful that he would recognize me, but then I realized: I've finally gotten my father inside my mouth, after years of dreaming about this!

My friend, Mona of the art department, had helped me devise my disguise. A long, brown wig with bangs floated around my shoulders. The tight, black dress I wore had a well-stuffed bodice.

With vivid make-up, we doubted Daddy could even recognize me under bright lights, let alone a darkened motel room. And my father and I had come together here because of Mike's gift of persuasion and Daddy's well-earned reputation for being a satyr.

Mike had raved to his buddy about this girl, Judy, who could give fantastic head. All the studs on campus were fighting over her to do them. But what made me unusual, Mike boasted, was that I was the daughter of a preacher and was naturally terrified someone would recognize me.

Therefore, I was famous for only doing my thing in complete darkness. And because I was so shy, I said very little. Daddy naturally had to meet this unusual fellatress.

Now, I was exhilarated to feel his hardness right between my hands and the tip of his universe inside my mouth. I savored everything about that moment…the smooth, warmth of his manhood, the firm resiliency of his balls, how I could take all of his shaft until my lips pressed against the pubic area I had shaven smooth the night before.

"Oh, Judy, you're incredible!" moaned my father.

It was at that moment I realized why my father was such a physical legend: I had been with only one guy, Mike, but my parent was writhing and gasping as if this were the greatest moment of his life.

His flesh was so warm, so smooth and it emanated an intoxicating aroma. I felt his organ pulse and like Mike, his abundance overflowed my mouth and dribbled onto his sac.

"Judy, you're fantastic!" he moaned and pulled me up against him and began kissing me. He had kissed me all my life, but always on the cheeks and occasionally a chaste peck on the mouth.

But now, his tongue went into my mouth and he guided my hands up and down his body and then he lay on his stomach and I knew what else he wanted.

Pushing the locks of my hair back from my face, I scooted down and ran my hand between his buttocks, then parted them and sank my face in there.

I wore very little lipstick that night for I didn't want to make him look like he'd been a casualty of war with slashes of red all over him. He gasped as my tongue found its target and I pushed against the opening hard.

If possible, he smelt even better and I felt his organ puffing up again beneath my throat. He made a guttural grunt and then I felt the sticky wetness spattering the sheets.He had ejaculated again and I pulled his organ up between his legs and sucked him for a second time. It was even better and Daddy quivered and writhed and threw his head back—and promptly unloaded once more.

He rolled over and grabbed me to him. "Judy, please let me fuck you, baby! I know you haven't done it with the other guys, Mike tells me, but when I hump, you'll want more!"

I had been dreading this question for there was no way I could fake that!

But how I wanted it, too, only I gathered up my discipline and stood up, shivering as he kissed my hand and fingers and guided my hands over his chest and nipples.

"I have to go," I whispered hoarsely. He got up on his knees on the bed and pulled my face down where he kissed me.

"Judy, Judy, you were fantastic! Please let me see you again! I'm getting hard just being close to you. Look!"

His organ was already swelling up. "Judy, you remind me so much of someone. I'm trying to think of who it is!"

It was then I knew I had to get out of there before he added two and two together. I gave him a quick kiss on those luscious lips and hurried out to where Mike was waiting for me in his car.

He was nearly hysterical to hear all the juicy details. As part of our agreement, I was to date him several times a week and he would take me to the motel where my father would wait for me.

So, within a month, I was not only going out with one of the most popular studs on campus. I was also bedding down once a week the college's notorious bad boy of the classrooms…the most oversexed professor on the faculty, who just happened to be my father.

#

Christmas Day.

I had never been happier, or more frustrated.

On one hand, I had finally achieved my goal: to have my adorable father make love to me. And he had been doing this once a week at the Dixie Dew Motel.

But on the other hand, we had to do this with so much subterfuge. While he was naked in bed, rampant and willing to ball all night, I had to wear my wig and full drag.

I was forced to disguise my voice, to be on guard constantly if he wanted so much as light up a cigarette or want to feel my boobs or pussy. The tight skirt inhibited his natural desire to caress me all over. So I became just a lascivious mouth and a pair of hands.

How long would he be satisfied with just that? Mike, of course, knew what was what and it tickled him to be able to strip me of my disguise in the backseat of his car and both fuck me and have me go down on him.

And by the time he got me home, all my make-up had been creamed away and I was wearing my boring boy clothes and my father would already be there, reading before the crackling fire while watching an old Bette Davis or Joan Crawford movie on television.

"Have a good time with Mike?" he'd drawl, looking up innocently at me and my "date."

"We fucked and sucked like crazy," Mike would grin.

"You found me a wonderful stud in Mike," I'd joke. Daddy beamed and acted like he'd been there all night. When Mike would leave, I'd curl up next to Daddy on the sofa and lean my head against his shoulder and we'd sip some wine like we'd always done and watch the movie.

But I would think: just an hour ago, my face was buried in his lap, between his butt cheeks, his tongue stuck nearly in my throat—and here we are playing this ridiculous game.

"Did you enjoy your night in?" I'd ask him.

"Oh, yes," he would lie. "Graded papers, did my exercise. Yes, a quiet night at home is just what I needed." He paused before asking:

"Is Mike treating you okay, son?"

"We have a great time together, Daddy."

A moment passed before he stammered: "Are—are you in love with Mike?"

"Mike? Gosh, no! He's fun. But, he's not my big heartthrob. That's somebody else."

My father's innocent eyes widened. "You mean, there's someone else?"

"Uh huh. But it's a secret. He's the most beautiful man I've ever seen. And he's so cute that—well, he's just too handsome!"

Daddy's little boy eyes widened, a shy smile played on those full lips, and then he blushed before looking back at the TV screen. He knew who I met.

#

It had begun snowing that Christmas afternoon.

Instead of going out to all the parties we'd been invited to, Daddy and I decided to stay in, which suited me perfectly.

Now that I was intimate with him in the most intense way, I couldn't get enough of being close to him. I adored the way he moved, the way his ass moved from side to side in the loose slacks he wore, how his glasses slid down his nose and his eyes would open wide when he was deep in thought or surprised.

And he was always so physically hot! I could feel his extraordinary warmth even when just a few feet away. No wonder there was always a moist, sultry look about him, even in winter.

I had given him a luxurious robe of dark blue satin, to match his eyes. His gift was also a robe, only mine was purple silk. It brought out the touch of lavender in my eyes and I spritzed on *Shalimar* perfume that he loved. We had both read that this was the very same perfume worn by the old Jazz Age movie stars—like Valentino, Gloria Swanson, Ramon Navarro.

We both cooked our favorite dishes and after gorging ourselves, we sat in front of our new big TV console and discussed which of the movie discs we'd watch first.

We agreed to begin with one of our favorites, Bette Davis in her tear-jerker, *Now, Voyager* and follow that with another goodie, *Gone With the Wind.*

We had a wonderful time, helped by two bottles of champagne and a platter of appetizers from one of his female students. We laughed at how she had shaped the cheese and bread slices into male sexual organs.

And of course we both wept when Bonnie Blue Butler was killed after she was thrown from her horse and we applauded when Vivien Leigh stared into the camera at the end of the movie and cried: "Home! Tara! I'll think of some way to get him back! After all, tomorrow is another day!"

With my eyes still wet, I took my champagne and went to the window. Snow had turned the world outside into a movie landscape that Hollywood would have loved. A group of singers from a church were actually were strolling by, singing "Silent Night."

Daddy came up behind me and kissed my neck. "Beautiful, isn't it?"

I trembled at the warmth of his lips and the closeness of his strong body for I now knew it as intimately as any of his countless lovers.

"I wish it could last, Daddy," I said, watching the red, gold and jade Christmas lights begin to glow in houses up and down the street.

"I know, I know," he whispered. Then I heard him yawn and stretch: "Will you hate me if I leave you and keep a date with someone?"

I felt like he had slapped me, suddenly destroying this romantic evening. "Oh, a date? You mean now, at this moment, Daddy? I was hoping you and I could spend some time alone together."

He leaned close to my ear and murmured: "She'll be here any moment and I have to get ready for her."

"She'll be here?" I muttered, growing even more distressed. "With us? Who is she?"

I heard him sigh: "Yes, right here, with you and me. And when you see Judy, tell her she doesn't have to wear her wig anymore. Or that make-up or that dress. I love her just the way she is."

For a moment, I was too shocked to move. But when I did, I whirled around. Daddy had already moved to the staircase, leaving behind him his robe on the steps.

I watched him coyly strip off his pink silk bikini briefs that he threw at me, so that he stood there naked, grinning at me, and pulling at his privates.

"Daddy! Did Mike tell you—"?

"We plotted the whole thing, my sweet little pervert!" he laughed in great amusement. "Now, is Judy coming up for her bag of Christmas nuts and candy?"

I picked up his skivvies and pressed them against my face. "I certainly am, Mr. Santa Claus!"

`And I hurried up into his waiting arms and grabbed his overflowing sack of holiday delights

ANGEL

— ◆ —

"Boo!"

I nearly dropped the lid to my outdoor trashcan and looked around me.

For two days, I'd luxuriated in being completely alone at this remote farmhouse—away from the big city bustle and dirt and humanity of New York. Away from pushing, bitching millions of human beings of every kind.

And now, human beings were invading me again and I wasn't exactly thrilled with the idea. Especially when the "Boo!" was uttered unmistakably by a child.

But there was no one visible among the row of pine trees and thick bushes near my back porch.

"Boo! Bang, you're dead!" I laughed now because I could make out the figure of a small boy crouched down behind a large fig bush. Aiming the nozzle of a red water gun over a branch, he sprinkled me.

"You're dead, you're dead!" he screamed happily and ran out into view. He looked like a Walt Disney kid, with a round face and big, dark eyes and wind was blowing his light curls around.

His body was fragile and little, though, and he barley came to my waist. A strong gust of wind could knock him down. His face was unusually pale which made his brown eyes so striking. They now danced as I pretended to clutch my arm and stagger around.

"Oh, you really hurt me that time!" I moaned and fell to my knees. "Please don't shoot me again!"

"You're supposed to fall down dead," he informed me seriously. "Fall down there. Now I'll kill you again. Bang, bang, yaa, yaaa, boom, you're dead again!"

Collapsing to the ground, I writhed and convulsed so convincingly my visitor squealed in delight. When I sat up, he pushed my shoulder. "Fall down again. Let me kill you again."

"Okay, but don't drench me, you big cowpoke you. It's freezing. Where's your coat and cap?" He ignored my question and sprayed me again and again with water.

The wind was bitter and slicing and I was shivering in my trench-coat—yet, this kid wore just a light sweater, jeans and Rebok tennis shoes.

"What's your name?" I asked after more minutes of playing Bang, Bang, You're Dead. "My name's Buddy Clark," he said seriously in that solemn way children have of answering a personal question like that.

"I'm Jason Fury. I'm happy to know you, Buddy." I held out my hand and took his cold paw. It was like holding some feathers in my hand, his fingers were so light.

His fingers were blue with cold which made me wonder again: what kind of parent would allow such a cute little poster boy like Buddy to roam around in freezing weather?

"Buddy? Buddy?" a man called out. "Where are you?"

"Uh oh," groaned Buddy. "Sounds like trouble. Dat's James."

"Is James your father?"

"Huh uh. He's my big brodder."

"Your big brother?"

And big he was for at that moment, a bear of a young man appeared and came over to us. His first concern was for Buddy, though, and after nodding his bearded face at me, he knelt down and hugged his brother's frail shoulders.

"Buddy, what's the idea of coming out here without your coat? Didn't I tell you to stay indoors? You don't want to get sick again. You know what the doctors said."

The little boy drooped against James who had pulled him inside his own jacket to warm him up. "I sowwy, James. I got tired watching cartoons all day."

He had that childish way of not being able to pronounce his "R's" distinctly. Cartoons sounded like "cawtoons." Sorry came out "sowwy."

Sternness left James face and a smile softened his rugged features. He took off his own red ski cap and pulled it over Buddy's tousled curls.

"It's okay, big fella," James smiled and kissed his cheek. "Let's hurry home and get you all nice and warm with some hot chocolate."

He now looked at me and held out his hand. "Sorry. Don't mean to be rude. I'll bet you're Jason Fury. I'm James Clark and this is my brother, Buddy. We live just over that field there. I read about you moving in." He paused before grinning: "I don't know how I stack up against those New York guys."

"Good God, but that girl reporter really got carried away about my background."

The journalist had interviewed me and seemed ga-ga by the fact I was a writer of boy-boy erotica and part-time stripper from New York who planned to live for a few months on Young Road in Lexington, North Carolina.

I grew up in that area and had always vowed that one day I'd come here to write and get away from it all. I loved the pastoral countryside, with its neat white houses, old farmhouses and its easy accessibility to more urban settings like Greensboro, High Point, Charlotte and Winston-Salem.

"Just what is it that article said you did for a living?" drawled James with an impish gleam in his eyes.

"Oh, that I just strip naked in front of a couple of hundred of men each night and I write novels about over-sexed cute guys. Want me to do my dance routine for you?"

He laughed with a roll of his eyes. "Maybe sometimes when it's warmer. I better get Buddy home. Don't want him to get sick again."

The little boy tugged at his brother's arm and James leaned down. He nodded and smiled at me.

"My brother here wonders if you could come by and visit us, maybe for supper tonight? I'm not a bad cook. Buddy would sure like to see you again. We don't get many visitors out here in the boondocks."

"I'd love to. Where do you live, Jimmy?"

He pointed toward a column of blue smoke ascending up into the gray sky. "Just follow the chimney smoke. Right across the field there. That's mine. Five minutes away."

He picked up Buddy easily who rested his head on his shoulder. It was touching to see two brothers so close like that and James was a handsome man who would be considered a catch even in New York.

Buddy glanced up and gave me a small wave before burying his face in his brother's strong shoulder.

#

The farmhouse where the Clarks lived was small but neat as if Aunt Bea on the *The Andy Griffin* show had cleaned it up.

A fire in the hearth perfumed the air with burning pine, and this mixed with the succulent aromas of baked ham, candied yams and other Southern goodies.

I was resigned to finding a Mrs. Clark, fussing around her husband or worse still, a possessive mother, but I was relieved to find neither. The only female there was a spry little black woman, Daisy, who lived down the road.

"She's part of my family," James smiled and gave her a big hug. "She's mothered me and Buddy here since we were both little but she wouldn't let me do anything in the kitchen tonight." Daisy cackled and pushed her glasses back on her nose. "I told him to don't even put a toe in the kitchen while I fixed supper because only ole Daisy knows how to cook for visitors."

"Hey, I make good fried chicken," joked Jimmy.

"Not like ole Daisy!" she sassed back and they both laughed.

"I think my baby brother wants your attention," whispered James and Buddy stood at the door of his bedroom and waved at me.

"Come on, Jason. Hurry! Let me show you my stuff."

He now wore a thick sweater, pajama bottoms and big slippers in the shape of the Lion King. Stuffed bears, cats and pandas crowded each other on the shelves with his collection of miniature cars. On a blackboard, he had made an attempt to draw trees and flowers.

"Here's my drum set," he bragged. "One day I'm gonna be a drummer like that guy on MTV, the man with long hair."

James joined us and pointed to the drummer for the Hockey Bop group. That was who Buddy worshipped.

"I'll show you how good I am," Buddy said and got behind a simple toy drum, imitating a rock drummer, complete with wild headshakes, rolling eyes and his tongue lolling out of his mouth.

James stood behind him and winked at me. "Okay, brother, I think Jason's heard enough for now. It's time for us to see what Daisy fixed for us."

Weight Watchers would have been appalled at our feast but we all had second and third helpings of Daisy's country ham huge biscuits.

While serving us her cherry and apple cobbler, I watched Daisy fuss over the two brothers like a real mother. So when we finished, she motioned to the front door. "You two men go on now, drive around some while I spend some time with my baby here."

"I wanna go with them! James, James, Jimmy, please let me go with you!" pleaded Buddy.

"You stay here with Daisy and I'll tell you ghost stories," the woman smiled.

"Will you tell me about Bloody Bones and the Ghost Train?" he asked.

"I'll tell you about those and about Santa Land! Because you know who's coming to see you in 8 weeks?"

"Santa Claus!" shrieked Buddy.

I stooped down and hugged him. "And we'll get together tomorrow, Buddy, and write Santa Claus a letter about what a good boy you've been and what all you want. We'll send it up the chimney there."

"I've already sent him a million letters," Buddy said solemnly. "But they get all burned up when they go up the chimney."

"Not the kind you and me will write. I'll see you tomorrow now. Be sure and have your pencils and paper ready."

On the porch, James lit up a cigarette. "Guess I could show you the night life here?" he said dryly.

"Are you sure we can cover it all in one night?"

We both laughed. There was zero nightlife along Young Road. After we got into his truck, he leaned across me to pull my door firmly closed. I caught my breath, for his ear brushed my mouth.

I felt immediately at ease with James. He was the big, rugged type of man you don't find in big cities. He was also quiet and reassuring, a man who would always be in charge of the situation.

He did show me the area, driving through downtown Lexington, which looked like a Norman Rockwell painting with its neat streets and sidewalks and buildings. We also passed through the small community of Denton, a picturesque little community where my favorite boyfriend, "Big" Bill Jackson had grown up.

Main Street was empty but the houses, which lined it, were lit up with Christmas lights and decorations. We could even see families sitting around big color TVs. How different all this was from the swirling pace of New York City.

He told me about himself, how he had grown up in that area, how his parents were killed in a traffic accident two years before and how he'd taken care of Buddy, and his own small construction firm which he hoped to expand in the future.

"Would you have a heart attack," I said dryly, "if I invite you in for a drink? I can promise you, my reputation for being on the wild side has been highly exaggerated."

"I'm a grown man," he grinned, "who can defend himself. What kind of poison do you have?"

In the den of my small farmhouse, he fixed a fire in the hearth since I knew nothing about this complicated ritual while I prepared us strong drinks at the small bar I'd set up in the corner, next to the window over-looking the field.

"Whew!" he gasped, as he sipped the strong concoction. "I thought we liked our brew strong down here. This tastes pretty powerful."

"Don't forget I'm a decadent writer who likes stripping in public. So watch out."

"You've got the place fixed up nice," he nodded. I'd put up my movie posters of Bette Davis, Vivien Leigh, Ida Lupino on the walls and he came over to see my work area.

"You look pretty busy," he noted, observing my computer and the dark green lamp and a shelf above the desk, featuring my books. He leafed through my latest novel, *His Eyes Were Dark, and He Licked His Lips*, scanned some of the love passages and grinned.

"Wow, you've either got a great imagination or you've got a fantastic love life."

"Combine the two and you'll have a typical Jason Fury masterpiece."

We sat together on the sofa and there was a definite quality of eroticism in the air. Without his jacket, he looked solid, but his eyes contained a sad quality. I wanted to see that expression go and a more romantic one to take its place.

"What do you people do here for fun?" I asked. "Is TV and shopping at Wal-Mart the only exciting things you do?"

He laughed. "That's about it. It sure ain't New Yawk City."

"How about the single scene? What do young guys, like yourself, do for fun?"

He had finished his drink and I refreshed it. "If you mean, what do we do for sex, our right hand is our best friend. Some of my buddies see the whores over in High Point. Sometimes I've thought about going over there, too, but—it costs money and I don't want any diseases. Frankly, doing it with a whore holds zero appeal to me."

"Do you know any guess who like other guys, James?"

He gave me an impish smile. "In college, I knew some. They'd approach me in the showers, sometimes they'd offer to give me a massage."

"Yes, I can see why. You're very good looking. And sexy. And you never took up any of their propositions?."

He studied his glass and his voice became weaker. "It was never the right time. Too many people around. No place to go. Yeah, I was tempted a few times."

A moment passed and the powerful sense of sexuality grew stronger. I saw his breathing had quickened, saw how warm his eyes looked.

"How about now, James? I'm safe. Nobody would know."

He stared for a second at the fire, then put his drink down. He leaned back and pulled me to him.

"I ain't had nobody for months and months so I might be a little rough around the edges.""I love men who're rough around the edges," I murmured. "It's those who've been around so much who bore me."

He pulled me to him and I thought: this guy is going to be a real treasure. His lips were shy but warm and as I responded he became more assured.

I ran my hand over his chest and shoulders and thought how wonderful he felt. For some reason, in New York, men always wore so many clothes and if you tried to caress their shoulders, you felt nothing but leather or wool or cotton.

Somehow we got out of our clothes and we laid down on my bear skin rug which always goes wherever I go. He made me think of a strong, macho wrestler with a solid body.

His neck and shoulders were glossy from sun and he laid back as I moved my mouth over him. His chest was hairy but just enough to shadow his chest and when my lips touched his stomach, he gasped and flung an arm over his eyes.

James would make his future wife happy indeed for his privates were as rugged and as healthy as he was. He was cut and the minute I covered the tip with my mouth, he gasped once more and muttered, "Oh, man, that's incredible, simply incredible! My first time."

I love to get down between a man's thighs and have them close on either side of my face, so that they brush my cheeks. James swelled bigger and when I glanced up, his mouth had fallen open, and his stomach was moving faster.

"Okay," he grunted. "I'm about ready, Jason."

I held his phallus up so we could both watch him ejaculate. It was a healthy stream which spattered his stomach and soon it was like he had body cream glistening there, waiting to be spread.

I used a towel to wipe him dry and he pulled me up to him and began kissing me again, only this time with more passion and confidence. He got over me and stared down at me.

"I guess screwing a guy ain't much difference than with a girl, is it? We'll soon find out."

"Just do what comes naturally," I smiled. "You're fantastic."

"I kinda like hearing them words," he grinned and began positioning himself between my buttocks.

He was gentle and careful, pausing now and then to study my expression and when I nodded, he continued on until he was all the way in.

I loved the boyish way he was doing everything, the slightly hesitant way he made love, as if afraid of disappointing. That was what endeared men like James to me, much more than their big city counterparts. To the latter group, balling is just a common routine. You pop it in, stir it around and then whip it out. End of the story with zero interest in the residual effects.

When he came this time, he pulled me closer to him and shuddered and I buried my face against his neck for a long time.

He was in no hurry to go. I fixed us another drink, he got out his cigarettes, and we lay there on the bear skin rug and talked for a long time, pausing now and then for me to "play" with him.

"I guess I'm just a green farm boy compared to those city slickers you're used to," he joked but there was seriousness behind his question.

"Stop that," I ordered. "You don't know how sick I get of the big city boys. Give me a hunk from Dixie any day. There's no comparison. Well, those Italian boys come close."

Rain was falling outside and freezing on the windows. It was after midnight and James finally sat up, yawned and scratched his chest.

"Gotta go and make sure Buddy's okay. He's been sick, Jason, real sick."

I put on a warm robe of black cashmere and wrapped my arms around him as he stood before the mirror, combing his hair.

"James, what's wrong with that little cherub? You mentioned something about doctors this afternoon. What's the story?"

My handsome neighbor was buttoning up his leather jacket and now held me again. "He's just gotten out of the hospital where he's been for three months."

He stopped and I looked up to see his eyes becoming wet.

"James," I repeated, "what's wrong with Buddy?"

"Leukemia. The kind they can't cure. The minute they operate on one tumor another grows back. He's only got a few months to live."

I was so shocked by this news I could only stare at him. "James, I can't believe it! He's such a little doll. And so active!"

James looked away, nodding and wiped his nose. "Yeah, he'll be like that for a spell because of medication. But it'll wear off soon. If I can just get him through this Christmas. That's all I want. To let him have one more Christmas."

I hugged him tight and vowed: "He will! Not just this one, but dozens of more to come."

James hugged me again before leaving. "Wow, I'm glad you came into our lives, Jason. Can I see you tomorrow?

"You'd better believe it!" I laughed. "And I'm coming by to visit with Buddy, too, and tell him some ghost stories."

I had trouble sleeping that night because I kept seeing a curly haired little boy running toward me, squealing: "Fall down! You're dead!"

I was lucky. I could pretend I was dead. But for Buddy, he didn't have a choice.

#

Big city people would have jeered at the Thanksgiving Parade that wound down the narrow Main Street of Denton. But to those rural residents, it was an eagerly awaited event.

I stood next to James, who held Buddy up on his shoulders, and as we shivered in the freezing cold, we beheld floats representing the various churches, with men in black-rimmed glasses and bathrobes and towels tied around their heads like burnooses posing as shepards...a float with a huge pig and around its neck the pennant: Big Bobby's Barbecue!...beauty queens like Miss Poultry...Miss Fertilizer.

The girls were pretty and wholesome looking, the young men husky and boyish. Then came the Denton School Band. Buddy clapped his hands when he saw the bass drum player who whirled his sticks above his head and from side to side. The young man winked and grinned at Buddy.

After eating barbecues and fries in Lexington, Buddy talked about nothing but the bass drum player.

"That's what I'm gonna do," he said repeatedly. "Maybe Santa Claus will bring me one?"

"You'd better write another letter again to remind him," suggested James.

Buddy had coughed all afternoon and now I thought he looked unusually pale. In the front seat of James's truck, the little boy fell into a nap and his head rested on my shoulder. I glanced down and saw blue veins beneath the translucent skin.

My eyes met James and he looked away. Neither of us had to say what was going through our minds. Was Buddy just tired or was he heading for another relapse?

#

Twice each week, I began to accompany James and Buddy to Duke Medical Center in Durham, an hour's drive away.

Buddy's specialist there was a handsome older man, Dr. Hogarth, world-famous for his treatment of terminally ill children. I'll never forget my first visit.

It was familiar grounds for the brothers since Buddy had spent three months there just recently and had been operated there several times before.

We passed by rooms where tiny children lay, sometimes alone, sometimes with nurses and visitors. Cursed by diseases, none of them ever left here "cured." I could barely look at these small creatures with tubes running into their bodies, surrounded by dolls barely larger than the patients.

They either died here or returned home to meet their maker. We walked by the door of one room where the door was closed.

"My friend, Simon, lives there," smiled Buddy. "I want to see him before we go. Can we, James?"

"We'll-we'll see," his brother replied with hesitation.

"Is Simon still here?" Buddy piped up after his examination by Dr. Hogarth. My little friend looked even smaller and more frail without his shirt on. His shoulders drooped slightly and I saw how thin his arms were. On the inside were dark bruises where syringes and tubes had been stuck during his last stay.

"Eh, no, Buddy, he's no longer here," said the surgeon.

James caught my eyes and shook his head and I sensed that Simon had passed away. But Buddy didn't know that.

"Did he go home, doctor?" he asked.

"Yes, Buddy," Dr.Hogarth said quietly, "he's gone *home*."

#

I accompanied the brothers to their country church that Sunday.

It was the first time the little boy had been there since returning from the hospital. Members fussed over him, hugging him and the women kissing his cheek.

Sitting between me and James, I thought how unusually small he looked in his Sunday suit, the polished shoes just barely hanging down over the pew and his hair neatly parted on the side. His brother had done a good job preparing him for church.

His eyes glowed big and dark from his face the color of snow. He drooped forward with his mouth slightly open and I thought: he's exhausted and feeling sick but he won't admit it to us.

From his pulpit, the minister recognized him. "And we want to welcome today, the return of Master Buddy Clark. Hope you feel better, son."

The little boy smiled shyly and James pulled him close while I took his hand. It was so tiny in mine. Daisy had trimmed his nails and I thought: it looks like a doll's hand.

#

In the first week of December, we all went shopping at the nearby Wal-Mart and K-Mart department stores.

After pigging out at yet another barbecue emporium, Daisy said she was taking Buddy to see the new Billy Jackson action movie, *The Pirates of Black Swamp.*

James and I hurried out to a store in Lexington that sold musical instruments. He had spotted this drum set months before and had been paying on it each month.

It was all glittering red and gold with cymbals and a foot pedal and all sizes of drums.

When we picked up Daisy and Buddy, the boy insisted that we stop at Rose's Department Store where he could shop "alone"—except for me. He wanted to buy his brother and Daisy their Christmas gifts.

He had taken the contents of his piggy bank, $2.82 cents that morning but he refused to let me add any money to his own.

"No," he said firmly, "this is my money. Santa wouldn't want anybody to help me."

He and I agreed that Jimmy would love a bottle of Old Spice After Shave for $1.02. And for 50 cents he found a pretty white handkerchief for Daisy.

"Now, I'm buying your present," he grinned, "so you go over by the door and wait."

But he was so small I didn't dare let him out of my sight so I followed behind him, sometimes barely able to see the top of his head above the counters.

When he joined me, he wore a proud smile. "You won't guess what I got you?" he giggled.

All the way home, Daisy, James and I pretended to guess what Buddy could have gotten us.

"Is it a monster from Jurassic Park?" I joked. "Uh oh, I can hear something roaring and growling in that package."

"No it's not!" squealed Buddy.

"Did you capture Frankenstein and Dracula?" gasped James. "I can hear them screaming!"

"Did you buy me a new microwave?" Daisy teased. "Maybe we could find a toad or a frog along the road and I could cook them for supper?"

"No, it's not a microwave!" crowed Buddy.

#

The next day, we went out into the woods to get our Christmas Trees.

James found me a beautiful evergreen and chopped it down with Buddy using a toy axe to help him.

For their house, they cut down a majestic specimen for the den and then they showed me another one growing right outside Buddy's window.

"We planted it here when Buddy was born," James explained. "Every Christmas, we put strings of popcorn and other food for birds and squirrels. It helps them out if the weather's bad."

"Can we put on the Christmas Angel now, Jimmy?" Buddy asked.

"We sure can. You know where to find it, Buddy."

The little boy ran with that endearing way of bending forward and he brought out an object from beneath his bed, wrapped in Christmas paper.

"Here it is, just waiting to be put back on the tree," he sang out.

When he unwrapped it, I was startled to see how strikingly similar the plastic angel with brown curls resembled Buddy. The large eyes of brown and the round cheeks and small mouth.

"Mama brought it right before she was killed, didn't she, Jimmy?" he asked quietly. "She brought it for me because she said it was like I had posed for it."

We went outside and James held his brother up so he could attach it to the very top of the tree. Then James made sure it was secured by tying it down with wire.

"Let the winds blow and the snows come," he sang out to Buddy, "but your Christmas Angel ain't going no place, is he?"

"He ain't, he ain't!" cried Buddy. "He's magic."

With Daisy assisting us, we baked cookies and made a pot of hot chocolate and then Buddy insisted we play a game of hide and seek. I finally begged off after an hour of this.

Daisy was staying overnight and she urged me and Jimmy to go off and "have some fun." I'll look after my baby. Don't worry."

We headed straight over to my place where we resumed a delightful ritual: after a drink, we stripped and laid down on my fur rug and tried to forget how sick Buddy was.

James seemed to improve with each session and in my mind, I could very easily see myself settling down with someone like him. I loved his quietness, his macho resiliency, the compassion he had for others.

"I hate to think of you leaving us," he whispered, as he kissed me.

"I'm staying on through Christmas," I answered. "You have a way of growing on me, James."

"On you or in you?" he teased, causing me to gasp as he moved his hips forward and driving himself deep into me.

#

All that day's excitement seemed to have injured Buddy's health for he began going downhill at an alarming rate.

When I went to see him the next afternoon, he was laying in bed, his face barely larger than the stuffed panda bear, Toby, he slept with.

"I've brought you some candy," I smiled and sat down on his bed.

He shook his head and stared at me from dark, sunken eyes. "Not hungry, Jason. Will Santa Claus come to see me if I'm sick?"

"Of course he will and if he even thinks differently, I'll get me a belt and beat him."

I pretended to lash the bed. A weak smile flitted across his mouth. I watched those small fingers knead the silk lining of his blanket. "I sure hope he comes. I hurt so bad."

A young county nurse who checked on Buddy each day, arrived just then. While she worked with him, I stood out in the hall with James and Daisy. We could hear Buddy moan with pain as the nurse administered syringes.

"If Buddy can just last until Christmas," James muttered. "That's all I want. Let him have one more Christmas. This morning, he told me he'll soon be seeing Mom and Dad. He knows!"

Other neighbors stopped by that day for a small community's grapevine works overtime when tragedy befalls one of its own. Daisy fixed coffee and sandwiches and one or two of the women made me want to scream when they began to sob.

"Oh, James, I hate to see him so sick!" one of them wailed.

I slipped in to see him once more that night before I left. "I'm going home, sweetie," I smiled and kissed his cheek. "I'll be back tomorrow. Can I bring you anything?"

"Is it dark over there, Jason?" he asked quietly. "I'm scared of the dark. Jimmy can't come with me over there, can he? He told me he would if I wanted to but it isn't time for him yet."

It chilled me to hear him talk about death like that. I hugged him tight. He felt like a small pillow and his hair and skin had that intangible scent of little child. As I tucked the blanket up under his chin, he pulled his Panda doll closer.

"Don't talk like that now, Buddy," I murmured. "James wouldn't want to hear you say that. You know you'll be up and playing around in no time."

"See the angel out there?" he whispered. "Right there, on the Christmas tree? Jimmy says it's my guardian angel."

I watched the glowing ornament bob in the wind.

"He'll guard you always," I told Buddy. "As long as he's out there, you won't have anything to worry about."

His eyes drooped, his fingers continued kneading the smooth lining of his blanket and he lifted up one hand to wave goodbye.

#

But overnight, his life began leaving him.

He underwent a relapse and we rushed him to the local hospital but there was nothing they could do. His energy was nearly gone and the disease had overtaken his immune system at a shocking rate.Dr. Hogarth had warned us to prepare for this. No operation could do anything to help him now. All anyone could do was to administer sedatives so that his end wouldn't be a nightmare of pain.

James brought him back home that night and nurses were assigned around the clock to care for him.

I was there when Dr. Hogarth drove in from Duke Hospital. Buddy had always been one of his favorites and now he had come down to help him out of this life with as little pain as possible.

Outside in the hallway, James stopped the doctor and cried out: "Why him, doctor? He's done nothing! He's just a scared little five-year-old boy! Why not take out some killer or bum or some lowlife. Why my little brother?"

#

Christmas Eve night.

Outside the Clark home, Buddy's little holiday tree bobbed in the wind and glowed with gold and azure and crimson lights. The vibrant lights dappled the white snow that had fallen enough to turn the plain farmyard into a post card.

I could see them even from the window of my house. Within the Clark house, though, the atmosphere was grim.

In the kitchen and dining room, tables overflowed with casseroles and platters of food brought in from neighbors and kindergarten children and members of the church where Buddy had attended.

They had not had much time to know him for he was only five years old.

The stream of visitors had been constant but touching to us all. People talked softly or whispered. Sometimes Buddy awoke from his heavy medication to stare bleary eyed at the well-wishers.

A few times he seemed to recognize someone and a weak smile flitted over his face and he'd raise his hand weakly to wave. When darkness came, though, his strength seemed to leave him for his breathing became more harsh.

Even standing in the hallway with Daisy and Jimmy, we could hear the little boy's chilling attempt to breathe. Dr. Hogarth and the nurse had asked us to wait outside because it would be a harrowing sight for us to watch them try to make his last hours peaceful.

Daisy and other women kept making pots of coffee and preparing us platters of food. We ignored the food but drank the coffee like an alcoholic in need of a drink.

It was two in the morning and the neighbors had long gone. Daisy sat in a stiff backed chair against the hall wall and James and I stood at the window, studying the snow that gleamed ghost like in the night.

I had tried to stop smoking but both James and I went through several packages during those hours. Finally, the door to Buddy's room opened and Dr. Hogarth and the nurse stepped out.

"We've done all we can," he said quietly, his eyes sad. "It won't be long now."

Daisy got clumsily to her feet and braced her hand against the wall for a moment. She had been praying silently for hours and now it would soon be over. With her head bowed down, she entered the room first and James and I followed. We all sat on the edge of the narrow bed that had been Buddy's for only five years.

His stuffed Panda doll, Toby, was clutched against his thin chest. All around him were the toys he had collected during his brief days on earth: the miniature cars, the dolls and the plastic guns. On the black board were the beginnings of chalk drawings of the moon and stars. He would never finish them. James took his hand. It looked so small in his big one.

"Buddy, can you hear me, little brother?"

We watched the eyes open slightly. He stared at his brother, as if trying to recognize him.

"Did—did Santa come, Jimmy?"

James couldn't speak and nodded his head.

"He certainly did, honey," I said and tried to smile. "And would you just look at what I'm wearing!"

I pulled open my cardigan sweater so he could see the white tee shirt with a picture of The Lion King on front. He had brought it for me with his last dollar.

"And see my beautiful white handkerchief?" cried Daisy, pulling the white square of cloth from her dress pocket. "How did you know I wanted a beautiful white handkerchief?"

"Smell me!" said James, rubbing his face against his brother's. "Can you smell that great after shave lotion? And Santa Claus brought you exactly what you wanted. See those drums over there in the corner?"

Buddy was too weak to move his head. I held him up and Daisy went over to the drums and showed him the drumsticks.

"These are just like you wanted, my baby boy!" she said but her voice broke and she turned her head away so he wouldn't see her tears.

"He brought'em!" he whispered. "Wow! He really did come after all didn't he? Can I play 'em, brother?"

As if he held a doll in his arms, James carried the dying child over to the drums. Too weak to hold a drumstick, James wrapped his brother's fingers around one of them and they tapped one of the heads.

"Do you like that, Buddy?" Jimmy asked desperately. "Is the color okay? We'll exchange it for another if—"

"Wow!" smiled Buddy. "I love it."

Then his mouth fell open and his eyes rolled.

"Hurt—hurt!" he whimpered.

After laying him back on the bed, James stretched out beside him and put his arms around him. Daisy and I moved closer for it was like the single lamp was darkening. Everything grew dimmer in the room.

Buddy's lips moved and he whispered something that sounded like, "Jim…Mama…"

Suddenly, he stiffened and there was a deep moan from him. His eyes opened slowly and as I looked into them, I saw life fading away.

"Don't leave me, Buddy!" cried James. "Stay with me a little longer!"

The small hand I held became cold and still. There was heavy silence in the room except for those of us weeping.

Daisy moved painfully to the door. When she spoke to me, her voice was hoarse: "Let's leave the brothers alone."

#

It was early January and I hesitated before entering Buddy's small room.

"At least we got him through Christmas," said James.

It was a freezing afternoon and I would be leaving for New York in an hour. I had walked over the field to the Clark home for the last time. Now, James and I stood in the room of the little dead boy.

Nothing had changed, except all signs of illness and death had been destroyed. James and Daisy had fixed the place up the way Buddy had loved it. His stuffed animals were everywhere, his Pacman and Mighty Morphin Power Rangers were all lined up on his dresser.

The framed picture of him with James still beamed on the nightstand beside the bed. And the bed was turned down as if the child who had slept there all those nights would return soon from some long trip he had taken. I tried not to look at the closet where his clothes and shoes were neatly arranged.

On the blackboard were still his attempts to draw stars and a moon. His new drum set still gleamed in the corner, untouched but still there. Waiting.

"Can I take something of Buddy's?"

"Sure," James murmured. His face was haggard and grim. He was the type of man who would never forget the death of his only sibling. If we met 50 years from now, I thought, he'll still be thinking of that little cherub who left us too early in life.

I opened the dresser drawer. A big mistake. Folded neatly were what looked like doll clothes: a child's underwear, socks, brightly colored jerseys. Quickly, I turned away. I thought I had built up my reserves from breaking down but it was no use.

I didn't want James to see me going on like this, though, and I turned to the closet.

It was even worse. On the floor were his Rebok shoes and hanging above were his windbreaker and jackets. Missing were his shiny "dress up" shoes and his Sunday's best suit.

He had been buried in those.

In his casket, he had looked like an adorable little doll but one whose face was too white, whose hands were too real and thin. I wouldn't think about that tombstone on the hill near the church and the epitaph: He was here not too long but while he was he spread sunshine everywhere."

My armor broke completely and when James saw what was happening he came to me and hugged me.

"I know, I know, it happens to me to every time I come in here."

After long minutes, I managed to pull myself together and then I went to the drum set. I picked up one of the sticks.

"Can I have this, Jimmy? There's another set of sticks."

"Yes, take it," nodded my friend.

Before we went outside, James turned on the lights of Buddy's Christmas tree for it was already growing dark.

Although there had been wind storms and heavy snows during those weeks he had lain in his grave on the hill, the small angel he had put at the top of the tree still remained there: strong and smiling and beautiful.

"That's how I'll always think of Buddy," I said. I kissed my finger and touched the small decoration and a gust of wind made it bob up and down, as if it were thanking me.

"He was like Christmas," murmured James. "He brought happiness to everybody he knew."

On the way to the airport, James stopped his truck at the cemetery and we walked to visit Buddy.

His grave was so small, the size of a pillow. Both James and I knelt down to kiss the little stone and I could imagine him sleeping beneath the dark soil. I hoped he hadn't minded the snow and the rain and the frost that had covered the soil during those past few weeks.

That was in 1991. Each year since then I've visited Jimmy Clark during the Christmas holidays.

It's become our ritual to kiss, to hug in my wooden cottage and then we walk over the fields to his house. Even in the dark, we can see that small winged figure on the tree, glowing in the night, surviving all the storms and winds that come its way.

RULES OF THE GAME

◆

His face convulsed with revulsion as he glared at me from across the dinner table.

He shoved his chair back, lit a cigarette while studying me—like I were a poisonous reptile which had suddenly slithered into the dining room.

"How can you say that kind of shit to me?" he spat. "I'm your father and here you sit, talking like that to me? You go off to college, you come back and you've changed. Christ, how you've changed!"

He did a vicious imitation of me eating my supper, with exaggerated flipping of wrists and pursing of lips and rolling of eyes. I know, I know I can be very piss elegant when I'm trying to piss somebody off—like this stupid asshole. So now, I exaggerated my weak-wristed movements and patted my mouth with very dainty gestures, all the time staring at my father with complete contempt.

"So why're you going off the deep end, my dear ole Pappy?" I sneered. "Huh? Huh? What'sa matter with my lil' ole Wall Street Tiger of a father? Huh? Just because I come out of the closet and want to ball with you, you're acting like some red-necked yahoo from Noo Joiseey!"

His eyes, those crystal blue orbs, which make women, go ga-ga and men go ah-ha, narrowed into slits. "I told you to stop talking that kind of shit around me! You understand what I'm saying? To think I've spent thousands for those goddamned shrinks to turn you around and you turn out like this!"

I stuck my pinkie out as I pretended to sip my wine. I rolled my eyes and touched the napkin to my mouth like a real flaming queen and flipped my wrists again.

Oh, did I know how to drive him nuts, this big he-man bull stud of New York City.

"Why, Daddy honey, you're always bragging to all your buddies about all the cunts you've been fucking with that big, juicy 10 incher inside your britches. Now come on! Gimme some of it! I'm a cocksucker from heaven and you'll feel like a million after I've sucked on it!"

I watched his hands knot up into fists. "Jason! I told you to shut the hell up!"

"I wanna put my hands around it, Daddy, and make you squirt out some of that Wall Street power down my throat. Remember when I was little and you let me play with it and I'd make you cum all over the damned place?"

He sprang out of his chair and leaned toward me. "For the last time, you faggot, I said for you to shut up!"

"And oh, how I'd love to put you in my mouth, oh, sweet, hot Daddy and—"

"I said for you to shut up!"

He jumped up, knocking over his chair and charged around the table to pounce on poor little me.

Throwing my boyish form over that formidable shoulder of his, he carried me kicking and pounding him upstairs and threw me on my bed.

He stood above me, panting and muttering insults about what a disgrace it was that here I was a Fury—where men were men and women were a nuisance except to be fucked—and now I was telling everybody I was a fucking fruit!

"You'd better believe it, hot shot!" I screamed. "I'm going to suck every cock in the world but your's is the one I really want. Oh, Daddy, can't you please just let me blow you for an hour or two to see if you like it? They say I'm the sleaziest queer slut to ever hit New York University. When nice boys see me, they run the other way and the horny ones mob me to make a date."

"I'm sending you to Bellevue Hospital for sure this time," he shouted. "Maybe those shock treatments will zap some of that queerness out of that little fag head of yours."

There was no way I could get past him. At six feet five, that heavily muscled, blue-eyed brute towered over me. A rugged face, with creases around the mouth, and those startling eyes the color of a winter's lake always made everyone stare at Nicky Fury.

A dashing moustache above those full lips had made God only knows how many idiot women drool over him and simper: "Lord, but you look just like Rhett Butler! Only you've got so many muscles you make Sly Stallone look like Dennis the Menace!"

Black curls now gleamed in disarray as he glared at me. He was such a big, powerful stud that his buddies called him the Tarzan of Wall Street.

That was why everyone was astonished to discover I was the son of the dashing, charming, over-sexed Nicky Fury.

My mother had bequeathed to me a cloud of golden curls and a hot little body that drew wolf whistles whenever I swished past the construction sites.

But a childhood accident had left me with a permanent limp. So when I hip-hopped alongside my father down Manhattan streets, it was certainly a head-turning contrast of beauty: he—so big, dark and heroic, and me—like a teenage kid, dressed in the latest fashions, limping along gamely beside him.

"Daddy," I pleaded, forcing tears into my eyes, "please let me go out tonight? It's Friday and—"

"Oh, sure!" he sneered. "A night out with the boys! A night to get gang-banged and go on a wild sucking spree where you'd probably blow all the winos on the Bowery! You're staying in this fucking room all weekend long so I can decide whether to have you locked up at Bellevue Hospital. We're having a talk Sunday. Now don't you bother me again. I'm going to bed."

"You bastard!" I shrieked and lunged for him, leaping upon his back. He whirled around, trying to force me off and when he couldn't, he grew nearly insane with rage. He managed to tear me off and threw me back on the bed. Then he slapped me good and hard, the way he had always done so when I went into a screaming tantrum.

I heard him lock the door. His blow had not been painful but it had been stinging enough to galvanize me into action. I waited impatiently for an hour to pass for he went to sleep early—when he wasn't bedding down half of New York City's high society cunts and secretaries and the clean-up women and any female who was around when he needed relief.

I dressed up warmly for January was bringing us another sleet storm. From my window, four floors above East 88th Street, I saw the streets turning into ice.

That wouldn't stop me. Nothing would block my way from being the most notorious slut in Manhattan and before the night was over, I was going to ball only with the biggest and the best.

From beneath my rug, I fished out the extra key I long ago had made to my bedroom. Carefully, I unlocked it. I tiptoed past my father's bedroom. I could hear Bette Davis spitting out the lines in his favorite movie, *Beyond the Forest*: "I'm gonna catch me a train! The choo choo to carry me away! At last I'm moving on!"

As I limped rapidly down the street to find a taxi, I thought: Bette hit the nail on the head. At last I'm moving on to find other men since the one I really wanted was already in bed, preparing for sleep, after brutally rejecting me.

From long experience I discovered that if I couldn't have him, Nicky Fury, then I would seek him out in other dark places—in the arms and between the legs of other hungry men.

#

Even at 10 p.m., the King's Cinema off Broadway teemed with sex-hungry sluts. I entered the theater just in time to see on the seamy screen the snarling, sadistic Jon Vincent feeding his lusty phallus to a drooling, gobbling boy.

I joined the small band of cruisers in the aisle and leaning against the walls. There was someone I had to find, someone I had balled with twice before.

He told he was always there on Friday nights, around 10 p.m. I didn't know his name, could barley describe his face. We said little because he supplied to me exactly what I wanted: a hot bull who thrived on exhibitionism.

In my mind, I called him Mr. Hot 'n Tot. He was hot, alright, and he had a tot that nearly glowed in the dark from heat. I could barely make out anything in that murky darkness but as my eyes became used to it, I smiled as I made out Mr. Hot 'n Tot, sitting alone against the wall.

He stood out even in that crowded, dark auditorium. He was a big guy with a slightly forbidding air about him. A motorcycle cap was pulled low over his left brow. A moustache made his lips look luscious and I made my way down to him.

At first, he didn't even glance at me but I saw him stiffen. You know how it is in a gay theater. Some creep plops down beside you and his cold fingers move over your thigh and all he wants to do is jerk you.

My mysterious lover had body heat so intense I could feel it even in that freezing hole. His black leather jacket was open. Beneath it, he wore nothing except his gleam of glorious muscles.

When he glanced down and recognized me, a big arm quickly went around my shoulder and he pulled me closer. Oh, how good that felt for I was trembling from the cold although I wore a fur-lined coat.

His moustache tickled my ear when he whispered: "Hey, little guy! Where you been so long? Been waiting here for you."

"My goddamned old man tried locking me up—the bastard. I told him I wanted to suck him off and get fucked by him and he nearly shit."

Mr. Hot 'n Tot snickered because he knew how hot I was for my father. Now, he pulled me even closer and kissed my cheek and then my mouth.

He had pulled his jacket away from his body and now my hands skimmed over his shimmering pecs and nipples. His tits bulged out like a woman's and I didn't care if I did make loud noises sucking those nipples.

My mouth traveled over his flat stomach, then lower so that he lifted up and pushed his soft leather pants down to his boots and then off.

His pubic was shaved smooth and I loved running my tongue over it because just an inch or two away was that juicy sucker which had already lifted up from between his thighs.

He only wore his biker's cap now as he leaned back and spread his thighs, ready for the action to begin. This guy always smelt clean and macho when I ate him and when he told me he only let one person do him—meaning me—I believed him.

Several men had stopped their eternal cruising in the aisles to watch our live sex show. A few even tried to move in and enjoy him, too, but he pushed their hands away.

This was strictly our treat that no one else could sample. His big hands were unusually gentle as he guided my mouth back to his jutting nipples and as I massaged the huge pectoral beneath them, it made me think of being an infant again and how I must have suckled my dead mother's breast.

I was aware of his manhood, though, growing bigger until it sprouted out from his hips like a big banana with a tip gleaming with honey. I covered the juicy head, with my fists grasping the stalk, and he grunted in delight as I began sucking hard on it.

My tongue darted deep into his slit to an unusual depth and he gasped this time. Gently, he humped my mouth. His balls were so large and resilient I squeezed them hard, steadily, as if trying to milk out the thick supply of sperm that simmered in his sac.

Mr. Hot 'n Tot writhed in his seat, breathing harsher with his cap almost hiding his eyes now. Faded colors from the cheap print of the movie on the screen spattered his white skin and I imagined to myself: this is Daddy, I'm doing! Wow, Daddy, I'm finally doing you!

Sticking my fingers deep into his foreskin, I brutally yanked it down from the sensitive head and once again began sucking on it as if it were a ball of pink candy stuck onto the end of a rubbery stick.

His stomach resembled an accordion as it rippled in and out. And suddenly, I felt his penis convulse as it lobbed out a thick spray of sperm—just as he had done it twice before during our trysts.

For several minutes, I let his organ soak in my mouth, felt it begin to soften as I tried drawing out the last remnants of his rare cream. He let me play with his prick sock like I had a handful of latex—stretching it, rolling it down, yanking on it until he took it away and began to dress.

Our rendezvous was over.

Before he left, he asked: "We'll meet again, in a week, on Friday night, same time?"

"I'll be here—if my father doesn't catch me!"

He kissed me then, smiled, squeezed my shoulder and vanished into the darkness. As I stood beneath the dingy marquee for a taxi, I thought of my father at home: his naked body curled up beneath a sheet, alone and here I was, listening to the invisible song of the streets, the one which only sidewalk whores like me can hear, and which made me want to live forever with a man sticking it up my arse or down my throat…

#

If Dante were gay, he would certainly have drawn inspiration for his inferno from the dark, sweaty, men-packed Beacon Baths near 42nd Street and Third Avenue.

Hidden away from the city, eight stories above the canyons of Manhattan, the wind and the rain whipped around the concrete building.

Like a city of dead men, pale figures glided relentlessly through the dim hallways, over moist carpeting, lit only by an occasional red bulb, past broken chairs stuffed away in dark corners, empty paper cups, a rare condom used and discarded, sticking to the foot of the zombie in front of you.

Putting on my towel, I joined this parade of anonymous men who wore one of two expressions: one of desperation so intense to find a sex partner that their eyes flashed with tears; the other one of arrogance and indifference so feigned I laughed out loud—especially when they groped under my towel to see if I measured up to the size of Long Dong Silver.

"Fuck off!" I hissed. "Go find some other stud with a 13 incher!"

I hated the type of men who were so mechanical about life that they wanted your private parts more than they wanted you as a person.

In the lounge, I paused to see what could possibly capture the interest on television of a dozen men in towels who had paid for lockers and rooms but who would never leave this area as long as they were there.

Why did they come here for? Companionship? Again, no one spoke to any others. They wore their invisible barricade which shouted: Do Not Touch or Speak to Me!

As I started to leave, though, I caught my breath in delight.

Standing against the wall was a blonde giant. He and I had gotten along passionately twice before. His name was Hans. Blonde hair hung to his formidable shoulders. His smooth, hairless torso was a dazzling monument to weight lifting. The skimpy towel barely covered his outstanding claim to manhood.

He might as well have been naked. You saw clearly the bottom of white, firm buttocks. Testicles weighed down so heavily in the soft sac one almost expected the tomato-sized balls to burst out.

Something even more thick and long glowed dully with a sheen of sweat. All of this was the object of many furtive glances from men standing close to him—but he was coolly ignoring them all while smoking a cigarette. Yes, I usually hated this arrogant type, whose body would forever be his main claim to glory and when his muscles would some-day sag, he would have nothing left.

He, too, was someone you would think was striking a pose, an insufferable exhibitionist but I knew his game by now and this act could be quickly dissolved if you knew how to do it. I did.

I went up to him and pulled the cigarette from his lips and stuck it between mine. I took a puff and let the smoke swirl above his big head. Looking down at me, he kept his face tight and inscrutable but I saw those blue eyes dance with great enjoyment.

The game was about to begin. He suddenly grinned, showing white, even teeth and he ran a pink tongue over his lips.

"Well, well," he said softly with a delicious accent, "am I actually being honored with the biggest slut in Manhattan? None other than the notorious Jason Fury who hates his Daddy but wants to ball with him?"

"Honey, I am none other than that fascinating creature and if you think I was hot the last time, watch out. Fasten your seat belt. It's going to be one fucking hot night."

I reached over and undid his towel, leaving him completely naked. He laughed for his "kick" was being a flamboyant exhibitionist. Nearly all eyes were on us now. I grasped his thick penis in my hand and used it as a pulley as I led him into the hallway.

He hugged me close to him, pushing me against the wall and kissed me for along time. "You hot little bitch," he whispered, "when you took off my towel, I wanted to cum right there. Everybody looking at me, wanting to rape me. Feel how hard I'm getting, Miss Hot Shit. You like playing games don't you, Miss Jason Fury? Hey, not too hard, I'm nearly ready to spurt."

He picked me up and carried me into the darkened game room. Several men paused their relentless cruising too watch this blonde Hercules holding someone who could have been his son.

Dozens of men were parked against the walls of the room that smelt of years of cum, piss, spit, sweat, even blood. I sensed their eyes on us and I wondered even in that moment what went on through their minds—never opening their mouths except to gobble, saying nothing, doing nothing, human question marks who glided away and who you would never in your life see again.

My golden-haired Atlas held me easily up in the air, against him, while he slipped my wrists into metal clamps. Then he brought my feet up and secured them into canvas ropes so that my ass was pointed directly towards his hips.

"Please don't hurt me," I simpered.

"You were born to be hurt," he laughed in genuine amusement for he had discovered I was nearly as decadent as he.

Pulling the sling forward, he guided the tip of his taut hard-on up against my anus. I cried out as the big head popped in. He paused for a moment, kissing me again as he drove more in until he was up to the hilt and I could feel his testicles brushing outside my buttocks.

Deep, deep he swiveled, as if he had a screwdriver of muscle jutting from his hips. He enjoyed letting his tool slip out so he could ram it roughly back in. A crowd of men had gathered around us now.

I could imagine what their eyes were fixated upon: a set of firm buttocks belonging to a gleaming giant; dimples quivering and wet as they fucked me, and his dark, taut penis slipping in and out in a steady rhythm, as if both of us were the parts of a well oiled clock.

I suddenly had an image of my father doing this and nearly fainted at the image of Nicky Fury, bare butt and rampant, fucking his own son in dark sleazy baths somewhere above a greasy, trash-filled street.

My real partner's breathing became harsher, his movements more intense and then he came. I could feel the swollen phallus pulsate but even more before he finished.I fell to my knees and began sucking him with no shame, exhilarated to be on my knees before this nocturnal god, behaving like a real 42nd Street tomcat.

Hans stood still and tensed and then he suddenly filled my mouth up with more of his nectar.

Taking the organ from my mouth, he brushed it across my face until it felt like I had syrup dribbled everywhere. I grabbed him again and stuck my tongue deep into his cock tunnel.

I wanted to slide down and live in his balls forever.

When I told him this, he smiled and said he would try to arrange it for our next rendezvous.

As we parted, I hugged him and sucked on his nipples once more.

"Hans," I teased with a laugh, "please don't hurt me!"

"Remember," he repeated, "you were born to be hurt. Ciao, baby."

#

In vain, I tried to find a cab on that desolate, wind-swept street as the freezing rain turned to ice.

There was no one around me except some drunken wino staggering down an alleyway. I was tempted to follow him and experience the thrill of blowing some filthy bum who probably hadn't washed in a year, for he had to have been a man once, someone who had enjoyed a love life, no matter how meager?

But then a green van passed by me slowly, driven by a man who stared at me very curiously.

The vehicle made a U-turn to return to where I stood. The driver rolled down the window near the curb and leaned toward me. He was a sex toy, alright—rough, macho, with black hair slicked back from his face that was sensual and hot.

"Hey, get in!" he said, snapping gum. "You need a lift somewhere?"

"I certainly do," I drawled, "but I don't know you. You could be a killer or a psycho or—"

"Fuck all that shit," he snorted, jerking his head for me to come closer. "You got nothing to worry about. I'm serious. Promise. I'm just Antonio, a nice Italian kid. I give you a lift home—you give me a blowjob. Fair enough. Look at my nice, big hard on. Look at it! I got it up just for you!"

Startled, but definitely intrigued, I approached him warily.

His jeans were around his ankles. With both hands, he rubbed his impressive organ over the lower part of the driver's wheel, bending it brutally and stretching and yanking at the foreskin.

"You like it, don'cha?" he whispered. "Come on in. I ain't no fruit. But I couldn't find any pussy tonight and I need some relief bad. Don't tell me you ain't interested. Yeah, you're licking those lips and drooling over Antonio's dick, ain't cha?"

"Antonio, I'm going to trust you now. Are you serious?"

"Get da fuck inside heah!" he snorted and pushed his pants on off and tossed them into the back. Then he peeled off his sweater to show me a dazzling chest and stiff nipples.

Dizzy from desire, I pushed my common sense aside and got in beside him. But I told him to drive to within a block of my home before I climbed into the back seat with him.

If he was going to prove to be a psycho, at least I'd be near home where I imagined that through some miracle, my father would hear my screams for help and rescue me. Yes, he could be a bastard but he always wanted to do the right thing. Imagine how it would look if the tabloids ran screaming headlines that Jason Fury, son of Wall Street Tiger, Nicky Fury, Butchered by Psycho and my father had stood idly by, listening to my piteous wails for help?

Antonio drove quietly, chomping gum, saying nothing and parked the van expertly between two cars. I could see my light glowing above and only then felt secure.

My Italian pickup was a wild, lusty stud, the type of macho hunk who puts his hand behind his head and spreads his thighs and lets you do anything you want to—just so you relieve him of his sexual tension.

He was already completely erect by the time I wrapped my hands around it and gobbled him down to his shaven pubic area. My partner grunted, snapped his gum, watching me with intense interest.

"I gotta blow," he grunted between crackles of gum.

He shot out so thickly that my mouth couldn't contain it all and it dribbled over his big balls and thighs.

"Eat my butt," he snarled and turned over. What a rear-end, this Italian stallion possessed! He was clean but hot and when my face sank down between the dimples, I felt like I had entered a city of sex and danger, excitement and mystery.

Where did he come from, where did men like Antonio go to after they left blonde-haired little tramps like me? He groaned as my tongue sank into his hole and he raised his hips slightly to push back his swelling phallus.

I pulled it up between his thighs and grabbed the juicy tip with my mouth. Then he turned over slowly until he was on his back and I managed to swallow him until my lips pressed against his pubic.

I felt him pulsing again and reluctantly drew my mouth after from this succulent all-night sucker. He pulled me close and I curled up in his brawny arms where I sucked on his nipples.

With a sigh, he pulled away and pulled on his torn jeans.

"Sorry, kid," he sighed, "but I gotta run. Got a date in about 15 minutes. In fact, the guy lives around here. He, eh, likes me to look a little scuzzy. Greasy hair, split jeans, you know the kind?"

"Oh, a guy, huh, Antonio? You go both ways, eh?"

My midnight lover shrugged and zipped up his jacket. "Maybe. This guy's a Wall Street banker. Big, muscle type. Black curls. A monster of a cock. Pays me $100 a visit. Nice. He even gave me a key to his apartment. He has a son home from school this weekend so I can't come by tonight."

For a moment, I couldn't move. "A Wall Street banker and he has a son?" I repeated slowly. "What's this guy's name?"

"No questions. You got maybe a $20 or $50 on you? Need some money for gas. Your wallet fell out back there and—"

"What are you doing with my wallet? You give me back my—"

He shoved me roughly away and calmly flipped it open and took out a $20, then threw me my wallet.

"Oh, I see,' I sneered. "You should have told me you were two-bit hustler, Antonio."

He slapped me across my face and smiled. "Hey, it's America, ain't it, you little cocksucking slut? You pay for certain services. I always deliver. Why complain? You got what you wanted. You're the type of homo who'd suck off a wino if you couldn't find a stud like me."

I jumped out of the van and screamed at him: "You two-bit hustler! You couldn't get it up for a woman anyway!"

Before I hurried away, I heard him call after me: "You shouldn't have said that! I'll get you! Nobody calls Antonio Gambino a hustler and lives!"

#

Silently I hurried past my father's room.

I saw no line of light beneath his door and it was quiet. He had probably been asleep for hours, little knowing what his wayward son had been up to.

Just as I threw on my new blue velvet robe after showering, I heard a slight noise in the hallway, like a door opening and closing in a stealthy manner.

My father wouldn't do that. If he wanted a drink he had his own bar. He had his own elaborate bathroom and sauna. None of our staff of 12 servants lived with us.

Cracking open my door, I saw a large figure moving quietly toward me.

It was Antonio!

He ran silently towards me, a murderous grin on his face.

I whirled around to slam my door but I was too late. He grabbed me and clamped a hand over my mouth. "Surprise! Guess who I've come to fuck tonight?"

I kicked him and tried biting his hand but he merely laughed and dragged me out into the corridor."

"I want your fag father to see what a queer son he's got!"

We were outside Daddy's bedroom now and Antonio kicked open the door.

"Daddy!" he hooted. "Look whose here and guess who I brought along? I got you a nice surprise!"

My captor clicked on the lights—

To reveal an empty bed.

#

Throwing me onto the gold comforter of my parent's bed, my tormentor stared down at me, smirking, as he tore off his clothes.

"Well, you gay nympho? What do you have to say for yourself?"

I threw my arms around my father.

"Ha!" I laughed, kissing him and running my hands up under his greasy jersey.

"You have fun tonight?" he laughed and fell on the bed beside me, pulling me close. "You like me in that blonde wig at the baths?"

"You were hot shit, Daddio, but I liked you even better as Mr. Hot 'n Tot at the theater."

"Damn, let me get some of this grease out of my hair!"

He jumped up and grabbed a towel and rubbed his hair with it. I went up to him and got on my knees. My fingers stroked the chiseled muscles of his stomach before caressing the thick length of his pride and joy.

"God you were sleazy as Antonio! And you swiped my $20, you bum!"

"Let's do it tomorrow night! New game, new disguises, new—"

I shook my head and put my arms around his neck. "Can't. It's the rules of the game. Next week. New game, new rules."

"And this time, I'll make the rules!" he snorted.

#

I glared at him from across the dining room table.

"How can you say something like that to me—your own son? I come home from college and—Christ, you've changed Daddy!"

Beneath the greasy red tee shirt, his big muscles danced. His handsome face was dark with a five-clock stubble. Guzzling a beer, he belched and stuck the toothpick into his mouth.

"What the fuck's bugging you, you slut? I told you I've come out of the closet and I'm a fruit and a fag and I wanna fuck that little bubble butt of yours. What's your problem? You gone and got religious or somethin'?"

I had gotten up from my chair and began backing away.

"I'm outta here," I said. "I don't want being around a pervert like you. I'll call up Jerry Springer or Ricki Lake and tell them if they're looking for a prick, you're the one they want."

He was already stripping off his shirt, jeans and boots as I began limping down the hallway.

But he caught me easily.

On the floor, his great white body lowered over mine and his hands ripped off my shorts and shirt. Digging himself into me, he kissed me rough and spit into my mouth.

He needed to bathe, to shave, his breath smelt like beer, cigarettes and—

The game was on.

THE STORY OF
SMOKEY JOE

◆

First, there was the father. Then came the son—and finally, all hell broke loose.

A rainy night in October began the chain of events which involved me with the fighting Johnson men. The empty lobby of an old building…a security guard's uniform…and a smile…these elements moved me quickly to the first link of that momentous chain.

He was a gorgeous black man, light-skinned in his early forties. A short crewcut topped a face both square and handsome. Above the full lips was a slight moustache. His torso was rugged and he certainly filled out his khaki shirt and trousers to the point of bursting.

I took all this in as I wearily left the elevator. Smiling, I greeted him and introduced myself as Jason Fury. For a security guard, he was a sizzling knockout. He returned the gesture, saying his name was Johnny and added: "So how we doin' tonight? You're really burning the midnight oil. You a college guy?"

"A struggling writer. Can't you tell by the bags under my eyes and pale complexion? I'm using a buddy's office here on the weekends to work on my novel."

"What kind of stuff you write, Mr. Jason Fury?"

Here came the test. When I told men I wrote stories about gay people, they registered one of two emotions: either they looked disgusted and nervous; or, their eyes flickered with interest and curiosity. Johnny's honey colored orbs registered the second.

"Sounds interesting," he smiled with a flash of white-on-white teeth. "Different strokes for different folks. I'd like to talk to you sometimes. Buy you a beer. Never met a writer before.""Ha, and you've never met one like me. I can promise you, Johnny, you won't be bored. Maybe next Saturday. About 10 p.m. That Okay?"

"Sure. I'll be ready."

Ready for what, I wondered as I hurried down the cold, rainy street to the Astor Place subway stop?

#

"You look like Clark Gable," I observed a week later. He led me out of the building into the dingy darkness of 14th Street.

"People tell me that," he smiled. "The black Clark Gable at your service."

Having changed from his uniform into a sensuous outfit of soft, black leather pants and jacket, he could have been a magazine cover boy. The jacket was unzipped halfway down his broad chest which was naked and shaven smooth. The material clung to his buttocks and thick thighs. It made his crotch look abnormally large, and as he moved, its contents shifted heavily from left to right.

Both of us were certainly attracting the attention of the drag queen whores and hustlers who inhabited that section of the block. They were whistling and making kissing sounds: "Hey, man, unzip those leather britches and let me swing on that!....Blondie, drop those drawers and let me dig into that boy's butt of yours!"

"You shouldn't be walking out here alone," he scolded me as we passed our admirers. "Killers and pill heads don't care who they murder for money."

"I can't even walk to the subway, Johnny, without a half dozen guys trying to rape me."

"Not with me around, they won't," he boasted and sure enough, the sidewalk inhabitants stared and called out, but they didn't try to touch the goodies.

My blonde looks and boyish torso had always drawn so much attention through my life it was like I had a neon sign above me, blinking: Look, Look and wonder! Over cans of beer at Mamie's, a bar that attracted cab drivers, men dressed up like women, yuppies and hard metal rockers, he described to me his brief heyday as a major boxing heavyweight.

Lack of discipline had made him loose it all. "I didn't want to give up booze, women and fucking. So here I am, working at $7 an hour as a knee-jerk guard."

He had a grown boy, a 23-year-old muscle child named Desmond, who called himself Smokey Joe. He wanted to be a prize ring boxer and fancied himself another Mike Tyson, the troubled prizefighter who had just been released from prison for attempted rape of a young woman.

From his wallet, Johnny withdrew two color photographs. Both were cracked and frayed. In one, he was shown ten years younger, a gorgeous hunk in boxing trunks. His gloved hands were ready to strike.

The second picture showed a sizzling dark Adonis in the very same pose. The pink lips of Smokey Joe pouted beneath a moustache. Eyes, black and angry, peered out from thick lashes. The same tawny-hued skin of his father's was present here in powerful musculature.

"Woo, Johnny, he looks terrific! Is he as mean as he looks?"

"Naw, he's a good kid. Wants to be just like me—as a fighter, I mean. Worries about me too much. Wants me to get married, stop drifting along."

"I've got to meet him, Johnny."

"Ha, no you don't. He hates guys like you. He gets real pissed off at me cause I've got some buddies who like other men. It just kills him. He and I fight, real fist fights now and then, but it don't mean nothing."

I hated homophobes and stuck a finger in my mouth. "Yucck. Keep that creep away from me. I can live without his kind."

Outside the bar, we approached the notorious Ring Cinema. This was a landmark in New York City, a legend among the city's gay community. Catering primarily to Manhattan's large population of deviant Asian, black and Latino men, it was well known that incredible sexual hijinks went on inside.

None of my white buddies would go near it, although they were fascinated by the stories they heard. Muggings and murders were routine. But it stayed opened around the clock.

"Johnny, let's go inside! It'd be great fun and I could tell all my friends."

Johnny snorted his amusement and said that what went on inside the Ring might shock me.

"So how would you know, hot shot?"

"Well, I go in there now and then to catch the flicks." His eyes danced wickedly and I burst out laughing.

"Sure you do. And you just sit there like a good little boy and watch, right? Please, Johnny. Nothing would happen to me if you were there with me. I mean, you're so big and tough looking…."

"Well…"

#

The cavernous like building literally teemed with men.

Was it steam—or just cigarette smoke—which swirled in the air? The powerful stench of piss, wine, cum, shit and spit was like an aphrodisiac.

Johnny put his arm around my shoulder for both of us were attracting many stares and I could see why: my companion was bigger than nearly anyone around and he filled out his leather outfit better than Marilyn Monroe in a tight sweater.

I was a walking symphony that night in a suede leather overcoat and purple beret which made my eyes look even bluer.

"If you wander around now," whispered my date, "you might get raped. Stay close to me. They don't see too many blonde-haired, blue-eyed dolls like you around—especially with an ass like yours."

Few members of the audience were watching the ancient, washed-out movie with Johnny Holmes and Seka. They were much too busy doing other things. We moved past a row of Latino boys who stood against the wall with their pants down around their ankles. In front of each one, men had squatted down and were sucking them greedily and rapidly.

Some men were fully naked and had leaned over the back of the seats while behind them, audience members fucked them.

In the balcony, it was even wilder. Several older men had crowded around one particular youth who wore nothing and sprawled in his seat with a quart bottle of Thunder Bird wine nestled in his arm. Two of his admirers traded the cock of the zonked out youth while others sucked on his nipples and toes.

In the corner, a black man lay nude on his back, with his legs pulled back. A beefy youth swiveled his fist up into the recipients butt. Others were pissing into the mouth of the fistee.

Husky drag queens in cheap clothes and big wigs prowled the aisles. Two of them fought over the swollen organ of an Oriental youth who resembled Bruce Lee. He seemed totally unaware of the battle since he was bare butt and another queen had already taken possession of his erection.

It was like a sexual jungle with animals fighting over their share of hundreds of tubes of meat, in all colors and sizes.

Johnny and I sat next to a grimy wall, speckled with glistening patches of old semen.

"Great place to bring your prom date," whispered Johnny and I laughed, while snuggling up to him. It was freezing in the theater and some of the drag queens were now engaged in a screaming, slapping fight while below us, another battle had broken out with wine bottles and beer cans being thrown.

With Johnny, though, I felt no nervousness at all. He sat near the aisle, as if making sure nobody was going to cross over him to get to me. My fingers pulled the zipper of his jacket all the way down. His handsome chest was completely exposed.

It thrilled me when he shrugged out of the jacket so that he was already half naked. My hands ran over his big biceps and caressed the trim pectorals which swelled out, each crowned with a thick nipple. I felt of them and fondled them and they seemed to get even harder.

"Johnny, you feel so warm—and hard."

"That ain't all that's warm and hard."

I was startled to see him raise his hips, peel down his leather pants and boots so that he was stark naked.

His phallus—thick, sticky and oval-tipped was rising up.

It was stunning for to behold this transformation—of big Johnny Johnson going from full clothed to completely bare-assed, without even any socks on his feet.

He was oblivious to the other men crowding the aisles who paused to watch him put his arms around me and pull me into his lap.

His kiss was intense—soft, warm, wet—and from his mouth mine moved to his nipples, down the firm stomach and on my knees, they found his fragrant erection.

During this time, he had helped me out of my clothes so that I was completely nude, with our clothes piled up in the seat next to the wall. The theater was notorious for queens who stole clothes from customers and then sold them off the streets.

Now, on my knees before him, I realized I was no different than the other whores there that night, acting like animals. Nor did I want to be any different. It thrilled me to see myself the neat, pretty, clean writer who popped his vitamins every morning, bare assed and nearly gagging with a black cock stuck in his mouth, kneeling on a floor littered with old and new sperm, empty wine bottles and paper towels stiff with dried spunk.

Johnny's organ was too thick to put completely in my mouth but the upper portion tapered to a bullet-shaped tip and this I worked on. My hands steadily milked him and my lips were relentless, so much so that he rewarded me with a sudden spurt of semen.

Johnny barely grunted as his dark pistol shot me full of its contents. Since I was the only white boy there that night, and one whose curls were so light it was like I wore silver neon, even more men had gathered around to watch our hot duo.

They wanted to turn it into a group thing but Johnny pushed their hands away and muttered ominously to those who couldn't take a hint.

Lifting me up onto his lap, I felt his hands moving around beneath me until I gasped when he edged himself up into me.

"Johnny, it hurts! You're so thick."

"Just hold on to me, baby, and I'll take care of everything. Hold tighter, put your head on my shoulder—ha, sounds like that song, don't it—yeah, I'm nearly there. Another few inches—Lord, it's there, it feels like magic."

Soon, his testicles bulged beneath my buttocks and he began to fuck me. For several minutes, we gave our watchers a treat since some had brought out their flashlights and beamed them at us. When he pulled out he blew out an impressive stream of whiteness up into the smoke filled air.

The crowd watching us clapped as if they had witnessed a stage act.

In a way it was like live entertainment during that wild night in the balcony of the most notorious den of perversion in America.

For this was only the first act in what became a three-ring circus.

#

Johnny began spending several nights a week in my small studio on Manhattan's posh Upper Side, located between Central Park and the East River.

He lived with his son in a rooming house in Harlem, just 20 blocks away, but Johnny said Smokey Joe got on his nerves.

"He's always getting on to me about my swish buddies."

"You've only got one swish buddy now, hot shot," I joked. "Don't go spreading your goodies elsewhere."

Usually I wanted no one near me at all when I wrote but he was different. Big, sexy, tender and thoughtful, he respected my need for quiet and at night, he waited in bed for me, enfolding me in those gleaming, strong arms, happy to allow me to scoot down and enjoy him.

He had a fighter's butt, one that was round and firm, and he liked me to rim him, just as much as I liked blowing him.

Together, we read the papers to follow the progress of his son in the boxing world. Smokey Joe had fought a string of anonymous amateur matches in New Jersey, winning them all.

Now, he was preparing for his first professional bout in Madison Square Garden. It would be one of several being held that month to display the rising young stars of the ring.

ABC's Wide World of Sports was even going to televise it as part of its series of unknown powerhouses, all on the brink of possible stardom.

Johnny would be 45 that January 27. I planned a big Southern feed for him for both of us were from the South. He hailed from Montgomery, Alabama and I came from that bustling metropolis of Denton, North Carolina.

On that cold but golden day, he went out to buy some champagne while I prepared some "White Trash" masterpieces: Mayonnaise biscuits, chicken livers covered with crumbled potato chips, a peanut butter pie and other dishes which only Dixie creatures like us could understand and love.

The doorbell rang. I opened it, expecting to find the birthday boy and his arm full of wine bottles. Instead, I was startled to find a stranger there, but what a stranger!

It was Smokey Joe. "Is my Daddy here?"

Reality was more flattering to the young boxer than his photographs. Like his father, he was big! A red windbreaker looked too small for those brawny shoulders. A scarlet sweatband made his shiny curls even more jet, glistening with mousse. Glittering in his right ear lobe was a blue diamond chip. A scar shaped like a small bolt of lightning made his pouting lips look even more pink and kissable.

But those eyes, peering at me from between thick, black lashes, were dark—and very hostile.

"You're Smokey Joe!" I sang out. "I've been wanting to meet you, you fighter you! Come on in. Your Daddy's gone out for some wine and stuff."

Smokey Joe pushed by me into my den. "Humph! Just what he don't need. Wine! I'm trying to keep him off the sauce. You don't need trying to get him back on it."

"My, my," I drawled sarcastically. "Don't tell me. You've come checking up on him, haven't you? You want to see if he's drinking and, eh, living with a queer? Is that it, Smokey Joe?"

I can't keep my cool around gay baiters and standing before me now was a perfect example of one. His whole look and attitude reeked of a super homophobe. He might be Johnny's son and he might look like a gay man's wet dream but I knew instantly that I wanted nothing to do with him.

I stalked into the kitchen where I went on with my preparations, try-ing to ignore this arrogant prick. Johnny was due back at any moment and I'd let him take care of his son.

He had followed me and leaned up against the wall and even through my blaze of disgust, I had to admit, this kid was an eye full. You could see he took care of his bod. His jeans were filled out alright and his black work boots and gleaming curls were then popular at all the in nightspots around the city.

"Watch out, Smokey Joe," I sneered. "Aren't you afraid you might catch some dread disease? I'm one of them flaming fags, you know and my germs are all over the place."

His face was hard and cold. "I wanted to take my old man out tonight to celebrate and I find him here with you."

"You poor little thing," I mocked. "Your old man's 45 today so don't you think he can make up his own mind?"

He was studying the casseroles and dishes I had prepared and I watched him pick up a fried chicken leg. "I don't want my Daddy eating this greasy, redneck food, fixed by somebody whose probably got AIDS."

I was dumbfounded when I watched him hold his fingers over the trashcan and drop the food into it. I slapped his hand and shoved him toward the door.

"Get the hell out of here, Mr. Black Pride! My redneck food will probably make you sick. Go fuck your girls and eat your goddamned health food and play the black macho stud elsewhere. I don't want your arrogant ass around me. So get out!"

I had thrown open the door but Smokey Joe looked murderous. His mouth tightened into a thin line and his hands curled up into fists. But just at that moment, Johnny entered the room.

"You like snooping around me, don't you?" he said and put his bags down on the table. "I heard what you said to Jason and I want you to apologize to him right now."

Smokey Joe had moved out into the hallway where a short flight of stairs led to the street. "You told me you'd finished that fag shit, Daddy?" he shouted. "You said that last queer, Jerry, would be the last homo who'd swallow your dick! And you're staying with this AIDS carrying cocksucker who—"

Johnny walloped him across the face, sending the boy reeling down the steps and onto the sidewalk.

That was when all hell broke loose.

Johnny had followed him down and it was like having a boxing match right there in the open. Bikers and joggers and pedestrians quickly gathered around as they usually do, to watch this drama of two big men, knocking the hell out of each other.

They fell down on the pavement, kicking, pounding, cursing and grunting. Blood gleamed on their upper lips and chin. When they staggered to their feet, Smokey Joe grabbed his father's shoulder, swung him around and struck him so hard that Johnny fell back between two cars and out into the street.

While trying to get to his feet, a Yellow Cab zoomed toward him, smashing into my boyfriend. He was thrown back onto the sidewalk where he lay crumpled up like a stack of old rags.

His left leg curved at a grotesque angle beneath him.

He was quickly surrounded by the gawkers but I pushed them aside and fell to my knees. "Johnny? Oh, my God, somebody call an ambulance! He's badly hurt!"

Smokey Joe had stooped down, too, and started to put his hands under his father's shoulders but I shoved him back.

"You keep away from him, you killer! It's your fault! You goddamned murderer!"

#

Johnny wasn't killed but he did suffer a broken leg and fractured ribs. At the hospital, I gave orders that Smokey Joe was not to be allowed to step foot into his father's room.

Several of Johnny's husky fighting buddies were there and they were only too glad to enforce my wishes. They didn't like the cocky, obnoxious son of their good friend.

One of Johnny's old girlfriends, Eula Mae, was a beautiful black woman from Harlem. She and I were his most constant visitors and we happened to like each other.

It didn't bother me that my boyfriend was bisexual and I knew there were probably others in his life. Someone as good looking as Johnny could hardly be expected to be monogamous. Eula Mae knew this, too, and she and I went off to smoke in the corridor each day while the nurses tended to their patient.

She wanted Johnny to come and stay with her in her big Brownstone home in Harlem where she ran her own beauty salon. This relieved me since my tiny studio was hardly the place for a recovering hospital patient.

When I told her how much I hated Smokey Joe she laughed wisely. "Oh, he can be a bastard alright. You want to strangle him, thinks he knows it all. But he's basically good. Really loves his father. You need to make him understand that being gay don't make you a monster."

"Ha, ha, ha," I snorted. "I'll never speak to that black bastard again."

Eula Mae howled. "Black bastard! Honey, that's a perfect name for him. Instead of Smokey Joe, those announcers should say: And over in this corner is the Black Bastard!"

When Johnny regained consciousness, he found me, Eula Mae and his buddies all around the bed. "Where's—where's my boy?"

"He's not getting anywhere near here, Johnny. It was his fault all this happened."

Johnny said nothing but looked uneasy. Eula glanced at me and raised her brows while rolling her eyes, as if saying: blood is thicker than water.

I was waiting alone at the elevator, after spending several hours with Johnny. Behind me was a crowded waiting room, filled with visitors leafing through magazines, babies screaming, nurses and doctors walking along the corridor.

A disheveled figure got up from one of the chairs and came over to me. I ignored him.

"Look, goddammit, I want to talk to you," growled Smokey Joe. "I want to get in and see my Daddy and they won't let me because you said so."

"Fuck off!" I snarled. "Don't bother me. You might get AIDS."

He grabbed my shoulders and whirled me around so that I was forced to look up at him. His face was gray and hollow-eyed. Those lustrous curls, which had gleamed with oil and gel before, were now matted. I liked seeing him looking like any other street punk.

"You're making it hard for me," he said. "I didn't mean anything to happen to my Daddy. He and I fight all the time."

"You arrogant prick! You ruined everything. It was beautiful before you came along, fucking everything up. You like playing God, don't you? Then go to some church and play it. We don't want you around."

He was staring at the floor and then without looking up, I heard him sigh: "If it makes you feel any better, I'm sorry about what I said to you. I wish it hadn't happened. You're—you're different from the other fags—I mean other gay guys I've seen him with."

"Gee, that makes me feel so great!" I sneered and sailed into the elevator.

#

But blood is thicker than common sense, I thought, and despite my arguing, Johnny insisted I let his son into the hospital room. When I protested, Johnny lectured me:

"He's my flesh and blood, Jason. Damn, I could just as easily have knocked him out into the street. Now, you go over there like my sweet Jason Fury can do and just open up that door—yeah, just a lil' bit. And let him in."

Reluctantly, I stood aside as my nemesis stepped warily into the room.

He saw not only me glaring at him but Johnny's old boxing buddies staring daggers at him. Eula Mae was the only to go over and kiss his cheek. She escorted him to the bed where he stood like an awkward kid.

Johnny winked at him. "I ain't gonna kill you, Smokey Joe, so don't go acting it. I want you and my good little buddy here, Jason, to shake hands. I know you're both as stubborn as mules but I want you to do it for me."

I looked away, preening in my indignation and Smokey Joe stared at the floor. Eula Mae smothered a grin but she grabbed my hand and Johnny took that of his son.

"I want you two stubborn mules to shake hands," he commanded again. "Or I ain't getting out of this bed."

"Johnny," I muttered, "I could kill you—"

"No, you don't because Smokey Joe's already tried it and see? I'm still alive. Now, shake."

I moaned and grimaced and looked everywhere but at Smokey Joe. He did the same but somehow I felt my hand in his. We shook. And then I whirled around and announced grandly that I had work to do.

Before I left, though, I heard Eula Mae saying to Smokey Joe: "Now, that wasn't so hard to do, was it?"

"I wanted to but he really is stubborn, ain't he?"

"He really thinks you're cute and just doesn't want to say it," snickered Johnny.I started to march back and correct them but I didn't want to see that hateful, conceited face of Smokey Joe ever again.

#

"Are you going to be in for the next few minutes?" Eula Mae said over the phone.

"Sure. I'm not going anywhere."

"Okay, I'll be right up. I'm at the corner where you live. I'm bringing you something from Johnny. A surprise."

"Eula Mae, he shouldn't have!"

"Maybe you'll wish he hadn't after you see what it is. Bye."

Now what did she mean by that?

When the doorbell rang, I opened it curiously. She stood there, in her mink coat and matching hat, grinning strangely.

"Come on in, honey," I said. "But where's your gift?"

"Right here and don't you dare send it back because Johnny won't take it."

She reached over and pulled someone into view.

"Oh, no, you don't!" I cried. "I shook hands with Mr. Mike Tyson, Jr., but that doesn't mean I'm going to be friends with him."

"You shut up and be nice to him or I'll tell Johnny," Eula Mae drawled. "You two guys act civilized and Jason, just give Smokey Joe ten minutes of your time. He wants to make up to you.""Did you say make me or make up?"

Eula Mae screeched and hurried away and even a glimmer of amusement danced in the young boxer's eyes as he stepped into my den, his arms laden with two brightly wrapped boxes.

"Look, I didn't want to come over here either," he muttered, "but they made me do it."

"Oh, be quiet and say your spill and then please leave. I'm very busy. I'm writing a story about how I accidentally castrated a certain young boxer who wanted to be like Cassius Clay but who had the personality of a rattlesnake."

He snickered with a roll of his eyes. "Okay, okay, I don't want to stay any longer than I have to."

He started to sit beside me on my sofa but I ordered him to take a chair across the room.

"You just stay right over there, Smokey Joe. I don't want to end up being thrown out the window and land in front of a taxi. I don't know why they don't call you the Black Bomber. Or the Black Tornado."

His luscious mouth tightened but I saw a grin tug at his lips. He gave me the first box and I saw that his fingers trembled. He was nervous! My contempt melted a little at that, but not much.

I tore off the wrappings and found a big box of Snicker Candy Bars—my only vice. Well, maybe there are a few others.

"Oh, my Lord!" I said, trying like hell not to smile. "Now I'll really have to join Weight Watchers. Did Johnny buy me this?"

"He most certainly did not!" huffed Smokey Joe. "I did it. He told me you liked Snickers and so—I brought it."

He looked so awkward and uncomfortable but proud that I felt a little sorry for him. "Well, I can't refuse it so, thank you, Smokey Joe."

"Hurry up and open up the second box so I can get out of here."

He looked around, trying to look cool and indifferent but I sensed he was very much interested in my reaction. He had sat down beside me but I didn't order him away.

This box was heavier, it felt cold and when I opened it I was startled to find two bottles of chilled champagne.

"Smokey Joe!" I squealed. "Is this from you, too?"

"Yeah, it's from me," he sniffed. "Now, I've done what I promised them I'd do and I'm going home. I don't want you to have to be afraid of the Black Bomber or the Black Tornado tearing up your place. 'Bye."

He stood up but I instinctively grabbed his arm. He wore his usual red windbreaker and had jazzed up his hair into curls of jet with gel and mousse.

"Listen, sit back down," I asked. "I've been a prick and so have you. Let's face it. We're both assholes but I think I had reason to be and—"

"You were mean and hateful and racist and—," he muttered but I grabbed his hand and squeezed it.

"Shut up! Let's don't get started again or my walls will be spattered with blood and I happen to like them gold. And so help me if you start that fucking racist crap I will crown you over the head with a bottle. How about some champagne?"

He rubbed his neck and rolled his eyes. "I shouldn't. I'm in training. But, maybe a small glass full."

In the kitchen, I got out two goblets but made an exaggerated gesture of scalding them beneath the hot water. "See, Smokey Joe? You won't get any diseases. They're all nice and sterilized. Of course, you know that by just entering my hell hole, you're being exposed to AIDS."

He raised a fist up and waved it at me. "You're really cruising for a bruising, ain't you?"

"I'm sorry. I just can't believe we're acting this way after we both wanted to kill each other a few hours ago."

He sat across from me, rather than on the sofa and we made small talk about his world of boxing and I told him about my boring life as a writer and how all of my stories were based on fact.

"You really writing a story about me?" he asked too innocently. Oh, what an ego, this kid had!

"Are you kidding? You're too boring. You don't like fags like me. Remember? Also, my stories have a lot of sexy stuff. You don't approve of that so that leaves out. But oh, boy, there is this older, former boxer I know and he's dynamite in bed although he was hit by a taxi."

He sighed and looked around. "Well, what else do you need? You've had the father, so you should know all about balling with him."

"The father has this very hunky looking son. But he's such a homophobe I don't see how I could write about someone like that."

Smokey Joe burst out laughing and put his glass down. "Knowing you, you'll find a way."

At the door, he stammered and hemmed and then blurted out his question: would I like to come and watch him workout at the gym? He understood I had several fans that hung out there who had read my stuff and they were all curious about meeting me.

"Maybe they're the aggressive type and come on too strong?" I said with a wide-eyed look of innocence. "Some of my fans, Smokey Joe—wow, they just get so carried away and all—"

"Don't worry," he boasted. "I'll be there. They won't try anything."

"Oh, you're such a macho stud!" I squealed and burst out laughing at his embarrassed expression. "Smokey Joe, I can look out for myself but thanks for the offer anyway. Yes, I'd love to come along."

"Come down in a coupla hours, then. I'll let them know you're on your own way."

When I met him there at Swanson's Gym, a sweaty, unpainted hole on Bleecker Street, several old and young fans that hung out there brought copies of my books to autograph.

Smokey Joe watched them gathering around me and when I finished, I went up to him. "How does it feel to have a famous and notorious pervert here to watch you practice?"

"Stop saying things like that," he demanded. "You don't act like the usual fags, I mean, gays who hang out here."

"You've said that before. Okay, I'll accept it as a compliment. Can I watch you change clothes in the locker room? As a writer, I want to experience everything. Or are you afraid I might try to rape you?"

"Geez, you really are acting faggy," he joked but he didn't mind at all when me and nearly a dozen others joined him in his room and saw him strip naked.

Wow, I thought, he looks exactly like his father did 20 years before. Smokey Joe was a gorgeous, dark Apollo with those smoldering eyes, full lips and body by Michelangelo.

His torso was shaven and powerful and he took obvious pride in his manhood which I watched him stuff into a jock strap. He glanced up just then and grinned.

"Am I as big as Daddy?"

"Ask me no questions and I'll tell you no lies," I joked. "To be serious, I can say for sure that you are a true son of Johnny Johnson."

He was, indeed, even down to the thick roll of foreskin, which tapered for several inches over the tip. While he was in the ring, sparring with a buddy, his other friends told me he was preparing for a big match with Kid Kalahari of New Mexico.

In one week, the ABC TV cameras would be recording it on tape for their popular Wide World of Sports.

In the locker room, he came out of the shower and seemed completely natural about his nudity. I didn't try to hide my fascination with him and when I jokingly asked if I could dry off his back, I was surprised when he handed me a clean towel.

"Go ahead," he said.

I let the fabric slide over his smooth skin, down to his buttocks which rose high and smooth. My towel went into his cleft and then I ran it between his thighs, over his genitals and when he turned around, his was visibly becoming aroused.

His friends saw this, too, and they snickered and nudged each other.

"I see that you're uncut, like your Daddy, Smokey Joe," I smiled. "Can you do the tricks he does with his foreskin?"

"You mean this?" We watched him stick his fingers into the soft folds of flesh and then he stretched it out, all the way up to his stomach.

"Yep, that's what he likes to do," I laughed. After he dressed, he took my arm and we went out to the curb.

"I thought we'd drop by and see the old man," he told me. He saw that I was in the cab first before joining me. He's treating me just like he would a date, or a girl, I thought with interest.

I was discovering that he was more like Johnny than he wanted to realize.

#

Eula Mae was sitting with Johnny when we entered the hospital room.

Both of them grinned big when they saw us.

"See?" hooted Johnny. "What did I tell you? If Jason liked me, then he's gonna love Smokey Joe."

"Slow down, old timer," I said dryly. "We've just decided not to kill each other, that's all. I don't want to end my writing career at Sing Sing Prison."

Smokey Joe had gone into his defiant, young hood mode. "Yeah, we shook hands and that's all there is. Ain't anything else to it."

"Yeah, sure," snorted Eula Mae. "Like father, like son, I always say."

Smokey Joe pretended to be indignant. "Now, I don't want you going saying that. Daddy can swing with fags, I mean, gays if he wants to, but that ain't my style."

I stared at them and rolled my eyes. "Please, don't anybody go off the deep end. Since we both are rather fond of Johnny, then it makes sense for us to try and get along."

We joked and laughed some more but when I had to leave, Smokey Joe insisted he escort me home.

In the cab, I explained to him why it wasn't necessary, although I was secretly glad to have him with me.

"I'm not some helpless, frail little fruit, Smokey Joe," I laughed.

"I know you ain't, but Daddy tells me how that blonde hair and that ass of yours gets you the wrong attention so I don't want you to worry any. I'm here since Daddy can't be."

"Oh, you Johnson men, I swear!"

#

But he began to visit me nearly every afternoon and we'd often go to the gym where I'd watch him workout for the big night. His trainer,

Gormo, a wiry little Latino man, studied his every move and then he'd rub him down after a workout.

While they talked and bitched, I'd stand by and drool over the way Gormo would casually slide his hands down within the upper thighs of the boxer, then into his cleft.

And when Smokey Joe would turn over, Gormo would continue babbling in Spanish and run his hands over the boy's heavy privates, leaving them all glistening from the baby oil.

When we visited Johnny the next day, he and Eula Mae informed us that he was moving into her townhouse that weekend where she had prepared him his own room.

She was also having a big party for the big night when Smokey Joe fought Kid Kalahari.

"Honey," she told me, "if you wanna see some really fine black men, you'll find them there. Most have been boxers and they're working as cops and construction workers. They're all big, sexy hunks. And they definitely will go crazy over a blonde gay guy like you!"

"Dahlin', I'll be there," I promised, "and I won't be wearing any underwear."

#

It was the night before the big fight.

I had invited Smokey Joe over for a light supper for he was comfortable with me. He had discovered that despite his convictions, I hadn't tried groping him or trying to seduce him.

Instead, I often even made this serious young man burst out laughing which wasn't easy. Even his doting father nicknamed him "Mr. Stone Face."

I regaled him with some of my experiences interviewing some of the movie stars. Even more hysterical were the Southern politicians and evangelists I'd written about when I was a star reporter in North Carolina, North Dakota and in Montgomery, Alabama.

I'd made us a zesty vegetable lasagna casserole along with a pasta salad and served it with Chablis wine.

In the den, I put on an old Clovers album and was surprised when Smokey Joe recognized the group, whose heyday was in the early 50s. They were singing "One Mint Julep" and my visitor nodded his head to the rhythm.

"Daddy loved that group," he smiled.

"I know. That's why I like playing it. Your father and I used to dance to it."

"Did he?" Smokey Joe asked. "Well, if he can, maybe I can to. Would you care to dance?"

"You boxers scare me," I smiled. "But all you black kids have rhythm, ain't that right?"

Johnny had screamed with laughter at my "black jokes" and even Smokey Joe snickered.

"And you gay white boys are always wanting a black man's cock, ain't that right?" he rejoined. He stood up and held out his arm. "Come on. I ain't never danced with a man before."

"And especially not with a blonde fag like me," I teased, "so you'd better protect your family jewels.""

He was wonderfully graceful and strong, just like his father. I felt the hardness of his muscles as we moved around the living room.

"What did my father like to do with you—in bed?" he murmured.

I looked up and saw his eyes staring down at me. "Sorry, Smokey Joe, but that's a secret."

"I mean, you have to have done something different for Daddy to have flipped out over you like he did? He knew a lot of white gay boys but you're the only one he dated regularly. Couldn't you just hint at what made you special?"

"Just what are you trying to say to me, you black stud, you?" I lisped and let my hand slide down to his crotch. I squeezed it and it didn't seem to faze him.

But he startled me when he grunted: "I don't mean just that. People squeeze me all the time down there. When you're a boxer, guys are always feeling me up. It had to be something else. How did you first two, eh, well, how did you start it all?"

I was thrilled that things were moving so quickly toward the bedroom for I missed Johnny terribly and here was his son, making it very clear that he wanted to carry on the tradition.

Quickly improvising, I ran my hand over his impressive manhood again. "Actually, he had seen me home because I told him about all these crazy whackos trying to rape me and I put on a record, the very one we're dancing to, and then—he kissed me."

"How?"

"Smokey Joe! I swear, sometimes you act so slow—oh, hell, like this!"

I pulled his face down and then it all began to happen, as if this were just the signal he had been waiting for.

His mouth was electrifying—strong, boyish but moist and sweet. He pulled me closer until he had lifted me off the floor. My hand slid up beneath his jersey, over the prominent pecs and felt the nipple stiffen.

It was clear that he had fantasized this happening, too, for he pulled me swiftly to my bed and laid me down while quickly stripping off his clothes and slut that I am, mine flew into a corner.

It was like having a younger version of Johnny there with me. His ebony body gleamed in the soft light and after passionate kissing, he guided my face down his torso.

His nipples were unusually thick, just as his father's were, and from there, I had his body rippling as he lay there, grunting and gasping in delight.

He had rolled down the foreskin so that by the time I reached it, the head was totally revealed, in all its pink beauty. Honey had oozed out of the slit and I covered all this succulent morsel with my mouth.

Unlike his father, Smoke Joe's phallus was more slender and longer, which meant I could take more into my mouth.

He whimpered, writhed and gasped as I began sucking him hard with no intention of being sensitive. I sensed tenderness was something he did not want. We rolled around the bed, he pushed himself up into me until his groin snuggled within my cleft.

When he prepared for eruption, Smokey Joe slowly arched his hips, so that I could see him burst. On my back and with my legs pulled back, I looked down to see his erection flip up towards his stomach.

A stream of whiteness squirted out, spattering my neck and stomach. Others followed until he fell on top of me and hugged me tight.

"Man, I never felt anything like that, Mr. White Gay Boy!" he murmured. "Let me try letting off steam in your mouth."

His tongue began licking my face and nostrils, the eyes and then he moved up until he sat gently on my chest and guided his sticky manhood between my lips.

My young lover wasn't as experienced as his father—but he made up for it in sheer passion and intensity, transforming my bed into a boxing ring of sensuality.

His hips moved back and forth slowly and he tried to push himself past my tonsils but when I gagged, he withdrew slightly. He startled me by suddenly ejaculating again, within only a few minutes after beginning.

As we lay there, recovering as if we had both endured a prolonged match on the mat, I rolled him over on his stomach.

If he was anything like his father, my lathering his anus with my mouth would drive him to near hysteria. And it did. His rump was highly mounted, two gleaming tributes to daily workouts. My face was buried in that succulent darkness and my hands had moved down beneath his hips and milked his organ until it was once more taut.

This time, I pulled it up and sucked him off like that, and watched his hole pulsate with each surge.

"Can I stay here tonight with you?" he asked. "I know I'll be a winner—if I can just think about being here—with you."

"If you try leaving me," I threatened, punching him lightly on that rippled stomach, "I'll knock you out."

He smiled, pulled me against his body again and incredibly, became rampant so fast that he was on top of me again, humping his hips and kissing me with passion.

Before we slept, I turned my face to his and after kissing him asked; "Smokey Joe, may I come to see you fight tomorrow night?"

He shook his head as his hips began their dance of passion. "I don't want anybody I know there tomorrow night I want to do it alone—and when I've made it big, I want you all there."

He sensed my disappointment because he took my face between his hands. "Look, just keep watching me on the TV screen. If I win, I'll blow you a kiss—like this and give you a big wink. That'll be for you and you only."

"And you won't be thinking of your Daddy?"

"Well, maybe I'll be thinking of him, too, when I do that."

"Oh, you Johnson men, I swear!"

#

A crowd of us gathered around Eula Mae's supper table the next night.

It was a dieter's nightmare because it was impossible to resist all that deep fried chicken, hush puppies, black-eyed peas and barbecued pork and chocolate pies and fudge cakes and puddings.

Tin tubs of iced beer were placed strategically so you didn't have to walk far for a bottle of brew. True to her word, there were a dozen or more gorgeous black men who all looked like they had just won physique or boxing championships.

They clustered around me, since word had gotten out that not only had Johnny Johnson flipped out over me, but his son, too.

Each of them gave me their telephone number, some thrust raunchy Polaroid shots of themselves into my hand and they all made me promise to call.

I was startled as they pressed up close to me, thrusting their phalluses brazenly into my hands, begging me to "do," them right there, or at least jerk them off.

"Please, guys!" I gasped. "Eh, not here, if you don't mind. I mean, I have a reputation to keep up!"

We screamed with laughter when Johnny pushed up against me and drawled: "What reputation?"

Then it was time to settle around the big TV set to watch Smokey Joe achieve either boxing stardom—or anonymity.

Johnny, the guest of honor, sat between me and Eula Mae and everyone in the room whooped and shouted when our young gladiator burst upon the screen.

Stunning in a red silk cape, matching trunks, he looked exactly like a café au lait version of Rocky Balboa with a moustache and blue diamond stud in his ear.

Something electrical, theatrical and magnificent jumped out at us as the camera moved in closer. Smokey Joe could have been a movie star…sweat glistened on his rippling physique, his black eyes flashed, his white teeth dazzled.

The bout with Kid Kalahari was vicious and draining to all of us watching. The combatants punched each other like they wanted to kill and quickly, we saw rivulets of blood on both their faces.

The Kalahari Kid gave Smokey Joe an unusually powerful blow and knocked him to the floor. Everyone thought this was it. We screamed for him to get to his feet and then he staggered up and went after his opponent with a hurricane blast of energy.

And when he knocked him out, both the spectators and us at Eula Mae's were jumping and shrieking with joy.

"That's the boy!" cackled Johnny. "Another Johnson male in the ring!"

Still watching the screen, I saw the TV camera move closer in on the champion's face. He put a gloved fist to his mouth, kissed it—and winked.

I threw my arms around Johnny and he hugged me tight. "You've got a winner on your hands, old man."

"Make that two," he laughed, kissing me. "He told me what he'd do if he won and it'd be just for you. So you helped put him there, buddy, with all those hot little sessions in bed! I told him you'd bring him good luck!"

"You mean you planned all this?"

He winked and I pretended to strangle him.

"Oh, you Johnson men, I swear!"

THE FINAL DAY

◆

September 1.

I slashed it out of existence on my calendar with a black crayon. Twelve more days and I would be a free man.

It was ironic, I knew to consider myself a prisoner. I was, after all, Jason, the dynamic, young director of the Carroll Halfway House for male convicts. I could come and go whenever I wished. The dozen men in my facility had to stay locked into a rigid routine through the week—and on Saturday and Sunday, it was back to the slammer.

However, after a six-months period, and if they were deemed qualified, these inmates were released from the jungle of brutal, degrading steels and live out probation in the free world.

We all carry our bars, in some ways, though, and I wanted out of this environment. It would be only a matter of time before I succumbed to temptation.

The twelve men in my house, especially one, were more than willing to help me give into my desires. And some of them were gorgeous, indeed, and starved for love. That could never happen, though.

It would destroy our professional relationship. I didn't want the word to go out over the prison grapevine that all one had to do get that crucial nod for freedom was to sleep with blonde, boyish Jason—he of the large blue eyes, trim torso and shapely rear end.

It had received numerous playful pinches in the house to indicate it was on the minds of all twelve men.

Three fifteen. Rufus was late—as usual. My office was like a steam bath since the air conditioner was again on the blink and the Mississippi sun in August is a horror.

I thought about my "men" for my dozen charges made up a big family. And as in all big families, there were those you liked, detested and adored. Some need little help to get by. Some need all they can get. Rufus was one of them and yet, despite his moodiness, he was the most popular man at Carroll House.

Just then, the door opened and Rufus sauntered in. My heart jumped as it always did whenever I saw him. Trying to act calm, I forced my face into a frown. "You're late, Rufus," I said quietly. "Your employer, Mr. Whatsisname at the bank, called up to say you were late this morning, too. That'll have to go on your record."

None of my words seemed to penetrate the consciousness of the magnificent black man who now walked to the chair in front of my desk. He was naked except for a pair of skimpy red nylon shorts and a towel around his neck.

His ebony skin shimmered with sweat. Pectorals and stomach and powerful thigh muscles all danced with each movement of his gait. Sprawling in the chair, his dark eyes studied me but they were nearly hidden by thick lashes.

It was always impossible for me to tell what was really going on behind that square face. There was a lot of fury, frustration and vindictiveness swirling around—but there was a strong thread of tenderness, too. I had seen it.

"Sorry," he said in that soft, musical voice which enchanted me. "Been lifting the weights." He glared at the air-conditioner. "Shit, ain't that fucker been fixed yet? Like hell in here."

Like a kid, he was trying to change the subject. I leaned forward. "Look, my dear buddy and friend, it's crucial you be on time in the real world. You'll be fresh out of prison. People are going to judge you much more severely than the most stupid moron in the office."

He smiled slightly, his black eyes glinting with an intense emotion. "Maybe I got a problem, man, and you ain't helping me with it."

"A problem?" I answered coolly but I knew what it was. We had gone round and round on this issue. In fact, it was this problem which had forced me to tender my resignation to the prison board. I couldn't hold out much longer. You see, I have this obsession about being a professional. I wanted nothing to mar my record, least of all, a charge that I had been romantically involved with one of my prisoners.

Watching me intently, Rufus put his hands on his crotch and began kneading it like he had a mass of rubber in there.

I was suddenly so exhausted with trying to dodge him on this issue and playing games with him, I sighed. "Okay, Rufus. What can I do?" I lit a cigarette with trembling fingers.

My visitor pulled down the front of his briefs. He tugged and stretched until his dark genitals overflowed the palm of his hand. He kicked aside his briefs. Standing halfway up, he plopped the heavy weight of his penis down on top my desk.

Glossy and smooth and thick, it was uncut. The big wattle of foreskin was securely tied with a length of thin leather. In prison ritual, this means no one but the loved one can suck on this meat—or have it crammed up the ass.

Rufus loved someone—and that was why I was having to leave because that someone was me.

"Untie the knot," he pleaded. "Please, baby, just help me some. It's really hurting, Jason. All you gotta do is untie it—and watch."

My hand trembled even more visibly as I loosened the sweat-drenched thong of leather. Rufus rolled the foreskin back. The tip, gummy and sticky with cock syrup, resembled a purple mushroom. I was startled by the enormous slit, which had parted slightly and was issuing bubbles of clear honey.

Silently, he continued his act of the frustrated lover. Bending over this chocolate-colored length of hose, Rufus put the palms of his hands on it and pressed it down hard—like he was trying to flatten a coil of clay. "Sometimes when I got me a load backed up in there," he muttered, as if to himself, "I gotta treat it real rough."

It was like he held a bloated sausage in his hand for he suddenly slammed his pecker down on the top of the desk so hard that the head bounced up—like a rubber ball. He winced, went "Ahhh!" and whammed it again and again. The glass top of my desk was becoming streaked with the sticky lubricant from his organ.

It was definitely swelling up bigger. A classic prick masochist, Rufus ran his toy over the sharp edge of my desk—and all the time staring at me accusingly. Then he put his palm on the tip and proceeded to bend the stalk double.

"Christ, Rufus!" I gasped. "You're gonna hurt—"

Quickly, he had stepped up onto the top of my desk. He squatted down, spreading his legs wide. He smelt like an animal—sweaty and sexy and wonderful. Both his hands were working brutally on his genitals. Then he edged back until he tottered slightly on the edge.

He thrust his hips towards me. "Grab it!" he ordered. "Or I'm falling back and people are gonna ask questions why I smashed my head on your cement floor."

Silently, I had watched this flamboyant exhibition of sexual abandon. I knew I should have been protesting and acting shocked. But I was thrilled with what he was doing. He wasn't trying to act like a stud.

He was one. But I attempted one last display of professional cool.

"Rufus, you can't—"

"I'm falling," he cried. "Better grab my fucker or I'm smashing down hard."

It was like something out of an X-rated cartoon because I had never seen anything like it in an X-rated movie. I jumped up and grabbed his enormous package of manhood—balls and pecker—with both hands and held them like a rope.

All that kept him form falling backwards was my trembling grip on a greatly stretched phallus and sac.

"Rufus, it's too slippery, I've got to let go!"

He grinned, clasped his hands behind his neck and leaned further back. Just when his slimy appendage was beginning to slip from my grasp, he moved forward and once again opened his thighs so that my face was directly between them.

His fists wrapped around his hardness. Brutally, he squeezed and pulled and treated his tools like they were made of leather and rubber. He was putting on a performance and knew that he had his audience of one hypnotized.

Rufus didn't pull any of the screaming, shouting crap you see in gay videos when every orgasm of the performer is like witnessing someone having a heart attack.

He just grunted a little and let it blow out. While this happened, I watched, too, his big, moist asshole pulsating like crazy.

When he stood up, sweat was running down his splendid torso. He stepped off my very wet desktop. Casually, he tied up the tip of his dork with the leather string, pulled on his shorts and threw the towel around his neck.

He walked to the door and paused for dramatic effect. As if he had rehearsed the whole thing, he turned to me and pointed a zinger: "Remember one thing, baby. Before you or me leaves this place, I'm fucking you."

I was so dazed by all that had happened I had sunk back into my chair. I ran a hand through my hair. "I'll be out two weeks before you are."

His face broke into a radiant smile: "Yeah, baby, I know, and thanks. I knew you'd find a way for us to get together after I'm free."

I hooted wildly because I was becoming hysterical. "Rufus! Please! It's just a coincidence. I've already told you it won't work."

He laughed softly, rubbing his genitals and squeezing them. "Sure, it will. You and me. I'll make it happen!"

After he left, I sat there for a long time, drinking cold diet soda, and running my fingers through the congealing wetness on my desk.

Black men, I thought. They've always been after my ass.

#

I have always adored the Southern black male. Not the northern ones with their street smarts, brutal attitudes and arrogant ways—but the simple sweet type of dark man you find below the Mason-Dixon line.

Like the white men down there, they're the most fascinating men anywhere.

Until I was eighteen, I grew up on a big farm in the Carolinas. My father encouraged me to work in the fields as much as I could—to learn the farm business.

He always hired plenty of black men. I loved watching their sensuous, dark bodies, half naked beneath the baking sun.

When I was sixteen, I began sucking many of them. They proved more than willing and their attitude was so casual and easy, it was as if they were just wanting me to scratch their backs.Buck naked, they'd lie back in the grass and let me gobble to my heart's content. And Good God, it's like Christmas when you rim a black man's ass. I can remember one unusually well built farmhand, in his late forties, who loved me to bury my face in his jet rear and eat him until he was squirming and squirting his seed all over the red Southern dirt.

He began bringing his two grown sons along to "help out" in the fields but actually they just wanted to be blown, too. And while I drooled over their privates, the father would be standing near, watching and impatient for me to drain him a few.

In college, I gravitated to the big black jocks. They were attracted to me, too. I'm a guy of medium height, with very white skin and light colored hair. These dark studs were obsessed with plowing up my butt. Relentlessly they would fuck me through the night until I had to beg for some rest.

But that was my fun phase. When I went to work for the corrections system, I was determined to be respected as a professional and was repelled by some of the gay employees I met who worked closely with the male inmates.

These workers snickered about "tricking" and "blowing" and getting "fucked" by some of the studs on the sly. I thought they were really exploiting these guys. To me, inmates needed to be treated with respect so they could respect themselves. Especially, those who were on the verge of being released.

That became my credo when I was appointed director of Carroll House. No matter how much I was tempted, I would refuse to ball with any of my men. Once that started, they had no respect for you. It was a fact of prison life.

Every time I went to the prison to interview inmates for my program, there was a big commotion. All the men in the yard would give me wolf whistles and yell bawdy invitations. "Say, Blondie, how about a quickie…Shit, he's got an ass I'm gonna fuck or kill for trying."

The dozen men I finally chose all picked up instantly on the fact that I was into the male animal. They're sharp about things like that. I can sometimes be pretty effeminate, too, but I made it clear from the beginning that there wasn't going to be any monkey business.

One whiff of scandal would destroy our pilot program since it was a first for our state. Others were watching ours closely to see how well we succeeded.

I was to give the men counseling, help them find jobs, see that they looked neat, did work around the house, and stayed out of trouble.

Rufus fascinated me from the beginning. A college football player, he killed another student during a drunken brawl. He was given five years, reduced to three on an involuntary manslaughter charge. Since I was hardly any match for the men physically, Rufus appointed himself my bodyguard.

Whenever there was a squabble, my bodyguard stepped in and squelched it.

•   *   *

Bets were being made in the prison system as to which of the 12 convicts would get "Jason's cherry." Rumors about my supposed promiscuity were spread by the gay workers who knew how I loathed their attitude toward prisoners. Everyone watched me constantly to witness me take my first false step.

Oscar Wilde was right. Being with men from the underworld is like "dining with panthers." They're beautiful and dangerous and totally unpredictable.

I felt Rufus watching me. One night, as he and I locked up the house, he turned off the kitchen light. Suddenly, I felt his big arms around me. His lips brushed my face and he started to kiss me. I slipped away, but not without difficulty.

"Rufus," I whispered. "I want it, too, but—we can't!" He looked at me, confused and furious and slammed out of the kitchen.

His record showed him to have a violent temper. Maybe that's why he was such an outstanding jock. But there was the night I was getting out of my station wagon in the garage. A figure slipped up behind me and whirled me around. It was Joey, a handsome mobster.

"Jason," he hissed, "please, just let's me and you do it and I won't bother you again." A huge black hand grabbed his shoulder and pushed him down. Rufus stood over him. "You ain't bothering Jason again, period. Now, fuck off."

Gradually, through indirect hints, I let all the men there know that regardless of what they thought about me, they weren't in prison anymore. You couldn't just rape a guy on whim. You had to live by rules again and respect each other's privacy. Everyone—except Rufus—finally accepted this.

We talked bluntly. I knew I could trust him and told him of my thing about black men. In turn, he told his biggest turn-on was to think of Marilyn Monroe. And since my coloring was almost exactly like hers, along with a spectacular butt, I flipped him out the first day he saw me at prison.

But I told him I couldn't ball with him—it would destroy so many things. Sullen and sarcastic, he taunted me constantly with his sexuality—just as he did in my office that blistering day. To him, I was like a shining good luck charm that he loved.

If we could live together, he said, there was no doubt he would be a success in the real world.

But I told him I couldn't live with anyone. I loved being alone and having my boyfriends leave after we'd had our fun. He couldn't understand this position. If you love someone, you sleep and live with them.

Neither could he understand it when I told him I came from a long line of eccentrics. None of us were the types who wanted or needed companions. All of us were the solitary types and we would drive any partner to drink or worse with our idiosyncrasies.

But still, Rufus was so incredibly sexy and desirable that maybe it would work out after all.

#

One more day—and then I would be free.

The men begged me to stay on. I told them maybe we could get together after they were out for good. Rufus had become quieter and sadder. He was seeing his dreams of our being together slip away and he didn't seem to know how to keep me anymore.

Supper on that last evening was over with. The dishes were put away. My men were watching some TV or studying for their college credits.

Rufus came in from his banker's job. Still in his suit, he had stripped off his coat and shirt and held up a brown bag in the air.

Grabbing my arm, he pulled me toward the garage.

"You're taking me on a farewell spin before you leave tomorrow," he grinned.

"Oh, I am, am I?" I joked. "Are we breaking out of prison or something? Damn, it's my last night here, so why not live dangerously."

But quickly, we were speeding out into the countryside. I parked in front of a river and Rufus pulled out a six-pack of beer.

I pretended to be shocked. "That's a no-no, Mr. Jail Bait. But what the fuck. I'll be driving off into the wild blue yonder tomorrow. Maybe the coast. Maybe the mountains."

But Rufus didn't want to waste time on banter. Neither did I. He pulled me next to him and began pulling off my clothes. His came next. I ate his nipples, my mouth traveled over that marvelous stretch of flat stomach, a slight bush of pubic hair and then engulfed his magic.

It wasn't like having a prick rammed into your mouth. With

Rufus, I felt like it was his heart. His semen spattered my throat and before I could even finish, I had turned him over and was slobbering between swellings of glorious black butt.

After nearly an hour of this, Rufus flipped me over and speared my ass deep, deep. Midnight and I lay in his arms."

In just two weeks, I'll be out of here, too," he whispered, nibbling on my ear, "and I'll join you and we'll live together, Jason. Man, I love you. I really mean that!"

"You're incredible, Rufus," I murmured. "But I don't know. I've told you my reasons."

"I'm talking about love," he muttered intensely. "Fuck everything you've said. We were made for each other."

Before I could, he pushed the point of his hardness up into me again.

#

The men helped me load my few belongings into my car the next morning.

They had gone in together and brought me a bottle of champagne. I poured us all some and several of the men got so choked up they had to leave the room.

The others, sensing that something was going on between me and Rufus, hugged, then left us alone.

In the garage, Rufus pulled me to him and kissed me. Angry, frightened, he gripped my shoulders and shook me.

"Your final day," he whispered, watching me intently. "Made up your mind, yet? We gonna live together or what? Listen, dammit, I'm out in two weeks. I can get a good job, man! I'll be good, Jason. I won't make you ashamed of me. You're my good luck charm, man!"

I started up the engine of my car. I leaned out and brought his face to mine and I kissed those full lips.

"Rufus, I don't know yet. You can be an asshole when you want to be. You're moody, you can be violent. I'm such a damned idealist. A neat little sissy britches. But—who knows? Maybe. Maybe. You'll be hearing from me—one way or the other."

I watched him in my rear-view window growing smaller as he stared after me.

Clouds of dust from the road finally made him disappear.

POSSESSED

◆

When Mama married her second husband, Charlie Jones, the town never stopped talking about it.

She was 42. With her bleached hair, Jayne Mansfield sized boobs and a reputation for going out with anybody who'd buy her a coupla brews, well the town just knew she was a rip.

Believe me, she was.

Her new husband was only 22. Yep, that is correct. And I was only 20 for God's sake. Can you imagine having a Daddy only two years older than you are?

But that wasn't the worst of it. And if the town knew about this little bit of dirt, they'd be calling up all the talk shows to get us on the air. You see, I had major hots for my new step Daddy. In the string of men Mama was always bringing home to our house trailer on the outskirts of Thomasville, North Carolina, cute, hunky Charlie Jones was by far the most gorgeous of the lot.

I first laid my hot little eyes on him the spring before I entered college. I had gotten a scholarship to Wake Forest and worked at the new Wal-Mart across town and was just counting the days when I could get out of that scuzzy trailer stuck in the middle of a field, along with a dozen other mobile homes.

There were no trees, flowers or even bushes out there in Paradise Trailer World. Just big aluminum boxes where people crammed inside.

Mama had never wanted me and hated my guts when she discovered I was into men. She had found me blowing a gang of boys in our mobile neighborhood.

I stayed out of her way by holding down after school jobs and working on school projects so that inadvertently, I became one of the school's brightest kids, thus helping me win a scholarship.

Mama had always worked at the furniture factory, which ruled the ugliest town in the South. I was used to her bringing home her boyfriends and most were slobs in dirty overalls and brown faces and white bodies.

A few, though, were cute, and they were fascinated as all the men were by her immense tits. Sometimes I felt sorry for her when I'd see her parading around in her bikini, pretending to hang up clothes outside on the line, but wanting all the men and boys to see what she had.

But I realized that was all she really had to be proud of. Two big swollen globes of fat flopping around on her chest. This was her only claim to fame, the one thing that made her stand out from the crowd. But the men loved it. Sometimes I'd peep out of my bedroom door and could see directly into our den.

There'd be Mama with her top off, the kinky head of her latest stud buried on one of her boobs. Her smiling and grinning like the town idiot.

Most of the guys should have been ashamed to take their clothes off. They looked weird with their white bodies and red necks and arms.

And then came that evening she brought Charlie Jones home.

He was gorgeous, I thought, as I put my schoolbooks down and began preparing supper. This was something I volunteered to do to keep Mama off my ass.

He sat there on the sofa besides Mama. She wore her blue halter outfit, with her bosoms nearly falling out and rolls of fat spreading over her briefs.

But Charlie…he made me think of one of those rock stars on MTV. Slender and tall, his brown skin was glossy and clean, set off by the white tee shirt and clean jeans and black boots he wore.

Long, dark hair was swept back into a ponytail. Eyes were deep set but it was his mouth that fascinated me. His lips were full and pink and he smiled a lot, showing off perfect white teeth.

He nodded his head at me and I exaggerated my sissy ways swishing around him. Mama saw what I was up to and muttered something to Charlie. He threw his head back and laughed.

"It takes all kinds, honey," he said and I knew at that moment, that he had accepted me instantly—much to Mama's irritation.

I was trim, of medium height with hair I had bleached to nearly a white mass of curls. A dash of blue mascara certainly didn't hurt the nearly purple hue of my eyes.

When people asked where did I get my looks since Mama bore zero resemblance to me, I'd shrug and drawl: "My father. She divorced him because he slept around and now she sleeps around so much she makes him look like Jesus H. Christ."

But what only Mama and I knew was that my limp resulted from one her bashings. She had gotten drunk one night, had seen one of her so-called boyfriends sneaking off after he and I had had some hot fun, and she went berserk.

She had knocked me over so hard, I crashed to the floor, right on top my leg, breaking it, and by the time I went on my own to the hospital a day later, it was too late. I would always have a limp and when I wanted to really stick it to my Mama, I'd exaggerate my handicap, hobbling around her like an 89-year-old goat.

At the table, Charlie complimented me on the baked tuna pie I'd made, along with candied yams and tomato pudding. I batted my eyes and we talked about some of the rock groups on MTV and I said he should be in one group because he was so cute.

Mama rolled her eyes and said: "Ain't it time you began your lessons? I'll clean up."

I ignored her. "I don't have any lessons tonight. And I'll clean up."

Charlie had been watching me with that adorable wide-eyed look of innocence and he laughed softly for no reason and Mama gave him a sharp glance.

Then she glared at me. "Look at him, Charlie. Such a damned little sissy. Can't do anything with him. I need to fix her up with some dresses and buy her some make-up."

I was so used to her taunts by this time that they meant nothing. I patted my hair with a delicate gesture, which I knew killed her and drawled: "Why don't you buy me a bikini like yours so I could show off my tits and really get the men in bed?"

She lunged at me, with her boobs dipping into the salad, but I danced around and went over to Charlie who was laughing hard again. Somehow I knew he would never let her hurt me and I was right. He put an arm on my shoulder.

"Okay now let's cut it out," he said easily. "Let's just finish up our meal which Jason so nicely put together for us."

Mama, though, could hardly be handled in such an easy manner. She leaned forward and dashed her large glass of iced tea into my face. But I was used to this, too, and kept right on nibbling at the lime pie I'd fixed.

"Angie!" muttered Charlie. "You shouldn't have done that."

"Oh, that's okay, Charlie," I shrugged. "It's better than the scalding coffee she used to throw at me when I was little. And iced tea is good for your make-up. Mama, you know you're nearly out of blue mascara? I wanted to wear it to school today but you didn't have any."

Charlie threw his head back and whooped with laughter and Mama jumped up again and chased me around the table until I finally fled to my room. I knew her well and she had no intention of letting Charlie notice me.

For several weeks, I didn't see much of Mama and occasionally I'd see her in the car with Charlie. Then one morning I was surprised, but delighted, to find him sitting at the table having breakfast.

Mama was serving him some bacon and she had changed into her pink bikini outfit. And Charlie…he wore just his jeans and his hair hung down his broad shoulders.

Oh, Lord, did he look good enough to eat.

With a cigarette in one hand, and a cup of coffee in the other, he leaned back and yawned. As he did so, his chest and stomach muscles danced in a fascinating pattern.

His nipples were erect and he rubbed them casually while throwing me a wink.

"You've got such a nice body, Charlie," I sighed. "You should be a model or something."

He laughed again but Mama rolled her eyes and dumped scrambled eggs into his plate. "Miss Queer here would notice that, wouldn't she?"

"Well," I lisped, "Miss Big Tits seemed to have noticed alright, so why not Miss Queer?"

"Why, you—?" she screeched and ran after me but I jumped up and got behind Charlie who grinned as if I had said the funniest thing in the world. He put an arm around my waist and put up a warning hand to Mama. "Now, let's cool it, Angie. Let's give Jason the good news."

He looked up at me, with those wide-opened eyes and told me I was his new Daddy. They had gotten "hitched" the night before in South Carolina.

"You mean that you—you're my new Daddy?" I gasped.

He nodded, watching me expectantly for my reaction. I threw my arms around his neck and kissed his cheek and he returned the gesture. But Mama yanked me back and shoved me toward the kitchen.

"That's enough of your queer shit," she fumed. "Real boys don't go around hugging their Daddies like that."

"I ain't a real boy, Mommie Dearest," I sneered. "I'm a two-bit faggot. Isn't that what you like to call me? A two-bit faggot or a sleazy queer? When you put it all together, that means I'm trouble for any hot-blooded hunk. Ain't that right, Daddy?"

I turned to Charlie and reached up and kissed him on the lips. "There, Charlie. Welcome to the Nut house."

Mama made a grab for my hair but I dodged her and got behind my new father. I immediately fell in love with him because: he smelt so good, like Lifebuoy soap, clean skin, freshly washed hair which gleamed dark, with reddish tints form the sunlight, the strength of those broad shoulders and tawny neck.

I wanted to kiss it but then that would bring him into Mama's dark shadow and I didn't want that to happen. He would go into it soon enough without my help.

"It's still morning and let's get the day off to a good start," he said and slapped the table. "Let's all go swimming at Oakwood Acres."

Glaring at me, Mama spat: "Over my dead body. You're taking that fag no place. And I've gotta work today, remember? Double shift. Noon until midnight. That freak is gonna stay here and clean up the trailer."

I held out my crippled leg toward her. In a baby voice, I lisped: "But Momsey, it's hard for little faggot here to work. My wittle weg hurts sooo bad!"

I watched her hand reach for a knife and I put my arm around Charlie's neck. He slid a hand over my waist and pulled me to him, as if saying: now that I'm your Daddy, I'll help look after you.

Oh, Lord, how she wanted to kill me. And as Charlie prepared to take her to work, I heard her threaten: "Don't you try sneaking that queer off for a swim. If you do—?"

But an hour later, Charlie returned and bounded into the trailer. "Hey, you little freak!" he grinned. "Wanna go for a swim?"

Impulsively, I threw my arms around his neck and he picked me up and swung me around. I kissed his cheek and he nuzzled it against my face.

If love is finding a man you feel natural and wonderful with, then I found it in the sturdy torso of Charlie Jackson.

Oakwood Acres was an ugly stretch of brown water at that time which was popular with the blue-collar crowd who couldn't afford to drive to the North Carolina coast.

There were few people around on that August morning because the sky was dark with storm clouds. Charlie stripped off his jeans and showed off his new black spandex briefs for me.

I whistled and when I took off everything except my red briefs, he whistled in turn and nodded his head. "You look really nice, son."

"Son?"

Both of us burst out laughing and he grabbed my hand and we waded into the dark water. But I stopped after a few yards. "Charlie, I can't swim. I'd better not go any further."

He held out his hand. "Grab my hand. I won't let anything happen to you."

That set the tone for our "secret" dates we had all that summer, never letting Mama know. We went into the water, he took me to the drive-in theater, on picnics and I got to know him better than any man before him.

It was during the night we went to the drive-in theater for their all-night Horror-Thon that Charlie and I became more than father and son.

Mama had quit her job at the "cheer" (chair) factory and was now working the midnight shift at the Waffle House on I-85, which was popular with the truckers. Charlie had no illusions about her fidelity: she should have been a trucker and fucked her way across America.

Charlie had put a mattress in the back of his truck and filled up a cooler with cherry cokes for me, beer for him. Beneath the blanket, under the stars, we began watching *The Thing*. Our bodies touched and I turned my face so I faced him.

His eyes were opened wide as the monster on the screen exploded out of the dog. I tickled his ear.

"Charlie, take off your shirt so I can feel your muscles."

With his eyes on the screen, he casually peeled off his jersey. I ran my hand over his chest. Still, he didn't resist, his eyes watching the action on the screen. My fingers rubbed his nipples, which were so erect I imagined they were miniature penises, up and ready for some relief.

Cautiously, my hand slid over his stomach and I knew he was very much aware of me for his breathing had become rapid. Beneath the waistband of his jeans slid my fingers. I undid his waist button and I realized he wore no underwear.

Lower my hand moved until they passed over the hair of his pubic and then onto that long object of passion that had so enchanted my mother. It felt so hot and firm and it was becoming stiffer.

I scooted under the blanket and sucked on his nipples, then slid my tongue over his stomach until I had reached that intimate secret which Mother enjoyed several times each night.

I thrilled to the taste of it—clean, sensual and perfectly shaped for my mouth. I took more and Charlie raised his hips slightly to drive in several more inches.

Every moment of that first encounter burned itself into my memory: the tawny beauty of his skin, the powerful scent of Charlie, boyish, clean and fleshy, how my lips kept moving downward until they were pressed against his pubic area.

I felt his phallus pulsing and tasted the wet thickness being spattered into my mouth. I didn't want it to stop, though, and neither did Charlie for I stayed on it again, sucking even stronger and he rewarded me once more, just minutes later with more of his elixir.

I came up for air and he pulled me tight against him and began kissing me passionately, not like he was a brother or a stepfather but a lover. There were no other people there on the back row and we had complete privacy.

His jeans had long since been discarded and he got up over me, and positioned his hardness between my buttock cheeks. I held on to him as he began to inch it in.

And when it was up to the hilt, he began screwing me deeply, his long hair hanging down on either side of my face. The light from the drive in screen glowed on his rump that humped steadily.

When he came, he rolled over on his stomach, breathing heavily and I got down below him and buried my face in his gorgeous rump. This had never been done to Charlie before and he went crazy.

He gasped and grunted and pushed his butt back so I could dig my tongue in even deeper. This naturally made him rampant again and I went down once more on him.

In his arms, I whispered: "Daddy, Daddy, you're wonderful!"

"My little sonny boy," he joked and we both laughed but grew serious when we agreed: Mama mustn't have a single clue as to what he and I were doing. If she did, there would be a fight to end all fights in that cramped little trailer.

Before we drove home, he confessed something so profound that I've never forgotten it. The only reason he had married my mother was so that he could love me and take me to bed.

"I'd seen you before at the K-mart," he whispered, "and somebody told me you were Angie's sissy boy. I just knew then, I had to meet and love you. And so I have."

That was one of the most beautiful moments of my life.

But I discovered my new stepfather had clay feet, too.

He was an alcoholic and a drug addict. I made this startling discovery over a period of weeks. I never saw him without a can of beer in his hand, but then most of the guys at the trailer court were the same way. You could buy a case of Red, White and Blue Beer for just $3.00.

He was also drinking liquor heavily and he and Mama would get drunk. But I came home early one afternoon from my job at Wal-Mart and found Charlie slumped over on the sofa, staring at a dark TV screen and giggling.

On a small mirror before him was the residue of white powder. His face was strange and flushed, his eyes glazed and he babbled about watching ghosts on TV and Cowboy Rangers and mixing up a gin and tonic.

He wanted me to blow him right there but I had no desire when I saw him like that. Charlie acted too weird for me to enjoy sexually at such times and he might do anything while on a binge and not remember it afterwards.

He worked on a construction firm each day, made great money but there was never any to pay bills. Mama began yelling at him about this. She was having to pay all the bills, while his mysteriously vanished.

Poor Mama. Her first husband was a slob and her second, a junkie. She never had any luck with men. Their fights grew so bad that she began staying out all night with her new boyfriends.

Charlie vanished for days and when he returned, his face was a sickly pasty color. If we tried having some fun in bed, he couldn't get an erection and he'd mutter something about being exhausted but I had read up on drug addictions. One symptom for men was that they were incapable of achieving a hard-on.

The night before I went to college I was alone in the trailer. The people at Wal-Mart had given me a set of luggage as a farewell gift and Mama was now involved with a trucker named Amos. She stayed over at his place in another trailer camp across town.

She had washed her hands of marriage to Charlie because "he couldn't get it up" for her and I heard her bragging to one of her women friends on the phone: "Oh, that Amos, you should see his hard-on. Looks like a big banana."

I hadn't seen my stepfather in two weeks but I knew he had a few brothers scattered around that area and he often stayed with them when he was on a binge.

A truck pulled up outside and when Charlie bounded in, tanned and radiant and gorgeous. I ran to him and hugged him.

"Hey, you little freak," he laughed. "I wanted to take you out and celebrate tonight since you're leaving tomorrow."

"Charlie, you didn't forget! I was so depressed."

He pulled me out to his truck. "Well, stop feeling depressed. I'm gonna give you a good time you won't forget."

I sensed he was "clean" and he told me he was. Hadn't touched either booze or dope in a month. He felt wonderful. He took me to a steak house near High Point and then we drove to nearby High Rock Lake.

At a small cabin, he stopped. "A friend of mine is letting me live here for awhile," he explained. "I got it ready for you."

It was cozy and small and he built a fire in the hearth. Nearby was a mattress neatly made up with bedclothes.

"This is my bed," he smiled. "I like it here because it's simple."

"Are you working now, Charlie?"

He glanced down. "Not exactly, but I got some interviews lined up for this week. Come 'ere. Let me hug you."

My hands slid up beneath his sweater and once more I delighted in the hard nipples which usually indicated how sexed up he was. His mouth felt wonderful, covering mine again and his dark hair falling on either side of my face.

On the mattress, he pulled me tight against him and it was like the first time in his truck. Firelight glinted off his skin and I moved down to taste him.

It was ready for me, taut and pulsing and the tip had slid out of its fleshy sock. I heard him grunt when I covered it with my mouth and began its memorable journey down to his pubic area.

He came quickly and I stayed on again until he produced another offering to me. Holding me again, Charlie rolled over on top of me and prepared me for entry.

I gasped as he pushed himself in deep and worked it around and I held on to him. He humped slowly, but steadily, seeming to enjoy the groans I made with each lunge.

Before leaving the cabin, we lay together and I studied his features, trying to photograph him permanently on my mind.

"You and me," he whispered, "we were destined to meet, Jason. I don't believe in God, but I do believe in fate. It's like—like—"

"We possess each other," I finished.

"Yes, possessed. That's a good word. Because even when I'm working on construction, I see you before me, just like you are now."

#

I was hardly surprised when Charlie wrote me a few weeks later at school that he and Mama were divorced.

Mama never wrote me a word which suited me fine. We'd never had a life together and she had no place in my future. My stepfather sent me boxes of candy bars, cartons of canned food, coffee, some clothes. His letters were short and sweet and sexy:

"My little blonde-haired sonny boy…I miss you a hell of a lot. I'm not wearing anything right now. I ain't gonna touch it, though. I'm saving every drop for you. Next time you see me, you'd better have a boat because I'm gonna drown you in all that white, hot stuff."

A week later, I was called down from my room in the dorm to the lobby. I had a visitor.

I was delighted to find Charlie standing there, looking luscious in a black windbreaker and tight jeans. His dark hair was pulled back into a braid.

"Daddy!" I squealed. "You finally came!"

'Not yet," he whispered, "but as soon as we can get to my motel, I'm blowing the tip off my cock."

Two of my gay buddies, a girl and a guy, were walking by and when I introduced them to my "Father", they were stunned. They couldn't believe this dazzling hunk was my parent.

It was a wild time we spent in the Holiday Inn that weekend. He had, indeed, been saving it up for me. I sucked him numerous times, he fucked me steadily and my face was buried for hours in that delectable rump.

When he was ready to leave, he told me his construction firm was going to New York City for its next project. He'd write me and send me airfare to fly up to visit him.

"We'll get together Christmas," he promised. "So mark it on your calendar."

Our kiss lasted for a long time and when he dropped me off at the dorm, he looked at me steadily: "I think of you too much, Jason. You've possessed me."

"But it's a beautiful possession," I smiled, "for I do the same for you, my handsome father."

I paused before asking: "Charlie, are you clean now? No booze, no drugs?"

His gaze wavered: "A little tiny bit. But not a binge. You saw the proof of that in bed, didn't you?"

#

Christmas approached. I was worried sick. I'd heard nothing from Charlie since early November.

He had sent me some amusing postcards from the Big Apple and then there was complete silence. I managed to track down the phone number of his construction firm in New York and got the secretary.

Charlie had left their employment two months ago. They had no address where I could reach him.

"Was it drugs?" I asked her.

She hemmed and hawed and then admitted that it was and they had tried to get him help, but he refused.

When holiday break came, I drew out some savings and flew to New York City. It was time I found my father.

The foreman of the construction firm was friendly and had been a good friend of Charlie. "He spoke of you all the time," he smiled. Then his face shadowed: "But he couldn't get off the booze and pills and crack."

The man gave me Charlie's last address. It was the YMCA on West 34th Street.

Outside, the sidewalks were scuzzy and filthy, winos and black punks hung around the entrance. The surly clerk at the desk snapped that Charlie Jackson was in 400 and I took the elevator up to his floor.

Along the threadbare carpet I walked to Room 400. Two drag queens were screaming at each other in the bathroom where they were putting on their make-up. Someone had vomited in the broken telephone booth and discarded chip bags and candy wrappers were strewn along the way.

I knocked on the door of 400. The door cracked open and a pale face peered out.

The face I had last remembered as glowing and boyish was the color of chalk, the eyes sunken and the silken hair was matted. A dark stubble of beard made his skin even more ghastly.

"Charlie?" I whispered. His dull eyes brightened for a moment and then he covered them.

"Oh, shit no!" he moaned. "I was hoping you wouldn't find me like this." I pushed on in and hugged him, kissing him. He smelt dank and his skin clammy.

"Charlie, what's been happening to you?

He was trying to kick his drug habit and the worst was behind him. His room was squalid, with clothes piled up in the corner, the desk covered with slices of bread, cookies spilling out of a bag and roaches running all over the place.

"How do you stay alive, Charlie? Where are you getting your money?"

He grinned bitterly and pointed to his privates that looked unusually swollen since my stepfather had lost so much weight.

"I sell my cock. Amazing how much tourists will pay you if you've got an impressive dick. In fact, I'm expecting a guy anytime."

Just then, someone knocked on the door and when Charlie opened it, a short Oriental man hurried in. He glanced from me to Charlie who gestured toward his penis.

He sat on the edge of the bed and the visitor, ignoring me, got down on his knees and began sucking off Charlie.

"I can get it up now," he told me, over the bobbing head of the China man, "and that means I'm getting better."

His breathing quickened and the sucker grew hungrier, chowing down harder and then Charlie yanked himself out and covered the face of the visitor with an impressive orgasm.

The man stood up, wiping his face with a handkerchief and handed Charlie a fifty-dollar bill.

"Can I do—again?" the man asked. "Will pay you more money?"

"You mean, right now?"

"Yes, yes, now! Please, I liked your thing so much. Right now, please, sir?"

Charlie shook his head and got up to show the guest out. "Sorry, I've got an important visitor. Come by tonight."

Charlie turned to me and held me close, but his cold skin made me think of a corpse. He pulled back and held out his genitals to me.

"You want this," he said eagerly, "I know you do. I'll let you take a crack at it now. I've got enough for a second and maybe a third load."

Most guys would have dropped to their knees and taken him up on his offer. But I gathered all my control and shook my head.

"Charlie, only after you've put yourself into a rehab program. I want you to be healthy again and then we'll get in bed and tear the place up."

He stared down at the floor littered with cigarette butts and the squashed bodies of roaches. "You really think that's gonna help me out?"

"You must do it for yourself, Charlie! I don't want you dying on me."

He laid back on the bed and stared up at the ceiling. "Let me think about it. Come back tomorrow, about this time. If I'm gone, it means I don't want any help. I can do it myself. If I'm here, we'll find help."

#

When I tapped on his door again the following day, my heart was beating so fast I felt sick. I waited and listened. There was no sound. I knocked again.

He was gone. He wanted no help.

I was turning away when the door opened and Charlie stood there, neatly shaven, pale but dressed up to go somewhere.

"Okay, my little sonny boy," he smiled. "Let's go and get it over with."

#

Our first night together after his release this afternoon from the rehab center.

He had been there for six months and it's like having the old Charlie back again.

In bed, we loved each other for hours and then he leaned over me, studying my face.

"The doctors told me I'm naturally addicted and will always be possessed by an addiction."

"You mean drugs and booze?"

He kissed me before answering: "No, I'll always be possessed—by *you!*"

CAPTAIN OF
THE CLOUDS

◆

So rarely did Mark Dumont descend from those gleaming towers he built all over Manhattan that we dubbed him Captain of the Clouds.

For each skyscraper seemed to outdo the last one as it thrust higher into the sky, piercing the void until the tips vanished beyond the cloud layer. And it was here where he dwelled in one of the most magnificent residences in the world: Dumont Towers.

A vicious murder trial a year before had turned him from party boy into such a recluse he made the late hermit billionaire, Howard Hughes, look like Donald Trump.

The trial was the reason I was in the private elevator of Mark Dumont last January as I ascended up toward his legendary penthouse. He had shocked me by agreeing to my visit to discuss a series of articles I wanted to do on him—America's most famous, but mysterious, building tycoon.

I had covered the trial for my New York newspaper. My syndicated column, "Crime Beat", had been consistently kind to this 44-year-old giant with jet hair and baby blue eyes. Each day, I studied him sitting at this table in the courtroom with his attorneys.

His glorious six foot five physique was always covered—darn it—in beautifully tailored suits. Always by Italian couturier's like Trezetiti,

D'Allasandra, Santagada. Several times our eyes met. A charge of electricity seemed to flash between us despite the grisly testimony which flowed around us.

On the night of April 23, 1995, he and his new wife, Claudia Dumont, were visiting their showcase mansion on the coast of Miami, Florida. Although numerous guests were there that night, the corpse of the new bride was found strangled in bed the next morning.

The nude bridegroom lay unconscious on the floor. He claimed he had come out of the shower when he heard sounds of a struggle and was struck on the head by a "bushy-haired" stranger.

Some witnesses testified the sexy, handsome Mark Dumont was actually a swinging bisexual with a ferocious temper. Two hustlers, in fact, swore he had tortured them, had them hospitalized, then paid them hush money.

Jurors were so confused by all the conflicting testimony they could reach no verdict. Enemies swore Mark Dumont paid a fortune for his freedom. Admirers like me contended he was the victim of a spurned lover, of which he had had many.

He wrote me a note, thanking me for my support. When I phoned him to request an exclusive interview, he charmingly agreed.

I had gone through all his extensive security screens to achieve my goal that afternoon and now two guards escorted me off the elevator into the penthouse.

"He'll be right here, sir," one of the men said and stepped back into the elevator. "Just wait for him."

I was startled by the opulence of my surroundings. When you're used to being on the sidewalks of Manhattan, with all the dirty garbage, the panhandlers, hustlers, pushing mobs, screaming horns, you often wonder who lives way up there among the clouds in those gleaming towers?

Now, I was getting a unique introduction. The walls and floors were of gleaming marble in hues of jet and rose, and along the walls glowed gold-shaded lamps.

Huge chandeliers glittered all along the corridor and above me gleamed the famous high ceilings I had read about, the ceilings festooned with paintings of Greek gods and scenes from mythology.

And suddenly appearing through the door before me was the man of my dreams. And oh, what a sight he was! Obviously having just worked out, he was attired in a pair of black briefs and a red tank top. His muscles were so well developed he could have been the star of any Terminator movie.

The press had often pointed out that if Mark Dumont ever wanted to give up building skyscrapers, he could make a fortune on the physique competition circuit.

"Well, hello there!" I sang out holding out my hand. "It was great hearing from you, Mark, and–"

"Get back into that goddamned elevator, you scumbag!" snarled my host. "What makes a gossipy little vulture like you think you can come and dig up all the dirt again? Huh?"

I was so astonished by my reception I could only stare at him in disbelief. But at that moment, a door behind him opened and out stepped his double.

Only this Mark Dumont was wearing a black turtleneck sweater and clinging pants of the same color.

"Cut it out, Bart!" roared this clone. "What the hell do you think you're doing, talking to my guest like that? I invited Jason Fury here so you be nice to our visitor or I'll lock you up again."

And suddenly things began to fall into place. Of course, this must be the twin brother of Mark Dumont—one who was supposedly an eccentric artist with emotional problems, who had been in mental hospitals for most of his life.

The press never wrote much about this sibling, though, thanks to the Dumont press relations corps, which was paid a fortune to keep these kind of things quiet. Now and then, buried at the end of an article, would be a brief reference to a "brother" of real estate magnate.

"Mark, Mark!" pleaded his twin brother, "You can't talk to this creep! All he wants to do is to run fucked up stories that'll bring you nothing but trouble."

"Jason, come this way!" Mark smiled as if his twin wasn't even there. But Bart followed us down the corridor, prancing around his brother with growing agitation.

"Mark!" cried Bart, grabbing his brother's arm. "This is just another faggy writer who wants to drool over your muscles and your big dick and write about how you should be Mr. Universe. He's trouble, Mark, I just know he is!"

As if used to such outrageous behavior, Mark was patient with his stunning looking sibling. "Bart, calm down now. You read Jason's columns. They helped me a lot. He was one of the few kind writers who stayed with me until the end."

Hearing nothing, Bart paced back and forth, his beautiful blue eyes snapping. Suddenly, he stopped before me. I moved closer to Mark who put an arm around my shoulder.

"I know what you want from my brother," jeered the charming Bart. "Wanna get your hands on his dick, right? Well, buddy, get a look at mine! I got one just like his. This big enough for you, fag, huh, huh?"

Stripping off his briefs and tank top, he stood before us in all his unclothed glory. He grabbed his impressive genitalia and shook it at me while rolling his eyes and sticking out his tongue. Instead of being enraged, I laughed for he looked exactly like a little boy who desperately wanted attention.

"Oh, goody!" I yelped. "I just love uncut men like you, Bart! Can we go somewhere more private? I'm the shy type."

This time Mark laughed at his brother's expression of shock and disgust. I had turned the tables on him, so flushing angrily, he grabbed his skimpy clothes and left the room—providing us with a stunning view of one luscious rump.

"Whew!" I gasped. "What an introduction! Is he always like this?"

Mark's smile was rueful. "Unfortunately, yes. He's been in therapy for so long I wanted to bring him out into reality to see how he adjusts. I'm getting worried, though."

I heard rumors in the newsroom about how Bart's hidden brother did wild things when in public: using the sidewalks for a latrine, dropping his pants and masturbating in crowds—and none of the incidents ever reaching the public because of Mark Dumont's very well trained—and paid—public relations staff.

An oriental man wheeled in a huge coffee cart, brimming with sandwiches and small cakes. As I enjoyed a platter of these goodies, I studied the handsome goody that stood against a wall of sheer glass.

Since his residence crowned the tallest building in America—Dumont Towers—a visitor could view four states stretching off in the distance into infinity. A wisp of cloud sailed by—below us.

Streets beneath us were the size of a human hair. Without a telescope, you couldn't even see the traffic and people bustling below. I felt completely remote from civilization up here, secure in a fortress of steel, marble and glass.

He listened to me outline my ambitious series of articles on him. I wanted to paint in words a real, flesh and blood picture of him—and describe how he had gotten where he had. It would take weeks of interviews and research, however.

I also made it clear I wanted no public relations flack hovering over his every word, making certain I painted only a rosy picture of the young tycoon.

"Okay, sounds good to me," he smiled. "If you're going to get an intimate look at me, why don't you move in? You could see how I spend every day, every night! Pretend this is your home for how ever long you want."

"That would be fantastic!" I enthused, having fantasized about doing just that. And I would also have a world exclusive scoop. For Mark

Dumont had let few media people invade his private residence. Now, I would be given the run of it.

"If you don't mind—?"

And by nightfall, I found myself living in the legendary guest suite in Dumont Towers. Only a few people had stayed here, including the U.S. President and his wife, a Saudi Arabian sheik and Antonio Rivera, the sizzling star of muscle movies.

The suite was actually in one of the four towers of Mark's penthouse. Overhead, the ceiling was solid glass, so the guest could look up at the clouds and stars. You pushed a button to have the ceiling covered with a canopy of dark blue velvet, studded with diamonds, shaped like the night sky.

My bathroom was the size of my tiny studio apartment. Besides a sunken bath and sauna, there were crystal bowls of incredibly luxurious soaps and oils and perfumes. I had the choice of a closet of imported bathrobes and nightshirts from around the world.

From my large bed with silk canopy, I could lay there and use my remote to operate the enormous entertainment center: a giant color TV console, rows and rows of laser movie discs, along with hundreds more of VHS cassettes.

I had mentioned to Mark how much I enjoyed the old Warner Brothers and Universal classics and to my delight, found all of the films of Bette Davis (*Beyond the Forest, In This Our Life*), Joan Crawford (*Humoresque, Mildred Pierce*), Ida Lupino, (*They Drive By Night, The Hard Way*) along with the great horror classics like *The Black Cat, The Mummy's Ghost* and *Captive Wild Woman*.

A bar in the corner surpassed any pub in Manhattan and pouring me a glass of champagne, I took it out to my balcony, wearing a new Russian style robe, which blew in the freezing wind. I pulled up the hood of my robe for rain had begun to fall.

I looked below me but saw only clouds drifting by and now and then the roof of another skyscraper, turning silver from the freezing rain.

God, I thought, to be able to live up here like this each day of your life and not have to worry about scrounging around for a living. Not having to worry about bills and looking out of your studio apartment window and seeing nothing but a Woolworth's Store across the street and filthy panhandlers and street punks milling around beneath you.

#

That night, after a sumptuous dinner in his dining room, served not only by the Oriental gentleman who had brought us drinks earlier but by two more exquisite Chinese women, he took me down to his gym.

"You see, I actually occupy all three top floors of the towers," he explained, "so my gym is in what I call the basement, but it's actually the lowest tier of my *home*."

The gym, like everything else I had seen, made all the health clubs I had visited in Manhattan look like bargain basement rip-offs. Everything here gleamed with money and newness.

Bart was already there, impatient to get going for their daily workout. It was there I witnessed the powerful bond between the brothers.

They were like two high-spirited athletes, eager to get their glorious torsos a workout. While his brother stripped, Bart skipped around us in black briefs, ignoring me, shadow boxing and punching Mark playfully.

"Come on, come on, big bro, get your cock in the jock sock, Mr. Universe, and let's get this show on the road."

It was an extraordinary experience—seeing two exact bodies that were breathtaking in their stunning proportions and musculature. Now, I understood how they could have identical physiques. Two heavy trainers worked with each of them—but they guided them through the same routines with barbells and exercise equipment

In the massage room, the brothers lay naked on twin tables. With hands wet from oil, their trainers slid fingers deep into the cleft of the luscious rumps. When the twins turned over, I was surprised to see the same wet fingers roll down the foreskins, slather a translucent goo onto the tips of their organs, and then tie the overhangs of flesh with leather thongs.

The masseurs handled the privates as indifferently as if they were a bundle of socks. The thongs made them swell up like dark sausages.

When I asked Mark about this, he explained that it was an old Oriental custom. The ointment applied to their penis tips was made from rare herbs found only in Asia. The oil was known to be effective in killing all germs and making a man more virile.

The cords were tied in order to keep the salve on for several hours in order for it to be completely absorbed.

Bart had listened impatiently to this mini-lecture and he suddenly burst out laughing, grabbing his brother's bound phallus.

"See, his old fucker is already puffing up. Hey, looka Markie Poo getting a big stiff."

Mark, in return, playfully grabbed his brother's trussed privates and within seconds, they were wrestling and gooching each other, like two high-spirited jocks.

How I wished I had me a secret camera to have photographed them like that. Playgirl or the gay mags would pay a small fortune for such sizzling hunks.

#

The Olympian sized pool looked beautiful as I prepared to dive in. It was not quite midnight but I was too excited from the day's events to sleep.

Since Mark had urged me to use his home as if it were mine, I was glad to take advantage. But just as I was about to hit the water, I paused at the sound of nearby voices.

The door to the massage room was cracked and a light was on. I moved toward it silently, curious as to who could be up.

I peered through the cracked door. What I saw made me glad for my caution. One of the brothers lay on his back on the table, while the other twin stood at his feet, with three naked young man.

A fourth stranger was giving the man on the table an energetic blowjob.

"Bart!" Mark called out. "I've already cum three times for you tonight. Let me take a break."

"Naw!" giggled Bart, watching the performance with dark, glittering eyes. "You've got two more boys who want to suck you off. That was our bet, remember? If I won the wrestling match, you'd do anything I asked you."

Mark was breathing harder and then he tapped his partner's head. The boy drew back and Mark held up his erection so that we could all see his ejaculation. If he had already cum three times that night, you wouldn't have guessed it from the volume of his fourth orgasm.

It squirted straight out and Bart stooped down to catch it in his mouth. Then he climbed up on the second table, spread his thighs and urged one of the boys in the group to do him.

And yet another one took over Mark.

I watched the twin brothers getting worked on and then I saw Bart grab his twin's hand and squeeze it. "We'll always be together, bro! Nobody will ever take you from me-not ever!"

The twins were soon covered with sweat as their paid admirers worked on them steadily.

Now and then, Mark and Bart leaned over and kissed passionately, their embrace becoming more intense as their partners built them up steadily to eruption. Then I watched Bart hop off his table, get up and mount his sweating sibling, and lunge his hardness up into him.

Mark whooped and gripped the sides of the table. After Bart came, he had his brother turn over and now Bart stooped down, grasping his brother's hardness with both fists and covered the swollen head with his mouth. His sucking was so powerful that he half lifted Mark off the table with each movement. Suddenly, Mark groaned and Bart drew back, letting everyone see his incredible brother ejaculate once more.

Then Bart lay down and this time it was Mark who used both fists to grab the enormous equipment of his brother and cover the tip with his mouth.

Quietly, I slipped away. I lay in my bed and thought: I witnessed something secret—a ritual the twins had probably started long ago and who had perfected it through the years from constant practice.

#

I was a physical wreck by the end of the week.

Trying to keep up with Mark Dumont on his frenetic pace was a feat that would have killed Henry Ford and floored Thomas Edison.

In his private helicopter, we flew to building sites in Manhattan where his skyscrapers competed with each other to pierce the clouds.

In his luxurious private jet, Mark and Bart's Bat Mobile, we skimmed around the country. Mark always wore his famous uniform: a black tailored trenchcoat, made of the finest cashmere and lined with mink fur, and dark glasses. A scarf of white silk was thrown dashingly around his neck.

I had not come prepared for travel and felt like I didn't have the right wardrobe. On his jet that first morning, over gourmet coffee and croissants, I expressed my concern. I only had a leather jacket with me.

"Look in the closet there," he said casually, glancing at the large units that lined the corridor between his dining room to the den, which was furnished with a big TV, a fax machine, a secretarial work area, and cozy chairs, and coffee tables. "You might find something there that will fit you."

I was astonished to find beautiful overcoats of fur, leather and wool bursting out of the closet, along with every type of hat and scarf to go along with them.

They were all suspiciously my size and when I pointed this out to my host, he grinned.

"Well, I wouldn't want you to freeze your cute little buns off and not be able to write your stories about the wonderful Mark Dumont, would I?"

"Oh," I joked, "you're thinking more about your reputation than my health, is that it?"

We both laughed and I found a gorgeous trenchcoat of tweed, with a huge collar of fox fur. A Russian type hat of the same precious material set it off perfectly and Mark complimented me on it.

One morning we flew to Birmingham to check on the mammoth stadium he was building for the University of Alabama. We breakfasted there at the nearby Biscuit Tavern where we pigged out on an old-fashioned feast of the eatery's famous biscuits, country ham, scrambled eggs and grits.

By lunchtime, we were in Atlanta where his lush Hotel Dumont rose above Peachtree Street. This time we grabbed a "bite" at Aunt Pittypat's Restaurant for yet another huge Southern meal, this time barbecued pork, Brunswick Stew and hush puppies.

By suppertime, we were in Williamsburg, Virginia, where his enormous apartment complex, The Furies, was rising steadily upward. Mark insisted we "try" out a nearby steakhouse where once more, I added thousands of calories to my diet but found the delightful culinary fare too scrumptious to turn down.

Not used to gorging so much, I could barely keep my eyes open by the time we arrived back at JFK Airport. In his stretch limousine, I fell asleep and when I awoke my head lay on the broad shoulder of Mark.

Ignoring my apologies, he insisted I keep my head there. "You're dead. It's the least I can do for you."

By the time he escorted me back to my room, I had lost all desire to sleep—not with him leaning in the doorway, smiling down at me and his body heat so intense I wanted to warm my hands between his thighs.

"Do you have everything you want now, Jason? Anything you need, let me know and I'll make sure you get it."

What a question? When what I wanted stood just a few feet away. So, it was now or never.

"Mark, you're a sophisticated male. So am I. I don't like sleeping alone. I enjoy having a man beside me at night."

He nodded slowly and rubbed his chin, staring at the floor. "Let me think. I don't know that many buddies who might be up at this time of night. I might be able to get you Gary, he's one of my architects and he's got a nice body, I understand, and—"

"Oh, Mark, can it!" I laughed and went up to him and put my arms around his neck and I had to reach up to do this, since I only came to his shoulders. "You're the man I'm thinking of."

"Me?" he drawled with deadpan humor. "I'm just some ugly building tycoon who doesn't have time for anything except work. Or so says the media. Well, I'll prove to you how wrong all the reporters are, Jason Fury!"

He kicked the door closed behind him and stripped off his clothes. Then he pulled me hard against him and covered my mouth with his. This was hardly the kiss of a cold, robot like builder. I sensed a sensualist had become aroused and he picked me up and carried me to bed.

Cradling me at first in his arms, he kissed my face while whispering; "That first day I saw you in the courtroom, looking like this sexy boy, with your gold hair and big, blue eyes, and that incredible ass I saw swinging in the courthouse hallways, I knew I had to get you somehow. Do whatever you want with me, honey! I've slept with no one since Claudia died."

The mention of his murdered wife startled me for he had not uttered it once since I had come to live there. A chill started to come between us for I still remembered the nauseating color photos of her corpse shown in the courtroom.

Even seasoned reporters had to look away from her butchered face and broken neck, with blood turning a once beautiful face into a Halloween mask.

But his kisses were electrifying and I pushed aside those disturbing memories. My mouth traveled down his famous body, which had been photographed thousands of times during the course of the sensational trial, which had consumed millions of TV viewers and newspaper readers.

Had he really killed her? Or was he innocent?

As my lips licked his big chest and the nipples, which had become hard and thick, he grabbed the back of the headboard with his fists and thrust his hips upwards.

When I kissed his stomach, it sank in sharply and then onto his penis, which was beautifully but thickly shaped—floppy, white, with the gleaming tip slipping out of its length of wrinkled foreskin.

Into his slit, my tongue darted to taste his abundant lubricant, which gleamed on the sides of the shaft. Then I began to suck him steadily. And beneath my oral worship, he writhed and panted—his handsome body rippling like that of a bodybuilder, posing before an admiring crowd.

He gave a little sigh of delight when he ejaculated. His phallus throbbed as it squirted its contents into my mouth. Mark grinned and winked at me when he finished and then he turned over to present me his much marked upon rump.

A survey of Manhattan female models said that of 10 current hunks, Mark Dumont had, by far, the most shapely rump of them all, judging from photos of him in a bathing suit.

Licking the white dimples, which showed no trace of even a pimple, I spread them and sank my face into the cleft. It was an intoxicating valley where I wanted to live and my tongue soon had him squirming.

I felt his privates swelling up again in my fists and when he turned over, he was ready to go again.

Through that memorable night, he whispered secrets to me that were not meant for publication. Few knew his brother was being kept there or that he was seriously unbalanced. Physically, he looked incredible. There were moments when he could talk like a normal man, never indicating he was psychopathic.

And his artwork had been hailed as that of a genius. Already, Bart's work was displayed in leading art galleries around the city, in the Metropolitan Museum and the Museum of Modern Art.

No one questioned his remarkable gifts as an artist.

But when Mark took him to obscure places in the city to test him out, it often proved disastrous. Bart could be talking and laughing like a normal person but would suddenly try stripping off his clothes and jerking off or crap on the sidewalks—usually when there was a crowd around. He loved having others watching him act outrageous.

I was to discover just how outrageous Bart could act the next morning.

#

I was leaving my room to have breakfast with Mark in the dining room. I stopped short outside my door.

Sitting in one of those large Tudor chairs which lined the corridor, Bart was completely naked. He was also frantically masturbating.

"Mornin' Bart!" I sang out. "Having a good time?"

He never looked up but I had to admit he was a luscious sight with the sweat gleaming on his powerful torso. His face was scrunched up and flushed, as his fist raced up and down the swollen length of dark penis.

Lubricant had oozed over his fingers. His nipples were stiff and his stomach danced faster as his breathing quickened. A stream of semen shot through the air to spatter a priceless tapestry on the other side of the corridor.

"A jerk-off a day, keeps the doctor away, right, Bart?" He was totally oblivious to me, though. Frowning in deep thought, his fingers stirred a gobbet of sperm on his thigh and he tasted it, then wiped more from his stomach and licked it from his fingers, too.

A half hour later, I was astonished when he joined his brother and me for breakfast.

Mark had told me about this amazing shift of mood and now I beheld it first hand. Bart had actually discarded his briefs and tank top for brown tweed slacks and a sweater of gold cashmere. His dark hair was slicked back and black-rimmed glasses made him look like a muscular Clark Kent.

He could have passed for a football player and his bright eyes of blue, which were usually blurred with medication and inner disturbances, were now clear and sparkled.

Bart performed vicious imitations of Marlon Brando and Michael Jackson and President Bill Clinton.

From Bart to Mark, I would look, and if a stranger had entered at that moment, it would have been impossible to tell which was which. It was only by their personalities that one could differentiate each twin.

But Bart giggled and even Mark snickered as they told me of years gone by when they'd completely fool their own parents, their nannies, their friends in school.

"That's how it was," Bart said quietly, "until I started getting sick. It just started happening and there was nothing we could do about it. My Mama went crazy in a nut house and we've had aunts and uncles who had bats in their belfry."

"That's okay, Bart," Mark said soothingly. "Now, show us your imitation of Arnold Schwartzenegger."

But Bart had become agitated and he jumped up from his chair and stripped off all his clothes. He sat back down and played around with his bowl of Cocoa Puffs, sticking one on each eyelid.

"Look, look!" he cried. "I'm Mr. Cocoa Puff!"

Then he became a pitiful little boy, his face contorting and tears welling up in those striking eyes. "Mark, Mark, don't leave me today! Stay here and let's play some. You never have time for me anymore, Mark! Don't you love me?"

It was heart breaking to see this young giant having to plead for companionship. Mark explained that he had to fly to Chicago that day on important business.

"But tomorrow, you and me and Jason will go down to Forty-Second Street and dress up sloppy and buy greasy hot dogs from the vendors and see some trash movies and guzzle some beers. How about that?"

Bart laughed in delight, nodding his head, and went back to sticking Cocoa Puffs on his eyelids and along his arm. He placed two on his nipples and giggled at how thick his tits were because the cereal didn't fall off.

Before his helicopter took off from the roof of his penthouse, Mark pulled me close to him. "Sure you won't go with me? I'd love to have you along, especially after last night. Feel!"

He guided my hand to his crotch where it felt wonderfully warm and firm. I unzipped him and took it out and could see it was already halfway hard. A bubble of sap sparkled in the slit and I stuck my finger there and put it to my mouth. It tasted clear and sexy, since it came from my boyfriend's most prized part of his body.

"You're making it impossible for me, you handsome SOB!" I joked. "No, I've got to start transcribing some of the dozens of tapes I've made. And Mark, I am really goddamned tired! I don't have your energy."

He kissed me again and promised to call me right before he returned, "So you can start getting ready for me."

I returned to the dining room. Bart still sat there but his head was resting on his arms. His shoulders shook as he wept and I hurried over to him and put my arms around him.

"Bart, what's wrong?"

He lifted his face and stared at me, weeping. "Nobody likes me, Jason! Mark won't play with me. I—I get so lonesome here. I don't have anybody to talk to!"

"Come on, you bad little boy!" I laughed. "Why don't you show me your paintings? Every time I ask you to, you say no. Now, this time, I really want to see them. Mark says you're wonderful!"

His face lit up. "Did he really say that? Would you really like to see them?"

He took my hand and led me to his suite, which was next to Mark's. Where my millionaire boyfriend had living quarters done up in black and gold, Bart's was that of a serious artist.

There was the same floor to ceiling windows, providing the visitor with a spectacular view of the world. But the other walls were plastered with magazine pictures and color photos of world famous body builders. There was exercise machinery everywhere along with weights.I hardly saw this because Bart had placed his paintings everywhere. All of them featured only one subject: himself. He had painted himself masturbating, screwing himself with dildos.

I sensed him close behind me, his breathing felt warm on my neck and suddenly his arms went around me.

I tensed at first, fully aware that he was considered a psychopath but his muscles and body felt so warm, exactly like that of his brother. His kiss made me shiver and then he whispered: "Will—will you play with me? I get so lonely here. Can we have some fun together?"

I turned and looked at his face. It glowed with longing and intense sensuality that was impossible to resist. His guided my hands over his nipples and his pecs, over his stomach and then down his erection, which pulsed against his abdomen.

"See, I'm ready to play and do anything you'd like me to do."

Without taking his eyes from my face, watching my reaction, he led me over to a corner where I saw a strange looking stool: protruding up from the middle was an enormous dildo, the size of a big thermos bottle.

"Wanna see something interesting, Jason? Just watch me take this up the butt! It's a real sight to see!"

I expressed my doubts that any human, no matter how acrobatic, could accommodate something that huge. But Bart squatted over it and in disbelief, I watched him grunt and groan and work his rectum over the football sized tip and then it gradually began to vanish up into him.

When he managed to suck it all up inside him, he beckoned me to come over and sit down on his swollen phallus. Intrigued and certainly aroused, I dropped my robe and sat down upon his hardness.

He gasped and rolled his eyes, his sensual mouth opened and moist. I kissed him, while holding to his shoulders. Beneath me, I felt him begin to move up and down on his dildo.

It was a bizarre but exciting experience, to be fucked by this uninhibited stud that in turn was being screwed by a phallus that few men or women could take.

Groaning, sweating profusely, his lunges were deep, and when he ejaculated, he gasped like he was dying.

Pulling himself off his artificial fucker, he carried me over to a sofa, laid down on it and begged me to suck him off.

When I did, it was like having a wilder version of his brother. Bart wanted it rough and sadistic, encouraging me to bite and nibble and stretch his genitals.

Taking me into his arms, he loved me up with abnormal excitement and pushed his hardness up into me. We kissed and then he began to talk, just as Mark had whispered to me the night before.

"I'm not as crazy as people think I am," he whispered. "Sometimes I exaggerate it because a brilliant artist is supposed to be a little nuts. But I'm being serious, Jason. I want to say something to you because I love you like Mark does. He and I feel the same things and I know he's fucked you, which is why I've got to fuck you. Are you listening to me?"

"Yes, Bart, go ahead and talk."

Into my ear, he murmured: "If you want to live, get out of that penthouse tonight."

His arms had tightened around me and he had rolled over on top of me, so I couldn't move. "What happens tonight, Bart?"

No one knew that Mark was actually the dangerously violent twin. Both shared the same madness, inherited from their mother. Only Mark could control his better. Once, every few months, his wild side would erupt and when it did, I didn't want to be around.

He could get violent, just as he had done the night he butchered his new wife.

Bart's penis was still hard within me but he wouldn't withdraw it. He played with my curls and kissed my face while smiling: "The killer of Claudia Dumont was never caught. Maybe he's living up here right now—and you're learning too much."

"Bart, you're hurting me. Please let me go."

He must have sensed the fear in my eyes and voice for after studying me, with his blue eyes reflecting the storm of different emotions whirling within him, he slowly pulled out of me.

While I sat up, trying to pull myself together, he remained on the floor, watching me, with both his fists whipping up and down his new erection.

"Don't you know who really loves you, Jason?" he panted. "Remember, if you need someone tonight, to help defend you or if you want some hot sex, you know where to find me. After all, I know how to handle my brother."

His hips arched and fell as his fresh semen spattered his stomach and thighs. When I left him, he was stirring the new gobs of sperm like a child who has suddenly discovered a new game.

#

I sat through a double feature starring Garbo at the Regency Theater but I saw nothing.

Usually, I never tired of watching her stunning wardrobe in *Mata Hari* or studying her final, extraordinary close-up as the tragic queen, standing at the helm of her ship, leaving Sweden forever in *Queen Christina*.

Was Bart trying to be honest with me? Or was he being the charming, sexual lunatic?Surely, Mark couldn't have fooled me that well? Yet, in the courtroom, the testimony of the hustlers had been so chilling and sincere. They described in casual but grim detail how they had been beaten, tortured with cigarettes and wire and cattle prods—yet, they had not brought charges because Mark had paid them both over $2,000 each to be quiet.

Mark, naturally, denied any of this. The district attorney had dug up these dregs on Forty-Second Street where the eccentric millionaire enjoyed "slumming" now and then, taking in the porno theaters and greasy hot dogs and just relaxing.

I checked by my own apartment in Chelsea to look through my mail and telephone messages. How could I live in this tiny hole in the wall after enjoying a taste of opulence at Dumont Towers?

As I made my way back to the skyscraper, I passed by squalling children, being pushed along by their single black and Latino mothers, past overflowing garbage bins and punks selling their drugs and bodies to the desperate.

How I wanted to be above all this, literally, and I fantasized about someday soon becoming a permanent resident of Dumont Towers, with my companion being the owner of the building.

The security staff greeted me warmly, the manager and the *maitre d'* all nodded and smiled my way for I must be someone very special indeed for Mark Dumont to allow to live in his own residence.

It was idiotic to worry about anything happening to me with such a large staff of security personnel in the lobby. Mark had handpicked all for their expertise in defense, karate skills, and at least two had recently worked as secret agents at the White House.

I didn't see Bart around, nor did I want to. His brother wasn't due home until nearly midnight.

The Oriental manservant, Herb Lee, brought a menu to my room and asked what I wanted for supper? He served me an elaborate seafood dinner, along with champagne, which I enjoyed alone.

He said that Bart had taken his medication and was already asleep.

"If there is anything you want, Mr. Fury," he said politely, "you have only to ring your buzzer next to your bed and somebody will be right up. Looks like a stormy night. Try the caviar, sir, and the shrimp. They were flown over from Russia just this afternoon."

I glanced at the silver bowl of black fish eggs, sitting in a larger container of crushed ice. "No thanks, Herb. It may be caviar to you, but it's just herring to me."

I went to my room and transcribed some more tapes, getting a thrill out of hearing Mark's voice crooning into my earphones. Nearly 10 p.m. and I tried watching part of *In This Our Life* with dear ole Bette but for once, I couldn't concentrate on a movie I had watched probably 100 times.

On the balcony, I tried to see below, but mist obscured my view. Raindrops spattered the tiles and I went back inside. Soon, the storm was roaring around the tower and I wondered how it would feel for the building to suddenly fall over and crash. I'd probably land in New Jersey.

I opened my eyes suddenly.

I had fallen asleep after all. My clock said 1 a.m. Still, the storm raged outside. Mark should have been home long before now and he had promised to telephone me ahead of time.

And then I realized how cold it was in my room. In fact, mist streamed from my nostrils. I threw on my big robe of black cashmere when someone rapped at my door. That was what must have awakened me.

"Jason, are you asleep? It's me, Mark! You okay?"

I hurried to the door, unlocked it and threw it open. Even though he sparkled with rain, Mark grabbed me to him.

He felt wonderful, even if his expensive leather jacket was wet, as were his pants and boots.

"I tried reaching you but you didn't answer," he said and began stripping off his clothes. "You must have been exhausted."

"It's been a weird afternoon, Mark. But what's happened to the power? It's freezing up here. The lights won't go on."

"It's the storm and we've got a new power system here that's giving me a big headache. They're working on it."

I hesitated but blurted out what Bart had said about him. To my relief, Mark merely snorted.

"That's okay. He tells everybody that. It's part of his illness. Although, I wonder why he believes that?"

I had been helping him out of his clothes all during this time until he was naked. Still freezing, I pulled up the collar of my robe and pressed up close to him.

"Mark, we all know you didn't kill your wife. But I'm thinking that maybe, well, Bart could easily have done it. He can get violent so easily and—"

Mark had been playing with my curls now he moved his hand down to caress my neck.

"Naw. I did it."

The room became completely still.

I could hear my breathing in the thick shadows, heard the rain and the wind spraying the French doors to the balcony. But even through the darkness, I could see him grin. It grew bigger.

Bart had been right!

The security button! If I could just somehow get to it but Mark seemed to have read my thoughts for he laughed and held me closer.

"It's okay, Jason. I turned off all the power to security. Nobody can hear you. And don't try crying out for help. Herb Lee and all the others live two floors down. Sorry, honey. You were determined to find out the truth about Claudia so I'm afraid this is the only way to end that."

I shoved him aside and ran out into the corridor and Mark followed me, but he did so in a casual way, showing that he was in no hurry at all. He must have had the power just to my room cut off for lamps gleamed here and there. I tried pushing open the doors to the hallway and elevator. They were locked.

I grabbed a poker from the fireplace and looked around frantically, as the shadow of Mark's figure grew larger on the wall.

Bart! He had told me to come to him if there was trouble. Thank God his door wasn't locked and I flew in there. It was dark but I could make out his comforting figure laying there on his back, with an arm draped over the side of the bed.

"Bart! Bart! Wake up! Please help me!"

He didn't move. I ran up to the bed and shook him. But he felt strange and when Mark threw open the door, the light from the hallway revealed a life-sized dummy, made up to look like him.

Mark stood in the doorway, watching me, not moving, but smiling in a strange way.

The cellular telephone rang beside Bart's bed. I grabbed the receiver.

"Hey, Jason, what's going on?" a familiar voice asked. "It's me, Mark. Sorry, I'm late, baby, but the storm has been terrible. I'm just a block away—"

I gulped and looked over my shoulder at the man moving slowly toward me. Bart had stripped off all his clothes and in the dim lightning, he could have been a Roman gladiator. The powerful muscles of his torso rippled. He shook his hands now and then, like he was getting ready to do battle.

So he wasn't the man I had fallen in love with. But Mark would never get to me in time....

"Mark, help me! Bart's trying—"

A strong hand ripped the phone from my hands and threw it across the room.

I backed away from Bart, holding the poker in both hands while he continued moving toward me only now he had covered his face with his hands and wept.

"I don't want to do it again!" he wailed. "I'm sorry, Jason, really I am. I liked you so much. But—but Jason, you're taking Mark away from me. His wife tried to, but I couldn't let her. He's all I've got, Jason, and—"

I slashed the poker against him but it merely bounced off his shoulders. He grabbed my weapon and threw it across the room. I yanked from a jar one of those long, wooden paintbrushes and rammed it at him like a stake. It sank into his shoulder but still he acted like he had felt nothing. Throwing his arms around me, he pushed open the doors to his balcony and dragged me out there.

I kicked him, punched at him but it was like he was a robot. With the wind and rain wailing around us, he suddenly raised me up above him and moved toward the railing.

"Bart!" I screamed. "Don't do this! I'll do anything you want!"

My horror increased as he stepped upon the narrow railing in his bare feet and swayed there, with the powerful gusts of wind causing him to move forward and then backward.

Above and beyond stretched a nightmarish abyss. I had often fantasized about how it would feel to fall from the 83rd floor and always breathed a sigh of relief for I knew it couldn't happen.

Now, I hung over it, held aloft by a madman, whose naked feet could barely steady themselves on the slippery metal railing.

I felt his arms begin to tremble, my robe flapped in his face. Before I died, I made one last plea.

"Bart, Bart, put me down and we'll play! I'll play with you and then I'll go away tomorrow."

Incredibly, my idiotic words seemed to sink into his madness. "You'll—you'll play?" he shouted. "And then you'll go away?"

Before I could answer, I saw several policemen move silently out behind us, onto the balcony, led by Mark. His brother was unaware of them and Mark gestured me to remain silent.

He lunged and grabbed me while the cops grabbed for Bart.

But just as this happened, a powerful gust of wind blew against us and Bart swayed. Mark had dropped me and turned to help the others pull Bart back, but he pitched forward into space, toppling over the railing and falling toward death, 83 stories below.

"Mark!" we heard him shriek. "Oh, Mark!"

#

Like the penthouse atop Dumont Towers, we see occasional clouds drift below us here in Mark's vast retreat in the North Carolina mountains, outside Asheville.

At dusk today, we walked down to the bottom of the steep drive to inspect the newly erected monument. It will greet any visitor who Mark permits to visit him.

It bears the name of this splendid estate: Bart's Mountain.

And above it is a lifelike bust of the late and tragic Bart Dumont.

Each day, for two months now, I've tried to erase that terrible pain in Mark's eyes. He'll never recover from the death of his twin.

We are aware Bart did terrible things in his life. He murdered once, he tried to again and it was he had tortured the male prostitutes in his zest for "games." Since the boys were unaware Bart had a twin, they naturally assumed it was Mark's picture they were asked to identify.

Had Bart not perished, we are certain he would have lived down all his mistakes. He loved his brother obsessively but fate had deemed him to live a life of darkness, shadowed always by the swirling clouds of mental instability.

Staring at the monument, Mark pulls me closer to him.

"Do you think he's somewhere near, Jason?" he asks again, looking around him. "You think I'm nuts, I know, but I sincerely believe that Bart's spirit is right here with us."

A mass of clouds, fringed in gold and pink, clustered on the horizon of blue mountains. They were so striking looking I called my companion's attention to them.

"Mark, maybe he's up there, looking down at us, from those clouds!"

"You—you really think so, Jason?"

"Of course! Look over there at that big cloud, the one apart from the others. It looks like this big, beautiful man. I'll bet that's Bart—the Captain of the Clouds, just like you!"

He stared until the stunning formation had drifted away.

Then we returned to the big house on top of Bart's Mountain.

FOR ADULTS ONLY

◆

I was worried about five-year-old Andy Swain.

Of all the kids who came to our day-care center, Kiddie Times, he was probably the most adorable. His face was round, like a little clown, his brows went up in a quizzical way, his mouth would open quickly into a big grin.

The fact he had two teeth out in front made him look even more like one of the original cast members of the old Our Gang comedy series. But from the first day he came to the center, I noticed disturbing things. He walked with a limp, his right arm was stiff and it seemed to give him constant pain although he wouldn't complain.

Bruises on his small shoulders and back naturally made me wonder how he could have gotten them. When he told us his brother caused them when they played outside, I took his word—until I discovered he had no brother.

When it was time for him to return home in the evening, he wailed and grabbed hold of our legs and begged us to keep him. We couldn't get him to tell us what terrified him.

And when his father, Hiram Swain or mother, Becky, arrived, the child would become instantly quiet, his face white and his eyes big and fearful.

What was his problem? Were his parents beating him?

I had returned to Edenton, North Carolina to take a needed break from the rat race of Manhattan where I worked occasionally as both a star stripper and a writer. It was the latter that drove me to find a quiet place for about six months where I could put the finishing touches to my short story collection, *Eric's Body*.

I had visited the beautiful old town several times because one of my favorite boyfriends, Craig, had moved there from New York City and fulfilled a life long dream: to work with children.

A strapping football player type, he had done outstanding volunteer work in New York with his passion for helping handicapped children get a foothold on life.

He knew someone in Edenton who told him how desperately the town needed a day care center for working parents and since Craig was raised in that part of the state, he jumped at the chance. His dream in life was to return to this part of North Carolina and live. He often called it "God's Country."

Since I had also grown up in the center of the state, I, too, could understand his desire to return to a place where life was much slower, people were friendlier, and some of the men were the most devastating to be found anywhere.

When I took up his invitation to spend several months as his guest there to work on my book, I also volunteered my time for his booming enterprise. I, too, had gotten a degree in English and Sociology in school and Craig and I had worked together on many a weekend with battered kids and those without parents.

We worked it out where I'd spend a few hours a week, when needed, but I wouldn't be a staff member. I didn't want that. It was more important to me to be able to come and go when I wanted to.

We made a "good couple." The children seemed naturally drawn to us and that was how I became a volunteer member of the Kiddie Times Day Care Center. I enjoyed reading stories to the little tykes and have them make up "scary" stories to tell the class and me.

Craig had also hired two sharp young women, Kitty and Linda.

They were married to each other, having met in college. Both were quiet, sweet gals with outstanding backgrounds in education. Kitty, in particular, had been physically abused by violent parents when she was growing up and had special empathy with children.

It was then I discovered our adorable little elf, Andy, and worried that he might, indeed, be the object of genuine child abuse. Not the phony, hysterical charges, which made shocking headlines for a while during the early '90s, thus giving legitimate child violence a bad name.

For it was during this era when America seemed to be rocked by one scandal after another involving inconceivable attacks against toddlers in places such as ours.

Craig and I and the girls followed the bizarre case in California where a jury sent to prison the entire staff of one center because of stupefying charges by children that they had been tortured, hung over crocodile pits and forced to swallow snakes.

I was amazed any jury could believe the accusations of toddlers who claimed they had been hung by their ankles above rivers of man-eating sharks for punishment; that they had been flown across the country during their lunch breaks and forced to submit to grotesque rituals conducted by a devil worshipper; that they witnessed each day the sacrifice of animals by staffers; and that the center had actually murdered and buried several children for misbehaving.

None of the moppets were found to have been abused in any way. No graves were ever uncovered of slaughtered youngsters or animals. On the days the kids were supposedly being flown by jet around America during their lunch break to participate in sexual orgies, witnesses claimed they had seen the "victims" playing happily at those times.

None of that mattered. Parents and jurors believed these fantasies. The center was shut down, the workers locked up all because one disgruntled parent had started the ball rolling until it had become the Salem Witch Hunt all over again. Identical scenes were played with terrifying regularity across America. No bizarre fantasy was too far out for hysterical parents and law enforcement officers to believe.

"That's never going to happen here," Craig told us, since we sat around over coffee and discussed this case and others like it for hours. "All it takes is one complaint and it can grow and grow and destroy a place like ours."

I had brought it to the attention of the center my suspicions about Andy. To my surprise, they had thought the same thing: that either his father or mother was using the adorable tyke as a punching bag.

"It's up to us to find out what's going on," Craig told us. "And if there's something wrong, we'll take it to court."

I adored Craig, big, burly and like a sweet teddy bear. In bed each night, it was always startling to see him strip off his "uniform" of Docker slacks and work boots and sweaters and slide naked next to me.

"Are you the same Craig Atkins who runs Kiddie Times? You're all naked and hot and sexy and…and you aren't a good role model right now for our little kiddies."

"Right now, it's time for adults only," he drawled and pulled me against him.

I loved the bigness of Craig for when he wrapped those brawny arms and legs around you, one felt completely safe and protected and relaxed for Craig was like a solid rock.

His neat beard felt soothing as he kissed me and nibbled my ears. Then I would move slowly down his well preserved torso, tasting his nipples and the licking the lightly tanned body until I came to his hardness.

Craig was famous for getting erect very easily and so part of his "uniform" in front of the kids each day was wearing a tight jock strap. Kids are always throwing their arms around you and hitting you unexpectedly in tender places.

In the past, my boyfriend would become mortified when his bulge grew bigger and he'd try desperately to hide it just in case any of the parents should see him.

But it was alone with him that I could enjoy this weakness, as he called it. I thrilled to putting it into my mouth and feeling it pulse slightly after awhile, watch Craig writhe and let out an occasional groan as I got him close to the edge.

And then we'd both watch as he used his fist to produce his first spurt of whiteness up into the air. Craig was a delightful lover for after this first orgasm, he would get over me and kiss me some more and then begin preparing me for his second entry.

He would move up so gradually that you were initially surprised when you suddenly felt it sliding in. He would take his time, grunting in delight as he edged ever deeper.

And when sleep came, you could drift off into dreamland knowing that the big shape next to you was there like a big, protective animal who, when he got up in the morning, would sit on the edge of the bed for a minute or two, shaking his mass of dark curls, rub his beard and then jump to his feet, yawning and shouting: "Up and at'em!"

Right after I came to Edenton, Craig had gone to great expense to make Kiddie Times "abuse proof." He wanted everyone in town to know that what was happening across the nation would never happen here.

He made the main activity area for the 28 kids—ranging in ages from three to five—completely visible by erecting plate-glass windows all around it.

Any motorist driving by, any pedestrian, could literally glance at the center and see what was happening inside. There was nowhere to hide anything, except the bathrooms. Even there, we decided not to have any doors as barriers, except on the cubicles and even here, they were half doors.

The children were basically your normals—always hungry, always with enough energy to make us workers long for sleep and a stiff drink, but none showed suggestions of abuse as much as Andy. Craig and I decided to visit his parents, Hiram and Becky Swain.

They lived in an average, one-story house with a green yard without trees or bushes of any kind. It looked bare and sterile. Inside, it was even more so. Sheets of plastic covered the sofa and chairs. The linoleum floor gleamed as if it were still wet. The air reeked of ammonia, pine disinfect, Ivory soap and Windex.

Becky was a heavy woman with long, dull hair and no make up on her white face. She waddled over to the sofa, smoking a cigarette and sipping coffee.

She worked as a nurse's aide at the local clinic. Her husband, Hiram was a neat man with short, dark hair and thick glasses, which magnified his gray eyes so they looked abnormally large.

Neither of them smiled or acted friendly. Andy sat in a corner, playing with a toy fire engine but I noticed he stayed very quiet during our brief visit.

A picture of Jesus Christ was prominent on the hospital white wall. Another frame contained a Sears Store Family Photo of the Swains: the parents and a grinning little Andy.

"I notice your son has a heavy limp," I began after the pleasantries dried up. "What caused it?"

Becky studied the TV screen showing a sobbing woman on Oprah Winfrey who was babbling about having murdered her two children because she was "temporarily insane."

"That clumsy fool fell down the stair steps upstairs," Hiram snapped. "I done told him a million times to stay away from them stairs. He just thrives on doing all the things he shouldn't."

"Where're your stairs, Mr. Swain?" Craig asked. And then I realized that there were no upstairs and therefore no steps for anyone to fall down.

"I meant the backstairs to the yard," drawled Hiram. I watched Andy who had looked up with fright in his eyes at this answer.

"How is Andy getting those bruises on his back?" I asked. "I know he's pretty active and all but—"

I watched a deep, red flush suffuse the face of our host. Uh oh, I thought. This guy has got a very short fuse. And he proved when he drawled sarcastically:

"I hear you do a kind of strip tease act for queer men in New York City. And you write books for queer readers."

"That's right, Mr. Swain," I smiled. "And I'll bet you've read them all." I waited. Men like him loved such a rare moment when they could jump on their soapboxes and start screaming about fags and cocksuckers.

"But Jason's also had wonderful experience in New York," Craig put in quickly, "volunteering his time with kids in hospitals and community centers."

"Oh!" Hiram leered. "Seems kinda strange to me that a person like you would want to work with children?"

"I've had no complaints so far, Mr. Swain," I said, "and I've always thought it kinda strange that some parents would even want children, considering how ill prepared the mothers and fathers are for raising a family."

The father's face flushed a deep red. "I don't really don't like a faggot accusing me of harming my boy."

"Did I suggest that, sir?" I smiled innocently. "Funny that you don't seem at all alarmed as to how your little boy is bruised all over, with welts on his back and scalp. Does that bother you at all, sir? Strange that I don't see any bully at the center beating him up."

Mr. Swain jumped to his feet. His thin, little mouth was a dangerous straight line. His eyes looked huge behind those strange looking glasses. "Are you accusing me—?"

"No, no, I'm sorry, sir," stammered Craig, "we aren't suggesting that at all. We just thought that you should be aware that Andy does seem to be in pain at times."

"He's just like his Mama," sneered Hiram Swain. "Jumpy as hell. Can't make him slow down."

All during this exchange, the mother sat chomping her gum, smoking her cigarette, like a big, heavy cow. Her dull eyes rarely left the TV screen where a sobbing mother begged the audience to forgive her for having murdered her children. She said she had been all "stressed out." I heard the audience go "Ahhhhhh!" in sympathy.

Craig and I were very uneasy over our visit with the Swains. We had an uncanny rapport when it came to other people. We got "good" vibes or "bad" ones. For the Swains, our vibes were definitely negative.

Hiram Swain was rumored to be a violent drunk, who had sent his wife to the clinic on several occasions although she always insisted she had gotten her black eye and fractured arm in a "car wreck" or fell off a bike.

I made little Andy Swain my project. If he was the victim of violence, then I would fight to put an end to it. Craig was startled when I told him that I had discovered from the State Child Protection Agency in Raleigh that our little mascot had already been removed once from his parents for possible abuse.

"You're kidding me?" gasped Craig. "What's the story?"

His grandmother, Reba Seagrove had filed charges with the sheriff's department that Andy had been beaten so bad his arm was broken.

"We should definitely visit the grandmother," said Craig.

She was a spry, earnest woman who lived on a small farm. Her cozy, warm house was the complete opposite of her daughter's and son-in-law.

"Becky may be my own daughter," she said to us over coffee and chocolate cake, "but you'll never find a more passive cow than her. When I discovered she was standing by, watching Hiram beat my little grand boy; I just hauled off and slapped her. That's how mad I was."

But the family court judge and the social workers had worked actively to get the little boy back with his parents again. Their reasoning: a child should remain with its own blood and flesh parents, even if they try to kill it.

"We've got to get him out of that family," Reba warned us. "If we don't, they'll kill him."

"You're damned right," Craig said. "We'll come up with something."

But Andy was not Craig's only worry. One of the mother's, Sheila Smart, was getting on everyone's nerves. Her hyperactive daughter, Judy, just wouldn't sit still and often bothered the other kids. One afternoon, when Judy continued to pull the hair and scratch the faces of several other moppets, Craig had grabbed her hand and smacked it.

Judy had screamed at the top of her lungs and when her mother came to pick her up, the child was hysterical.

"What did you do to my baby?" squealed the mother who always made me think of a rabbit. She had two big buckteeth in front, wore large, black-framed glasses and no make-up. She was also fanatically religious.

On her sweater that day she had knitted the words: Jesus Is My Savior.

Craig and the girls tried to explain but the mother was furious. "I want an apology from you. I want you to tell me you did wrong in attacking my baby."

But Craig and Kitty and Linda felt there were no apologies necessary. If anything, they wanted the mother to apologize to the staff for having to put up with such an obnoxious brat as Judy Smart.

"Well, I'm taking her out of your rotten day care center!" squeaked the mother. "Imagine, a grown man like you attacking my little baby girl."

A baby girl who made us all think of a crocodile.

To get away from it all, Craig enjoyed driving the two girls and me to Wilmington every other weekend, a beautiful city on the North Carolina coast.

We'd rent rooms at the big Blockade Runner Hotel at Wrightsville Beach and chill out. We all loved the water and it was fun going to the Mickey Ratz bar and The Palladium, watching the cute surfers and the handsome young Navy men and Marines who cruised the streets. The girls enjoyed watching other females in their bikinis.

Having let Kitty and Linda off at their home one Sunday night from one such trip, Craig parked the car and we were going into the house when he impulsively pulled me to him and kissed me. There weren't any homes around but just at that moment, a car drove by and seemed to slow down when the headlights caught us.

"Uh oh," Craig muttered. "That wasn't so cool. I keep forgetting I'm not in New York anymore."

I wasn't able to make any light jokes for the person behind the wheel was none other than Hiram Swain.

#

Strangely enough, Andy didn't come to the center all that week. When we called home to find out why, his mother told us he was suffering from earaches.

He showed up the following Monday. Something was definitely wrong. He was pale and looked thinner than usual. Dark circles were under his usually bright blue eyes.

We all clustered around him. "How you feeling, honey?" I asked.

"I just had an earache," he said dully. But he moved awkwardly, slowly and Craig and I were instantly alarmed.

"Craig, something is definitely wrong with Andy!" I hissed. "He's real sick."

"I'll check him over in the bathroom," Craig said. He took the little boy away from the group and then after several long minutes, he beckoned me to join him. "Get in here!" he muttered. "Look at this."

I wanted to vomit when I saw our little elf sitting on the toilet without his clothes. There were dark bruises around his genitals and when he turned around, a clumsy bandage had been fixed between his buttocks. It was soaked in blood.

"Oh, my God, Craig!" I gasped. "What could have happened?"

We called up Andy's grandmother and Reba Seagrove rushed over to the center. Then we took Andy to the emergency room of the clinic and the doctor and nurse were concerned—but not shocked.

"We've seen Andy in here several times," Dr. Kinard snorted. "He's been terribly brutalized and if he goes back home, he'll soon be dead."

Suddenly, the door to the room burst open and Hiram Swain roared in.

"What the hell are you bastards doing with my little boy?"

He grabbed Andy and pulled his clothes on. "We're going home, son," he shouted. "I'm getting a warrant for your arrest, you cocksuckers," he snarled to Craig and me.

"And we're getting one for you, you gutless scumbag!" I shouted. I went up to him and stood inches from his face. "You're a disgrace! Using your little boy for a punching bag! We're putting your ass behind bars if it's the last thing we do!"

His face was purple, his lips quivered but he snarled: "You shouldn't have said that—faggot!"

After he stormed out with Andy, the rest of us gathered around the doctor, protesting this outrage but the physician was hardly comforting.

"There's nothing we can do," muttered Dr. Kinmar. "We don't have proof Andy was really beaten by his father. Every time we complain to Social Services, they say their aim is to keep the kids with their natural parents. In this case, God forbid!"

Craig and I and Reba Seagrove persuaded him to at least fill out a police report complaint. But the state workers quickly let us know where their priority lay: Andy would be far better off at home with his parents. It was the goal of the Social Services Department to keep the family unit intact.

We were furious and frustrated. Reba Seagrove went to Andy's house several times, but was met with insults and threats. Her daughter, Becky, and son-in-law filed a complaint with the sheriff's department to keep her away from their house.

Andy stayed home for another week and in the meantime, our center began to receive strange calls and we noticed that mothers had begun coming in at different times through the day, watching us steadily through the plate glass windows

Suddenly, children were staying at home and when we called their parents, they seemed evasive, if not downright hostile. But one of them mentioned two names, which set alarms going off in our minds: Sheilah Sharp and Hiram Swain.

Craig called Sheilah to ask if she had anything to do with the sudden drop in attendance.

She laughed and said: "You should have apologized to me, Craig. You shouldn't go around attacking little girls. Hiram Swain doesn't like it either that you stripped his little boy naked in the bathroom and played with him."

"What in hell are you saying?" he roared. She giggled and hung up. He found me and told me what happened. Chills prickled my skin. We had only to think of what had happened in California, in New York, at the other children centers.

The very next day, I was fixing a pot of coffee in the center's kitchen when a team of uniformed officers marched into the nearly empty activity room and went up to Craig.

"Are you Craig Atkins, the owner of the Kiddie Times Center?"

"I am," Craig said in a voice that shook for I had come out of the kitchen, fearful of what I suspected was going to happen.

"We have a warrant for your arrest and the entire staff. You have been charged with sexually and physically abusing two of the children here. Their names are Judy Smart and Andy Swain."

"What? What are you saying?" gasped Craig. "That's something I'd never do!"

"You're queer, ain'tcha?" sneered one of the deputies. "Your whole staff is queer, ain't they? Why shouldn't you be suspected of messing with kids? Fags do that kind of shit."

"You fucking louse!" I snarled. "It's straight, hetero scum bags like you who do all the messing around."

"What did you just say?" he hissed and Craig turned around and told me to shut up until we got our lawyer there.

It's a good thing we did. By the next morning, 20 other parents filed suit against the center, accusing the staff of also perverting the morals of their youngsters and sexually tormenting them.

\#

All it had taken were two psychotic misfits to strike a match to explosives to cause it to blow up into another day care child abuse scandal.

On TV screens across America, the rabbity face of Sheilah Sharp could be seen oozing tears as she told viewers how her darling little moppet, Judy, had been terrorized and abused by 'the den of homos."

Right behind her was Hiram Swain, who also wept and sniffled about how his little boy had been stripped naked one afternoon in the bathroom and forced to have sex with all the center's staff

When one reporter asked him why would two lesbians be interested in raping a male child, Hiram Swain screamed: "They're homo's! Everybody knows the homo's are after our children! They want to brain wash and make them homo's, too! It's their agenda!"

Caseworkers at the Child Protection Agency, so lazy and indifferent to my complaints about Hiram Swain, now went into a frenzy of activity.

They counseled each of the tykes who had been enrolled in our center. And you know what? New headlines shrieked that not only had Andy Swain been raped and tortured, but so had all the others!

Now, like an episode from "Twilight Zone," we began to hear the very charges we had derided in other cases now leveled at us.

We had carried on Satanic rituals in far off woods, like California, we sacrificed animals and even children who had misbehaved. Although all the tots were alive and well, District Attorney Brian Chavitts, who was up for re-election that fall, insisted there were children buried in the backyard of our center.

We had also built a network of underground tunnels to take the children for devil worshipping sessions. If anyone disobeyed, we hung them by their wrists above a pit of snapping sharks.

Another form of punishment we used was to put children into our microwave oven and turn it on high. When we tried to explain that our oven was one of the "mini" type, big enough for just a casserole bowl, let alone a grown child, no one listened.

We also routinely sacrificed animals and buried them in the tunnels and we had also been seen torturing and murdering children. Who were these children, we asked?

Parents also discovered, somehow, that Craig and I and the girls enjoyed dancing naked before the children and forcing them to strip off their clothes so we could have sex with them in the middle of a circle.

As if that wasn't enough for the few hours they were there at the center, we inserted sharp objects into their lower orifices, forced them to read pornographic books and flew them to California each day at lunch period to join a devil-worshipping cult.

Our attorney countered that this would prove slightly difficult to accomplish, since Los Angeles was a 6 to 7 hour trip on the fastest jet. Our lunch break was only 30 minutes.

Of course, the fact that I was a 'notorious" exotic dancer" and "author of gay books" was seen as something hellacious. Why had I flown to Edenton, of all places, to work at a center? Why had I been the one to force Andy Swain to strip naked in the bathroom so I could examine his injuries?

What did Craig and I and the female staffers do when we went to Wilmington? Was it true we tried to lure little boys into our motel room and seduce them? It was pointed out that since Craig was revealed to be a "homosexual", his favorite past time was to drive to the coastal beaches on the weekends and "oogle the sailors and Marines."

We had actually been seen by Hiram Swain kissing and having sex right in public in front of our house.

Was this supposed to be the sign of a depraved child molester? Asked the gay newspaper in Raleigh, The Front Page? Yes, we had somehow managed to do all these perversions right there in the glassed in area of our center, which was visited each day by visitors, parents, people in the neighborhood.

Incredible as it may sound, parents and the district attorney and a team of social workers actually believed these outlandish charges. Therefore, it took no stretch of the imagination to believe that we were the ones who caused the injuries to Andy Swain.

Nowhere did any of the newspaper articles cite any of Craig's outstanding background working with kids. The fact that he was a homosexual obviously nullified anything fine and noble in his character.

There was never a mention of his passion for helping abused children and the fact that he had spent thousands of dollars of his own money in buying food and clothes for toddlers whose parents couldn't afford it.

He was a "homo" and therefore it was to be expected that he thrived on seducing anyone of any age who belonged to the male gender.

When it came out that our female staffers lived together and were reputed to be "married" to each other, this brought out more howls of horror. This proved that they worked at the center to pervert the morals of the lads and lassies.

During the first week of grand jury hearings, Hiram Swain was called to the stand to state his case. I watched with nausea and revulsion as he put on his act. His wife sat in the packed courtroom, chewing her gum like a drugged rabbit, remembering to occasionally wipe her eyes so she would look grief stricken.

The father went into his tragic mode, weeping and wringing his hands. He told the court how he had been destroyed by the terrible thing that had happened to his boy at the hands of a nest of "degenerates."

The mother of Judy Sharp also proved to be an effective witness. She wept, too, and said that all she wanted was an apology from the center for "beating up" her little female terminator.

No, she answered the center's lawyer, she had no private vendetta against Craig or the center. It was just by accident that she discovered all the terrible bruises on her little girl and listened in horror as Judy filled her in on the "monstrous" activities that occurred at the center.

Each day, as I went with the day care center staff into the courthouse, we faced howling, shrieking mobs of parents and the religious right. They carried placards which screamed: "Stop AIDS! Kill a Fag!" or "Keep Your Hands Off Our Kids!" There was even that hoary old favorite of anti-gays printed on posters and held aloft by former kiddies of our center for the TV cameras: "God Made Adam and Eve, not Adam and Steve."

We were pelted with rocks, bottles, spattered with plastic bags of human waste and blood. The smirking cops looked the other way. These All-American mothers and their husbands spit in our faces, grabbed for our hair and told us what they would do to us if they had just 'ten minutes." Yet, TV cameras recorded them filing into their churches on Sundays, all neat and serious an sometimes tearful.

I stared into those all-American faces, usually placid and pleasant and saw their features snarling and vicious and it struck me: they want to believe all this is true! They don't care if we did it or not. They're determined to believe these atrocities!

We became used to hearing ourselves referred to as "Queers… Cocksuckers …Baby Killers…Scumbags…AIDS carriers…Degenerates…Freaks…Faggot Animals…"

TV reporters interviewed weeping mothers and fathers who had once been Craig's biggest supporters and friends. Now, they considered him worse than Jeffrey Dahmer and Charles Manson. Somehow, they had become brainwashed with little coaxing into believing the amazing lies spun by Hiram Swain and Sheilah Sharp, coaxed by an unscrupulous District Attorney and vindictive social workers.

The grand jury excluded me from the charges since I was merely a volunteer, who worked a few hours a week there. But Craig and the girls were found guilty on dozens of charges.

Two months later, a Circuit Court juror found my friends guilty. They were each sentenced to prison for 20 to 30 years. For two weeks, I listened as the district attorney and his staff screamed at Craig and the girls about all the horrible things they supposedly had done to more than 20 little innocents.

Parents hissed and glared at the trio, while giving interviews about how they'd love to see the center staff hung or "fried."

After the verdict, TV cameras showed the mothers hugging each other and clapping and jumping up and down, grinning broadly and congratulating themselves. In the background, their children played happily. They showed no signs of having been hung over a pit filled with snapping alligators and sharks, as they had testified.

These families were so thrilled that justice had been done that they held parties all weekend long and in churches, the preachers extolled the wonderful judicial system of America, which had sent to prison "three degenerates."

Naturally, I was hardly invited to any of these festivities. The residents of Edenton knew how I felt about their railroading three innocent people into prison for crimes that were completely fabricated.

Sheilah Sharp, posing in the bedroom of her little girl with that adorable little tyke mugging for the camera, had become a local heroine. She was interviewed for magazine and newspaper articles and told everyone: "The Lord told me what to do. If it hadn't been for my sweet Jesus, I wouldn't have had the strength to endure this hell on earth."

Hiram Swain also enjoyed a sudden burst of fame. He and his mousy wife and Andy were shown in their sterile living room with the plastic sheets covering the furniture, as he solemnly accepted the praise of a grateful town for ending a "reign of terror."

"I just did what I felt like I had to do," he intoned. "When you've got a bunch of degenerates running a child center, you can't expect nothing but trouble."

None of the media wanted to talk to either Andy's grandmother or me about what a travesty of justice had been done in Edenton.

But two days later, right after I had visited Craig and the girls in jail, something terrible happened.

Little Andy Swain was rushed to the hospital from his home.

His grandmother had brought him there. Someone wearing work boots had kicked the child viciously in the stomach. The boy's stomach was completely severed, his kidneys smashed.

He was in a coma. Then his breathing stopped. This time Hiram Swain couldn't put the blame on someone else.

He claimed, first, that he had himself been abused by his parents when he was little and so he didn't know any better. When he saw this wasn't going to wash with the jurors, who had recoiled at the horrifying color pictures of his dead little boy, he then claimed he had been temporarily insane.

And he told us what that reason was. His little boy. Andy just wouldn't stop moaning and weeping from the pain from other beatings. Therefore, the father wanted to stop hearing those "pitiful" sounds and therefore he began stomping his own son.

Yes, he admitted he had gotten a "little carried away." He had no idea his attack had torn his child's stomach in two or that his kidneys were destroyed.

And his wife? She admitted she had watched this final beating and had wept and wrung her hands—but she did nothing. Even on the stand, she chewed her gum.

Ironically, since the center staff was now imprisoned, I was drafted as a witness because I had already described to anyone who would listen all the things I had seen wrong with the little dead boy and my confrontations with the killer.

I remember attending this final day of his trial. The judge asked the grandmother and myself if there was anything we wanted to say to the murderers. Andy's grandmother, Reba Seagrove, was the first to say her piece.

She went to the front of the courtroom and looked at the parents of her dead grandson.

"If there was a death sentence, I wish you would both get the chair," she said. "Yes, even if Andy's mother is my own daughter, the fact she did nothing makes her as guilty as that animal she married. You're both worthless garbage. I wish you both were dead."

Then, it was my turn.

An army of media people were there that afternoon, not only because of the horrific nature of the case, but because I was the "gay author" from New York who was writing a book on this travesty of justice.

The packed courtroom became hushed when I went to the podium. They knew by now that I spoke my mind and had read my interviews in the newspapers and seen me on TV. My remarks were certainly not what the Chamber of Commerce or the churches of Edenton wanted to hear.

For this grim occasion, I wore complete black: from my beret, to my turtleneck, pants and boots. Some said later, I looked like a movie star preparing for his big scene in the courtroom.

"You call yourself parents," I spat. "You're nothing. You're brainless jerk offs who should never have even a pet puppy, let alone a child. People like you should be sterilized. You don't beat up on humans your size. You take it out on your own flesh and blood too little to fight back. Andy didn't choose to come into this world. You brought him in. And look at what he got. What a welcome! I hope you both fry in hell. If not that, just give me 10 minutes alone with each of you. Just 10 minutes. That's all I ask. A murder like this can't be forgiven. And for those of you in this town who rushed to judge the center without even giving them a chance to defend themselves, you certainly don't deserve any forgiveness. You're nothing more than a lynch mob. God might forgive you, but I can't. And if there was any real justice, Sheilah Smart and Hiram Swain, who helped get this nightmare rolling and ruined lives right and left, should both be shoved into a garbage disposal and ground up. The electric chair is too gentle a sentence for these monsters."

The courtroom exploded into shouts and curses while a few brave souls applauded and cheered. A small group of supporters for Craig and us from nearby towns and cities, hugged me, while most of the preachers in town would condemn me in their Sunday sermons.

I didn't care. I'd seen lynch mobs before, in college and elsewhere so I wasn't surprised to find it here in this beautiful little hamlet.

Hiram Swain was eventually sentenced to 60 years in prison while his gutless wife got l0.

Several newspaper editorials bashed my appearance, saying that I sounded like a vigilante and that I should show forgiveness. Reba Seagrove and I, in reading these excoriations, just looked at each other and thought: they still don't get it!

At the airport, I was waiting for my plane to take me back to New York when a TV crew from Raleigh approached me and asked me for comments on the "Edenton Three," as Craig and Kitty and Linda were now called.

"Why don't you take your crew back to Edenton," I smiled,

"and ask the parents of the so-called victims to show you all these terrible scars their little darlings received during their endless hours of torture? Try to find just one of those underground tunnels that the staff used for demonic sacrifices and murder. And then why don't you ask Sheilah Sharp why she started the witch-hunt? I thought lynchings were a thing of the past but you can now proudly point out that there were three hangings in Edenton in the past few months. What a town! What a mob!"

I returned to Manhattan, delighted for once to find that fast and grungy, in-your-face charm, exhilarating.

And I moved into a new high rise building on the Upper East Side, tucked away in a studio in a tower, high above the crowds.

I chose, it, too, because no children are allowed to live here.

It's for adults only.

CHRISTMAS AT THE YA'LL COME MOTEL

◆

Two big Marines in the back of the bus grimly chewed their gum.

Across the aisle from me, the minister who resembled a football star bit his knuckle. Me and two other members of our college rock band, The Heart Throbs, stared glumly out the window.

Even the "star" of our group, Mr. Elvis Presley look-a-like James LeRoy McRae, had stopped his relentless flirting with the coeds surrounding him. Concern over our situation had made even him forget to keep his lip curled in that famous Presley snarl.

On Christmas Eve of 1961, light snow had thickened into a howling storm. An hour before, we had led the passengers in singing Yule tide favorites with Kenny and James playing guitar, Joey blowing sax and me on the harmonica. Now, we all fully expected to end up in one of those steep ditches outside Siler City, North Carolina.

"Hey, looka that motel just ahead!" shouted someone. Through the thick whiteness, we could make out the cheerful blinking of gold and crimson neon, which formed a man's grinning face. Ya'll Come Motel were the words formed in his gaping mouth. Beneath his chin brimmed more jolly lights: Ya'll Get Inside—Ya Heah?

We all whooped and cheered when the bus wheezed to a stop before the long, low building. "Everybody out!" barked the exhausted driver,

Ben. "End of the line. We ain't going anywhere until this shit, I mean, snow blows over. Maybe tomorrow. Trailways is paying for ya'll's rooms tonight."

For a mom and pop operation, the motel wasn't half bad. It was more like a cozy home than the usual concrete and plastic boxes that called themselves motels.

In the lobby, a hearty fire roared in the hearth where four stockings of red flannel hung. Scarlet, amber and azure lights twinkled on the large Christmas tree. On the big TV console, Lawrence Welk was leading his orchestra and singers through a rendition of "Winter Wonderland."

Standing behind the registration desk was a white-haired, smiling woman who said she was Miz Callie. There were rooms, she said, but some of us would have to double up.

I hurried up to her, turned on my charm, told her that I had been deathly ill and needed my rest, and managed to wrangle a single room. I was going to have some fucking fun.

At that time in my life, I was of medium-height, had light blonde curls, was sassy and swish and had more boyfriends at Brevard Junior College in North Carolina than the Homecoming Queen. Kenny, the cute guitarist of The Heart Throbs, ambled over to me.

He and Joey always hung out together and so they were going to share one room. Maybe, he suggested I'd let James LeRoy—"Brevard College's Very Own Elvis Presley"—bunk with me?

I threw my head back and hooted. "Ha, I'm not going near that big, fat, ugly slob! He makes me sick! I wish he were dead! I wish those Marines over there would just kill him! I wish somebody would give him a barbed-wire enema! I'll sleep out in the snow before sleeping in the same room with that big, fat, greasy, no-talent redneck hick!"

"Sweet Jesus!" muttered Kenny with a roll of his eyes. He had become the peacemaker in our group since James LeRoy and I fought all the time. What no one knew was that I had already balled three times with my gorgeous heartthrob and each time it was better than a hundred Christmases rolled up into one.

But after each roll in the hay, James ignored me and treated me with contempt—until he got horny again and then he turned on his charm. You know how it is with a straight boy. You make him feel like a million bucks in bed and when it's over, he starts singing them Oh-God-How-I-Hate-Myself-For-Doing-It-With-A-Queer Blues.

Yet, you could bet he stopped singing once he got all steamed up again. He hated him for this hypocrisy.

"Okay, so what's he done now, honey?" sighed Kenny.

"You heard him call me a yaller-haired cocksucker from Mars last night at the dance, didn't you?"

We had performed for one of the big fraternities at North Carolina State University the night before.

Kenny bent over laughing. He always thought I was funnier than comedian Jerry Lewis. "Now, now, you gotta remember you called him some names, too, when you found him making out with that girl. So just be reasonable for once and go over there and ask him to room with you."

As I hesitated, Kenny quickly added: "He likes you, Jason. Really, he does. He told me so."

"Yeah," Joey agreed, "he sure does."

"Did he really say that?"

Kenny and Joey nodded too quickly but I was eager to believe them. The two boys took my arms and pulled me over to where James LeRoy stood against the wall, watching me intently from beneath his dark brows.

He knew he looked a million times better than his god, Elvis. Black hair formed a gleaming pompadour and he worked for hours to make that lock of hair fall over his forehead that way.

His square face startled not only for its striking beauty but also because of those eyes—dark brown, they gleamed like smoldering embers, from between thick lashes. You just knew he had nothing on his mind but sex. And those lips of his, full and pink, he licked to make them moist and when you saw them move, it was like he was urging you to kiss him.

Beneath his red windbreaker and skin tight jeans bulged his formidable young torso. His eyes lit up now as I came up to him. That sexy smile of his began to form. Already, my resolve was melting. I had only to think of our last coupling, with him naked, on his back, that glorious torso of his tensed and rippling and that wonderful toy between his legs standing to full attention and…

"Jason's got something to say, James Leroy," Kenny began with a squeeze of my arm. Joey nudged me in the ribs. "Go on and talk to him now, Jason."

"Eh, James," I smiled, "I'm sorry I said you were dead from the head down last night although you did call me a yaller-haired cocksucker from Mars. But if you're interested in maybe, eh, doubling up with me and—"

At that moment, one of the cute Marines I had flirted with on the bus all the way from Raleigh called over to me: "Hey, Jason, are we still gonna party tonight? We've got the booze, if you've got the time!"

He and his other buddy grinned and winked knowingly but when I looked up at James, his expression was murderous.

"Yeah, whyn't you get together with those Marines and that preacher man you flirted with? You know what they think of you. You're so damned brazen!"

God, how I wanted to kill him! Instead, I smiled. "James, I really didn't mean it when I said you were dead from your head down. What I meant to say was that you're an ass-hole with the sex appeal of the Three Stooges."

I whirled around and caught up with the handsome minister who was leaving the lobby. "Wait, preach, and I'll walk with you."

"Little queer!" hissed James LeRoy, loud enough for me to hear.

"James," I trilled, "I'm real sorry your mother never could have any children."

Kenny and Joey howled and slapped their glowering buddy on the back. It was a game we played—who could get the last jab. Suddenly, it wasn't so funny anymore.

#

The Reverend Reggie Green surprised me by eagerly accepting my invitation to come by my room later and "unwound." I had barely gotten out of the shower and into my white terrycloth robe when he was knocking at my door.

After entering, he startled me further by pulling out a half-empty bottle of bourbon and filling up two Dixie cups. I hated the stuff but pretended to sip it.

"Just what we need," he smiled, "on a freezing Christmas Eve."

"You don't act at all like the preacher's I've known."

"Everybody tells me that. Just because you're a minister, doesn't mean you're dead." He told me of his days as an athlete at The Citadel Military Academy and later at East Carolina University.

He was sturdy and well built with an easy, wet grin. His brown hair was cut short in the style popular at that time with the "clean cut" or Pat Boone kind. But I could see him easily in the Elvis Presley mode, like my hateful James LeRoy.

Glasses gave him a studious look but his dark eyes were hot and glistened with lust. Or so I hoped, for on the bus he had been unusually warm and friendly, laughing hard at some of my comments.

We tapped our Dixie cups together. "May we all get home safely for Christmas," he toasted.

"May we all have a good time at the Ya'll Come Motel until we do!" I rejoined.

The warm glint in his eyes became to burn. "Any suggestions?"

"Sure, but let me change into something more comfortable," I drawled and let my robe fall to the floor. His eyes swept over me and when he moved closer, his brows had risen and he ran a tongue over his lips.

"You, eh, you look real, real nice," he murmured and pulled me against him. His voluptuous mouth pressed against mine and it was as thrilling as I imagined it to be. Soft, warm, moist sinking down harder, his tongue moving expertly into my mouth and his hands sliding down to my buttocks.

I undid his gray slacks and he kicked off his shoes. His sweater was pulled off and it was clear he had come ready for fun for he wore no socks or underwear.

On the bed, it was he who took over, laying me on my back and his delicious mouth moving from each of my nipples then down my stomach and finally onto my hardness.

To say I was startled would be an understatement. I was usually the one who did all the mouth stuff and the sucking but this time he became the dominant partner.

Like other preachers I knew then and have known since, he used his lips and tongue like sex organs. His well-shaped head moved steadily up and down while his fingers caressed my groin and buttocks with the skill that one can only acquire from much practice.

His breathing was loud and labored since he was breathing through his nose. I couldn't hold it back any longer and raised my hips slightly. He knew what was happening and pressed his mouth even tighter against my pubic. When I came, he gulped several times, moaning out his delight.

Finally, he released me from his mouth and raised my crotch closer to his face. This time, he licked my groin and cleft—his wet lips moving from one to the other steadily, for several minutes until he had made me hard once more.

He crammed my erection back into his mouth and began to work his magic again only this time his fingers massaged my buttocks. Once more, he helped me produce a powerful orgasm, even better than before, and he wouldn't move his mouth away until he had licked up the last drop of my coming.

Reggie moved up to me now and fell back, breathing hard, smiling and he grinned when I scooted down and began to do to him what he had done to me. His was a sturdy erection but not a memorable one, which may have been the shadow, which hung over him.

For even in that brief time, I came to know Reggie, it was clear that he was not cut out for the ministry. He was too normal and sexy for such a cloistered life.

But he was so charming that he made balling with him terrific fun. I was just beginning to enjoy his hardness when there was a sharp knock on my door.

"Shhh!" I whispered. "Maybe they'll go away."

"Jason, it's me, James!" shouted my moral babysitter.

"Oh, God, this is one bastard who will not go away!" I muttered to Reggie. Just a month before, he had nearly torn down my dorm room door when I refused to let him in.

"Come on now, Jason!" bellowed James again. "I know you're in there. I know you're mad, honey, but let's talk this thing over. It's freezing out here."

I recognized the mating call. James LeRoy was horny as blue blazes and was wanting to get it on! What could I do? Motioning Reggie to remain silent, I threw on my robe and ran to the door.

"Oh, hi, James. I was just taking a little nap."

God, he looked gorgeous standing there against all that whiteness. His moist hair had whipped over his brows from the wind and those sexed up eyes were sending out the message: sex, sex sex!

And I couldn't help but glance down at his basket. Yep, this boy was ready to tie one on!

James grinned and pulled out a bottle of champagne from behind him. All of us Heart Throbs had received gifts of wine from the fraternity the night before.

"Still mad at me?" he grinned boyishly. "I thought maybe we could have some of this here champagne and—"

Before I could stop him, he had pushed the door open—and his words broke off. Color drained from his face, which had hardened into a mask of fury for he was once more furious at Jason Fury.

I looked around. There was a mirror right behind me, which reflected perfectly my bed. And laying there, playing with himself was my very aroused young sinner.

"Shit, baby!" snarled James LeRoy, "You work pretty damned fast! Want me to go around and round up all the other guys and have'em gang bang you—you little slut?"

It was like being slapped and I winced. "You go tell every guy you see, including Kenny and Joey, that I'm open all day and all night and it won't cost a fucking penny. So get in line, bub! First come, first served!"

Reggie was putting on his clothes when I slammed the door. "Me thinks," he grinned, "that your friend is just a little bit jealous."

"That redneck slob? The only person he loves is that prick who stares back at him in the mirror."

"I think you love him and he loves you," Reggie smiled.

"Ha, ha, ha. That's the funniest joke I've heard all year."

After Reggie left, though, I thought: he's right. I do love that conceited slob but what good does it do me? All he wants is a quick blowjob when he's horny and then he hates my guts for doing it.

The tiny coffee shop of the motel was jammed and it took me forever to get a cheeseburger and a big bowl of home made vegetable soup. But who cared? It was like a big party and I forgot for a moment my turmoil of emotions regarding James LeRoy.

There were nearly 20 of us there that night, with the crowd spilling out into the lobby. Someone was tinkling the ivories of an old piano in the corner, next to the Christmas tree, and a crowd had gathered around to sing holiday favorites.

Even Ben, our short and hefty bus driver, had become a human being. He was smoking a stogie and showing off pictures of his family. In on one of them, he grinned happily, wearing a big pair of swimming trunks, surrounded by his three daughters and wife.

As usual, James LeRoy had attracted his cluster of glazed-eyed coeds in bobby sox and loafers and tight skirts and sweaters, the uniform of all young girls back then. I should know. I wore them around my football buddies in the dorm on weekends and they loved it.

I nearly burst out laughing when he went into his hyper Elvis Presley mode, curling up his lip and trying to talk like 'The King': "Yes, ma'm…No, ma'm…I sho' do think you're kinda nice…wal, that's real sweet of ya, honey…people always tell me I remind them of ole Elvis…can't imagine why…"

If he sounded anymore like that singing sensation, I thought, I wouldn't have been surprised to see Colonel Parker leaping out from behind the counter and selling photo's of "his boy."

There was something about James LeRoy, however, which made him a favorite with kids. Despite his impressive size, children always ran up to him. This happened now as a little black boy and girl went up to him and he picked them up in his big arms.

I had talked to their mother, a thin, sad-eyed woman from Chicago, named Eunice, on the bus and knew something about their story. They were heading toward a tiny whistle-stop, near Denton, North Carolina, called Southmont where her mother lived. They were going to stay there indefinitely until Eunice could find work somewhere.

"How can Santa Claus find us here?" piped up four-year-old Esther.

"He can find you anywhere!" James LeRoy assured her.

"Can he get a pig and a tent down the chimney?" wondered five-year-old Lester. "That's what I want for Christmas."

"Well, we'll have to wait and see," smiled James LeRoy. After the kids left him, I couldn't resist going up to him. "James LeRoy, I wish you were always as nice as you were just then."

His face seemed sad, for once, and lost its conceited expression. "Maybe you expect too much out of me, Jason."

"I expect? Maybe you expect too much out of me!" I snapped back. Before another fight could erupt, Kenny grabbed my arm and dragged me over to the piano. People were urging The Heart Throbs to perform some songs. Kenny and Joey had already brought their instruments out and I sat down at the piano.

James strummed his guitar and led everyone in such holiday favorites as "Jingle Bell Rock," "Rocking Around the Christmas Tree" and the more traditional fare of "I'll Have a Blue Christmas" and "Have Yourself a Merry Little Christmas."

Several of the girls were members of the glee club at North Carolina State University and provided beautiful harmony. Eunice's little kids danced and jumped to the fast numbers and tried joining in the chorus of the others.

When James LeRoy performed his Elvis favorite, "Are You Lonesome Tonight?" he stared at me, crooning the words with obvious meaning. I shook my head emphatically and even he broke down to join the other Heart Throbs in hysterical laughter.

They knew I would never be lonely at night—not at the rate I was going!

I was heading to the men's room during a break when the two Marines came out. They were actually two brothers, Leo and Larry, from Camp Lejeune and I discovered they were basically fun-loving farm boys. With their sturdy young builds and freckled faces, they made me think of Tom Sawyer twins.

"Hey, you!" grinned Larry. "Whar you been? Me and Larry here thought we could get together for some fun."

"What kind of fun?" I drawled, batting my eyes innocently. As if expecting my question, those young studs unzipped themselves and pressed their country grown endowments into my hand, as if they were offering me thick sticks of bubble gum.

"Our cocks will give you more fun than a barrel of monkeys," snickered Leo. "And you can play with 'em all night."

"Since I'm not all that wild about playing with a barrel of monkeys, fellows, I think you've got yourselves a deal. Whoopee, let's go!"

On the way out, we bumped into my over-sexed preacher. "Hey, Reggie, wanna come to an orgy?" I whispered. "It's gonna be a blast!

With a roll of his eyes, he laughed. "Sure, why not? If you stay at the Ya'll Come Motel, you might as well do what the name says!"

#

Imagine if you can, a dimly lit motel room with mesh curtains from Woolworth's, a neon green spread on the bed, a black and white TV set with the sound off showing a Perry Como Holiday Special.

And laying before you on the bed are not one, not two, but three bare-assed men in their prime.

My Marines had playfully decided to keep their military caps and boots on. Gleaming against his young chest was the minister's gold cross. I had sprayed myself with Jungle Gardenia perfume and dabbed make-up on my face.

The brothers giggled and joked about actually having a preacher present for our orgy.

"I've never fucked a preacher before," drawled Leo.

"Well, you're fucking one now, Mr. Marine!" I howled. With Larry's help, we had Reverend Green to lay on his back and pull his legs towards his shoulder.

Then we guided Leo over to him and helped position him so that he could easily just slide it on in. And he did with the preacher wincing, then gasping and then nodding his head.

"Man, you know how to fuck, you jug-headed kid!"

With those two men taken care of, Larry laid back and beckoned me to enjoy him. Like his brother, Larry was uncut and enjoyed the way I played with his foreskin. I stretched it out with my fingers, then I rolled it down around the head and then I covered all this good stuff with my mouth.

He had a delightful organ to work on—strong, thick and clean and it seemed in no time, he was filling my mouth to overflowing with cream from the United States Marines.

But he wanted to do what his brother was doing to the preacher. So, Larry had me lay down beside Reggie Green and then he got on top of me and quickly, he had synchronized his humping with that of his brother. Reggie glanced over at me, his face flushed and excited. "I wasn't expecting much on this trip, Jason. But wow, I'm glad we stopped here."

His fucker wanted to try me out for size, though, so he and his brother traded places but you know what? I couldn't tell any difference. The brothers were so alike, they must have been trained in the same school of sexual experience.

What startled me was watching the two brothers pull out at the same time and begin spurting out their stuff all over my and Reggie's stomachs.

Reggie had a new bottle of bourbon on the nightstand and he reached over and took a big swig and then passed it around. Leo and Larry must've gotten a quick high for they both fell forward and began kissing us madly, humping their hips and preparing for another hot session.

But at that moment, the door to my motel room swung open. A gust of wind blew in, along with James LeRoy.

"Hey, Jason!" he was saying. "Where'd you disappear to?" He had been brushing the snow from his face and as his eyes adjusted to the dark, he froze.

"Jesus H. Christ!" he gulped, staring at us four naked men. "You—you're simply amazing! I mean, you never take a break, do you?"

He slammed the door behind him. The other three men snickered and the Marines resumed their energetic butt motions as they screwed us but for me, the orgy was over.

Damn James LeRoy! He screwed up everything.

#

It was nearly midnight and I was surprised to find guests still hanging around the lobby. Obviously, they couldn't sleep either.

"Come on over here," said the clerk, the charming Miz Callie. "I want you to try some of my hot apple cider and some ginger bread I just baked."

She, along with James LeRoy, Kenny and Joey, were stuffing two stockings with candy and fruit.

Kenny came over to me. "Jason, you got something small, like a gift, we could wrap up for those lil' black kids? James LeRoy's given some packs of Juicy Fruit Gum, I've got a pen and pencil set, some of the girls have rounded up some make-up for the Mama."

I hurried back to my room and found a dozen new comic books I had planned to give to a favorite nephew. I had other gifts for him, though and brought the books back to the group.

At least the Mama and her children would have something for Christmas.

James LeRoy pretended to ignore me, yet I felt him watching me. He was strangely quiet and was actually indifferent to the three coeds fluttering around him. Each competed for his attention, and hopefully, a tussle in bed later on.

I felt depressed, though. Reggie had gotten drunk and the Marines had taken him back to his room and God only knew what they were doing now. Kenny, who resembled an adorable elf, had gotten a little smashed on his bottle of wine and had put a Christmas wreath around his head.

I went up to him and hugged him. "Merry Christmas, my dear friend Kenny." And then: "Will you still love me tomorrow?"

He hugged me and kissed my cheek. "I'll always love you, Mr. Jason Fury, tomorrow and forever and a day. You sure are the most original guy I've ever met. Merry Christmas, baby."

His buddy, Joey, came over and embraced me, too, for none of us were used to spending Christmas away from our families and in this strange situation, we had become one big family.

He rubbed his chin against my cheek. "I love you, too, honey, even if you are a weird little sumbitch."

I grabbed his basket and he and Kenny whooped and laughed. I threw them a kiss but ignored James LeRoy who had watched the whole thing.

On the freezing walkway to my room, a strong hand suddenly grabbed my arm.

"Come on!" muttered James LeRoy, dragging me along. "We got some talking to do and I'm gonna do it before some other guy beats me to it."

"You're hurting my arm, James LeRoy!" I wailed—but not too convincingly. I was thrilled at what was happening. Shoving me into my room, he slammed the door behind him, locked it and set down a bottle of champagne on the dresser.

Then he began stripping off his red windbreaker, black muffler and gloves.

"Get out of them clothes!" he barked. "There's somethin' I wanna do and you know damned well what it is."

"You told me you wanted to talk, James LeRoy," I taunted him. "Start talking. My Marine buddies just might want to drop by, along with that cute preacher and—I resent being called a yaller-haired cocksucker from Mars."

He laughed softly. "Well, you came from somewhere, you crazy lil' cocksucker, you!" He peeled off his white BVD's and threw them at me, striking me in the face. I pretended to swoon as I pressed them against my nose and mouth. James LeRoy was completely naked now and Christ, what a Christmas present that was!

As a football player at Brevard College, he was in great shape, with round pecs and a flat tummy. His shoulders, arms and legs were muscular and smooth and I could hardly wait to run my mouth over them.

He pushed me against the wall and ground his body against mine, while thrusting my wrists behind me.

"Stop treating me like a yaller-haired cocksucker from Mars, James LeRoy!" I meowed. "You're hurting me, you big stud, you! Would Elvis Presley treat a cocksucker like this?"

He laughed for he knew I grooved on his intense machismo. He lowered his face and then kissed me hard. This amazed me for he had never done this before. And it wasn't a tender kiss, either, but one of passion.

James released my wrists and I slid my hands up and down his strong back and beautiful rump.

I fell to my knees and covered his manhood with my mouth. It was already half hard and it was the type that stood straight up when fully erect. I brought my hands up between his thighs to bring him even closer.

His body tensed and trembled some and then he grunted as my mouth was suddenly filled with thick wetness.

"I've been wanting to cum all day," he muttered.

"I wanna do it again, James LeRoy! You know you can do it again and again."

"Well, let's get in bed before I freeze my butt off."

It was wonderful curling up against him between those sheets and breathing in his young essence: he made me think of clean skin and Vaseline Hair Tonic and Juicy Fruit Gum—and that indefinable scent of aroused male.

He got over me and while kissing me, worked his hips over mine until his erection had found its entry between my legs. We both forgot about the howling of the winds and the snow against the window of that small room and after he emptied himself inside me, he slid his face down and got me off with his mouth—another first that astonished me.

Later, as we kissed and he fucked me again, I whispered into his ear: "Thank God we found this little motel."

"Yeah, and it doesn't hurt any when there's a yaller-haired cocksucker along, either!"

I gooched him, he yelped and I put my hands around his buns to bring him in deeper.

#

I pulled the curtain back from the window.

Dawn was touching the white landscape with pearl and blue light. A sliver of pink glowed on the horizon.

I could see the bus parked in the courtyard but the lights were on, the tailpipe was spewing out smoke and several men were working to clear a trail to the highway.

We would soon be on our way.

"James, look! The storm—it's over!"

He raised himself on his elbow and for once, his hair wasn't greased into place. It fell over his forehead, making him resemble an adorable teenage punk. And this, I thought, is what his future wife will see when she wakes up in the morning.

"I'm mighty glad to hear that, honey," he yawned. "Now, jest get your little self on back here to bed."

I danced over to the dresser and poured the rest of the warm champagne into our Dixie cups. I gave him his and kissed him on the cheek.

"Merry Christmas, James LeRoy. May your future be bright and wonderful."

His beautiful smile dazzled me as he kissed me. Even tonight, as I write this, I can still see his white teeth, his face radiant with emotion, and his dark eyes glowing with something deeper than pleasure.

"And Merry Christmas to you, Jason Fury. One day, I want to read a story you've written about our wild Christmas here at the Ya'll Come Motel."

"You will, Sweet Baby James. You will."

I snuggled up against him, his big arms pulled me close and soon, his warm breath kissed my cheek as he slept.

And I thought of my young lover who would one day become a grandpa and a run a small hardware store in Mocksville, North Carolina. And Kenny, who would start his insurance firm in Spartanburg, South Carolina and Joey who would soon die of cancer in less than five years.

But I also thought of the others...the preacher whose days in the ministry were obviously numbered...the fun-loving Marine brothers...the thin mother and her two children living in a community not even on the map...all of whom would vanish into oblivion in just a few hours after I got off the bus in my hometown of Denton, North Carolina.

Whatever became of them?

Tonight, perhaps they, too, wherever they are, remember the Christmas of 1961 when we all stayed at the Ya'll Come Motel...which was razed to the ground in 1974 to make way for a highway.

If only those walls could have talked, what stories they would have told!

MY FATHER'S HOUSE

◆

Each time I made that long journey from New York to the North Carolina coast, I asked myself: why go through hell?

Although the old homestead by the sea is fully furnished, no one lives there anymore. I visit it a few times a year.

Despite countless offers from people who want to buy the plantation-like residence with its stained glass windows and spectacular view of the ocean, I've refused them all.

You see, I keep hoping that one day he will return.

My father has been gone for 15 years now. With each passing day, he becomes more of a dream person than a man I thought once was the greatest guy in the world.

Perhaps he really did run off with another woman, like Mama said. Maybe he's been dead all this time. I don't know because in 15 years, I've never received a single card or phone call from him.

Yet, I keep this house furnished with his possessions. The Johnsons down the road maintain the place beautifully. When they know I'm coming down from the Big Apple, they clean the house from top to bottom and stockpile enough food for an army.

On December 22, of this year, I unlocked the front door for the first time in six months.I could have stayed in New York for the holidays, going to parties and seeing some old flames that all want to drop by to have some fun. Something powerful, though, propelled me here to this remote place near Wilmington to a house filled with old wounds and rare joys.

Standing in the dark hallway, I heard a board creak overhead. Could it be my father up there at last, waiting for me?

I climbed the steps to his room, which I always occupy when I return.

He made everything in it, just as he built this house with his bare hands, with assistance from our neighbors. Everything in this chamber, from the four-poster bed, the fire place, the window seat and the rocking chair—he constructed them all.

That's why his suddenly vanishing without a word to me always haunted me. Daddy was passionately in love with both his house and with me and even when I was a child, I had fantasies of just he and I living here together for the rest of our lives.

Beside the dormer windows in this bedroom, with their cushioned seats, is his large bed, with the patchwork quilt still there at the bottom, and the bedclothes turned down by the Johnsons. The sheets are stiff and cool with starch, smelling faintly of lilac.

From the window, I can see the ocean out there, gray and icy. On the nightstand, I placed the framed picture of my father, which I've had since childhood. It's actually a crumpled Polaroid I had rescued from the garbage when Mama had gone on her rampage.

She had thrown every photograph of him into the fire, not wanting a single image of him left in his house

The cracked and blurred picture shows a young giant dressed in football uniform. Dark curls brim over his forehead. A shy smile plays around his lips that are full and slightly open, like a small boy.

And looking directly at me are those startling eyes that always make me think of candles glowing behind blue crystal. His are opened wide, enhancing that adorable quality he possessed of being an innocent who never grew up, despite his strapping torso.

When I was small, this big bear of a man would take me into the shower with him. Later, he hugged me close against his naked body, kissing my face and mouth, taking me to bed with him, where he would murmur old fairy tales and describe scary movies he had seen as a child.

As long as I was with him, I knew nothing would go wrong in my life. He would always be there in my corner, offering me his formidable protection.

"We'll always be together," he whispered to me, kissing me, guiding my hands over his chest and back. "We'll grow old together for you're the only person in the world I love. You and me—we'll live together in my house and nowhere else. Because this is your father's house."

Why did you leave me without a word, Daddy? Where are you tonight?

For I remember:

Black, shining hair combed back from a square but boyish face…a moustache above white, even teeth…his dazzling body always smelling of MacGregor Aftershave lotion and a lingering scent of Dial Soap…his mouth perfumed with the ghosts of bourbon, tobacco, the hard cherry candy he loved to suck on and when he came into a room, he brought with him the cold wind and the pine wood he had chopped for our fires.

One day he was there, the next he was gone.

One day he was wrestling with me and throwing me on his back and running around the yard.

The next day, it was like he had never existed.

At a towering six foot five, he had a physique so outstanding, he had entered amateur weight lifting competitions—and always won.

That's what drove Mama crazy. She was convinced this dazzling young Hercules was sleeping around because both women and men drooled over him.

In his tiny black bikini, his muscles oiled and inviting, he took your breath away, as he posed beneath the spotlights. Daddy didn't sleep around, though. He was so naïve and child-like, I don't think he even realized men were cruising him, as they felt of his muscles or took Polaroid shots of him in the locker rooms.

"We've separated," Mama told me bluntly, that horrible day when I was 13. "He's run off with another woman. We'll just pretend he's dead because he will never come home again. We won't mention his name again."

I called her a liar and said I was going to find him because he would never leave me or his house he loved so much without some explanation.

Something was terribly wrong. And I told her that which sent her into one of her terrifying rages. Screaming abuse at me, she tore through the house, throwing everything she could find of his into the fire.

I managed to hide some of his personal possessions, which convinced me more than ever that a tragedy had occurred.

He would never leave behind his pipe collection, his clothes, his physique trophies or his dog-eared collection of Hardy Boys mystery books.

And he would certainly never leave me. I had heard neighbors whispering about his "obsession" about me.

So close we became that it preyed on mother's dark side.

"You and you father act like two homo's," she liked to jeer.

Having her constantly at my throat had taught me how to dish it back to her.

"It takes a homo to know one," I shot back. "You jealous or something?"

Her slap was the usual way she reacted to my jibes. I learned how to use a baseball bat to defend myself, though, and she very quickly stopped beating up on me.

After my father vanished, she had me shipped off to a series of private schools, then colleges and then I escaped to New York City where I became a writer.

As the years passed, Mama's mind steadily deteriorated until I was forced to put her away into a nursing home. Although she had plenty of money, she allowed our home to go to seed. After her death, I used a good portion of my inheritance to restore our estate to its former grandeur.

It quickly became a major showplace of the Southern coast but I never allowed it to be included on the tourist roster. I hated the idea of strangers tramping through the rooms, gaping at the bedroom where my father and I had slept, where he had taken care of me and calmed my fears.

All this time my father haunted me.

Where was he? What was he doing? I ran ads in national publications, seeking information. I hired a private investigation firm who could find nothing. I offered large sums of money from anyone who could help me.

There was nothing except bogus claims from scam artists, wanting easy money. Yet, I never gave up hope.

He'll come back and when he does, I thought, I'll be here in the house that the built.

#

After I arrived that December night, it began snowing. The house was warm and cozy and the sound of the waves made me enjoy the snugness that my father had built.

I was preparing to microwave some Brunswick stew that Mrs. Johnson had frozen when the doorbell rang.

It was probably Mr. Johnson, the caretaker, wanting to see if I had everything with the snow starting. Beneath the porch light, I made out the figure of a large man, a stranger.

He wore a ski cap pulled low over his forehead and the collar of his jacket was pulled up high. Putting my chain lock on, I cracked open the door. He stood away from the light, as if hesitant about being recognized, which made me nervous.

It was isolated out here and there had been a string of robberies of some of the big show places in this area.

"Can I help you?" I asked.

"Sorry to bother you," the stranger murmured nervously, "but, eh, are you Jason Fury?"

He moved closer now, taking off his ski cap and I stared silently, too stunned to move. For I began to suspect who this man was. Those startling eyes of innocent blue...the black curls...the same moustache...and that handsome figure which few men possessed...

"I'm Jason," I whispered, "and you—oh, my God, it can't be! You're—?"

A beautiful smile lit up his whole face, which was incredibly young and unlined. "It's like a dream," he murmured, shaking his head in wonder, "but I'm your father! I know it's been a long, long time but—"

I threw my arms around his neck. He picked me up and crushed me against him, kissing my face and then my mouth and for a long time we said nothing. Both of us were weeping when we separated.

"Was—was it okay," he asked hoarsely, "to come back home?"

"Oh, my God, what a question, Daddy? This is your home and don't ever try leaving it again!"

#

Age withers most men, giving them potbellies, balding heads and double chins. A rare few, like my father, escape such ravages. In fact, they look even better in middle age than in youth.

At 46, Jim Fury was the spitting image of a mature Mel Gibson; only my parent was much bigger and more muscular than that film hunk.

Granted, his hair had thinned some above the brow but that merely gifted him with a more naked and sensual look. After he removed his jacket, I was startled by the size of his shoulders and arms.

Beneath the red flannel shirt, his pectorals strained the material and a dusting of dark hair matched the color of his moustache. Attractive creases had formed around his full lips.

Hardly knowing what I was doing, I fixed us both bowls of Brunswick stew and made us huge turkey club sandwiches. While he sipped a beer, his beautiful eyes never left me.

Over our feast, we tried to cover 15 years of lost time.

"Where have you been, Daddy? Why didn't you ever try to write or call? I never knew where you were! I didn't know if you were alive or dead!"

His eyes clouded over with distress. "Didn't your mother ever give you any of those letters or gifts I sent? She told me you hated me for leaving you and wanted to never see me again. I just stopped trying after awhile. She had become so vicious and jealous I just couldn't take it anymore. We separated and then I went over seas and worked on the oil rigs in Saudi Arabia."

He kept trying all those years to make contact with me but mother had sworn out an injunction with the sheriff's department, forbidding him to even step foot on this property. She insisted I hated him and wanted to never see him again.

"Daddy, don't you see what she was doing? You know I'd never hate you. She never gave me anything you sent me."

"Well, she's gone now, son. We'll pretend she never existed. Wow, I'm tired. Could you put me up for the night?"

"Of course not," I joked and then hugged him again. "You'd better believe I will. Let me show you something."

#

Silently, he moved around his bedroom. Nothing had changed in it since he left it fifteen years before.

A lamp with a gold shade spattered amber light on the red and orange patchwork quilt. In the white marble hearth snapped a hearty fire, a welcome sight with the freezing wind whipping against the windows.

When he saw the picture of himself on the nightstand, he embraced me again and held me hard against his body.

I slipped my hands beneath his flannel shirt and massaged the warm muscles of his back.

"You didn't forget me after all, did you?" he murmured. "You're the only person I thought of all those years I was gone. Remember the nights when you'd get scared of the dark and snuggle up to me for protection? Let's pretend it's fifteen years ago—and we'll sleep together again."

As I lay in bed, waiting for him to finish his shower, I couldn't believe this was finally happening. There was something very mysterious about his sudden appearance, but I wasn't going to allow that to mar our reunion. I wore nothing but had spritzed myself a little with *Aqua di Parma* perfume. Every man I knew swore they got hard just smelling it on me.

My father emerged from the shower. Except for a skimpy towel, he was naked.

I caught my breath and whistled. His muscles still swelled and gleamed like a prize body builder. In fact, his chest was even bigger than when I last saw it.

His chest tapered to a narrow waist, enclosing a flat stomach. From beneath the towel swayed his loose sac, weighed down by testicles shaped like large eggs. What had impressed me profoundly about my father was that his powerful torso was so natural looking. It didn't look like he lifted weights. He had always reminded me of the ravishing Clint Walker, the cowboy star, whose bare-chested scenes were always my favorites.

"Those oil rigs must have agreed with you, Daddy," I laughed.

"You look bigger than Superman or Conan the Barbarian ever were."

Pleased with my admiration, he made his stunning pecs jiggle, his stomach to sink in sharply and flexed his biceps for me to feel.

Then he casually removed his towel and folded it neatly before sliding beneath the sheets next to me.

My breathing definitely quickened. Even on soft, his manhood made a stunning sight, hanging heavily between his thighs…dark, moist, with the foreskin forming a large snout over the tip.

He put his hands behind his head, thrusting his chest to full display and gazed at me with eyes, which sparkled.

"Is this any way to greet your long lost father?" he smiled.

He slid an arm beneath me and pulled me close to him and once again, I felt like a small boy and I probably looked like one, since I am of average height and my father was like a giant.

"Do you still really love me?" he asked, staring down at me. "I wondered if this would ever happen again? Me, you, in bed together again on a snowy night, me keeping you warm and—"

His mouth suddenly covered mine. I had dreamt of this happening and now it was…tasting his warm, moist lips and feeling the tongue sliding deep into my mouth.

Pressed against me was his phallus. I reached down to squeeze it and this seemed to release my father from any other inhibition for he groaned and wrapped his legs around me.

He guided my fingers down to his foreskin and together, we yanked it down, releasing the tip that slid out, all pink and lustrous and gleaming with sparkling lubricant.

I rolled over on top of him. And after kissing him for a long time, my mouth went quickly to his nipples, so luscious and thick, and then on down to his stomach which moved in and out faster.

By now, his phallus was swollen into full erection and pulsed against his stomach, like a mallet of flesh tapping a drum.

It was so thick, I could barely wrap my fists around it. I covered the head with my mouth and pushed my tongue deep, deep into the slit.

By now, my father writhed on the bed and had grasped the headboard with his fists. I worked his hardness between my lips and surprised myself when I was able to take nearly all of it, almost down to his shaven pubic.

He came fast and I was so surprised that his semen was spattering his thighs and stomach before I could catch it all. Without hesitation, he flipped me over on my back and got on top of me.

While he kissed me, I felt him guiding his new erection up between my cheeks and then he pushed it in.

I gasped and held on to him tightly and he paused for a moment, letting me become used to his size. Soon, though, he was in all the way, and as he humped, he continued kissing my throat, face and mouth.

And I thought: My father is literally within me now!

I explored him thoroughly through that night…using my mouth as a compass, I began with his feet and worked myself up to his ears. Once more, I was exploring that sacred territory that I had thought lost, and now discovered again.

His mouth was always open for me to enjoy. He held forth his privates for me to enjoy. He turned on his stomach, displaying to me again that spectacular behind that had always attracted so much attention at the physique competitions.

I licked and nibbled and savored it all. The warm wetness of his mouth, the unforgettable resilience of his phallus, the enormous testicles that resembled baseballs, the deep navel I loved to tongue, the deeply buried opening between his cheeks.

I was like someone drunk, who couldn't get enough—for I was afraid it would vanish again.

At dawn, I fell asleep with my face pressed against his heart.

Its steady thump-thump accompanied me on a dream journey. I stood before a locked door. Someone was on the other side, pounding on it. I didn't want to, but my hands unlocked the barrier, and I didn't want to see the enemy on the other side for I was certain this person wanted to do my Daddy harm.

I awoke to find Daddy shaking me.

"You okay, son? You've been moaning in your sleep."

He wrapped his corded arms around me and with my mouth on his nipple, I again fell asleep. This time, though, it was a wonderful dream, of a ravishing hunk kissing me and pushing himself up into me.

After a few minutes, he pulled out so I could see the size of his organ and then behold him beating out a thick stream of whiteness.

When I awoke, I smiled, for it had been no dream at all.

#

Christmas morning and snow covered the grounds outside.

Slipping on a warm robe, I hurried downstairs to the kitchen.

I wanted to prepare an old-fashioned holiday breakfast like Daddy used to make for us when I was little. I had left him, curled up beneath the electric blanket, looking for all the world like a gorgeous young boy—one with the body of Hercules and the face of an oversexed Boy Scout.

The night before, we cut down a Christmas tree and had a wonderful time trimming it with decorations we found in the attic. Then we drove into town to buy gifts and groceries for our holiday feast.

I brought him a red turtleneck sweater which I wrapped and put under a tree. He had purchased me something but would not tell me what it was.

And during the night, like we had every night since his arrival, we had wonderful, exhausting sex. It amazed me to see how he could act like a teenager during the act itself. His stamina was amazing, even out matching mine.

Something bothered me, though. In bed, he was like a football stud, wanting to hump all night. During the day, though, he would lapse into strange moods, and when he was in such a phase, he rarely talked and stared off blankly into the distance.

He took pills.

I caught him several times slipping a capsule into his mouth. I didn't know if they were illegal drugs or some kind of medication. Another habit which puzzled me was that in the mornings, when he shaved, he missed parts of his face which gave him a straggly look.

When I teased him and offered to re-shave him, he surprised me by agreeing, as if there were nothing unusual in this.

Going through the jumble of items in the attic, he found an old basketball he had played with during high school. Sometimes he would sit on the edge of his bed for an hour or more, bouncing the ball slowly, up and down, saying nothing, completely lost in his thoughts.

That night, we had been in bed, kissing and loving each other and I let my hands move down to their favorite area of his body, that warm spot between his thighs and I caressed the muscle which embodied all the strong things about him.

"What's wrong, Daddy?" I asked. "You seem worried. Can I help?"

"It can't last," he sighed and looked at the window, encrusted with ice. Beyond that was the steady pounding of the waves. "You know it can't last. Your mother hated weak people. That's why I had to leave. Will you make me leave, too?"

He looked at me with the expression of a frightened child. I hugged him and he pulled me tight against him. "Don't say that, Daddy! You know I never would."

But now, as I put the rolls into the oven, I tried to forget that dark dream I kept having, of running down a long corridor and someone was pounding at the door. Beyond the door was the reason my father was so fearful of leaving me again.

I nearly dropped the tray of rolls when I heard a loud knocking on the front door.

For a moment, I couldn't move. It was like the dream and if I opened it, something out there would destroy the relationship between my father and me again.

On the porch were two sheriff deputies and another man dressed in a parka, jeans and ski cap. So this was the nightmare.

Daddy was running from the law. He had done something in the past and this would explain all those lost years.

"Sorry to bother you on a Christmas morning, sir," the man in the parka began, "but I'm Bill Thrush from the state mental hospital in Raleigh and these deputies and I are trying to locate someone. His name is Mike Sutton. He escaped from the grounds a few days ago."

I was so relieved I nearly laughed. "Sorry, but I've never heard that name before. It's just me and my father here."

The man flipped open a thick folder and held it before me. "Are you sure you haven't seen this man? Big, muscular, about six feet five, black hair, very good looking? Somebody saw him at the New Hanover Mall last night in Wilmington. They thought he might be with you. You are Jason Fury, aren't you? The writer who comes down here a few times a year?"

"Sure I am, I visit about three times-"

My words stopped when I saw the colored Polaroid stapled to the report.

I had trouble breathing because the man in the picture was my father. "There's—there's something wrong, sir. This man, he, well he looks like my father, Jim Fury. But my father's just returned from Saudi Arabia. I'm his son, Jason."

The three men glanced at each uneasily and shifted their feet. "Oh, Lord," sighed Bill Thrust, pushing his hat back from his forehead. "So ole Mike wasn't making up tales after all. He really did have a son. We thought it was just a crazy man's fantasies."

"Crazy man?" I cried. "I'm telling you my father has been overseas—"

My words broke off when Bill turned some pages and held them up to me again. This time it was the face of a woman. Beneath it was the name, "Elizabeth Sutton."

But it was a picture of my mother. Helen Fury.

"Do you know this woman?" Bill asked quietly.

"What—what's going on here? Of course I know her. She's my mother. She died seven years ago. She always swore my father had run off with another woman and that we weren't to mention his name again. Ever."

Bill's face softened and the deputies looked at me with troubled expressions. "Son, can we go inside and talk some. I think I'm beginning to understand what happened."

#

I didn't taste the bitter coffee although I drank four cups of it. I was vaguely aware of getting out three extra cups and pouring my visitors some of the strong brew.

I was trying to comprehend all that I was hearing. It was a tale so bizarre that not even the National Enquirer could match it for its Can-You-Believe-That turns and twists.

Bill Thrust was at the state mental hospital 15 years ago, the day "Elizabeth Sutton" brought her brother, "Michael Sutton," in for treatment. He had been judged insane by a probate court that also decided he was incapable of looking after himself.

"He was really a sick guy," Bill told me. "You were too young to remember the signs of mental illness but your father suffered from progressive psychosis. He was exposing himself to kids, masturbating in public, trying to force men to have sex with him."

All these incidents were kept hidden from me. I knew nothing about them. But I understood then why my father and I had always gotten along so well in my childhood.

Because his mind was that of a kid.

"I think your mother was terrified of anybody finding out what happened to your father," Bill theorized. "Her family had its share of mental illness. That must be why she changed his name and pretended to be his sister. She probably fixed it with the probate judge to have him put away."

She had a phobia about family scandal and I knew that in her eyes, having a husband who was a basket case would have been disastrous to her peace of mind.

And for a number of years, my Daddy had been given massive dosages of medication, electro-shock and insulin treatments, so that he really was incapable of looking after himself. Neither was he able to remember anything of the past.

But his mind had cleared somewhat in the past few years and he had begun talking about me and his house and the staff all thought he was still nuts. "Mike Sutton" had no family and his sister, "Elizabeth" had died.

So, for 15 years, my father had lived only 100 miles away, locked up and forgotten—until he had somehow managed to escape to come home and spend Christmas with me.

"But he doesn't look like a mental patient," I protested. "Good God, he could be a contender for a Mr. Universe contest."

Bill explained that over the years, my father had improved a lot and even held classes in weight lifting for the other inmates. But he still needed adult supervision.

In some ways, he had reverted to being a child again and depended on others to do things for him. Like shaving.

"So that's why he let me shave him," I murmured, "and that's why he took those pills."

Bill had heard my father talk many times about how he wished he could work in Saudi Arabia on the oil rigs. And how he wished he could see his son again. Especially at Christmas.

I stood up. "He's not going back to the hospital, Bill. He's staying home with me. I'll take care of him."

The men all looked relieved and I walked them to the door. Bill thrust into my hand a bag of medication for my father to take and would arrange with a doctor in Wilmington to oversee his treatment. After the holidays, we could visit probate court and make it official: I would be responsible for my father.

Before they left, Bill turned to me. "Remember something. Your relationship has changed. You're the father now. And he's the child."

Upstairs, I peered into his room. He sat naked on the edge of the bed, bouncing slowly the basketball, looking for all the world like a Mr. America winner pausing for a moment to relax.

Glancing up at me, though, his eyes glittered with fear.

"Don't let them take me back," he pleaded. "I heard Bill's voice down there. I want to stay here in my own house. I—I'll behave myself. I won't embarrass you or make you ashamed. I'm not a weak person. Really I'm not."

I hugged him tight and sitting together on the bed, we rocked some, both of us unable to speak because of the powerful emotion of that moment. My hands moved over his incredible torso, feeling the power in his biceps, his shoulders and chest.

"This will always be your home, Daddy."

Like a child, his mood suddenly changed. Wiping the tears away with the back of his hand, he suddenly smiled.

"Hey, this is really a great Christmas after all!"

He sprang to his feet and began dribbling the ball around the room, laughing and whooping with joy.

#

Christmas Day is nearly over.

I've walked around the house for the past hour for I've needed to be alone and ponder all that's happened on this extraordinary day.

The cold is bitter but it feels clean and sterilizing. Ice has formed along the shore and I smile at the snowman Daddy and I built this afternoon.

Its impish grin reflects my father's killer charm and sense of little boy humor. We've put a jock strap on the front and made him a moustache from bits of coal.

Through the window, I can see him.

A fire crackles in the hearth nearby. He wears the new sweater I gave him and sits in his lounge chair before the TV, smoking his pipe and smiling at the antics of Spanky in an old *Our Gang* comedy.

For my present, he presented me with a box of Snicker Candy Bars and has naturally managed to consume nearly half of them.

You're the father and he's the child now, Bill told me.

I'm going in now to be with him for this is the way I've always dreamed it would be.

Me and him, living our lives together, growing old together, loving each other forever…in my father's house.

Author's Note

◆

Many readers have written to me during the past two decades—with mail and e-mail coming to me from as far away as Australia and often from within my little home town of Manhattan. My real name is **Jery Tillotson.** I was raised in Denton, North Carolina. All my stories are based on fact. **Jason Fury** is probably my best-known pen name. Another one is **Andrea D'Allasandra** and there are yet a few others that I like to keep secret. I live on New York City's Upper Eastside, in a strange, little hotel between the East River and Central Park. I rarely leave my apartment these days and about the only visitor I see is the marvelous 'Big' Bill Jackson who lives a few blocks away. We're working together on a new book. His memoirs, **Eighth Wonder,** by the way, is still a big best-seller, even though it was first published in 1994.

Printed in the United Kingdom
by Lightning Source UK Ltd.
121342UK00002B/26/A